Torquere Pres

911 by Chris Owen • Amn

An Agreement Among Gen[illegible] Owen

Bad Case of Loving You by Laney Cairo • Between Friends by Sean Michael

Bus Stories and Other Tales by Sean Michael

Bareback by Chris Owen • The Broken Road by Sean Michael

Caged by Sean Michael • The Call edited by Rob Knight

Catching a Second Wind by Sean Michael • Cowboy Up edited by Rob Knight

Deviations: Discipline by Chris Owen and Jodi Payne

Deviations: Domination by Chris Owen and Jodi Payne

Deviations: Submission by Chris Owen and Jodi Payne

Don't Ask, Don't Tell by Sean Michael • Drawing Closer by Jane Davitt

Faire Grounds by Willa Okati • Fireline by Tory Temple

Founder by Jodi Payne • Galleons & Gangplanks, editor Rob Knight

His Beautiful Samurai by Sedonia Guillone

Historical Obsessions by Julia Talbot • Hurricane by BA Tortuga

Hyacinth Club by BA Tortuga In Bear Country by Kiernan Kelly

Jumping Into Things and Landing On Both Feet by Julia Talbot

Latigo by BA Tortuga • Living in Fast Forward by BA Tortuga

Locked and Loaded edited by SA Clements

Long Black Cadillac by BA Tortuga • The Long Road Home by BA Tortuga

Making a Splash: A Going for the Gold Novel by Sean Michael

Manners and Means by Julia Talbot • Music and Metal by Mike Shade

The Name of the Game by Willa Okati • Natural Disaster by Chris Owen

Need by Sean Michael • Off World 1 & 2 by Stephanie Vaughan

On Fire I & II by Drew Zachary • Old Town New by BA Tortuga

Out of the Closet by Sean Michael • Perfect by Julia Talbot

Perfect Ten: A Going for the Gold Novel by Sean Michael

Personal Best I: A Going for the Gold Novel by Sean Michael

Personal Best II: A Going for the Gold Novel by Sean Michael

Personal Leave by Sean Michael • A Private Hunger by Sean Michael

PsyCop: Partners by Jordon Castillo Price

Racing the Moon by BA Tortuga • Rain and Whiskey by BA Tortuga

Redemption's Ride by BA Tortuga

Riding Heartbreak Road by Kiernan Kelly

Secrets, Skin and Leather by Sean Michael

Shifting, Volumes I-III, edited by Rob Knight

Soul Mates: Bound by Blood by Jourdan Lane

Soul Mates: Deception and Soul Mates: Sacrifice by Jourdan Lane

Steam and Sunshine by BA Tortuga

Stress Relief by BA Tortuga • Taking a Leap by Julia Talbot

Tempering by Sean Michael • Three Day Passes by Sean Michael

Timeless Hunger by BA Tortuga

To Serve and Protect edited by T. Mitchell

Tomb of the God King by Julia Talbot

Torqued Tales edited by SA Clements

Touching Evil by Rob Knight • Tripwire by Sean Michael

Tropical Depression by BA Tortuga

Under This Cowboy's Hat edited by Rob Knight

Under This Cowgirl's Hat edited by SA Clements

The Velvet Glove Vol. I by Sean Michael

Where Flows the Water by Sean Michael • White Tiger by Sedonia Guillone

Windbrothers by Sean Michael

This is a work of fiction. Names, characters, places, and incidents either are the product of the author's imagination or are used fictitiously. Any resemblance to actual events, locales, organizations, or persons, living or dead, is entirely coincidental and beyond the intent of either the author or the publisher.

To Serve and Protect
TOP SHELF
An imprint of Torquere Press Publishers
PO Box 2545
Round Rock, TX 78680

Cover illustration by Rose Lenoir
Published with permission
ISBN: 978-1-60370-167-9, 1-60370-167-2
www.torquerepress.com

First Torquere Press Printing: October 2007
Printed in the USA

To Serve and Protect

Edited by T. Mitchell

Torquere Press Inc.
romance for the rest of us
www.torquerepress.com

Table of Contents

Foreword by T. Mitchell

To Serve and Protect.

The phrase brings to mind a myriad of images for me: of badges, of uniforms, of brave men and women who go out every day to put their lives on the line for the safety and well-being of others. But what happens when the uniform comes off? When the gun and the badge are put away? When the helmets and turn-outs are locked up at the end of a twenty-four hour shift?

Odd hours, shift work, middle-of-the-night calls to rouse a detective out of bed for a case that's just breaking... Sometimes it's hard to balance that time between work and life.

It might be hard, frustrating, or even lonely at times, but these men do it every day. This collection of stories shows another side to the men behind the badges and the uniforms, be it couples who are just trying to make things work, or men in search of romance.

I hope you enjoy the stories as much as I did!

T. Mitchell

On the Clock by Chris Owen

Chapter One

"Strang, you're up! Grab your coat." Lieutenant Williamson's voice cut across the room, impossible to ignore even though Cort was tempted to try. He'd been just about ready to head home with a stack of files to read from the comfort of his armchair, and now he'd have one more folder to add to the pile and wouldn't see home for hours.

"Where?" Cort asked, standing up from his newly cleaned off desk and reaching for his jacket. He was pretty sure that Williamson hated him. His shift was over in five minutes and there were already fresh detectives in the room, coming in for the next watch.

"Oakplace." Williamson handed him a sheet of paper with the address and the bare details on it. "Patrol's already there and the ME is on her way. The victim's a white male in his thirties, patrol reports no suspect at the scene when the body was found."

Cort nodded and stuffed the paper in his pocket. "On it." Arguing wouldn't get him anywhere but put on notice, and Cort had learned a long time ago to just go when he was told to, no matter what.

"Oh, and Strang," Williamson called, just as Cort reached the door. "Don't bitch about not having a partner on this one. If it looks like you need one, Samuels and Turner will be wrapping up something this year, won't you guys?"

Cort tried not even to look toward where Samuels and Turner's desks were, but couldn't quite stop himself. As expected, they were looking grimly at him instead of shooting their glares at Williamson, which was probably safer for them if not wonderful for Cort. "It'll be fine," Cort said weakly and made his escape.

It had better be fine, he told himself as he drove to Oakplace. He hadn't had a steady partner in months and was barely keeping up with his workload, but it had better be fine. Passing off his active cases didn't look good, and putting work on the others would only earn him more grief from Williamson. He hadn't even had time to look at his cold cases in weeks, and there wasn't any telling when he'd get a partner he could tolerate. It was looking more and more like it was time to put in for a transfer. The bullshit was becoming unbearable.

His mood wasn't the best when he arrived at the crime scene; he was tired and fed up, which wasn't his favorite way to start a case. The uniformed officer waiting in the hallway outside the apartment saw him coming and straightened up, clipboard in hand.

"Relax, I'm with Homicide," Cort said, showing his badge. "What's it like in there?" He scrawled his name and badge number on the sign in sheet, making the officer hold the clipboard steady for him.

"Pretty clean, no blood. The medical examiner's waiting, and the forensic team got here about three minutes ago. Everyone's kind of wound up that no one from Homicide's here yet."

Cort rolled his eyes. "Yeah, well. No transporters, last I checked." He lifted the yellow police tape and stepped into the apartment, taking a moment to snag a pair of latex gloves from a box just inside the door. The apartment seemed at a glance to be typical: kitchen to the side, nice but not new furniture, a comfortable home. There were photos and art prints on the walls and the accumulation of possessions most people had were scattered here and there. He could smell stale coffee under the unmistakable odor that a dead body created.

He walked down the short hall by the kitchen and into the living room, where all the action seemed to be centered. At a desk in the far corner sat the body, back turned to Cort, and looking at the body was the medical examiner, Sherry Lachlan.

She glanced up as she passed personal effects to a uniformed police officer gathering evidence for her. "Strang," she said. "Nice to see you. Good to know that Homicide still attends scenes."

Cort sighed and went over to peer at the corpse. "Lachlan," he said, eyeing the computer keyboard dangling behind the body and the chair he was sitting in, apparently held in place by the way the cord was wrapped around his neck. "Should I skip the cause of death question?"

"Asphyxiation," Lachlan said crisply. "At least, unless I find something unexpected during the autopsy. Meet Mr. Vincent Dinsmore. Not a pleasant way to die." She pointed to the cord wrapped so tightly around Dinsmore's neck that it had cut in, almost vanishing into the skin under his left ear. "Whoever did this was standing behind him. They looped the cord around his neck, pulled back and yanked the ends as hard as they could, then twisted them tightly for good measure. That's why the keyboard didn't just fall to the floor after."

Cort nodded and stepped back to give her room. He hated strangulations; something about the popping eyes and the discoloration of the skin gave him the heebies in a way that other deaths didn't. It wasn't a plus that this one featured dried spittle around the mouth, a protruding tongue and scratch marks where Dinsmore had tried to claw the cord off his throat. "Time of death?" he asked, looking at Dinsmore's face and resisting the urge to shudder.

"According to the liver temperature, he died about two hours ago."

"Around four," Cort said, looking around the room carefully. He dismissed the body for the moment, trying to take in the larger picture. It looked like Dinsmore spent a lot of time where he'd died. On the desk in front of him was a very nice flat screen monitor, a cordless mouse and keyboard, and to the right of the monitor was a fax machine. "Where did the keyboard come from?" Cort asked, pointing at the one on the desk. "He's got one already."

"By the couch," one of the forensic investigators said, pointing with the brush he'd been using to lift prints from the stereo. "There's a whole box of stuff right there."

"Huh." Cort stepped over to it, carefully staying out of the way while a second man took a fast series of photos, and then bent to see what was left in the box. "Nice collection of power cords, keyboards and drives. What's up with that?"

"People save that shit," the tech said with a shrug. "At least, most do. They can't bear to part with a perfectly usable keyboard, and the drives might come in handy some day. It's like keeping textbooks from college."

Cort raised an eyebrow but let it go. He hadn't saved anything from college other than his degree. "Okay, what else?" he asked, mostly to himself. He looked up at the body from where he was crouched, trying to imagine what had happened. "He's working at his computer, someone's here. Someone he knows or not?" He stood up and looked around again, noting that there was no sign of a struggle other than right where Dinsmore had died, which tentatively pointed to someone the victim knew.

He also noticed a man standing well out of the way, back to the wall and his hands carefully shoved in his pockets. The first thing that occurred to Cort was to take everyone to task for not letting him know there was someone in his crime scene. His second thought, right on top of the first, was that the man had a gold detective's shield on display, hanging from his breast pocket.

The man was standing there quietly, watching and not doing anything at all that looked like police work. He saw Cort looking at him and nodded once in acknowledgement, but didn't say a word.

Cort nodded back and picked his way around evidence markers to get to him, cataloguing details by reflex. The detective was about the same age he was, in his early to mid thirties, and a bit taller, with broader shoulders. He was fairly unremarkable aside from deep brown eyes that didn't quite go with the light hair. Certainly good looking, but not stunning like a model. Just an average guy with beautiful eyes.

"Cortland Strang," Cort introduced himself when he reached the man, offering his hand. "Homicide."

The detective's handshake was firm, odd feeling with Cort's latex glove between them. "Patrick Gallagher. Computer crimes."

Cort raised his eyebrow and looked back at the body significantly. "There's a tasteless joke here, somewhere," he said.

"Several. I've been making them up for half an hour now," Gallagher said with a fast grin. "But none that are good enough to share." His voice had the barest trace of an accent, more from his diction than pronunciation, and the grin made his face change from almost bland to something very attractive. This was a man who should smile more, Cort decided.

"Too bad," Cort said, returning the grin with one of his own. "I could do with a laugh." He gave Gallagher a quick look, up and down, and pulled out his notebook. "So what's your interest here? And how come you got the call before us?" If people were stepping into homicide cases before the homicide detectives even got to the scenes, Williamson was going to lose his shit in a pretty spectacular way.

Gallagher shook his head. "Not work related at all, actually. I found the body and called it in."

Cort tilted his head. "You knew something was going down?"

"No, I live across the hall." Gallagher grinned at him again, apparently finding the entire line of questioning amusing. He tilted his head to look down the hall toward the door and added, "I came home from work, found him, called it in and waited."

"Well," Cort said, finally catching up. "At least you knew what you were doing and didn't fuck up my scene." He gave Gallagher a hard look. "Did you? I don't see gloves on your hands." But at least the man had done the next best thing and shoved his hands into his pockets. Even when people were trying not to touch anything, it was surprising how often accidents happened.

Gallagher sighed and rolled his eyes. "I didn't fuck up your scene." He held his hands up and turned them over, showing them off before jamming them back into the pockets of his coat.

"Okay." Cort glanced around again and watched the ME and the paramedics load the body onto a gurney. He hated the familiar sound of the body bag zipper, and braced himself for it as Lachlan started at the feet and worked her way up. "All right," he said, looking back at Gallagher. It seemed easiest to treat the guy like any other witness. "Tell me what happened when you--"

"Strang," Lachlan called. She had stopped with the zipper and was looking over at Cort, her hand hovering near the victim's waist. "You might want to see this," she said as she waved the investigator with the camera over to her.

Cort left Gallagher and walked over, around the medic waiting patiently, and looked where she was pointing. "Huh," he said, leaning over and turning a bit to see better. With one gloved hand he lifted Dinsmore's arm. "Names?"

"Looks like," Lachlan agreed. "Tattooed."

The letters were neat and uniform but the variations in the color suggested that they hadn't been done at the same time. Starting just under the elbow, the list was four names long, but it wasn't like any list Cort had seen on skin before.

He stepped back so the investigator with the cameras could shoot a series of photos and then asked for some from the Polaroid. "Three," he said, fishing out his pen to label them. "Gallagher, come here. Take a look."

Gallagher looked faintly surprised but came over, taking Cort's place when he stepped back. The tech handed him the photos one after another and Cort wrote on the strip at the bottom as Gallagher made an interested noise, his gaze on the victim's arm.

"What do you think?" Cort asked, eyeing the image taking form on the photo card he had in his hand.

"What you do," Gallagher said, backing up so the ME could

zip the body bag closed. "Those names are online handles."

"Any idea from where?" Cort asked, not really holding out any hope.

"Not a chance," Gallagher said with a headshake. "Usernames can be from anywhere." He eyed Dinsmore's computer. "Bet that can tell us, though."

"Likely," Cort agreed. The whole system would go into the evidence locker and hopefully be looked at that night. It was a faint hope, but the case was a homicide; the names on Dinsmore's arm would bump it up the queue, too. It was related evidence and had a priority.

The picture finally stabilized as the gurney was taken away and Cort put the two extras in his pocket. "When's the autopsy?" he asked Lachlan as she packed up her things to go with the body.

"Hopefully tonight. Are you planning to attend?"

"Not unless you think I should."

She shook her head and picked up her bag. "I don't think you need to be there," she said. "I'll call if something unexpected turns up. Other than that, you should have a preliminary report sometime tomorrow."

"Thanks," Cort told her, looking around the room. "I'll be here for a while, then at the station. You've got my numbers."

"I do." She nodded to both him and Gallagher, then left.

"Let's go to the kitchen," Cort said to Gallagher. "Get out of the way in here."

"Thank you," one of the forensics team said, not quite under her breath. She smiled sweetly when Cort gave her a look, clearly not bothered about being caught.

"Can you leave the computer hooked up for now?" Gallagher asked her. "Not long."

"My scene," Cort sighed. But he nodded at the tech to leave the computer and moved to the kitchen, leading Gallagher along.

"Sorry," Gallagher said as they leaned on the counter, side by side. "I overstepped."

"Yeah. But you want a look, don't you?" Cort said, letting the issue slide. He had no interest in a pissing contest; it just didn't mean that much to him.

Gallagher nodded but didn't say anything, so Cort fished out his notebook again. "All right, take two," he said. "Fill me in."

"I got home at about five-twenty," Gallagher told him promptly. "Maybe a couple of minutes later, but not five-thirty, for sure. I checked my mail in the entry, started up the stairs. I could hear music as soon as I walked out of the stairway onto our floor, which is only notable because it wasn't muffled, like it would be if it were behind closed doors. I walked to my door and was unlocking it when I realized the music was coming from this apartment, which is directly across from mine."

Cort nodded, taking notes quickly in his own mix of shorthand and actual text. "So you looked."

"Yup. Just a glance, 'cause I've never heard loud music from here, let alone known the man to leave his door open. It was open an inch or so and I kind of assumed that he'd just run down to the laundry room, you know? So I went into my place and then started thinking."

"That's the trouble with being a cop," Cort said, still writing.

"You know it. I went back, called out a general hello. I didn't touch the door. I couldn't hear anything but the music, so I leaned on the door with my shoulder to open it a bit more and looked in. Called out again, identified myself, and asked if everything was all right. When I didn't get an answer I drew my weapon and went in. I identified myself again in the hall, yelled loud. Last thing I wanted to do was scare the shit of the guy."

"Sure." Cort had heard more than a few stories about people just not answering when the police were at their door and then freaking when confronted.

"I went slow, looked into the living room and saw him. Cleared the room, made sure he wasn't alive and called it in."

"Phone?"

"My mobile. Called at five thirty-one by my watch."

Cort nodded and made a note of the time, then asked, "What next?"

"I took a look around, touched nothing, waited for the patrol car and the medics in the hall. The music was driving us all batshit by that point, and the first thing forensics did was unplug the stereo."

"And everyone sighed with relief." Cort finished writing and looked up at Gallagher. "Thanks. That was the easiest statement I ever took."

Gallagher grinned. "The rest of it won't be quite so neat and full of handy clean details."

"The investigation?"

"That, too. But I meant the part where you ask me what I know about the victim, what kind of guy he was."

"That part is rarely neat and tidy," Cort agreed. "Shoot. Give me what you've got."

Gallagher looked thoughtful for a moment and it suddenly occurred to Cort that he'd probably been going over everything he knew since the moment he'd gotten off the phone with 911. He would've known what he was going to have to do.

"Well," Gallagher said slowly. "I'm pretty sure he'd lived here two years, but I might be a few months off on either side. He worked mostly from home, and once a week or so I saw him coming or going with a laptop case, so he might have only been part time here, part time at his office. He was quiet, never had a loud party or people in that I can remember. And aside from one woman that stopped by regularly, there weren't many visitors. I don't think the woman was a girlfriend."

"What makes you think that?" Cort asked.

Gallagher shrugged. "No pet names, the goodbyes were of the 'see you when I see you' sort, and usually in the hallway. Plus the time of day -- she was usually by or leaving when I was coming off shift in the late afternoon."

Cort wrote it down and made a note to find the woman, whoever she was. "Co-worker, do you think?" he asked.

"Maybe." Gallagher didn't look like he was going to put his money anywhere, so Cort stopped fishing that pond.

"Ever work a homicide?" he asked, glancing out to the living room to see what the forensic unit was up to. Aside from bagging evidence and writing notes on the little jars and envelopes they were filling, it didn't look like much. Cort was grateful for it, though. An entire case could depend on that team and one of their little jars.

"Not really," Gallagher said, looking as well. "Did the fetch and carry bit on a few scenes when I was on patrol, though."

Cort nodded and watched the activity in the living room, trying to judge when he could go back in and not be in their way. It looked like most of the latents had been lifted; at least, the dust was thick over everything and he didn't see anyone using the brushes. He flipped to a clean page in his notebook and passed it over to Gallagher. "I need your numbers, please," he said. "In case I need to talk to you again."

"Is that likely?" Gallagher asked, taking the pad from him and holding out his hand for the pen.

"Not really," Cort admitted. "You can pretty much leave any time now, actually."

Gallagher made a humming noise and nodded, his gaze fixed on the notebook as he wrote his name and three phone numbers. "Home, mobile and desk." He passed the book back but didn't release it when Cort took hold. "Feel free to call," he added, when Cort looked at him.

Cort didn't even blink, which pleased him to no end. He wasn't exactly used to being hit on, but it had been known to happen. "I will," he said, hoping he got the tone right. Tone was a little tricky; he always thought that he came off as more smarmy than interested. "Thanks."

Gallagher smiled and let go of the notebook, grinning more broadly when Cort wordlessly handed him one of his business cards with all of his numbers on it, other than his home phone. "Are you going to take a look at his computer?" Gallagher asked, shoving his hands back in his coat pockets and making the card vanish.

"Yeah," Cort said with a nod. "But unless he typed out the name of the guy who killed him while it was happening, I'm only going to glance at it. I have to get to the next of kin ASAP, then head back to the station to start working this out. The computer will be a big part of my night, probably. Or not. Hard to tell at this stage."

Gallagher nodded. He also made no move at all to leave, so Cort rolled his eyes. "Come on, then," he said, pushing away from the counter and going back into the living room. "Take a look if you want." He led the way to the computer and checked with the forensic team to make sure they were done with it before he got himself in trouble.

After carefully moving the chair Dinsmore had died in out of the way, Cort stood in front of the desk and looked at the monitor. The screensaver wasn't anything fancy, just a randomly shifting image that Cort knew was on his own computer at the station. He made a mental note of it and looked at Gallagher. "You do realize that there's a ninety-nine percent chance that he was just looking at work, right?"

"Sure," Gallagher said. "And there's a hundred percent certainty that I'm just nosy."

Cort grinned and gave the mouse a nudge. "There you go," he said, stepping back so Gallagher could get a good look. "Told you." As expected, the screen was filled with a chart and some kind of text document. No porn, no handy e-mail open with the name of the killer in red letters.

Gallagher didn't even glance at Cort, just bent over and moved the mouse around, minimizing some windows and bringing up others. "He's running an IBM clone, but he's a Mac lover," Gallagher said absently. "Linux is on here, and probably

Unix, and he's dressed the desktop to mimic OSX. Look."

"What?" Cort asked, already lost.

"Well, you use a PC at work, right? And have icons all over the desktop? If he worked from home he was likely using some programs that aren't compliant with a Macintosh system," Gallagher explained. "But he probably liked the look of the Mac operating system, so he's got a plug-in running to give him a dock." He moved the cursor to the side of the screen and a neat line of icons slid into view. "Like that. It's just a tidier setup if you have a lot of programs going."

Cort nodded slowly. "And this is going to show me how to catch his killer how, exactly?"

Gallagher blinked and then shrugged ruefully. "It's not. I'm just telling you what I see." He looked at the screen again and ran the cursor along the icons in Dinsmore's dock. "He has three chat programs here, but none of them are open. The e-mail program is open, and the program he was working with. The browsers are closed, both of them. He's got Internet Explorer and Mozilla."

Cort wrote that all down in his notebook and took a guess at the chat programs. "Yahoo, AIM and MSN?"

"Yahoo, AIM and IRC."

"Damn. I don't know that one."

"It's messy. Well, for what you're looking for, assuming you're planning to track down those usernames." Gallagher gave him a look that was tinged with more than a little sympathy. "The forensics lab has some great computer techs, though, and hopefully Dinsmore saves some chat logs. Plus, if he's using any of the smaller chat software like Jabber or something, you really want the techs doing it instead of going it on your own. And that's ignoring the possibility that the names aren't messaging related at all, but from forums, message boards, e-mails or even games."

Cort started to feel slightly ill looking at the computer screen. "Do you do this stuff?"

"Sort of. Not the forensics, though. Well, not exactly." Gallagher clapped him on the shoulder and stepped away from the computer. "Get a good tech. Good luck, Strang."

"Thanks." Cort glared at the computer and turned to watch Gallagher leave. "Hey, Gallagher," he called. "Thanks. Really."

Gallagher smiled at him and waved one hand as he kept going. "Call me."

Cort had an idea that he would, actually. He'd even make the effort to keep work out of it, if he could.

With a shake of his head, he looked around the apartment and got himself back on track. There were steps here, things he had to do. Pretty high up on the list was contacting the next of kin and breaking the news, then finding out everything he possibly could about the victim. After that, if he was really lucky and didn't have to spend hours with the family waiting for them to calm down enough to talk, he could get to the station and start working his way through the information.

"So, okay," he said out loud, looking around the room. "Do we have a name for the next of kin?"

In moments, he'd forgotten about Patrick Gallagher and was hard at work, trying to unravel the last few hours of Vincent Dinsmore's life.

Chapter Two

It was almost eleven-thirty that night when Cort made his way to the department gym, intent on getting on the treadmill and running until he'd made some headway or was so dead exhausted he had to stop. He figured twenty minutes would do it, either way.

At that hour of the night, the gym was almost deserted. Only two other cops were there, making their circuits of the weights and spotting each other. He nodded to them and said hello, then went to his favorite treadmill and made sure that the nearest TV was off. From his gym bag he pulled one of the Polaroids of the crime scene, another of Dinsmore's arm, and a sheet of paper with the preliminary information from forensics on it. There wasn't a lot, so he'd used a large font and made a nice little chart with his notes added in.

With a roll of tape that was on the shelf behind the treadmill, he stuck the pictures and his notes over the treadmill display, making sure he could still use the arrow keys to control his speed and incline; it was something a lot of the detectives did, thus the availability of the tape. That done, he got on, set himself a nice height and started to run, his eyes fixed on his case.

He wasn't sure how long he'd been at it when the two men using the weights left, or when someone got on the treadmill next to him. He was looking at Dinsmore's arm and the sheet from forensics, turning ideas over in his mind and trying to figure out how he was going to reach the anonymous people behind the usernames.

"He saved logs?"

Cort almost missed his stride as he whipped his head around to look at Gallagher, jogging beside him and looking over at his display. "What the hell are you doing here?" he demanded, not so much annoyed to see him as surprised and a little startled to be jerked out of his own headspace.

"Running." Gallagher gave him a sunny grin and picked up his speed a fraction.

Cort snorted and wiped sweat from his forehead with the hem of his T-shirt. "At damn near midnight."

"All right, I'm here because you are," Gallagher said, going as far as to wink at him.

Cort looked around the empty room. "You took a chance with that stunt at the scene, you know," he said.

"Yeah," Gallagher admitted. "I did. Paid off, though. Maybe. Interested?"

"In men in general, or in you?" Cort knew the answer, but the easy way Gallagher just seemed to be so sure of him was a bit much to take. Cort liked his men to be confident, but arrogance wasn't really a turn on, even if his body was kind of waking up.

"In me. I figure I already know you're into men, since you didn't deck me, and you knew I was flirting. Straight guys either don't even notice or they get a little panicked before politely brushing me off."

"So you hit on guys a lot." Being outgoing was good, Cort told himself. A slut was bad. And still, his body was getting a nice hit of adrenaline from the workout.

"Often enough to know a returned flirt when I get it."

"What if I tell you I'm involved with someone?" Cort asked, curious.

"I call you a liar and accept that I dragged my ass down here to get sweaty for nothing other than improved cardiovascular health."

"What makes you say that?"

"The returned flirt. The way you're not actually telling me to fuck off. The hard-on you're working up and the way you're thinking about the steam room. I'll warn you, though, there might be someone in there at the moment. Although maybe not, given the hour."

Cort stared at him. "You're really something else, aren't you?" He hadn't once thought about the steam room. Although now that the idea was in his head, he was finding it hard to dislodge.

"Yeah, I guess. Too forward?"

It took Cort almost two minutes and almost a quarter mile before he could say, "No. Not too forward."

He got another sunny grin and Gallagher shut off his treadmill, riding the runner to the end before hopping off. "I'm going to shower and see if there's anyone in the steam room."

"I'm going to finish my run," Cort said. He was absolutely not going to go panting off after some detective from computer crimes just because he had a nice smile and gorgeous eyes.

"Okay," Gallagher said, walking away from him toward the locker room.

"Damn," Cort said to himself, watching. He might just finish his run as soon as Gallagher was out of the room, after all. The man had a pretty spectacular ass, too.

He made himself run for a little while longer, trying to force his mind back to the case, but it was hopeless. He looked at Dinsmore's arm and didn't see it at all, looked at his neat table of information and saw only clouds of steam and Gallagher in the middle of it, naked.

When the gym door opened and two female officers came in, he fled. Ripping the photos and paper off his treadmill, he stuffed them in his gym bag and grabbed the spray bottle to wipe down both his treadmill and Gallagher's, listening while the women talked about what to watch on the TV while they worked out. With a nod to them for the sake of being polite and not a jerk, he made his escape to the locker room.

The room echoed as he walked to the row of lockers closest to the showers and pulled open a random locker to shove his kit into. By the time he'd stripped naked and found his towel, his cock was damn near insistent, making an unseemly bulge that he tried to tame by the way he fastened his towel. He just wasn't prepared to walk into either the shower or the sauna with his cock leading the way. What if Gallagher wasn't the only one there? What if he was? Cort honestly wasn't sure which would be worse, until he had a mental image of a senior detective eyeing him up and making a joke about working out not being the same as sex.

Shuddering at the thought, Cort walked through the empty shower room to the sauna, noting that the small glass window was already dripping with condensation. Gallagher had to have used about twice the amount of water the sign recommended in order to create that much steam in only a few minutes. After glancing furtively over his shoulder to make sure he was alone, and then rolling his eyes at himself for doing it, Cort pushed the door open and walked into the humid, foggy air.

Only in movies had he seen that much steam in a sauna. The room really wasn't that big at all, small enough that the rules listed a limit of four people at a time, and the floor space was minimal before one walked right into the double layer of wooden benches. However, the fog of steam was thick enough that Gallagher was an indistinct shape, sitting on the second tier of the benches.

"This is really stupid," Cort said, stepping up onto the lower bench. It was warm and slick under his feet, like clean summer rain on a deck. The steam was beading on his chest, and his towel felt heavy with moisture already. He looked down at Gallagher and felt his cock push against his towel with renewed enthusiasm.

Gallagher was looking up at him with heavy lidded eyes, his towel in a heap on his lap and not wrapped around his hips. A long length of thigh was a tease, the shine of sweat and water on his smooth chest an enticement. "Stupid can be fun," he said, reaching for Cort's towel. "And besides, not that stupid, really, given the time of day. There's next to no chance at all that someone will come in."

Cort batted his hands away before his towel could be yanked off. "Still not very smart," he said, leaning over to plant one hand on the wall above Gallagher's shoulder. The other he pushed against the white bundle on Gallagher's lap, shifting folds until he felt only one layer between his hand and Gallagher's cock. "Are you always this pushy?"

Gallagher's eyes closed and his hips lifted a bit. "Not really," he said, his voice sounding muted and thick in the steam.

"Why now?" Cort asked, massaging his dick and admiring the way Gallagher's chest was lifting, his thighs parting slightly. His own cock was happily still pushing at his towel and he had doubts that the towel would remain in place, with or without Gallagher's help.

"Dunno." Gallagher's eyes slitted open and he grinned. "Maybe because I'm smart."

"I suspect you're full of shit," Cort told him, returning the grin and giving his cock a long, slow stroke with the towel. "There's no way you turned up at the gym knowing I was here."

"Just got lucky, I guess," Gallagher said with a gasp, his hands once more reaching for Cort's towel. "Really, really lucky."

"Must be the Irish." Cort let him touch this time, bemused that Gallagher's hands skimmed his hips over the towel before loosening it.

"No ethnic jokes." Gallagher's tongue darted out to lick his upper lip, just a flick before it vanished again. "You going to touch me for real, or do you have a thing for cotton?"

Cort smirked and dragged the towel over Gallagher's erection, knowing full well that the friction would be a mixture of sharp pleasure and irritation. "Just setting the pace."

"The pace needs to pick up, Strang. Public space and all that." He tugged Cort's towel and let it fall, his hands immediately going to Cort's cock and balls.

Cort moaned and pushed through Gallagher's hand, his mind skipping over the part that rebelled at being called by his last name when he was getting off. Before he could form words to tell Gallagher that, though, another part of his mind took over and got rid of the towel hiding Gallagher's attributes from him. "Oh, nice," he murmured, both about the hand on him and the cock he was admiring.

"I like it," Gallagher said, possibly for the same reasons, his breath catching when Cort took him in hand and started to jack him in earnest.

Gallagher wasn't circumcised, which was sadly still a novelty for Cort; most of his partners had been, as he was, and it was with near delight that he started to play. The head of Gallagher's cock was mostly exposed, so on the upstroke he was gentle, lifting the gathering of the foreskin as he went, and tugging slightly on the down. "How do you like it?" he asked, his gaze fixed on what he was doing, although his attention was split. His own prick was making happy leaps every time Gallagher smoothed his thumb over the sweet spot just under the head and squeezed hard at the base.

"Just like that," Gallagher gasped, his hips starting to rock. "Oh, God. Yeah, like that. Little faster."

Cort let go of the wall and bent his knees, finding an odd rhythm where he could thrust into Gallagher's hand and stroke him off at the same time. He palmed Gallagher's balls up and rolled them, too, tugging gently when they got tight and hard in his hand and Gallagher's dick throbbed. "Not yet," he whispered, "Too soon."

Gallagher whimpered, his hand stuttering on Cort's dick. "Please."

Cort groaned, lust surging through him. Please, for Christ's sake. He moved back, shifting out of Gallagher's hand so he could concentrate. Gallagher's chest was heaving, his moans never quite dying off as he tried to get Cort to move faster on him. He was almost ready to blow, and Cort hadn't even really done anything yet.

It was a boost to his ego, if nothing else.

With a tight grin Cort curled his fingers tighter around Gallagher's cock and pulled, sliding his other hand back and down. He had every intention of just teasing the man's ass, giving him a hint that he might be willing to go further, but his finger hit slippery heat.

Gallagher's moan turned into a grunt and Cort's eyes went wide. "Jesus, you are pushy," he whispered, shoving two fingers deep into Gallagher's ass. "Or really sure of yourself."

Gallagher made a strangled noise and started to come, his

cock flexing and his hips jerking as spunk poured out, first in tight arc and then in a flood over Cort's hand.

"Nice," Cort said, both hands still working, though slower.

Gallagher merely made a contented noise and went a little limp, both cock and body.

"Oh, no, you don't." Cort gave him another stroke and reached for the nearest towel. "My turn."

"Of course," Gallagher purred, every movement languid as he took the other towel and swiped it over his belly and balls. "That definitely calls for reciprocation." But instead of reaching for Cort's waiting and increasingly impatient cock, he took him by the hips and turned Cort's body. "Sit," he said, nodding to the length of bench beside him.

Sitting sounded like a damn fine idea, given that Cort's knees were a little wobbly. He moved to Gallagher's side and sat, then lay back as Gallagher almost crawled over him. "What--" he started to ask, but the word broke off when Gallagher went down on him, all wet, eager mouth. "Oh. Oh, yeah."

Gallagher's penchant for noise didn't seem to be limited to just when he was getting close to coming; the more he licked and sucked, the more noise he made, even over the sound of Cort panting. The room was insanely hot and wet, but it didn't have anything on what Gallagher was doing to him.

"Jesus," Cort gasped, his hand firmly in Gallagher's hair, encouraging him with probably too much force. He'd had a lot of good head in his life, but Gallagher's enthusiasm and undoubted skill was making him almost dizzy.

Gallagher dragged his tongue up Cort's cock and licked at the head before sucking him again. But it was the hand suddenly on his balls and the deep groan that finally sent Cort over the edge, his body tense and coiled as he started to shoot.

He thought he should let go of Gallagher's hair, let him move out of the way, but Gallagher didn't seem to mind. He swallowed and licked some more, sucking gently as Cort tried to breathe properly in the damp and far too hot room.

"God," Cort said, the world drawled out as his body relaxed. "Good."

Gallagher laughed softly and licked him once more before sitting up. "Little rushed."

"Public place."

"Uh huh." Gallagher seemed pleased about that part, beaming at him. "Catch your breath. We should get out of here soon."

Cort nodded and made himself sit up, pulling his towel into

his lap just in case someone came in. "Smells like sex in here," he noted. They were so busted if anyone even stuck their head in.

"Leave the door open when we go," Gallagher said, leaning back. "Be all fresh in the morning."

Cort nodded, thinking that morning was only a few hours off and he really should put in a couple of more hours work before then. "What are you doing here, really?" he asked curiously.

"I got a call that one of my cases was showing some activity, and as I'm off tomorrow I had to come check the files." He shrugged. "Then I figured I'd sneak in a workout here before going home. I saw you and changed my mind."

Cort almost laughed. "You're brazen."

"Sometimes," Gallagher admitted. "But usually smart."

"You got your ass ready," Cort pointed out. "That's brazen and not terribly smart. Distinct lack of rubbers in here; if I weren't who I am I would have fucked you bareback."

Gallagher nodded. "But you are who you are and I'm a good judge. Plus, I'm not exactly a shrinking violet; if you'd tried I would have stopped you."

Cort nodded and let it go. Gallagher had to have known himself, at least. "I have to get to my desk," he said, not standing up yet. He didn't quite trust his legs.

"Really?" Gallagher looked at him. "It's midnight."

"It's a homicide."

It was Gallagher's turn to nod. "I'm going to head home. Will you call me?"

Standing, Cort gave him a steady look. "To hook up again?"

To his surprise Gallagher shook his head. "Wouldn't say no to a repeat, but I think maybe we could have a decent time hanging out. Do you like Italian?"

"Chinese. Italian's good, though. Harder to work off."

Gallagher laughed. "Yeah, okay. So? Will you?"

Cort nodded and stepped off the risers. "Yeah, probably. Can't promise when, but you know that. The job. You can always call me, you know."

"Yeah, I know. Still. I chased you down this time; the ball's in your court."

"Okay, point taken. See you, Gallagher." Cort pulled the door open and let in a blast of cool air tinged with locker room. "Thanks."

"Thank you," Gallagher called back, laughing. "Close the door, it's cold out there."

Cort smiled and shook his head to himself. If he didn't know better, he could imagine them fighting about temperatures and how many blankets to put on the bed.

But that wasn't going to happen. That never happened in Cort's life. Putting the thought aside, he went back to work, hoping to catch a killer.

Chapter Three

The good thing about working a case in the middle of the night was that the squad room was pretty quiet. There were a few guys around, but they were doing the same thing he was, going through files and trying to track down evidence.

Cort went to his desk first and checked his voicemail for messages, jotting down the order they came in and the times. Often, he'd get a call about something and a later call would be from the same lab with more conclusive information.

Lachlan had called to tell him that the cause of death was as expected. "The paperwork will be on your desk tomorrow," her recorded voice said, "but basically he was strangled. There wasn't anything in his blood work, and until his death he was perfectly healthy, if a little unfit. Probably went to the gym three or four times a week, but had a sedentary job. Watch for the file, Strang."

The next message was a call back from Dinsmore's office, Rookwood Corporation, saying that of course they would see him at his convenience, and what a tragedy it was. They would do all that they could to help. He wrote it down, wondering if their lawyers would meet him at the doors as soon as someone twigged that he might just possibly want to poke around their systems and financial situation, not to mention talk to everyone Dinsmore had even waved hello to.

Cort wasn't surprised that the labs hadn't gotten back to him yet; even given the current hour, the case had come in at a bad time of day. Gathering up his papers and forwarding his phone to one of the mid-sized rooms available to the homicide department, Cort crossed the hall to set up camp.

Ten minutes and a roll of tape later, he sat on the table and looked at the wall. He had neat little charts of information he'd gathered with big gaping holes in important places. He knew that Dinsmore worked from home. That he'd lived in his apartment for two years and a month, that he paid his bills on time and was a good tenant. He knew that the only living relative was his sister, Georgia, but he hadn't been able to get in touch with her yet; her phones both went to voicemail and her boss said that she was on vacation.

He knew that Dinsmore had been working when he died, and he was reasonably sure that the killer was someone he knew and had let in. There was no sign of forced entry, and Dinsmore had clearly turned his back on his attacker. He hadn't seen it coming. Someone he trusted, probably.

Cort wrote down *friend, family, coworker* and carried on.

There was a huge gaping white space next to the photos of Dinsmore's arm. Cort had written out the names in a nice thick marker, all neat and tidy, but it didn't help to give him any ideas.

Suzie3624
Swampmonster
Brokenrecord2
Puddin1975

He was reasonably sure that Suzie3624 was a female, but that was all. He wouldn't be surprised if she turned out to be a sixty-year-old man, though, given that the Internet was what it was. The other three gave him no ideas at all, other than maybe Puddin' was born in 1975.

He really, really wanted to hear from the computer tech. Soon. Maybe he should have had Gallagher at least try to find logs.

Cort looked at the next photo and wondered about the music that had been playing. It seemed odd that the perpetrator would leave loud music on and the door open; it was sure to attract attention. But the door could have been an accident. The whole thing felt like it had been spur of the moment, an act of rage.

"So," Cort said out loud as he climbed off the table. "Vincent is working. Someone knocks, he lets them in because he knows them. He feels safe. He goes back to his desk, they talk. Vincent says something the other guy really doesn't like, but it doesn't turn into a fight, 'cause Vincent stays where he is and doesn't mind that the person is behind him. Perp rummages in the box, gets the keyboard and does the deed. Panics. If the music is on, he doesn't turn it off, just goes. If it's off, he turns it on and runs."

Cort nodded and grabbed his pad.

Music on. Find out if it's a CD or radio. Find track if it's a CD.

He rubbed his eyes and tossed the pad down, suddenly exhausted. A look at the clock told him it was just after one in the morning. There was no hope of getting a hold of Dinsmore's sister at this hour, and if there was anyone working in the lab they would assume he was home in bed. Which was exactly where he wanted to be.

With a sigh he started taking down the mostly blank map of the case, putting everything back in the file. It was sparse at that point; if he didn't close the case within forty-eight hours it would grow to be inches thick. He hoped it wouldn't merit a blue cold-case tag; with an unpremeditated murder he had a certain expectation of himself. Crimes of passion tended to be sloppy, and sloppy meant that he had a better than average chance of a collar, even if he was working alone.

He went back to his desk, changed the phone back to normal and put the case file dead center on his desk with a sticky note attached to it that said he'd be in by seven. Then he went home, yawning and idly wondering how Gallagher was sleeping, across the hall from a crime scene.

* * *

Cort actually got back to the station by six-thirty, gritty-eyed and in desperate need of coffee. The coffee he found easily enough in the squad room, although he couldn't have sworn that it had been made in the time since he'd left. When he felt fortified he started taping again, covering the walls nearest his desk with his crime scene and notes, adding sticky notes with reminders to himself in the appropriate places.

It took him about fifteen minutes to get it looking like he needed it to, and the blank spaces were once more a taunt to his knowledge. He stood by his desk and finished off the coffee in his mug, reading things over and waiting for seven o'clock to arrive so he could get down to the lab and start cracking a whip over whoever had been assigned his evidence.

With a fresh mug of stale coffee in his hand, he left the squad room at five to the hour and took the elevator down, then wandered the maze of hallways to find the forensic lab that had the computers. He was more than sure that the prints lifted from the scene would have been run the night before and someone would call him if, by some miracle, they'd matched anything in the system.

He finally found one of the forensic investigators hard at work, music turned down low as he sat at a long table stacked high with computer components.

"Hey, Marty," Cort said, walking into the lab and stepping over cables.

Marty looked up, blinking rapidly behind his glasses. "Oh, hey. Strang. You're in early."

"Yeah, well. That my case?" He peered at the monitor and learned exactly nothing from the lines of code.

"Nope. Yours is over here." Marty shoved with his feet and the wheeled office chair he was sitting on shot across the floor to another table. He nudged a mouse and the flat-screen monitor came to life. "God, I love computers. Actually, I love the way people keep absolutely everything on them."

That sounded good. "Tell me," Cort prompted.

"Well, your victim liked blondes, has a healthy savings account and worked a lot. He didn't listen to much music via mp3s stored here, but he might have had a nice collection of CDs. He collected movies and had a nice little commercial database on here to organize them. And he had a thriving social life via the Internet."

Cort nodded slowly and tried to pick the important bits of information out of the litany. "Porn?"

"I like the way your mind works, but no. Not really. Just a few pictures, nothing memorable. They actually looked like amateur shots, but the file names didn't give anything away." Marty clicked a couple of icons and brought up text files. "You sent the Polaroid of his arm, so I concentrated on the chat logs and anything I could find from message boards."

"Anything?"

"Just the final name." Marty indicated one of the text files with the cursor. "He had a whole file dedicated to saved AIM chats with whoever puddin1975 is. They're from more than a year ago, and I couldn't find anything more recent attached to that username."

Cort tilted his head and started scanning the document as best he could. "Were they romantic?" he asked, not seeing anything other than small talk.

"Oh, yeah. Romantic in the sexy way of cybering."

Cort snorted. "Great. Anything else?"

With a nod Marty pushed his chair again and woke up another monitor. "This is from one of the other drives in that box," he said. "He had the same programs on here and by the dates on some of the files -- like the movie database -- this was the prior drive. I'm running a search to gather all the chat logs and find the rest of the names. Interesting thing, though..."

Cort stepped back two paces as Marty wheeled himself back to the table with Dinsmore's working computer. "Warn a guy!"

"Sorry. Anyway, like I was saying, this guy chatted a lot. A lot, a lot. Like almost eighteen hours a day, lot."

"That's a lot," Cort agreed, mostly because Marty seemed to expect him to. "About what?"

Clicking away, Marty opened more files. "He had a constant window open with his office, strictly work things. Usually there were also private message windows open with his co-workers, one each. Also all work related. And at the same time, he had three other chat programs open, maintaining conversations with other people. Going by timestamps on the conversations in the logs, it wasn't unusual for him to have up to four other things going on while he worked, and then several more in the evenings."

Cort found himself impressed. "What did he talk about?"

"Depends on the person. He had geek friends, movie buff friends, people who he just said hi to, his sister, a few people he was talking to about getting a puppy. And there's a fair amount of the sex talk, too."

Grimacing, Cort nodded. "Great. I can hardly wait to read them. Can you send me the files?"

Marty laughed and reached for a disc. "Too big for e-mail, my friend. I burned them for you. The interesting part you want to know about, however, is that it all stopped. Dead stop on everything other than his AIM talk with work, about two months ago."

"Really," Cort said slowly, looking at the disc in his hand. "No idea why?"

"Nope."

"Huh." He put the disc in the other hand and looked at the tagged drives on the table. "What's next?"

Marty sighed and looked forlorn. "Next I go through these and try to find those other names. But honestly, I'd say you have the important stuff. I'll poke around the drive he was using some more, see if I can pull up anything he deleted that might explain the sudden silence."

"Thanks." Cort didn't envy him. "I'm out of here. See you, Marty. Call me if you get anything."

"You know it."

Cort left him there, wheeling around like a mad man, and went back up to his desk to load the disc and try to make some headway before Williamson got in. Looking busy and actually being busy were two different things, and Williamson knew it.

By nine, Cort had drunk three more cups of coffee, one of which was fresh, and read the autopsy report between rounds of scanning the chat logs. What he hadn't managed to do was find Dinsmore's next of kin. His sister had well and truly gone on vacation, completely unreachable by her job and, apparently, her brother. All he'd been able to do was file a notice for patrols to watch for her car, in hopes of locating her that way.

For a couple of hours, Cort sat at his desk and scrolled through pages and pages of text, looking for some reason why Dinsmore had been killed. He'd started with the chats from his coworkers and found only that their job was complicated and very, very dull.

"Strang!"

Cort's constant infusions of caffeine had him awake, but it made him jittery, too. Williamson calling his name over the buzz of the room made him twitch so hard he almost sent his tidy cup full of pens crashing to the floor. "Sir," he called back, grabbing the cup and the pens before they could escape.

"What are you still doing here? Rookwood opened at eight." Williamson was out of his office, bearing down on Cort's desk with all the grace of a bull in a fury.

"I'd planned to be there at some point this morning," Cort said, keeping his tone even. "I wanted to get a hold of the sister first."

"Yeah, well, she's MIA. Get going. Talk to the people who knew him best." Williamson turned around on his heel, causing a near collision between three other people who'd been following along in his wake, heading for the door.

Cort sighed and put on his coat. He didn't really think Williamson was in the mood to argue about who knew Dinsmore best, given that the man had worked from home. Chances were that no one really knew him well, not in the sense Williamson meant. It certainly didn't look like it was his coworkers based on the conversations he'd been reading over.

He thought about that as he drove, the whole idea of who knew a person best. He supposed that an argument could be made that his own coworkers should know him best, given that he also lived alone, like Dinsmore. But they didn't, not by a long shot. His family didn't, not really. Cort figured that the people who knew him best were the ones whom he allowed to know him at all, and that number was slim. There were a few ex-lovers out there who could say they knew him, but only two or three. Mostly, Cort decided, the only person who knew him really well was himself.

Which wouldn't really come in handy if he was ever killed.

In a suitably muted mood he arrived at the building the Rookwood Corporation called home and made his way up to the third floor, looking for a woman named Eileen Summer. She'd been Dinsmore's department head, and was therefore a likely place to begin talking to people. If nothing else, it was the politic thing to do.

She saw him at once, taking him into her office and closing the door behind them. "Such a shock," she said, seating herself behind her desk.

To her credit, Cort thought that she did, indeed, look shocked. Unraveled and clearly upset were accurate terms as well; her hair was neatly styled and her clothes were as fresh as anyone's were at noon, but her eyes had dark smudges under them and she was pale.

"I'm sure it is," Cort said sympathetically. "Were you very close to Mr. Dinsmore?"

He expected her to either go with the typical boss and employee relationship comments or to suggest something deeper, a real friendship. He wasn't at all expecting her to shake her head and say, "No. I didn't like him very much, actually."

Cort felt his eyebrows go up and quickly schooled his expression into something bland. "Really?" he asked mildly. "Were there personal issues or professional?"

Ms. Summer blinked at him for a moment and then flushed. "I didn't mean it like that," she said, looking away from him. "Vincent was a good guy. He was a fantastic employee."

"Then what did you mean?" Cort asked, trying not to be accusatory or pushy. It wasn't often that initial interviews went odd right off the bat. He'd found out very early in his career with the homicide unit that people tended to make saints and heroes out of every victim. They were always model citizens who were on perfect terms with everyone. Until, of course, it was pointed out that the victim was a crack-dealing liar and thief who'd never paid his child support.

She sighed and picked up a pen that was on her desk, then put it down again. "He just..." She rolled her eyes, apparently at herself and leaned forward to look at Cort intently. "He had very poor people skills. He never did anything inappropriate, don't get me wrong, but he was socially awkward. That's a big part of why he worked from home, to be honest. The sad thing is that he knew it. He knew he was bad with people face to face and chose to do his work out of the office. It worked out very well for all of us, though it's pretty pathetic when you look at it. I felt bad for him, but at the same time, I couldn't bring myself to actually enjoy being around him."

Cort made a note or two in his book, mostly so he could look busy while he thought. "Was he aggressive at all? Did he upset any of his coworkers?"

"Good Lord, no," Ms. Summer protested immediately. "Damn, I shouldn't have said anything. We didn't dislike him, Detective. We just didn't... like him. If you know what I mean."

"No, I'm glad you did say it," Cort told her. "Anything at all is a help. You have to remember that we, the police, didn't know him at all. Anything you can tell me is a help. You said he was a good worker?" He hoped that by moving to something more positive she would relax a little; he could always circle around again to the other side of things.

Ms. Summer nodded. "Yes, he was," she said, sounding utterly certain. "We actually had him headhunted about five years ago when we did an expansion of our development team. He came with very good references and had a lot of potential, which he more than lived up to. He requested that he work out of the office when we made him the job offer, and we were reluctant to go ahead with that. We've found before that a team tends to work better if they are actually together. In Vincent's case, however, it was better to do it his way."

"You say he knew that he wasn't good with people?" Cort asked before he could remind himself that he was supposed to be holding off.

"Oh, yes." Ms. Summer shrugged one shoulder and added, "He related much better through the written word as opposed to the spoken. He was in constant touch with his team via e-mail and instant messaging programs and, despite my initial reservations, was very productive. He was concise and clear in his communication, and I suspect that by keeping all of his work relationships firmly within the scope of his job we avoided a lot of interpersonal things which get in the way."

"Hmm." Cort made another note and asked, "Do you know which messaging program he used for work?" He knew, of course, but it would be interesting to know how much of their chatter had been monitored, if any at all.

She looked surprised and shook her head. "We had to have everyone take AIM off their computers last year because of a virus someone downloaded to the server, but they have it back again. I really don't know."

"Okay," Cort said, giving her a fast smile. "It's probably not important. Can you tell me what kind of work Mr. Dinsmore did for you?"

"He wrote some highly specialized database software for us," she said. "That's why we hired him, initially. In the last two years he's been doing more and more work on outside projects, developing programs for internal use for clients of ours. He even brought in two fairly important contracts over the last while." She looked thoughtful for a moment. "I'd say that if anything he's been more focused over the last several weeks. I'd even made a recommendation to my boss that he be considered for team lead position, although that would have meant he'd be in the office more."

Cort felt a fast tingle shoot into his spine, nice and low. "I see," he said mildly. "Was he aware of that?"

"No." She shook her head. "I don't think anyone was. Just myself and my superior, Mr. Ling."

The tingle eased off. "All right," Cort said. "Can you think of anything else? Do you know if Mr. Dinsmore had a romantic relationship at all? We've been unable to reach his next of kin, so we're unaware of his personal life at this time."

She stared at him. "How sad is it that I'd never once even thought of Vincent in a relationship with anyone?"

Cort took that as a no. "May I speak with his coworkers now? I'd like to talk to his team, particularly."

"Certainly." Ms. Summer stood up and led him through a short warren of cubicles, apparently ignoring the looks they got as they walked past desks. She seemed immune to the looks, which was intriguing to Cort. He, of course, was used to people stopping to stare when he was working, but she seemed to be merely in a daze.

She took him into an area where three cubicles opened off a central faux room with a printer table and a coffee pot of its own, and cleared her throat. Instantly, three people emerged, looking at Cort and not Ms. Summer.

"This is the team Vincent worked with," she said. "Nick Weston, Marcie Wong and Joseph Reeves. This is Detective Strang, and I believe he has a few questions for you." She only waited long enough for them all to nod and then excused herself, which Cort appreciated. People tended to talk a lot more freely if their boss wasn't hanging around.

"Just a few questions," Cort said easily, not even flipping open his notebook again. "Did you know Mr. Dinsmore well? How was he to work with, that sort of thing."

The three of them looked at each for a moment and both of the men each shrugged a shoulder. The woman, Marcie Wong, moved a little to the left, a little closer to Weston. They were both in their late twenties, Cort guessed, and he mentally took a guess and decided that they were fucking. It was just an impression based on nothing, and it certainly wouldn't go into his file, but he thought it anyway.

"He was all right," Reeves finally said. "He did his job, didn't make it hard for anyone else to do theirs."

"He was helpful," Wong put in, biting at her lower lip. "And he was always online, so getting a hold of him was never a problem. It actually worked kind of well, with all of us in a chat room, plus the three of us able to talk out here as well."

Cort nodded. "How about personally? Did he ever share anything with you? Do you know if he had a girlfriend, boyfriend, money trouble? Anything like that?"

The three of them stared and Weston hid a laugh behind a cough and then turned red. "Uh, no," he said when Cort looked directly at him. "I don't know anything like that. Vince was... kind of asexual, actually. I doubt he'd had a date in his life, unless it was online."

"How about that?" Cort said calmly. "Do you know if he did? Date online, I mean. If he was online all day, it wouldn't be hard."

Again, the three of them stared at him.

Cort stifled a sigh. "Was he ever absent from a chat? Did he take a long time replying sometimes?"

As a unit, they shook their heads.

"How long were you all a team?" Cort asked.

"The four of us?" Weston thought for a moment. "At least two years. Before Marcie was hired, me and Joseph and Vince worked together. Five years for us."

"Since Vincent was hired," Reeves agreed.

Cort nodded, wondering how the three of them could know so little about a man they worked with all day, regardless of if he was in the office or not. Hell, Cort knew all about Samuel's marital woes and even what Turner had for takeout on Fridays. "So, the four of you were a team. Is there an actual team leader? One of you kind of in charge?"

"Me," Reeves said, straightening a little.

"So Mr. Dinsmore reported to you?" Cort asked.

"Sort of," Reeves replied. "I plot and outline the work that needs to be done, assign parts and check up on progress. If there are issues with the way things flow, I have to rework the plans to find solutions and keep things on track, under budget and on time."

Cort glanced at the other two and took in their bland expressions. "Did you have any issues with Mr. Dinsmore working within your frameworks?"

Reeves shook his head. "No. He did his job. And like Marcie said, he was helpful. He was really good at the technical things, kind of solved a lot of little troubles that would have added up to bigger problems."

Both Wong and Weston relaxed minutely and Cort nodded. "All right, then," he said, trying to read between the lines to get at the real story. No one was lying, he thought, but there was something not being said. "Do you have any idea what could have happened yesterday?"

Three heads shook at him, Wong looking faintly troubled.

"Ms. Wong?" Cort pushed.

"Nothing," she said, still looking thoughtful. "Everything seemed to be going fine. He was in the chat room, then said he was going offline for half an hour or so. He came back, said he'd figured out the code error I'd been having trouble with, and e-mailed me the section I needed to replace. Then things were quiet until it was time for me to leave. I told him I was going home and signed off."

Cort nodded, waiting.

She shook her head. "He didn't reply to say bye, but sometimes he didn't. I didn't think anything of it."

"What time was that?" Cort asked, finally opening his notebook.

"I left early yesterday for a dental appointment. I can check the log for the exact time, if you'd like."

"That would be helpful, yes," Cort said.

She went into her cubicle for a minute and then called out, "I signed off at ten past four, and the last message from Vincent was at ten to."

Cort made a note and did some fast math. According to the medical examiner's estimates, Dinsmore probably died between the two, if not immediately after sending his last message to Wong. "Thank you," he said, keeping his voice distant and professional. "What time does the office typically work until?"

"Five," Reeves said. "Yesterday was odd, though, because we were at an imposed lull in the project. We can't do much more until the client is ready to test, so we were all in and out a bit."

Cort felt his eyebrow go up. "I see. What time did you leave?" he asked both Reeves and Weston.

Weston looked back. "I actually came in a little late, around ten. But I was here until five, except for lunch."

"I took a long lunch, with Mr. Ling, one of the bosses. And then I was here, but left again around three," Reeves said.

"Did you go home at that time?" Cort asked, using his briefest shorthand so he could look utterly casual about it. It never really worked; people didn't generally like it when the police wrote down what they said, regardless of how casually they did it.

"Sure," Reeves told him. "Well, after getting some groceries."

Cort closed his book and put it in his pocket. "Thank you," he said again. "I may have more questions later, and if you think of anything, please call me." He handed out his business cards, suddenly flashing on the way he'd given one to Gallagher the evening before.

This was far less exciting.

He made his way back out of the cubicle farm and stopped at the front desk to smile winningly at the receptionist. "I'd like to see Mr. Ling, please."

Chapter Four

Fifteen minutes later Cort was in his car, headed back to the station. As he sat at a red light he scrolled through the phonebook on his mobile phone and called the forensic lab. He was two blocks farther along before he got through to the person he wanted to; lucky for him, it was one of his favorite scientists.

"Cortland!" she said cheerfully when she came on the line. "And how are you today, Apple?"

Cort winced and then grinned. "Tart and juicy, Karen. Don't call me that."

"Whatever. Had a good night, huh? What's his name?"

"I'll never tell. Unless you have good news for me, anyway." That was a lie; he wasn't about to tell Karen that he'd gotten off with someone she likely knew.

"What kind of good news? I have good news and... well. Regular inconclusive news."

"I want to hear that you got prints off the keyboard," he said, pulling up at the next red light, one block farther along.

Karen laughed. "I have a dream, too. It involves Johnny Depp, a sword, and those things he had in his hair when he was playing Captain Jack."

Cort snorted. "I had that dream. He wasn't very good."

"The hottest ones rarely are," Karen said with a long sigh. "In lieu of prints from the murder weapon -- and thank you, by the way, for adding to my list of objects which can take a life -- I can tell you that most of the latents from the apartment were the victim's. I do have a series of unidentified ones that are currently running through the system, though. Nineteen of them from three different areas, so likely it's at least that many people. Did he have a cleaning lady or anything?"

"I have no idea," Cort said, chagrined. "I can find out. How long do I have to wait on the prints?"

"A few more hours. Did you get the autopsy report?"

"Yeah."

"Okay, so you know the blood was clean."

"Uh huh." Cort moved with the traffic again and swung onto the block the station was on. "Do you have anything to do with the computer stuff on this one?"

"Nah, they're down the hall. Marty's working on it."

"Yeah, I talked to him. Did any of your unidentified latent prints come off the stuff in the box?"

"Four," Karen said. "And nine from the bookshelf in the living room, and six from objects on the coffee table."

Cort frowned and eased his car around a delivery van. "None from the stereo?" he asked as he pulled into the parking lot.

"Nope, just the victim's. Why?"

"Gallagher said the music was up loud, which is what got his attention in the first place. I wondered if it was up to cover the sound of the murder, or if the vic turned it up."

There was a brief pause and he could hear something being shifted, metal on metal. "Gallagher? From upstairs?"

"If that's where computer crimes is," Cort said, driving in a slow circle to find a space. "He found the body, lives across the hall."

"Oh, ew," Karen said. "That's gotta suck."

Cort grinned. "Sucks," he agreed, thinking about Gallagher's mouth in very general terms and thinking he really did have to find time to call him. Soon.

"Wish I could help you. Nothing funky about the stereo, though."

"Was it taken in to you guys?"

"Nope," Karen said with a grunt, the metal sound happening again. "No reason to, right? Why?"

Cort pulled into a spot and parked his car, crookedly. "Nothing, I guess. I'll figure it out."

"You always do, Apple."

If only that were true. Cort rolled his eyes and turned off the car. "Do you have anything else for me?" he asked, making sure he had his notebook. "I'm just coming in the building, so I can come down."

"Jesus, no. I mean, you can come down, but I don't have anything but a big fucking metal box of crap to sort through for Delaney. Head found at the recycling plant. Disgusting. You don't want to see it."

Cort shuddered. "You're right, I don't. Thanks, Karen. Call me about the prints, all right?"

"Don't be simple. Of course I'll call." She hung up on him and Cort found himself grinning as he stuffed his phone back in his pocket. He liked Karen a lot; she was high on the easy to talk to list, and low on the bullshit. It was actually kind of too bad she wasn't a guy. She was just his type.

He walked into the building and took the stairs up to his squad room, hoping he had time to grab some lunch before he went back to work, or at least a doughnut. There were four pink message slips on his desk, though, so he sat and read them without even taking off his overcoat.

Two hours later he was still sitting there, but he'd had coffee and added to his notes. His case map on the wall had a lot less white space, and he'd followed up on two tips for other cases. He'd also called Georgia Dinsmore again, at all three numbers he had for her, but only her office line was answered. They hadn't heard from her either, and were beginning to recognize his voice.

Cort taped up his notes and impressions of Dinsmore's coworkers and leaned back in his chair, stretching. He hadn't heard from Karen, he hadn't heard from Marty about the other names on Dinsmore's arm, and the sister wasn't anywhere he could find.

He was temporarily stalled, save for reading chat text. That kind of work required food and a very tall bottle of something to drink, preferably with more caffeine. He kind of wanted to take a nap, too, but that wasn't going to happen. He felt a little twitchy, restless and wanting to be working the case harder than he was, but he wasn't sure what he should be doing.

Standing up, he opened up his web browser on his computer and did a search for Rookwood. It came up easily, so he clicked and went to their homepage, and then left his desk to go hunt for a sandwich. He'd poke around the site between rounds of reading chats when he was fed. It was probably a good idea to get some exercise too, so he decided that he'd walk down the block to the deli to get some takeout.

However, walking wasn't the kind of exercise he wanted, he realized as he headed down the stairs. He wasn't at all interested in a walk down the street; he was looking for something a bit more intense, more full bodied. Something distracting. His mind was busy and his body was agitated, geared up with nowhere to go.

"Jesus," he said to himself, almost automatically turning down the hall that led to the farthest hallway from the public areas. "This is such a bad idea."

But it wasn't as if it hadn't been done before, and it wasn't like that lonely, out of the way bathroom hadn't been used by overworked and jazzed up cops before. Cort just hoped that there wasn't anyone else in his particular mood as he pulled the door open. It would be just too embarrassing to whack off next to someone he'd have to nod to for the next twenty years.

The bathroom was empty, thankfully, and Cort went right to a stall, leaning on the door as soon as he'd closed it. He wasn't going to take his time, either. Just a nice, fast jerk off, and then back to work. All he needed was his hand and something hot to think about.

Hot and steamy, really.

Eyes closed, his cock heavy in his hand, Cort admitted to himself that a lot of little things had been bringing Gallagher to mind, all morning. But the biggest thing, the undeniable thing, was that Cort had gotten off on him in a big way. His mouth, his hands, the noises he made when he was getting jacked off. It had made an impression.

It took no time at all to sink back into his memory, to see the sweat on Gallagher's chest, to hear him. Cort pulled at his cock and kept his eyes closed, using the sex he'd had less than fifteen hours earlier as the best jerk-off fantasy he'd had in years. He licked his lower lip and then bit it, his hand tight and his strokes long and full.

In his mind, he could see it all again and he could hear Gallagher talking to him, see the smile and the spark in his eye. He could feel what it was like to be pursued. And in the stall of a bathroom, his balls pulled up tight and hot.

"Yeah," he grunted, remembering too late where he was. He leaned forward, hips shoving his cock through his fist, and came, splashing into the toilet.

Panting, he wiped his hand carefully and flushed, then took another few moments to wait for his heartbeat to settle before going to wash up and head back to work with a sandwich from the vending machine.

He really did have to call Gallagher when he got a chance.

* * *

The chats varied between the incredibly dreary work related conversations that had no life in them at all to a pornographic tour of the man's imagination.

Cort seriously worried about what exactly Karen was going to find on that keyboard. It was a good thing she wore gloves.

He read steadily for an hour, scrolling through folders labeled with usernames. He started with the work ones and found nothing that hinted at any of Dinsmore's teammates having it in for him, and moved on to scan through the relationship Dinsmore had with puddin1975.

The two had apparently found each other on a Yahoo group devoted to James Bond movies and had taken their discussion about the merits of the villains to a private chat room. How they'd managed to talk for almost three hours exclusively about the bad guys, Cort wasn't sure, but they'd done it.

They'd chatted again a few nights later, mostly about James Bond but a little more about things like TV shows and books, and within a week or so they were logging on to just say hi. It was almost three weeks before they clarified that they were, in fact, of opposite genders, acknowledged geeks, and into computers. They then proceeded to talk code and share jokes Cort didn't understand for another week or so.

Finally, they met up as usual one evening, but it seemed that Puddin' had had a very bad day. She talked in circles and apparently wanted to vent a bit, and Dinsmore invited her to do just that. What followed was about fifteen messages in a row of job angst and spilled coffee on her purse and her best friend nagging her about something silly and missing the bus home because her boss had her stay late for some meeting she wasn't really needed for and then finding out that her hot water had been shut off because the people in the next apartment were idiots.

Dinsmore was sympathetic.

Puddin' was grateful.

And thus, a friendship was born.

Cort scrolled down farther, looking for key words to jump out at him. It was hard to find actual full sentences though, due to a huge use of emoticons that didn't look nearly so neat as plain text.

"Whoa," he said out loud as one word caught his attention, leaping out from the scrolling text. He backed up and leaned forward, making a fast note of the date. It looked like a little less than two months after their first talk about Bond's bad boys and girls, the two of them split a bottle of wine and got down to business.

As sexy talk went it was a little uninspiring, in Cort's opinion. Puddin' liked the word 'cock' too much, and Dinsmore had an affinity with 'pussy' that made Cort wonder if he'd ever heard of other words for it. Still, it seemed to get them going, and if the sudden utter lack of capital letters really did mean they were typing one handed, he didn't want to think about it too hard.

The post screwing sweet talk was interesting, though. He learned that Puddin's first name was Nancy and that she was, in fact, born in 1975. Dinsmore didn't lie about his first name, and they said a few very sweet things to each other, and signed off.

The conversation was more of the same. As was the next and the one after that. Cort was finding the similarities to an offline relationship intriguing. They talked a bit, flirted, fucked around. The energy of the conversations was geared to sex for a few weeks, then they calmed down a bit and started talking more, sharing their lives. It was like they were settling down.

There were a few references to the sounds of each other's voices and gaps in information that indicated they'd also spoken on the phone. Curious to see what happened to them, Cort started scrolling faster, his eyes now adjusted to seeing the word 'cock' all over the place.

The dates on the left hand side did a funky thing though, and he slowed, back tracking. There had been a four day gap in their conversations, which was immediately explained by the first conversation after that. They'd actually met up, in Chicago for a long weekend.

Fairly sure that actually seeing each other in person would herald the end, given the way Dinsmore's coworkers had talked about him, Cort was oddly pleased to see that they'd maintained their relationship for another three months. The last two weeks were horribly awkward reading, however, as it was clear by the long silences and stilted conversations that they were in the final stages.

And oddly, it was Dinsmore who wanted out. Puddin' seemed like a nice girl, other than the way that she spelled during sex, and Cort found himself feeling a little bad for her. The actual break-up was gentle, with Dinsmore full of apologies and no lies that Cort could see at a fast glance. He was honest enough to tell her that he really liked her but that the distance was an issue, and that he didn't think they had the strength to endure one of them actually moving. He thought it best if they just part and keep each other fondly in their hearts.

It kind of made Cort want to roll his eyes.

Puddin' took it okay though, and that was that.

Cort closed the files and sat back, his eyes burning and his legs stiff as he tried to work the kinks out from sitting too long. He had no idea how people like Marty -- or even Dinsmore, for that matter -- could stare at a screen all day.

Idly, he wondered if Gallagher's eyes ever burned.

With a sigh he reached for his phone and called down to Marty.

"Hey," Cort said when the line connected. "How's it going?"

"Tedious. I have a couple more discs for you, though. I found the other usernames on the vic's arm."

Cort sat straighter. "Yeah? Did you read?"

"Just a bit. They were also relationships." Marty sounded pleased with himself.

"Oh, good. Because I haven't read enough about pussy today."

Marty laughed. "Yeah, well. He wasn't real good at finding the thesaurus. Too busy, I guess."

Cort nodded and stretched his back a bit. "I'll come down and get them. Did you manage to retrieve any deleted files from the newest drive?"

"Working on it. No rush to read this stuff, if you ask me. They all broke up and never contacted him again, at least, not under those names."

"Ah, but under other names is why I have to read them." Cort made a face.

"That's why you're the detective," Marty laughed.

"Yeah, lucky me. Hey, can you do something for me?"

"That would depend entirely on what it is you want," Marty said. "If it's computer based, probably. Cook dinner, not so much."

Cort pulled the phone away from his ear and looked at it, then held it properly again. "You're weird."

"That's why I stay in the lab. What do you need?"

"A snapshot. Can you draw me a picture of his life in the two weeks or so leading up to his sudden halt with the chat programs? I'm looking for anything offbeat; you know, work, money, a spike in some other interest he might have kept a record of."

Marty didn't say anything for a moment. "Yeah, I can do that," he said eventually. "It won't be hard at all, just take me a couple of hours to pick out the data. Give me... say three hours? The retrieval of anything deleted but not written over should be done by then. And as it's almost quitting time I'll be ordering in if you want to share a pizza later. I had a late lunch."

Cort grinned, pleased that he wasn't the only one working insane hours. "Great. I'll come by the lab in a few hours then. If you finish up fast, just call my mobile, all right?"

"Yeah, okay. Get back to work, I'm busy."

Cort hung up and made a few notes, smiling to himself. He didn't have anything concrete yet, but at least there was a promise of incoming information. He called Dinsmore's sister again, both at home and on her mobile, and hung up before the voice mail could kick in. He'd already left messages; more would just add to her stress and panic when she finally checked them.

He looked over his notes once more and decided that it was time to move, to get off his ass and out of the station. He still wanted to check on the music that had been playing, so he took that as an excuse to leave, reasoning that it wouldn't hurt at all to take another look at the crime scene.

Chapter Five

Cort cut the tape that sealed the door of Dinsmore's apartment and went in. He stood in the narrow hall for a moment, listening to the quiet as he pulled on a pair of gloves, and thought about how being in a crime scene by himself was always a little creepy. That no one in Dinsmore's life was clamoring to be let in was just sad.

After a moment he went through to the living room and took a look at the stereo, still covered with dust from the techs. Turned off, its LED display showed nothing at all, not even the time, which was odd. Cort tried to turn it on, but nothing happened; he wanted to slap his forehead when he remembered the techs had unplugged it to shut it off.

Once it was plugged back in, the time started flashing and the display cycled through its settings for a minute before finally settling on CD. Cort could only assume that's where it had been when it had been used last, although it was entirely likely that it was the system default. He pushed the eject button and the tray slid out, showing only one disc in the five disc caddy. "That makes it easier," he said out loud.

Carefully, he lifted out the disc by the very edge and the center, hoping there would be prints on it. The disc didn't have a label; Dinsmore or someone else had burned it themselves. He put it back in, after making sure there were no markings on the other side, and pressed play.

"Jesus!" he yelled as the music crashed through the speakers. He turned the volume down from fifteen to six and tried to get his heartbeat under control. No wonder that had gotten Gallagher's attention. It was basic generic club music, heavy on the bass line and with no discernable melody, but the volume alone was worth noting. He let it play for a few more minutes, hoping there would be some hint why Dinsmore had put it on, or why the killer had.

"This is ridiculous," he muttered to himself after the song ended, replaced with silence. "Probably had it on repeat. But why?" He took the disc back out and slipped it into an evidence bag, neatly labeling it for the lab. He'd have them dust it for prints and pray that if there were any they'd match one of unknowns. Other than maybe placing someone at the scene at the right time, the music angle was feeling pretty useless to Cort.

Frustrated, he looked around the room and absently took a

few books off the shelves, trying to get a feel for Dinsmore and why someone hated him enough to wrap a cord around his neck. He walked through to the kitchen and poked around in the cupboards, then to the bathroom, which was mostly empty, everything being at the lab. The bedroom was the same, most of the personal items cleared away in case they had any bearing.

There wasn't even a photograph left in there, if there ever had been.

Slightly disturbed by how empty Dinsmore's life felt in the aftermath of his death, Cort left the apartment, resealing the door behind himself and signing the tape.

He didn't know he was going to turn right around and knock on Gallagher's door until he'd done it. And he didn't know what he was going to say if the door actually opened.

"I wondered if that was you over there," Gallagher said as the door opened. "Loud music, huh?"

"Yeah, it was," Cort said, his mouth going dry. Gallagher was wearing jeans and a t-shirt, not exactly a seductive outfit but it seemed to be working anyway. "I wanted to see if the music was more important than I'd thought or not. Was it the same as yesterday?"

Gallagher stepped back and held the door open for him, inviting him in. "Sounded like it, yeah. You turned down the volume before I could really hear. Come on in."

Cort nodded his thanks and went in, careful not to keep going into the living area, in case Gallagher simply wanted to talk about the case out of the public hallway.

"I said come in," Gallagher told him, rolling his eyes and walking deeper into the apartment. "Unless you actually like the claustrophobic space that they call an entry?"

"Jeeze, you are pushy," Cort said with a sigh. "I was being polite." He smiled and took off his coat, tossing it over a handy chair.

"You don't have to be polite, I've had your cock in my mouth." Gallagher threw himself onto a comfortable looking couch and glanced up at him. "Nah, polite is good. Forget I said that. Come in, make yourself at home. Get anywhere on the case yet?"

"Not really," Cort said, glancing around. Gallagher's apartment was a mirror image of Dinsmore's but they had a completely different feel. Gallagher's was tidy but lived in, and there were piles of books and magazines on every flat surface, along with coffee cups and pottery. The art on the walls was also different from Dinsmore's, most of it a collection of framed posters, mixed in with what looked like original watercolors showing a lot of countryside. "I'm waiting on the computer lab, mostly," Cort added.

Gallagher nodded. "Sit down," he invited. "Did you manage to find any chats to go with those names on his arm?"

Cort made and face and sat, taking over the other half of the couch. "Yeah. I've read the ones for the last name, apparently the most recent of the four. Some of the most illiterate and unimaginative porn ever, and Marty says that the others are about the same."

"Hell, it's probably better than some of the stuff I've had to read," Gallagher said sympathetically. "Was it kinky?"

"Sadly, no. Just straight up vanilla heterosexual cybersex." He looked at Gallagher curiously. "Do you wind up reading a lot of that?"

"Sometimes," Gallagher said with a nod. "Usually, though, if I'm reading for sexual offenses or predators it's a lot worse. And sneaky, too. In the beginning, when you're just starting out on perv patrol, you don't see a lot of things that are flags and then suddenly you're reading some disgusting little snippet that makes you want to throw your computer across the room."

Cort winced. "It must get disturbing."

"Yeah, for sure. That's why we have to rotate on and off that sort of work, as well as see counselors. The rest of the job isn't bad that way. Lots of work, for sure, but a lot easier on the head. I'm working some fraud cases right now, which means we've got to deal with the federal agencies; also hard on the head, but it doesn't give me nightmares."

Cort looked back toward the hallway and Dinsmore's apartment. "Did you have nightmares last night? He wasn't pretty."

Gallagher laughed softly. "No, I was a little too tired to dream last night. Someone wore me out at the gym."

"Wow, it must have been the late hour," Cort said with a broad, satisfied grin. "That was hardly a workout." He relaxed a bit more into the couch and eyed Gallagher up smugly.

"It was the rush of adrenaline," Gallagher explained, eyeing him back. "Must have been the setting that got me all fired up."

"Oh, so it wasn't the actual sex you liked?" Cort cocked an eyebrow at him, daring him to say the sex itself hadn't been stellar in its own right.

Gallagher laughed, his head going back a little bit and his eyes crinkling at the corners. "I didn't say that," he protested. "Although you did point out that it wasn't particularly athletic."

Cort nodded and pushed himself up, then leaned over the space between them, not quite touching. "If you want athletic, I have some time."

"Enough time? The word athletic makes certain promises, and I'd hate to be rushed again. Nothing worse than being in mid-workout and getting a call from the office." He leaned, too, the space between them vanishing.

"There's a difference between rushing and going fast," Cort pointed out. "Yes or no?"

"I'm not stupid," Gallagher said, moving forward the necessary inch or so to kiss Cort. It was hardly a shy kiss, and it wasn't so much an invitation for more of the same as it was a blatant demand. "Take off your gun and get your weapon out."

"That was really pathetic," Cort said, trying not to laugh. But he did take off his gun and its belt, setting them on the table before he dove back for more. He pushed Gallagher back, hands and body moving to cover as much of him as he could. The couch wasn't exactly big enough for both of them, and Cort sincerely hoped that the actual fucking would take place somewhere they wouldn't have a fifty-fifty chance of falling off, but it would do for a start. He shoved his tongue into Gallagher's mouth and one hand into his hair, making the most of what leverage he could find.

"That's it," Gallagher said, tearing his mouth away long enough to speak. "I knew you weren't a tease."

"A tease? Jesus Christ, when did I ever manage to give that impression?" Cort grinned down at him and circled his hips to make his point. Gallagher's point was impressive, too, Cort observed.

Gallagher inhaled sharply and moved against him, his hands grabbing at Cort's ass. "Sorry," he said roughly. "My mistake. Oh man, do that again."

"Do what?" Cort ignored the way Gallagher's hands were trying to guide him, trying to make him thrust and give him some movement to work with.

"Tease!" Gallagher accused, laughing. Then he braced one leg on the couch and shoved, tumbling them to the floor. "Now," he said, looking down at Cort and not waiting for him to catch the breath that had been forced out by the impact. "I suggest we move to the bedroom. It'll be easier on your back than on the carpet."

"My back?" Cort raised an eyebrow.

Gallagher raised one right back at him. "Don't tell me we're going to argue about who tops."

"No, no. Just about who's assuming he's going to top." Cort beamed at him and moved his hips, making it seem like he'd be just as happy to rub off. It was a blatant lie, of course; he at least wanted to get his pants undone before he came.

Gallagher sighed and rolled his eyes. "Please, Strang. May I shove my cock up your ass and fuck you stupid?"

"Sure," Cort agreed magnanimously. "That would be lovely."

"I don't know about that," Gallagher said, rolling off and standing up. "But it'll be fun." He held out a hand for Cort to haul himself up from the floor, and beamed at him. "Really, a lot of fun."

"I love it when guys make promises," Cort said, following him to the bedroom and shedding his shirt as they went. "Makes them try hard to live up to the hype."

"Whatever gets you going," Gallagher said over his shoulder, his belt coming off and landing on a chair. "Personally, I'd rather be doing than talking about doing."

"Pushy," Cort reminded him. "Careful, or I'll start calling you that."

Gallagher looked honestly shocked for a moment, staring at him with wide eyes and his mouth open. "I'll show you pushy," he finally managed, his eyes gleaming. He moved fast, shoving Cort to the bed and pouncing on him with a laugh.

"Oh, this is more like it," Cort taunted, laughing back and wrestling with him as they worked to strip each other. It wasn't easy, between the laughing and the nearly constant struggle for superiority, but they managed to stay on the bed and not injure each other.

"Stop wasting precious departmental time," Gallagher said, still laughing as he tried to pin Cort to the bed.

"God." Cort stared up at him for a moment, looking at his face and then lower, admiring his skin and nicely defined abs. "I don't think I've ever fucked around on the clock before, you know. This could send me right to hell."

"Right, because the butt sex wasn't enough." Gallagher snickered at him and blatantly flexed, showing off. "Done looking?"

"Not by a long shot." Cort added hands and tongue to his perusal, licking what he could reach and feeling up where his mouth couldn't go with Gallagher's weight on him. Tight nipples got bitten, and the curve of Gallagher's ass got squeezed while Cort attempted to shamelessly rub his own erection along Gallagher's hip.

Gallagher rolled slightly to the left and Cort let him, following along until they were both lying back on the bed. The move seemed to settle them both and Cort allowed himself the pleasure of long, luxurious kisses with a lot of tongue. His hands were still on Gallagher, for sure, and Gallagher's were on him, roaming and touching, but the kissing was captivating.

They tangled their legs together, cocks brushing and bumping as they made out, and Cort found himself smiling into the kisses. He really hadn't expected Gallagher to be a snuggler.

"What?" Gallagher said as he ran his hand up Cort's spine, pressing lightly at each vertebra.

"Nothing." Cort smiled more broadly and then buried his head in Gallagher's neck and bit him lightly. "Nothing at all."

"You're thinking too much," Gallagher said, his head tipping back to give Cort easier access to his neck and jaw.

"So make me stop," Cort taunted. He dragged his teeth over skin wet from his tongue and noted how Gallagher froze in his arms, swallowing hard to smother a moan.

"Doing is better than thinking," Gallagher insisted, his voice rough. He moved away from Cort's mouth and pinned him to the bed again, pushing mostly with his hips. "No marks above the collar," he warned.

Cort nodded, going up on his elbows to lick the center of Gallagher's chest. He could do that. He could mark well below the collar, in a variety of ways.

"Little oral?" Gallagher gasped out.

Cort laughed, hoping that Gallagher wasn't trying to pretend that was a protest, what with the way he was holding Cort's head to him, guiding him back to his nipples. Still laughing, Cort did as Gallagher so clearly wanted, suckling hard as he slid a hand around Gallagher's hip and found his erection, slick and hot.

"Oh God," Gallagher panted, his body arching and curling in turns as Cort played with his cock and tortured his chest.

"Thought you were going to fuck me," Cort said, grinning up at him. "Can just keep doing this, though, if you want." He dragged the palm of his hand over the head of Gallagher's prick, pushing fluid around and down in a sticky smear. Gallagher's foreskin had completely retracted and Cort had no doubt at all that the head was intensely sensitive.

"Jesus," Gallagher hissed, his hips jerking, his thighs tight on

Cort's hipbones. "Stop that. Want in your ass."

"Do it then," Cort teased, stroking him again. "I'm waiting."

"The hell you are," Gallagher said, edging away. "You're teasing me. If you were waiting, you'd be slick and ready."

Cort grinned broadly and let him go. "That's your trick. But okay, I can do that one, too. Where's your lube?"

Gallagher's brown eyes went murky and dark, just like that, and he pointed to the shelf beside the bed. "Toss me a jacket," he said, his accent a little stronger as he moved to the end of the bed.

So he could watch, Cort realized. A sharp needle of lust drove up Cort's spine and then down again, right to his balls. It was almost painful, how much the idea suddenly turned him on. He'd done it before for plenty of guys, but the way Gallagher was watching him, one hand cupping his own balls, was different. Intense.

He reached to the shelf and tossed Gallagher the strip of condoms he found there, and then grabbed a palmful of lube. It was nice stuff, too, not cheap KY quality. It was slippery and wet, and Cort was careful not to spill it all over as he moved to the head of the bed and lay back. "Get ready," he said, reaching down.

Gallagher nodded and watched him, not moving.

"No, really," Cort said, smoothing lube over and around his hole with two fingers. "I'm no virgin. This won't take long." He changed his angle, drew up a knee and gathered his balls in free hand. When he pushed two fingers into his own ass, he started stroking his cock.

"Jesus," Gallagher breathed. He was staring, mouth slack and eyes dilated, one hand motionless on his cock and the other holding the strip of rubbers.

"Come on," Cort said, fingering himself. "You did it. You do it. Can't tell me you've never seen it before."

Gallagher nodded, finally tearing one wrapper open and getting the condom out. "Seen it. Just not... God, do it faster."

Cort closed his eyes and did it faster, his cock jumping. He could feel the pressure of his own hand, the drag of skin on his hole and the wet, slippery fluid he was pushing into himself. His prick twinged and he gave it a quick jerk just to keep things calm, but all that did was feel really, really good. So he did it again.

"Oh no, you don't," Gallagher protested. "Wait for me."

Cort moaned and shoved his fingers as far into his ass as he could manage, but then Gallagher was there, between his legs, his weight making the bed move. Cort opened his eyes when Gallagher's hand wrapped around his wrist, dragging his fingers out. "Come on," he said again. "I'm ready." Even to his own ears he sounded drugged.

Gallagher's hands dug into Cort's hips, and with a growl from Gallagher and a cry from Cort, he was dragged down the bed and pretty much right onto Gallagher's cock. There was only a slight moment of fumbling, Cort trying to move onto him and Gallagher letting go of one hip to guide himself, and then Gallagher thrust into him, piercing him with a hard push.

"Christ." Gallagher groaned the word instead of saying it, and then he moved, hands braced beside Cort's shoulders as he fucked Cort with long, ragged strokes.

"Uh huh," Cort agreed, his legs circling Gallagher's hips and his heels digging in, pulling him deeper, faster. His head was already spinning, his ass grasping and clutching at the cock that was invading every sense. He couldn't hear anything other than their panting and the roar of his own breath, and he couldn't smell anything other than sex.

It was far, far better than the faint hint of antiseptic and chlorine from the gym at the station.

Cort had figured out pretty damn fast that the entirety of their encounter, messing up a nice set of sheets and what felt like a really good quality quilt and all, was going to be rather quick.

But it wasn't going to be disappointing. Not at all, not with the way Gallagher's cock was banging up against Cort's prostate with almost every thrust, sending waves of sharp longing through his body. He wasn't sure how long he could withstand the pounding, the rising fury of his orgasm already gathering, but he was sure as hell going to take as much as he could get. His ass was twitching, grasping, and his cock was getting a quick rub every once in a while along Gallagher's belly, but that part was lacking. He reached down, making a grab for his erection, needing just a little bit more.

"Fuck," Gallagher panted, pushing himself back to rest on his heels and yanking Cort's hips with him. "Slow down."

Cort shook his head. "No slow. Slow bad." He stroked himself quickly, his back arched by the angle Gallagher had him, his cock rigid and aching in his hand.

"Too fast!" Gallagher insisted, pulling out.

Cort swore, squeezing his cock tightly at the base. "Jesus

Christ, almost there! What's your problem?"

"Too fast," Gallagher said again, but he was grinning wickedly. "You want fast and hard, roll over."

Cort stared at him, blinking rapidly. Then he rolled, legs bent at the knee and his ass high.

"Thought so," Gallagher said smugly.

"Just do it," Cort ground out, bracing himself. "And don't forget my dick."

"Hardly," Gallagher said dryly. Then he shoved in hard, fucking Cort fast and just as hard as Cort could have begged for, one hand immediately going around to jack Cort's cock.

"Jesus, yes!" Cort yelled, holding on for everything he was worth. He felt like he was about to burst into flames, about to implode, and then Gallagher circled his hips, cock deep inside, and lights flashed.

"Yes," Gallagher panted, his hips circling again. "Just like that. Come on, Strang. Give it to me."

Cort couldn't even draw breath to yell as he came, streaks of come spilling and shooting onto the quilt as he clamped down hard on Gallagher's prick. His eyes were closed tight and he knew he was going to shake with the aftershocks; he didn't even care if he managed to keep himself up while Gallagher finished.

Gallagher chanted at him, fucking him through it roughly for a handful of thrusts, apparently enjoying the way it felt when Cort came on him, around him. "Yeah," he finally yelled, his cock throbbing so hard Cort felt it. Then he followed Cort down to the bed, lying on his back, gasping.

Cort struggled to get his breath, his face half buried in a pillow. He hadn't been fucked like that in a long time, hadn't even really noticed that he'd missed it. But now that he knew, he had a feeling that he'd be making time to get to know Gallagher a lot better.

"Goddamn," Gallagher said roughly, sucking in air. "Best way to spend my day off, ever."

"Not my day off," Cort said, slurring a bit. "Oh, fuck, it really isn't. Shit."

Gallagher groaned and rolled away from him. "Fuck and run?" he asked, reaching for a box of tissues.

"I don't want to," Cort told him, not quite ready to move yet. "I really, really don't." Staying right where he was and waiting until they could it again, or a variation on the theme, sounded much better to him.

"That's flattering, at least," Gallagher said as he cleaned up.

"The yelling was nice, too." He grinned and rolled back to Cort, kissing him softly. "So, how's the case going, anyway?"

Cort made himself shift enough to get an arm around Gallagher. "Well, let's see. His coworkers know nothing about him, other than he was good at his job. His boss says he was socially inept. His sister is unreachable. All I've got so far is a huge amount of internet chatter, really. Too much of it; I'll be reading for days unless something more tangible turns up. Marty's trying to pull up recently deleted data for me, and to be honest that's where all of my hope is. That and the sister."

Gallagher made an interested noise and kissed him again. "What's next?"

"Back to see Marty," Cort said with a sigh. "Then lots of reading."

"Want some help?"

Cort leaned back to see Gallagher's face better. "Are you serious?"

"Sure. I was going to do laundry and clean the kitchen, but that can wait." He seemed sincere, and added in a smile. "If you get it all read, then maybe you'll have time for a late dinner out with me. Hell, order in and we can eat at your desk, even."

"You have a very odd idea about dating," Cort said, smiling back. "All right. I could use another set of eyes. Will your squad back you up on helping me if Williamson has a cow?"

"Sure," Gallagher said as he got up and headed to the bathroom. "I mean, I'm not going to ask for overtime. Just helping out is all. Want a shower?"

"God, yes." Cort followed him, his body aching pleasantly and his attitude very nicely adjusted.

Chapter Six

Cort stopped by Karen's lab to drop off the CD he'd taken from Dinsmore's stereo, then he and Gallagher made their way down the hall to the forensic computing lab. Marty was hard at work when they got there, both of them smelling of the same shower gel and Gallagher with still damp hair. Cort didn't think anyone would notice.

"Nice dinner hour?" Marty asked, barely glancing at them. "Must be good, having free time like that."

"It's my day off," Gallagher said mildly, pulling out a chair and sitting at a free computer.

"I was waiting on you," Cort added, rolling his eyes.

"Don't touch that," Marty snapped, reaching for Gallagher's hand before he could move the mouse in front of him. "Don't you have your own computers to play with?"

"Sure, but they aren't as nice as yours," Gallagher said grinning. "Plus you have that nice plasma screen and all. That you don't use."

"It's too big and fiddly," Marty sniffed. "But I do use it. It impresses people like you."

Cort found himself rolling his eyes again. It was like suddenly realizing everyone at the party was there because they loved the same movie, but it was one you'd never seen. "What have you got for me?" he asked, trying to bring Marty back to the matter had hand.

"Masses of data," Marty said, swinging back to where he'd been, his chair rolling smoothly. "This guy saved everything. I love it when they do that."

"Yeah, me too," Gallagher chimed in. "I especially love the ones who keep spreadsheets of their money and where they spend it. Even better than budgeting software, usually."

"I'm thrilled for you both," Cort said. "But I need it to make sense."

Marty handed him a disc. "Here, these are the old chat logs from the other drives. Same as before, but it's for the other three names. Happy reading."

Cort sighed. "Wonderful. Did you get that timeline snapshot thing done for me?"

"Yep." Marty pulled up a screen on the nearest computer and Gallagher came over to peer over his shoulder. "Made a nice little chart for you, too."

"Use the plasma," Gallagher begged, actually clasping his hands in front of him and making his eyes go wide.

Marty turned and looked at Cort. "And you're chasing after him?"

"No," Cort said with a thin smile. "I just randomly decided to use his shower. Can we please see the evidence now?"

"Touchy," Marty muttered, picking up a remote. "For you, Patrick," he said, giving Gallagher a nod. "But only because you asked so nicely." He used the remote and a very nice graph suddenly appeared on a large plasma screen mounted above the work stations. "There you go. Mr. Dinsmore's last three months."

Cort stared and then squinted as he tilted his head. "Help me out here."

Marty pointed. "The green line is money. Nice and even, same as always. He got paid every two weeks, paid his bills, had some left over. No huge dips or peaks."

Cort nodded. "Okay, got it. Blue line."

"Work. His logged hours that is -- the time he was actually counting as his work day and getting paid for. Also nice and steady, put in his time well and there's chat logs with his coworkers time stamped to fit in with a normal business day. By the way, that is some of the driest reading ever."

"Right," Cort said, mostly to himself. The graph started to form itself into something he could read, and he pointed to a yellow line that curved neatly with very regular dips and rises, about four times a week. "That's the gym."

"Very good, Detective," Marty said with approval. "And now you can tell me what the very exciting purple line is."

Cort looked, conscious of Gallagher watching him. "Social chatter," Cort said, actually walking closer to the screen. "Nice and high for a while and then a dead stop." The purple line didn't even so much as waver, let alone have a sudden drop below the mean average of the amount of time Dinsmore had spent talking to people; it merely came to an abrupt end, ten weeks before Dinsmore's death.

"What's this one?" Cort asked, lifting his hand and pointing. It was a hard to miss shade of orange, one of the smooth lines that just flowed without a lot of activity until it suddenly curved upward, starting about a week after the social internet chat stopped.

"That," Marty said, coming to stand next to him, "is an interesting little thing I found while poking around. It's not hard data, but something I put together from some scraps of information in his work logs and from things he said to his coworkers. I marked the passages in the chats on the disc I gave you."

"Careful, Marty," Gallagher said softly, coming to stand by Cort's other side. "You'll wind up out of the lab and working for Computer Crimes."

"You lot wouldn't keep me and the rest of them would fight to keep me here," Marty said, grinning at him and looking pleased.

Cort waved his hand in a hurry up motion. "But what is it, Marty?" he asked again. "My case is going as cold as the corpse, here."

Marty pointed. "That is his work performance. Your victim got offline and started kicking some serious ass at work."

Cort nodded slowly and pulled his notebook from his pocket. "His boss said he was doing really well the last couple of months," he said, flipping through to find her statement. "She's recommended him for promotion, too."

"Good for him," Marty said, leaving him there and going to one of his computers. "I'll give you the information I have to back up the graph, in case you need it."

"Yeah, of course," Cort said, frowning to himself. "Thing is, I still don't know why he stopped chatting. Did you find anything in the deleted stuff?"

"Bits and pieces," Marty said over his shoulder. "The data is raw and jumbled up right now. I'm working on it."

Cort sighed. "Okay. We're going to read this stuff, I guess."

"Fun times," Gallagher said, heading to the door. "I can burn a copy, right?"

"If you know how, you can do it," Marty said, not looking up. "I'm sure you'll figure it out."

Cort tried not to smile as Gallagher rolled his eyes. "Come on, let's go burn our retinas," he said, leading the way out. "Call me, Marty."

"Yeah, yeah, I know the drill, Strang," Marty said without any real annoyance.

Cort pushed the elevator call button and looked at the disc in his hand. "How much data do these things hold?" he asked glumly.

"A lot," Gallagher said, looking at the elevator doors. "But it won't be full. We'll split it up."

"Yeah, okay," Cort sighed, not really looking forward to

reading it all. "I owe you dinner."

"You owe me dinner and a blowjob."

Cort grinned. "Yeah, okay. You work cheap." In his pocket, Cort's mobile phone rang and vibrated. "If that's Marty, I'll either kiss him or kill him," he muttered, getting it out and open. "Strang."

"Are you in the building?"

Cort nodded, his back straightening by reflex as soon as he heard Williamson's voice. "Yes, sir, just heading up from the lab now."

"Good. Georgia Dinsmore waiting for you in my office. She finally checked her voicemail and came right in, so get up here."

"Yes, sir." Cort hung up and looked at Gallagher. "Well. I'm going to have to put a hold on the reading, dinner, and even the blowjob."

"Got a break?" Gallagher asked, not looking surprised.

"Dinsmore's sister finally showed up." The elevator doors slid open and Cort stepped in. "With any luck at all, it'll be a break." He pushed the number for his floor, nodding to himself when Gallagher pressed the button for a floor lower. "I'll call you when I know what's going on."

"Sure," Gallagher said easily as the doors closed. "I'll be at my desk. Want me to start on the logs?"

"Nah." Cort shook his head. "No sense in you wasting your time if you don't have to. It's not your case."

They went up, the elevator stopping at almost every floor and filling up. When Gallagher got off at his floor he nodded to Cort and said, "Call me. I'll be home later."

"Will do," Cort told him, watching him go. He hoped he wouldn't be working past midnight again.

Cort didn't waste time getting to the squad room when he reached his floor; Williamson would have his balls, and it wasn't like Cort didn't know how important it was to talk to Georgia Dinsmore. He wasn't surprised to find Williamson hovering near the entrance, either.

"Use my office," he said gruffly. "But don't take too long."

Cort nodded, still walking. "How is she?" he asked.

"She can talk."

That was good enough for Cort. He dismissed Williamson from his mind, tapped twice at the closed door, and opened it. "Ms. Dinsmore?" he said quietly.

She was sitting in the visitor's chair, looking a little shell-shocked, but wasn't in tears, for which Cort was glad. She looked up at him and nodded, her brown hair back in a tight ponytail that bobbed in a far too cheerful way. "Yes," she said. "Georgia."

"I'm Detective Strang," Cort told her as he closed the door behind himself. "I'm the detective investigating your brother's death. Thank you for coming in, Georgia."

She nodded jerkily. "Of course," she said, barely above a whisper. "I was out of town, up in the mountains with my girlfriends. There wasn't any mobile reception and I didn't leave the hotel number with Vincent."

"I'm sorry for your loss," Cort said gently as he leaned on Williamson's desk. She really did seem mostly together, if a little stunned.

"Thank you," she said, swallowing hard. "He was a good man."

"I'm sure he was," Cort agreed. "His coworkers said he was very hard working and reliable. I've had a hard time finding out anything about his personal life, though. Can you tell me about him?"

Georgia blinked slowly, her hands twisted together in her lap. "He was... he was kind. He had a difficult time with people face to face, but Vincent was a kind person. He never hurt anyone. I can't believe this is happening."

"It's hard, I know," Cort said sympathetically. He moved to the other visitor's chair, pulling it around so he could sit next to her instead of looming. "Did he have many friends?"

Shaking her head, she said, "Not offline. He spent a lot of time with his friends on the computer. Vincent was very literal and abrupt in person; he found it a lot easier to make friends when he could write to them. He had girlfriends, though, nice girls he met online. I met one of them, a couple of years ago. She came to visit."

"What was her name?"

"Judith," she said after a short pause. "She was nice. They seemed happy. They broke up a few months later, after a few trips to see each other. There were a couple more after that, but I didn't meet them."

Cort nodded, careful not to lean in too close to her. "Was he seeing anyone recently?"

Georgia shook her head, then nodded. "He talked about someone a few months ago, maybe three months? He didn't tell me her name, just that he'd met someone nice."

"He didn't talk about her again?" Cort asked casually. Three months would have put the new lady friend on the latest hard drive, but he hadn't seen anything.

"Not really. Actually, he brushed it off when I asked him about her, about a month ago. He said he'd been working too much to keep up a relationship."

Interesting. Cort thought for a moment. "Did your brother ever talk about work stress, or some random run in with someone? Was there anything bothering him, in your opinion?"

"No," Georgia said, shaking her head vehemently. "Nothing. If anything, he was happier with his work. He said he was doing a lot, that he'd brought in a contract that was really interesting. The last time I talked to him, it was all he wanted to discuss. Most of it went way over my head, but it made him happy."

Cort filed that away, thinking he'd have to make another trip over to Rookwood. "Thank you, Georgia," he said. "Is there anything else you can think of that would help?"

Her ponytail swayed as she shook her head again, her eyes filling. "I don't know," she said. "There's no reason for anyone to hate him. He's a good person."

"I know," Cort assured him. "Do you have someone to take you home?" He wasn't entirely sure that she was in a fit state to drive.

"My friend Alice is waiting downstairs," she said as she stood up. "Will you call me when you find out who did this?"

"Yes," Cort promised. "And I may call you if I have more questions." He gave her one of his business cards. "If you think of anything, no matter how small, please feel free to call me."

She took the card and nodded. "Thank you, Detective. I will."

Cort walked her out and took her all the way to the lobby, neither of them talking. When she was safely handed off to her friend and crying freely in her arms, Cort fled back to his desk, his mind racing.

He moved paper on his desk, the phone wedged between his ear and shoulder as he tried to find his notes. "Marty," he said as soon as the line connected. "I need that data. I don't even care if it's in order at the moment, I need to see any deleted chat transcripts from about three months ago."

"I'm working on it," Marty said. "I told you -- "

"Now, if not sooner. I'm on my way down." Cort pushed the disconnect and started dialing again, Gallagher's number in his hand. As soon as he'd pushed the last button he got out the disc from Marty and put it in the disc drive, tapping his foot while he waited for it to load and for Gallagher to pick up his line.

"Gallagher."

"Hey, it's me. Busy?"

"It's my day off."

"Great, meet me in Marty's lab in about four minutes." He hung up and scrolled through the disc menu, then pulled up Marty's colorful graph of the way Dinsmore had lived his life. "There you are," Cort muttered, setting it to print. "The question is: what was so horrible that you turned your life upside down for it?"

Three minutes later, Cort walked into Marty's lab, the sheet of paper in hand. "It's basic," he said, looking at Marty. "He stopped his social life cold and started working hard. Someone didn't like it. I need to know who, and I need to know what happened."

"Basic for you," Marty snapped, pointing at the plasma screen. "Recovered data isn't in neat little folders, Strang. It's an out of order mix of data, some of which has been overwritten and is gone. I have everything I could get, but it's a mess. There's video, text, graphics, downloaded files, a lot of stuff from his work. I can't give you just the chat or just the video yet."

"What's up?" Gallagher asked, walking in and going right to the chair he'd had before.

"I need you to help Marty find me chat logs."

Gallagher raised an eyebrow. "How?"

"I don't know, you're the computer experts. I need to know who he was seeing online a couple of months ago. The week before he stopped chatting is key. Find it, please." Cort turned and headed to the door. "I have to check into something upstairs on that disc you gave me. Be back in an hour."

"For crying out loud," Marty muttered as Cort left. "All right, sit down. Let's split this up."

"You owe me," Gallagher yelled after him.

Cort knew. But if they could find what he needed, he didn't care.

An hour later, Cort went back, feeling a bit more secure with his theory. "Tell me you have--" He stopped dead, met by Marty and Gallagher sitting on the table and looking smug. "You found it."

"We found it." Marty looked very pleased with himself.

"So?" Cort looked from Marty to Gallagher and back, his body suddenly tight with anticipation. "Show me. What happened to him?"

"Abrupt and total social faux pas," Marty said, lifting his remote. "Gallagher likes the plasma. I'm indulging him because he found the transcripts through clever use of a keyword search."

"Yeah?" Cort gave Gallagher a wide smile and got a modest shrug in return. "What word?"

"Tell you later," Gallagher said as a page of text filled the plasma screen. "It's choppy," he said, pointing to a wide gap in the text. "And we're not sure it's all in order, as some of it was apparently overwritten. But the important part is there."

Cort moved closer to the screen, his eyes catching random words as Marty scrolled slowly through the document for him. "Looks like a budding relationship," he said, remembering how Dinsmore's relationship with Puddin' had read at the beginning.

"Oh, yeah," Marty agreed. "Hang on." He scrolled more rapidly and stopped at a long stream of text. "Their first time. Isn't it sweet?"

Cort scanned the text and made a face. "Someone really should have given him a thesaurus for his birthday. Okay, so new girlfriend. And then he deleted everything that had to do with her, so give me the why."

Marty smiled and scrolled to the end of the document. "Note the date," he said. "As far as I can tell, this is pretty much the day he took himself offline for anything other than work."

Cort nodded absently and read the last page. Then he read it again, smiling. "Oh, ouch."

"I'll say," Gallagher said with a wince. "It just doesn't get better, no matter how many times I read it."

Cort shook his head. "I'm pretty sure I would have hidden from the world, too." he said as he checked his watch. "I think she's probably at home by this time. Can you print that for me?"

Gallagher handed him a folder, grinning. "Here you go."

"Thanks," Cort said as he took it. "Nice job, you two."

Marty snorted. "We kind of got the impression that it was important, what with you barking at us and all. And now, if you'll excuse me, I've been here for more than thirteen hours and I'm going home."

"Sorry about that," Cort said as he lifted the file in a salute. He turned on his heel and headed out the door, calling back, "Gallagher, need a lift home?"

"You're not going to let me ride along for the fun part?" Gallagher asked. He caught up with Cort just outside the lab, Marty joining them as he turned off the lights.

"I was being discreet," Cort pointed out.

"Not on my account, I hope," Marty said, rolling his eyes.

"You kind of blew your cover earlier."

Both Cort and Gallagher turned to look at him, each with an eyebrow raised.

"However," Marty went on, pushing the elevator call button. "There is such a thing as too much information."

Cort grinned and let silence reign for a moment, then said, "I need to go to my desk and get the home addresses, then we can go ask her some questions before I swing by your place."

Gallagher snorted. "Sure. And when you make your arrest and wind up doing paperwork all night, I'll just take a cab home."

"That works, too," Cort agreed, still smiling. He loved it when a case started to fall into place.

Chapter Seven

It was getting close to nine p.m. when he and Gallagher knocked on Eileen Summer's front door. She lived in a trim townhouse in one of the up and coming areas, her home one of the few that had achieved the polished look of newly completed renovations. Three doors down, a rented dumpster stood, advertising the continuing work on her block.

"Detective," she said when she opened the door. She looked from Cort to Gallagher and back again, her teeth worrying at her lower lip.

"Ms. Summer." Cort smiled politely at her, noting that she wasn't exactly holding the door wide open for them. "This is Detective Gallagher, from Computer Crimes. May we come in for a moment?"

She stared at Gallagher for a moment and stepped back. "Of course. Computer Crimes? Did you find something else while you were looking into Vincent's death?"

"No, no," Cort said, stepping into her entryway and making room for Gallagher to close the door behind them. "This is still in relation to Mr. Dinsmore's murder. But Detective Gallagher did find some information of interest when he was going over data from Mr. Dinsmore's computer."

Eileen Summer turned her stare to Cort and he watched as she made the leap from confusion to complete understanding. "Oh," she said, looking away. "That."

"That," Cort agreed. "He had deleted everything, but some of it wasn't overwritten yet. I imagine it must have been a huge shock to you both when you figured out you actually knew each other offline."

Gallagher said nothing, merely stood behind Cort's shoulder and held his hands behind his back.

She nodded and walked away from them, not objecting when they followed her into the living room. She got a tissue and sat on the couch, holding herself stiffly. "We were both incredibly embarrassed," she said, looking at her knees. "Him more than me, I think."

"You're probably right," Cort said, lowering himself onto a chair across from her. "Can you tell me about it?"

She shrugged, still not looking at him. "I met a man online. We talked, became friendly. We traded stories about our days, things we'd read, things that happened. It was just like having a face to face friend. And then one day we were both online while we worked at our jobs and had a chat window open with each other as well. I told him I had to work for a bit and could talk in an hour or so. He said he had to work, too. I finished what I was doing and sent a file by e-mail to Vincent, flagged for questions. And a couple of minutes later, my friend said he'd just gotten the stupidest e-mail from his boss. I laughed, and told him a story about one of my staff. He said he knew people like that. A couple of minutes later I got a message from him that was just my name and a question mark." She glanced up at Cort, tears starting to roll down her cheeks. "I stared at it for almost a minute before I typed in Vincent's name. He went offline at once."

"Did you talk to him about it later?" Cort asked gently.

She nodded. "He came to my office a few hours later and offered to quit. It was very awkward."

"I imagine it was."

"I told him there was no need for that," she said, wiping her eyes. "That we could just put the whole thing behind us and pretend none of it had happened."

"Did that work?"

"For the most part," she said, looking down again. "He never contacted me online again and when we did deal with one another it was strictly business. He apologized for saying my questions were stupid." She started to cry in earnest, her shoulders shaking. "He always was smarter than me. He proved it over and over the last two months, too. His work was so good I had no choice but to try to get him promoted."

"And then he'd be out of your office?" Cort asked.

She shook her head violently. "If anything he'd have to work more closely with me. But it didn't matter, he deserved a better position. He earned it."

Cort looked at Gallagher, hoping he'd have something to offer in the face of a woman's grief, but he looked as uncomfortable as Cort felt. "Thank you, Ms. Summer," Cort finally said. "Can I call someone for you? A friend or neighbor to stay with you?"

Her head shook again and she swiped at her tears with the tissue. "I'm fine," she said, obviously trying to get herself under control. "Besides, what would I say? I'm sort of overreacting to losing an employee."

"But not to losing someone you cared about," Cort pointed out gently. "I'm sorry for your loss."

She looked at him with wide eyes and nodded slowly. "Thank you, Detective. That's nice to hear."

Cort stood up and got the box of tissues. "Please call someone you can confide in," he said as he handed it to her. "It will help."

"Thank you," she whispered. "Please find out who did this to him."

"I will," Cort promised as he gestured Gallagher toward the door. "Hopefully very soon."

* * *

Cort let Gallagher drive after they left Eileen Summer, choosing to spend the drive to Gallagher's building on the phone checking his messages and making some fast notes. As he'd expected, the messages from Karen were particularly unhelpful in terms of the physical evidence.

"Easy," Cort murmured as Gallagher took a turn faster than Cort had expected, his pen leaving a jagged scrawl across the page.

"Sorry."

Cort nodded and dutifully wrote what Karen's recorded voice told him. None of the unidentified prints were in the criminal justice system. The only prints on the music CD were Dinsmore's. There was no traceable organic matter on the keyboard, other than the victim's. There was nothing in the apartment that gave them a name for the unknown person or persons at the scene.

"Well, that sucks," Cort said as he disconnected. "I'm past the twenty-four window here and running on five hour's sleep and three orgasms. I need food."

"Three?" Gallagher glanced at him as he pulled into a parking space.

"I jerked off at lunch."

Gallagher smiled. "Me, too. Come on up, I've got some pasta we can reheat. You can lay out your case, it might help you see something."

Cort nodded and gathered up his pad and pen, shoving them into a pocket along with his phone. He was suddenly starving and just the idea of sitting somewhere comfortable for a bit and talking out his theory had an appeal that almost rejuvenated him. They walked up, both of them pausing to look at Dinsmore's door, still resealed with police tape.

"I think I might move," Gallagher said as he unlocked his door. "But maybe it'll be less weird when the tape is down."

"It'll be less weird when I catch the killer," Cort told him. He followed Gallagher in, kicking off his shoes in the hall and loosening his tie.

"True. Get on that, will you?" Gallagher said, going right to the fridge and getting out dishes to heat up. "Wine?" he asked, taking off his jacket and gun.

"Yeah, thanks." Cort did the same, grinning as he realized it was the second time that day that he'd started stripping down in that apartment. "This is becoming a habit."

"A habit takes three weeks. And you now owe me two dinners."

"And a blowjob."

"I'm beginning to think the blowjob will be easier to collect on." Gallagher grinned at him and winked as he turned on the oven. "Tell me about your case," he invited, crossing to a cupboard and getting two wine glasses.

"What parts are you missing?" Cort wandered into the living room, grateful that the fairly open floor plan meant he could walk and talk at the same time, and not have to yell so Gallagher could hear him.

"Uh..." Gallagher poured wine, something red, and came out of the kitchen. "It's not money, or at least not his money. His girlfriend didn't kill him, just got him to get offline. His sister?"

"I don't think she knows anything about it," Cort said, shaking his head. "Call it a gut feeling. She seemed to love him a lot as a brother, but I don't think she knew him a whole lot better than anyone else. Hey, can you tell me what the girl you saw visiting looked like?"

Gallagher passed him a wine glass and looked thoughtful. "Not terribly tall, late twenties. Brown shoulder length hair, medium build. No glasses."

"Sounds like his sister." Cort nodded to himself and shrugged. "Only one other thing left, really."

"Work?"

"I think so," Cort said with a sigh. He tasted the wine and nodded. "This is good."

"I like it," Gallagher agreed. "So. Want to stop thinking for a bit?"

Cort blinked and shook his head wryly. "You don't believe in subtle, do you?" he asked, taking a much bigger swallow of wine. "All right, then. Blowjob?"

"I might even forgive the dinner debt, if it's a good one," Gallagher said, setting his glass down. "Little fooling around, a glass of wine, supper. Then your head will be ready to get back to work."

"But my body will be ready for sleep," Cort pointed out, following him to the couch. "Just for future reference, most homicide cases don't include me spending so much time fucking around."

"Noted." Gallagher sprawled on the couch and reached for Cort's hand, dragging him down, too. "We have twenty minutes before supper's ready."

"Timed sex acts. A personal favorite." Cort put his hand on the bulge in Gallagher's pants and grinned. "Yours as well."

"Most sex acts are my personal favorites," Gallagher said, shifting his hips up. "This will work better if my pants are open."

"God, you're so fucking helpful," Cort praised sarcastically. Instead of undoing Gallagher's pants, though, he undid his own. "Need room," he explained, not at all shy about shoving his hand in his boxers and adjusting himself.

"Me, too," Gallagher pointed out, looking down at himself. "Whenever you're ready."

Sadly, Cort was pretty sure he'd been ready since about the time he'd finished washing off in Gallagher's shower. "Oh, all right, then. Let's see what you've got." He sighed dramatically and ignored the way his own erection was pushing at his open fly as he got Gallagher's open.

"Same as what I had earlier," Gallagher said, his voice getting nice and husky as he lifted his cock free of his clothes.

"Same as what you had last night, too." Cort settled himself on his knees by the couch and nuzzled Gallagher's balls. "I like it."

"Me, too," Gallagher said, the teasing evaporating as they began to touch. "A lot."

"There's a lot to like." Cort licked delicately along the rapidly hardening length, Gallagher's cock going from mostly hard to really fucking hard in about the time it took for Cort to reach the tip, mostly exposed as Gallagher's foreskin drew back.

"Flatterer," Gallagher gasped, his hips twitching as Cort licked over the sensitive head.

Cort didn't bother with a reply, too busy tasting to keep up the banter. He licked and kissed and used one hand to stroke slowly as he got Gallagher's dick all nice and wet. "I don't think I can suck any cock for twenty minutes," he said, nuzzling again. "I'm out of practice."

"I'm pretty sure there's no such thing as a bad blowjob," Gallagher said, his fingers sliding through Cort's hair. "I won't bitch, swear."

Cort laughed softly. "Good point," he said, licking once more. "But there is such a thing as really good head." And moving his whole body closer, he set out to prove it.

"Oh, God." Gallagher groaned loudly as Cort went down on him, his fingers tangling tight for a moment before letting go and grabbing the couch. "Yeah, like that."

Rolling his eyes at how Gallagher liked to stage manage, Cort kept doing what he was doing. He used a lot of tongue, a little variation in the suction, and did his level best to make Gallagher incoherent enough to stop giving orders and just give it up for him.

With both hands, Cort grabbed Gallagher's trousers and pulled them down over his hips, sucking hard enough on the cock in his mouth that Gallagher helpfully lifted his hips, thrusting deeper with a long moan. Then, having bared a lot more skin, Cort went exploring. He held Gallagher's prick in a loose fist and licked his way over one hip and then the other, waiting until Gallagher practically begged before he went back.

"Please," Gallagher whispered. "Come on, Strang. Suck me."

Cort nodded and scraped his teeth over the soft skin of Gallagher's belly. He like the sounds Gallagher made, but the words themselves went right to his own balls. He took Gallagher in, sucking hard and going down as far as he could, tasting Gallagher's pre-come all along his cock and then going back up to find more at the tip.

"Jesus, yes," Gallagher hissed, his hips starting to rock rhythmically. "Do it, suck me."

Cort moaned and jammed a hand into his own pants, stroking off as he sucked. He usually thought it kind of rude to do that, preferring to center all of his attention on the cock he was sucking, but this time he ached for it. His balls were heavy and tight, his cock hot and hard and demanding a palm to grind up against.

Gallagher gasped again, panting and fucking Cort's mouth, and Cort found himself panting right along with him, his chest burning as his balls pulled up. He was going to ruin a good portion of Gallagher's couch if he didn't hold it.

"Shit! Yes!" Gallagher arched and Cort sucked hard, feeling the first twitch and pulse. As he swallowed, Cort made himself squeeze hard at the base of his own erection, waiting until

Gallagher was done. He licked and sucked and swallowed, listening to Gallagher praise God and take the names of several Celtic deities in vain.

"Flatterer," Cort panted when he finally let Gallagher slip from his mouth. "Oh God." With another moan he fell back onto the floor, his feet braced under the edge of the couch as he fucked his fist. It only took a few strokes and Gallagher's hand landing on his thigh before Cort came in a tight arc, his eyes wide and unseeing.

"Nice," Gallagher said, still breathing hard. His hand squeezed Cort's thigh for a moment and then relaxed. "Oh, man, I want a nap."

"No time." Cort closed his eyes and swiped his hand through the mess he'd made on his shirt. "Damn it."

"I'll lend you a shirt," Gallagher promised. "And put food in your belly. And I'll even listen while you talk out your case. But no way am I leaving home again tonight."

"Lucky you," Cort said, rolling over and getting to his feet to go get washed up. "Put your dick away, it's distracting."

"That's what it's there for. I wouldn't want you to get bored."

Cort laughed and went to the bathroom. He was far from bored. Overworked, underfed, in serious need of sleep and verging on over-sexed, but not bored.

When he came back out of the bathroom with clean hands and no shirt, Gallagher was in the kitchen, dishing out reheated Italian takeout. "So, I think I've got it pretty much figured out," Cort said, leaning on the counter. "Where did my wine go?"

"Living room. And good. Can you make a case?"

"I hope so. It's all circumstantial, though. I'm crossing my fingers for a confession." He went to the living room and got both glasses of wine. "I'll be going as soon as I eat," he said regretfully as he passed Gallagher his glass.

"Okay," Gallagher said with a nod, apparently accepting that as due course. "So, who did it?"

"One of his team." Cort sipped his wine, his brow furrowed while he put thoughts in order. "When you were going through that stuff for Marty and finding out about Vincent's last great love affair, I was going over my notes and looking through as much of the recent online talk within the team as I could."

"And?" Gallagher handed him a plate and fork, then led the way back to the living room.

Cort sat on the couch and put his plate on the coffee table. "And Dinsmore was outshining them all," he said, taking a forkful of something cheesy. "One of them had to be pissy about it, right? Look at the way he was killed: unplanned, violently, with the tools at hand. I was pretty sure that the woman, Marcie Wong, was simply too small to pull a cord that tight, but then I took another look at the photos and reconsidered. Reeves is the one with the loosest alibi, but really any of them could have managed it. So I went through all the chats and tried to read between the lines."

Gallagher nodded, eating steadily with one hand and not even setting his wine glass down with the other. Cort had to wonder if he'd had lunch.

"I wish I had access to their computers," Cort said, mostly to himself as he chewed.

"So get them." Gallagher shrugged. "It shouldn't be too hard."

Cort thought about that while he ate, turning over reasons and counter arguments before he finally decided it was worth a try. "I hope there's a sympathetic judge working late," he said, reaching for his phone.

There was, thankfully, or at least one who thought that examining the computers was a reasonable step. Cort double-checked how long the paperwork would take and grabbed his notebook while finishing off his wine.

"I'll get you a shirt." Gallagher went to the bedroom while Cort riffled through his notes and made another call, this time for patrol to meet him at Rookwood to take care of the acquisition. As an afterthought, he also called Mr. Ling as a courtesy, making sure someone would be there to let them in.

"Thanks," Cort said, putting on Gallagher's shirt. "For supper, too. Hate to eat and run, but..."

"It's the job," Gallagher said easily. He moved forward and kissed Cort quickly, then handed him his gun. "Call me later. Come back if you want."

"Yeah?"

"Yeah. I'll be up for a few hours."

Cort grinned and finished getting dressed. "I thought you were ready to crash."

"I was." Gallagher smiled back. "Okay, maybe being up is a lie. But come back, if you want."

"I just might," Cort said, kissing him again. "But I have to go now."

"So go." Gallagher followed him to the door, taking one more kiss. "Just to keep you from being bored."

"Being bored sucks," Cort agreed. He made himself leave,

once more pausing to stare at Dinsmore's door. It was odd how surprised he was to keep seeing it there. He looked forward to seeing it without the tape.

Chapter Eight

Cort was the first to the Rookwood building and he stood outside the door, peering in as he waited for both Ling and his search warrant to arrive. There were lights on inside, but the door was locked tight and there wasn't a bell. He assumed there was a guard in there somewhere, but until the guard showed up to see Cort standing there, he was stuck counting how many minutes he could have spent with Gallagher instead of out in the night.

Two police cruisers and two sedans arrived at about the same time, and Gallagher nodded to Mr. Ling as an officer handed over the paperwork.

"This is our lawyer, Dennis Gifford," Mr. Ling said as the man who drove the other sedan joined them. "He's just here to make sure everything is in order."

Cort nodded and shook the lawyer's hand as Mr. Ling opened the door and led them all in. "This won't take long," Cort said as they went up the stairs to the third floor. "Sorry for the inconvenience."

"If it will help find out who killed Vincent," Mr. Ling said, his voice trailing off. "Although I sincerely doubt that anyone here was involved."

Cort didn't have any such doubts, but refrained from saying anything. They went into the maze of cubicles, Cort leading this time as he made his way to where Dinsmore's team had been stationed. "Three of them," he told the officers with him. "Just over here."

As he rounded a partition wall he heard someone working, the click of a keyboard loud in the room, devoid of people. By instinct, he reached for his gun, the officers doing the same.

"Who's there?" Mr. Ling called before anyone could stop him. His lawyer was already pulling him back, well behind everyone who had a weapon.

The typing stopped and there was a very brief pause before a voice called out, "Mr. Ling? It's just me."

Cort recognized Reeves voice and nodded to the officers, but kept his hand on his gun. "Mr. Reeves. Sorry to interrupt, but can you step out of your office for a moment?"

"Uh, sure." Joseph Reeves slowly appeared in the opening to his cubicle, looking disheveled and confused. When he saw Cort and the uniformed officers, his eyes went wide and he darted back in.

Cort moved at the same time the officers did, grabbing for the man's hands before he could do anything to the computer. "Mr. Reeves," Cort said firmly. "We are here to serve a search warrant and take this computer as evidence. Do not impede us."

Reeves stood trembling, held by two of the officers. "The computer?" he asked, licking his lips. "I need it for my work. You can't take the computer. Mr. Ling, tell them."

Cort glanced at Ling and Gifford, who were exchanging looks of their own, suddenly glad that there was a lawyer there. Reeves was about to come apart at the seams.

"Mr. Reeves," Cort said, speaking slowly and clearly. "I need to ask you some questions. You are not under arrest at this time, and you do not have to answer them. That man over there is a lawyer, okay? If you have a question about what you should or should not say, you can ask him."

"Do not say anything at all, Mr. Reeves," Gifford said immediately, coming over to them.

"But they can't take the computer," Reeves insisted. "My work. All of it is on there, and I'm going to get that promotion now." He turned his gaze on Mr. Ling. "Right? Golden boy is gone and now it's just me again. Bastard."

Gifford sighed and Cort nodded. "Joseph Reeve, I'm arresting you on suspicion of murder in the death of Vincent Dinsmore." He watched as one of the uniforms handcuffed Reeves, and recited the Miranda rights while Gifford attempted to keep the man quiet.

"Mr. Reeves, shut up," Gifford finally snapped. "You can say what you need to say after you've been processed and your own lawyer is there."

Cort nodded, hoping that Reeves would be just as chatty at the station. Reeves had a wide variety of names for Dinsmore that would come in useful at some point, likely. "Take the computers," Cort told the uniforms. "I'll call for transport."

Beside him, Mr. Ling looked at Reeves and shook his head. "I would never have thought you capable, Joseph," he said softly.

Reeves, leaning on a wall with his hands cuffed behind his back and an officer holding his arm, nodded. "Me neither," he said quietly. "Stupid bastard didn't even know. Just wanted to work insane hours and take over everything and hide from the world. He was pathetic."

"And yet, someone loved him," Cort said, suddenly angry. He pushed it all down and made his call to the station, then stood and waited. It was going to be a long, long night.

An hour later he was in an interview room, sitting across from Reeves, who had a pad of paper in front of him and his own lawyer next to him.

"You understand that you're under arrest?"

Reeves nodded and looked at the pad. "Yes."

"Do you wish to make a statement for the record?"

"Yes." Reeves looked at his lawyer and shrugged. "Not much point, anymore."

"My client is speaking to you against my advice," the lawyer said stiffly, glaring at the recording equipment.

"Noted." Cort looked at Reeves, took a moment to state the names of everyone present and the time, and then sat back. "What happened, Joe?" he asked.

Reeves shrugged. "Don't know. Well, I know, but." He sighed and held his head up with one hand, elbow on the table. "He was always so fucking lame, except for with work. They said he was helpful. That means he did everyone's job. He did his work, most of theirs, and everyone was kind of coasting. Then he started doing more, and weird shit. He was pulling in clients, fixing things that wouldn't be a problem for weeks, making up new programs out of thin air."

"And that was bad?" Cort asked.

"Not until he got fucking noticed," Reeves snapped. "He was on my team. I was team leader. And he was going to be promoted over me. I got him hired in the first place."

"Killing him seems like a bit of an overreaction," Cort observed.

"I didn't go there to kill him," Reeves said sullenly. "I went to pick up some work. And he just sat there in his apartment, babbling about the project and all these plans of his and making me listen to some shitty music over and over. I just... I couldn't stand it anymore. Not the way he worked, the way people let him do what he wanted, the way he talked to me."

"What did you do?" Cort asked, keeping himself still.

For a long moment Reeves didn't say anything. He picked up the pen and turned it over in his hand, once. "He sat at his computer and opened the file. He said, 'look at this', talking to me like it was an order. And I stood behind him, watched him tell me shit I already knew, and I got so mad I wanted to punch the back of his head."

"Why didn't you?"

"Because then he said he was going to talk to Mr. Ling about an idea he had, and I knew he didn't know about the promotion. No one knew -- I wasn't supposed to, but I saw the e-mail about it on Mr. Ling's desk. He'd printed it out and just left it there; I think he wanted me to know, so I'd work harder. He likes me better than Dinsmore. Everyone does. And I didn't want Dinsmore to talk to Mr. Ling or anyone else, and certainly not me. I was just... done. Angry and done."

Cort nodded and waited, watching the pen in Reeves' hand flip end over end again.

"I grabbed the keyboard from the box and asked him if it worked. He didn't even look at me, just told me to look at the screen. So I wrapped the cord around his neck and pulled. Hard."

Cort pushed the pad a little closer to him. "Write it down," he said.

Chapter Nine

At three in the morning, Cort sat in his car and rubbed his eyes before dialing a number on his mobile phone. It rang three times and he was about to hang up before the line got picked up.

"Gallagher."

"Hey, it's me," Cort said.

"You sound like shit."

"Just tired. Did I wake you up?"

"Not really," Gallagher said with a yawn. "I was just dozing on the couch. Where are you?"

"In my car outside your building."

There was a brief pause and then Gallagher snorted. "Don't be stupid. Come on up," he said, and hung up.

Cort nodded to himself and turned off his phone; the last thing he wanted was an early morning wake up from Williamson. He'd file his paperwork whenever he managed to drag his ass into the station and not a minute before.

Gallagher met him at the door with a critical look and didn't say word. He took Cort's jacket and gun and dragged him into the bedroom, not even minding the way Cort was mostly asleep before he even lay down.

No pillow had ever felt so good. He remembered thinking that Gallagher's pillows must be made of some luxury fabric, but he didn't stay awake long enough to ask.

The next thing he was conscious of was that the room was filled with sunlight and the pillow was still the best ever. He turned his head, just to feel it squish, and the rest of his body started reporting in.

Starting with his cock, which was hard and warm and very, very wet.

"Oh, man," Cort said, grinned and peeking under the sheet. "Best wake up call ever."

Gallagher's hand curled on his hip and Cort saw a wicked flash of his eyes just before Gallagher nodded. The nodding turned into bobbing, and Cort's head fell back with a groan as he enjoyed the blowjob, his legs falling apart to let Gallagher do whatever the hell he wanted. "Nice," he said, his hand tangling in the sheets.

Gallagher's tongue traced a lazy line up over his cock and then down the other side, pausing to lap at Cort's balls. His hands were in there too, Cort noted as another moan made its way out. One was stroking him, the other was massaging his thigh like a kitten kneading.

Cort lifted the other leg, bending at the knee. He knew it was a bit of slut move, but Christ, when had he and Gallagher been shy? They'd only known each other about thirty-six hours; they seemed to communicate just fine. Gallagher's tongue slipped over his balls again and then lower, and Cort grinned at the ceiling. Just fine, indeed.

When Gallagher licked over his hole, Cort grunted, his hands making fists. "Yeah," he tried to say, the word mostly lost in a gasp. "That."

"This?" Gallagher asked, his voice muffled and indistinct under the blankets and against Cort's ass.

"Yes, that!" Cort yelled, Gallagher's hands suddenly holding him open and Gallagher's mouth everywhere.

Licking. Biting. Kissing. Nibbling. And then, finally, when Cort was about to go mad and start looking for something to shove in his ass, Gallagher started tongue fucking him.

"Fuck, yes," Cort rasped, grabbing his cock and jerking off fast and hard. "Lick me. Oh shit, yes!"

Gallagher moaned and licked him, the lump of his body shifting under the blankets at the bottom of the bed. He licked again and again, and then a wet finger slid into Cort's ass, pushing hard.

"Yes!" Cort yelled, clamping down and coming in a rush. "Yes, yes, yes."

"Yeah," Gallagher said, emerging from the blanket and breathing hard. "Hell, yes. Hang on."

Cort nodded, not caring at all about what Gallagher was saying. "Hanging," he said, his chest heaving. "Why?"

"Because." Gallagher sucked Cort's cock quickly, keeping him from going soft. He waved a condom in the air and lifted his head, saying, "I'm not done yet."

"Oh," Cort said easily, watching as Gallagher rolled the rubber down onto him. "We can take care of that." He was utterly relaxed, though, despite his erection. "I hope you don't mind doing all the work."

"I'm getting used to it," Gallagher said dryly, straddling Cort's hip and grasping his cock. "Oh, shit," he breathed, lowering himself down.

"See? Good sex." Cort tried to keep his eyes from rolling as Gallagher sank down onto him, tight and warm. "You've been playing with the lube again."

"Shut up. I'm working here."

Cort laughed, his body shaking as he planted his feet and pushed up. Gallagher cursed at him, his hands flat on Cort's chest as he slammed down onto him rapidly.

"Come on," Cort teased, reaching for his Gallagher's cock and squeezing hard. "Come for me."

"Damn it, you bastard," Gallagher yelled, his back arching. "I hate you."

"I hate you more," Cort said, stroking him off and attempting to find some sort of rhythm. "Damn. Nice ass."

Gallagher just moaned, his eyes closing and his fingers digging in.

"Close?" Cort asked, watching him and pulling on his cock. "Hang on." He let go and grabbed at Gallagher's hips, fucking him deeper.

"There!" Gallagher yelled, one hand going to his prick and stroking himself rapidly. "Oh, shit, yeah, there!"

Cort nodded, grinding into him and doing him hard, watching Gallagher's cock getting redder and harder, leaking all over the place. "Come on, baby," he said roughly. "Want to feel you come around me."

Gallagher gasped, his eyes flying open. "Now," he said, come spraying up Cort's belly and chest as his ass grew impossibly tight.

"God," Cort gasped, his own orgasm sweeping through him, entirely unexpected. He tried to breathe, rocking through it as Gallagher kept coming, squeezing around him. "That's it," Cort crooned. "Beautiful."

Gallagher made an agreeable noise between pants and tumbled forward, sticking them together. "Damn. Good."

"Uh huh," Cort agreed, kissing him happily. "And before breakfast, we'll see if we can do it again in the shower."

"Insatiable." Gallagher rolled off him and sprawled on the bed, still panting softly. "Hey, you fell asleep before you filled me in."

Cort blinked and found himself smiling again. "Went to get the computers and ended up with an arrest and a confession. Reeves, one of the guys he worked with, killed him over a promotion and a damaged ego."

Gallagher laughed softly. "Workaholics, man. Never know when they'll snap. Good for you, though; you closed your case fast."

"I did indeed," Cort said, utterly content. "I wish they all worked out that fast."

"It would be nice," Gallagher agreed.

"Mind you," Cort said, rolling to his side and kissing Gallagher again. "I'm pretty sure I'm going to be needing my sleep."

"You think?" Gallagher asked, his eyes twinkling.

"Yeah. I'm looking forward to seeing that door across the hall without all that tape. Often."

"I think we can work out some sort of visitation."

"Oh, good." Cort kissed him again, thinking that it was possibly the best morning he'd had in his life, and he hadn't even had his coffee yet.

NOTHING'S EVER EASY BY CB POTTS

Part One

The music was loud -- so loud it shook through the club's chairs, sending the few empty ones on short, vibrating dances of their own; so loud that it resonated inside every dancer's head, obscuring all but the most urgent of thoughts. It was, and always was, so loud that neighbors for miles around planned on spending their evenings at the club, since they knew they'd spend those hours listening to the music anyway.

Grant couldn't hear it. Not one single note. His ears were too busy listening to the stunningly hot guy who'd accepted his offer of a drink and was now sharing a far-too-crowded corner of the bar with him.

"Mmmm," the guy said, licking his lips. "They do make a good mojito here."

Grant signaled for another. "Glad you like it."

"I do." Incredible brown eyes turned on him, almost, but not quite, the absolute black of morning coffee. "So tell me about yourself. What do you do?"

"Oh, it's boring." Grant waved a hand. He liked what he saw of this guy -- the close cropped hair, the wiry frame, the shirt open enough to reveal a golden nipple ring -- to be cautious. "I work for the state." He let his eyes slide over the guy's short torso, dallying for a delicious moment at a very promising bulge in black jeans. "What about you?" he asked, drawing out the last syllable to fish for a name.

"Alejandro," Brown eyes smiled, "But my friends call me Ali." He dismissed the matter of naming with a shrug. "Right now, I'm sort of between jobs. But I've just finished up a photo shoot for GayStud.com." He grinned, preening a bit. "I'm pretty sure my schedule will pick up a bit after the shoot goes live."

"Me too," Grant agreed. He made a mental note to check out GayStud.com as soon as he got home.

That is, if he didn't manage to get Alejandro out of those tight black jeans in a timely fashion.

"That's enough about me, though." Ali leaned in close, letting his hands sneak in under the hem of Grant's shirt. "Let's talk about you. You didn't get these abs sitting at a desk."

"No," Grant replied, enjoying the feel of soft hands on his skin. "I work out a little bit."

"More than a little, ese."

Grant nodded, agreeing as Ali's hands moved higher. Knowing fingers sought out pectoral muscles, worried at the nipples. "You could say that."

"So what is it?" Ali dipped in for a teasing, biting kiss. "Highway department? Water and sewer?" His voice dropped a fraction. "What do you do for the state to get these big muscles?"

Grant swallowed. In for an inch, in for a mile. "I'm a corrections officer."

Ali's hands were off him so fast Grant never even felt them move. His shirt was still settling back into place as Ali whirled on his heel and started toward the door.

"Hey, man!" Grant called. "What the fuck?"

"What the fuck? You ask me what the fuck?" Ali glared at him. "You're a prison guard. I'm not taking up with no thug like that."

"You're judging me," Grant said, willing himself to keep his tone calm, a trick he'd long ago mastered, "before you even know me."

"Who's got to know you?" Ali turned back toward the door, disdain evident in every gesture. "Man's got a job like that, you know he's fucked in the head."

* * *

"Buddy, I'm gonna have to cut you off." The bartender's hand was gentle on his shoulder, but Grant glared at him anyway. "You've had the better part of the bottle, mate, and last call's in ten minutes."

"All right." His feet knew the way to the floor, and sheer willpower pulled Grant off the bar stool. "Have a good one."

"You want me to call you a cab, man?" The bartender shot a look -- a look that Grant totally missed -- to the bouncer. "You're in no shape to drive."

"I'll be fine," Grant slurred. "No worries."

He made it to the door without falling on his face. The only problem was navigating around the bouncer, who managed to position himself between Grant and the door.

The bouncer was a tall man, head a few inches shy of the ceiling. He was broad, nearly four feet across the shoulder blades. His stomach was roughly the size of a pony keg, strapped horizontally to a tree-trunk spine.

"You're going to want to move, buddy," Grant snarled, speaking directly into the man's ribcage, "Or I'm going to have to put you down."

"Can't do that, boss." The big man shrugged, the muscles on his shoulders moving like boulders tumbling down a mountain. "You're way too drunk to be getting behind the wheel right now. Not gonna happen."

Grant hit him.

The bouncer smiled.

"You see, that right there is impaired judgment. If you were sober, you'd never even consider doing that."

Grant looked up at the bouncer, and up some more, and up a few more inches. "What the hell do you think I do all day long when I'm sober?"

"I don't know," the bouncer shrugged, "And I don't care. What you're doing right now is getting in this here cab."

The bouncer put his hands on Grant's shoulders, lifting him bodily and turning around in one smooth motion.

The cab driver had the back door open.

"Pour him in here, Bucky. I'll get him home."

Grant landed on the plush seat face first, folding into a crumbled heap. The cab driver shut the door and crossed round the front of the car, moving away before Grant managed to pull himself upright.

"Where are we going, friend?"

Grant shrugged. "Fucked if I know." He glared out the window. "I live in Champlain, but that's no good."

"Well, it'd be a long walk back to get your vehicle, that's for sure." The cab driver laughed. "And I reckon you'll want to get to work in the morning." Brown eyes shot up to the rear view mirror. "Although you're going to be a hurting unit when eight a.m. rolls around."

"Doesn't matter," Grant replied, speaking automatically. "I'm not on again until 2300."

"Night owl, huh?" The cab driver smiled. "Me too. I've always been that way. My mother used to flip me over, try to get me to sleep at night, but it never took."

Grant nodded. "Me too." He smiled up at the cabbie. Even through his whiskey goggles, he could recognize what was happening. The guy was trying to talk him down, the same way he did inside when one of the guys was riled up. "I always thought it was insomnia, you know? But no."

"And sleeping pills?" The cab driver shook his head. "They're not for shit. Makes me climb the walls, I try to take a Unisom."

Grant laughed. "Me too!" He leaned forward. "Maybe we're brothers, separated at birth."

Incredible brown eyes met his own. "I don't think so, buddy. No brother of mine would be as good looking as you are."

Grant fell back in the seat. "Fat lot of good that does me." He shrugged. "Guys go running once they find out I'm a CO." The words were out of his mouth before he realized he'd outed himself on multiple levels. "Uh, I mean…"

"I know where I picked you up, man." There was a grin in the rearview mirror. "And it don't bother me one bit."

"Which part?" Grant leaned forward. "The fact I'm queer or that I'm a CO?"

"Both." A sharp curve put Grant back against the upholstery, clutching his stomach. "Either. But it is going to bug me if you lose your lunch all over my car, dude."

"Then you'd better let me out." Grant reached for the door handle. "Like right fucking now."

* * *

Much to Grant's surprise, the cabbie waited by the side of the road, keeping vigil while he lost an evening's worth of liquor and anger.

"Thanks," he said, climbing back into the car.

"We've all been there, man." The cab driver handed him a Mountain Dew. "From my personal stash."

"Liquid Gold, right?" It tasted good -- sweet and cold -- splashing down his throat, washing away the worst of the bile. "I needed that."

"Now, don't go thinking you're sober enough to drive now." Brown eyes flickered back up to the mirror. "That shit's still in your system."

"You're a mind reader, are you?"

"Blind man could read your mind right now," the cab driver replied. "You're tired, you want to go home, and you want to get that fine ass of yours to bed."

"Two out of three." Grant held up a finger. "I'm tired. I want to go to bed." He shook his head, only to instantly regret the gesture. "But I don't want to go home."

Home was lonely, with empty, echoing bedrooms. Home had a bed that was too large by half. Home was too orderly, too controlled, too damn stifling without someone to mess it up a little bit.

"No," he reiterated. "I don't want to go home."

"Well, man, you've got to go somewhere." The cab driver shook his head. "Pick something. You want to go to up to Champlain, I can take you. You want to go somewhere else, I can do that too." He shrugged, nodded out the window at the half-darkened strip they were passing. "One of the cheap hotels. Flop for a couple hours, get some breakfast in your stomach before you hit the road. Or Wal-Mart. It's open all night. You can walk around. Do your Christmas shopping."

"I don't want to do my motherfucking Christmas shopping."

"Easy, big guy." There was a little smile pushing up the corner of the cab driver's mouth. "Course, there's always another alternative."

"And what's that?"

"I could bring you back to my place, give you what you really need."

Part Two

"Man, I must have been piss-ass drunk when I agreed to this." Grant tugged his wrist, feeling the total absence of slack in the chain attaching him to the bed frame.

"Nah." The cab driver grinned. He'd stripped down to his blue jeans, bare feet silent on the carpeted floor. "Maybe you weren't 100 percent sober, but you knew what you were doing."

"Did I?" Grant turned his head to follow the cabbie's progress around the room. "Man, I don't even know your name."

"Right now," the driver said, selecting a bandana from the dresser drawer, "why don't you just call me sir?"

There was no answer, just a groaning assent as the blue cloth covered his eyes.

"I didn't quite catch that, boy."

"I said, 'Yes, Sir'," Grant replied. His cock was stiffening under him, flattening against the mattress.

"That's better." A hand, bare and soft, landed on Grant's shoulder, fingertips tracing over the bulging top of his bicep. "Just relax, friend, and let it happen. I'll get you out of your head for a while."

Grant didn't know how this had happened -- how, in the space of an evening he'd gone from rejected loser drowning his sorrows at the bar to tightly bound sex toy -- but he wasn't complaining.

It had been a long time since he'd been with anyone, anyway. And if he tried to think back to how long it had been since anyone had wanted to tie him down and do him up -- well, right this moment, Grant couldn't recollect that far back.

Sir's hands were everywhere, tightening straps around his thighs, cupping his ass cheeks, sneaking underneath his bound form to pluck at aching nipples.

"Look at you," Sir said. "You must be so tired. Tired of having to be in control all the time. Tired of people judging you. Tired of people seeing a uniform instead of a man."

"I am tired," Grant replied, stifling a groan as Sir's fingers traveled up the inside of his thigh. "But I don't want to sleep right this minute."

Those knowing fingers slid over the sheet and wrapped themselves around Grant's trapped cock. "No, I imagine that you don't."

That hand started to move, pulling on Grant. He closed his eyes, instinctively, despite the blindfold. The sensations had him squirming, enjoying and hesitant at the same time.

"Is that strange," Sir asked. He was leaning over Grant, his lips scant inches from Grant's ear. "To know you can't do anything about me touching you? That you're helpless to stop me? That I'll do what I want to, and you can't stop me?"

"What are you going to do?" Grant breathed, barely audible. "Sir?"

"I think," Sir replied, quickening his hands, "That I'd like to see you come."

That was all it took -- the gently phrased command, the fast moving hand, the fact that Grant was bound and naked -- it all conspired to send Grant over the edge. He went rigid, every muscle stiffening, legs pushing against the footboard, forgetting to breathe for a long moment.

"God," he said, after, his own heat cushioning him, "That was something."

"Yes," Sir replied, "A little something to get us started."

* * *

"Nice thick thighs." Sir's hands slid up Grant's legs, starting at the back of his knees and slowly ascending until he was brushing the underside of Grant's ass. "You're on your feet all day, of course."

Grant nodded.

"Walking around, stared at all day long, by people who hate you." Sir was massaging Grant's ass now, working each cheek gently. "It's a tough beat."

There were no words, now. Grant wasn't sure why the blindfold was starting to get wet against his eyes. He wasn't about to think about that.

"You've got to remember, we're not all like that."

Grant's cheeks were spread, cool air sneaking in. A finger, slick with cool lube, followed.

"Some of us are looking, and we really like what we see." Sir's words fell soft and easy now. "We see you. We see how hot you are. How tough you are. How strong you have to be."

Sir's fingertip was pushing in now, slowly.

"And we want that. We want to touch you. We want to taste you. We want to have you."

Sir's knuckle passed Grant's pucker, forcing a moan out of him.

"Did you know that?"

"No," Grant managed. "Sir."

Chains rattled and bedposts creaked as another finger slid in beside the first.

"Easy, big boy." Sir ran a reassuring hand down Grant's thighs. "I'm just opening you up now, getting you ready for a little fun."

Grant was hard again, his cock stabbing at his stomach. "Don't stop," he said, a little note of pleading breaking through the command. "Please."

"Oh, I don't plan to. Not for a while yet." Fingers slid in and out, slowly widening the passage. Every now and again, Sir's fingertips would brush a particularly sensitive spot, making Grant jump like a fish on a line. "Not when you dance so pretty for me."

Grant's hips were coming up to meet Sir's hand, countering every thrust with one of his own.

"I should have tied your belly down," Sir murmured. "Keep you still. But you've just got to have some kind of control, don't you?"

Suddenly, the fingers were gone. Grant's ass was completely empty, the absence of Sir's fingers a larger presence than his fingers had been.

"Sir?" Grant yelped. "I'm sorry. I won't move…."

"Shhh," Sir replied, his knees settling onto the mattress between Grant's thighs. He was still clothed, the stiff denim of his jeans almost abrasive against Grant's bare flesh. "I like it when you move."

Something new, soft edged and rubbery, nosed between Grant's cheeks. "This will make you move, I bet."

"What is it?" A cold sweat started running down Grant's back, pooling at the base of his spine. His forehead was dripping. Suddenly, not being able to see became unbearable. After all, Grant realized, he didn't even know this guy, didn't even know his name, nothing. He was far too vulnerable and found himself aware of that all at once.

Grant tensed up, ready to push himself off the bed. He might not be able to break the chains holding his wrists, he reckoned, but he was pretty sure he could pull the bedposts out of place if need be. His palms flattened on the mattress, scrabbling for purchase, and he dug in his knees as much as the leg shackles would allow.

"Hoo -- Hold on, Grant." Sir was suddenly off the bed, bare feet padding around to the head of the bed. "I'm sorry." The blue blindfold was off in an instant, landing with a sodden thud on the floor.

Grant blinked against the light, vision clearing to find Sir crouching in front of him.

"I didn't mean to freak you out." Sir smiled. "I was trying to get you out of your head, if just for a bit. But you're wired pretty tight."

Grant panted. "I guess."

"We'll ditch the blindfold, okay?" Sir reached out, steadying himself with a hand on Grant's shoulder. "No surprises. You're going to know what's coming."

"Okay." Grant let out a breath he hadn't realized he'd been holding. "I think that's what got me, not knowing what was coming." He smiled, weakly. "I've been told I have trust issues."

"Why wouldn't you?" Sir shrugged. "That's who you are. But I want you to trust me." He held up a small butt plug, a few inches long with a gentle flare. "This was it, man. I want to see what you look like with that pretty ass of yours plugged up tight."

"Oh." Grant blushed, the crimson heat crawling across his face. "I, uh…"

"Don't be embarrassed." Sir's voice was steady, his gaze direct. "I could have had anything back there. I should have known better." He looked at the plug. "Should we try again?"

Grant looked at the plug, and then at Sir. If he let himself think about it -- and there was no reason not to, really -- his ass was missing Sir's fingers something fierce, at this point.

He swallowed.

"I think so, yes."

"Good," Sir said. He leaned closer, his face a few inches from Grant's. "I'll push you, big boy, but only as far as you want to go. Understood?"

Grant looked up, searching Sir's brown eyes. There was nothing but truth there, shining bright. "Yes, sir." A pause then, the import of Grant's words ringing loud in his ears. "Thank you, sir."

Sir smiled. "Thank you." He stood up, circling around to the side of the bed. "Thank you."

Knowing what was coming had Grant half hard again before Sir regained the bed. His cock swelled fully erect at the first touch of Sir's hand, a contented sigh accompanying the reintroduction of slippery fingers.

"Christ," Grant sighed. "That feels so good."

"Mmm." Sir took up a slow rhythm, letting his fingertips push a little deeper with each thrust. "It does. So hot, so tight."

Grant's hips were already raising off the bed. "Would you fuck me," he asked, the need suddenly overwhelming, "Sir?"

"I will," Sir replied. He withdrew his fingers. "But not just yet." The end of the plug was back. "First, let's fill you up."

It had been quite a while. Sir's fingers were wide, but not nearly as wide as the rubbery plug. Grant stretched the chains a few inches more, grunting and biting his lip a bit, but not protesting a bit as Sir pushed the plug in.

It didn't quite fill him -- but he was surely aware of its presence. Such a small thing shouldn't weigh so much, he thought, feeling his ass muscles clench convulsively around the rubber.

"That's fucking hot." Sir groaned. The sound of his zipper descending filled the room. "You should see yourself, Grant."

Grant had no reply. He was too busy letting himself accommodate to the plug inside him, reveling in the sensation of being opened this way.

"God." Sir had himself in hand, stroking his cock as he got off the bed. "Look what you do to me."

Grant turned his head to see. Sir's pants were unzipped just a fraction, enough to let his cock spring out.

It was a thick shaft, fully erect, set round the base with wiry black hair.

Grant thought it was the prettiest thing he'd ever seen.

"Please, sir," he said, eyes riveted on Sir's cock. "Let me suck you."

Sir smiled. "Tempting, big boy. Tempting indeed." His thumb slid over Grant's lower lip. "You've got the sexiest damn mouth I've ever seen."

"Thank you," Grant replied.

Sir smiled. "But I'm not as young as I might be," he said. "If I go off in that pretty little mouth of yours, I'll never get to replace that plug," he added, with a nod toward Grant's ass. "With this one."

"Oh."

"Besides which," Sir said, "We've still got to get you into some good head space. Shift some of that burden that you've been carrying off of your shoulders."

He tucked himself back into his jeans, zipping back up. "I can put myself on hold while we take care of that." He walked out of Grant's field of vision, standing between the bed and a dresser.

"You've got a lot of tension here." Sir's hands were confident, cupping a shoulder blade. "Stress, guilt. It accumulates, builds up." He started to massage Grant, kneading at the muscles. "Toxic, after a while."

"That feels good," Grant replied.

"Yeah, but it's not what you need." Sir stood up abruptly. "Hard men can't be fixed with soft solutions." There was a soft sound, a leathery slither, off to one side. It took all of Grant's willpower not to turn his head and look. "You need a more direct approach."

Sir moved in front of Grant, a thick, black belt dangling from his hands. "Do you agree?"

Grant swallowed. "The massage would feel better," he said, eyeing the leather strap. "Sir."

"I'm sure it would." Sir bent his knees, crouching on his heels to bring himself eye level with Grant. "But is that what you need? Are tender touches and sweet loving going to pull you out of your pain?" One finger, thick and callused, yet light as a feather, traced over Grant's cheekbone. "I don't think so."

Grant bowed his head. "You're right." A rush of air slid out of his lungs, tumbling past his lips to fall onto the floor at Sir's feet. It wasn't a need he'd known he had, but hearing Sir's voice made it suddenly true.

Perhaps new pain would wash away the old: the rejections, the nagging self-doubt, the plain old feeling bad about everything.

Anyway, Grant figured, it couldn't hurt.

Much.

* * *

"Here it comes." Sir's voice was firm. "You tell me if this gets to be too much. You let me know when you've had enough."

Grant nodded.

"Talk to me, big boy." There was no arguing with that tone. "I need to hear that you understand me."

"I do. I will."

The first stroke took Grant by surprise -- both lighter and sharper than he expected, square across the broad of his back. It was bright and crisp and somehow, completely wonderful.

"All right?" Sir asked.

"Better than all right," Grant replied, pulling on the chains just a bit. "Do it again."

From there, they found their rhythm: Sir's arm falling steadily, Grant goading him to action. "Again...Again...Again."

Each hit freed him a little bit, scourging away negativity. Grant could feel the pain washing him clean, a sharp-edged caress reassuring him that under all the baggage, he, Grant, was all right.

The strokes covered Grant's back, reaching from shoulder blades to the plump curve of his ass. They'd made the journey three times, down and back and down again, when the edge of the belt caught the fleshy side of Grant's stomach.

"Yipe!"

Sir dropped the belt. "What happened? What's the matter?"

Grant rolled, as much as he could, up on one side. "You got a tender bit."

"Shit." Sir bent over and examined Grant's side. "It didn't break the skin, but it's pretty pink."

"S'alright." Grant was sliding back toward the blissful daze he'd been approaching under Sir's belt. "You can give me some more."

"No," Sir said. "I don't think so." He smiled. "You've had enough -- and you're not going to stop me until I beat you into hamburger. I can see that." His hand dropped to his crotch. "And I'm too horny to have to work that hard."

"We can't have that, can we?"

"No." Sir's voice dropped, thickened. "We sure can't."

Grant could feel Sir climbing onto the bed behind him. "Your ass is so red," he purred. "It's hot when I touch it." His words were like growls, possessive, animalistic. "Like fire."

Grant growled back. "Take it, then." His hips arched upward. "I can't wait anymore."

The plug was out in a fraction of the time it took to go in, discarded without a thought. "Me either, big boy. Me either."

Sir slid in, quick and deep, taking Grant's breath away.

"Damn, sir!"

"Fucking right, boy!" There was no gentle build-up here, no tentative teasing -- they'd sped right past that to hip-slamming, full-throttle fucking.

"Give it to me!" Grant planted his knees under himself, hearing the bed's footboards crack as he pulled his legs closer. His ass went high in the air. If it weren't for Sir's iron grip on his hips, the smaller man would have gone flying.

"Here you go!" Sir was drilling him, pounding in for all he was worth. "Here it comes."

Grant pushed himself further backward. The footboard gave way on the left hand side, bringing a splintered board up against his bare, bound foot. "Motherfucker!"

"Goddamn!"

Sir changed his pace, a few quick rabbit strokes signaling the end. "Holy holy holy," he breathed, collapsing onto Grant's back after sending a warm flood deep inside Grant.

That did it for Grant, who lost it again. "Hot damn," he said, collapsing under Sir's weight. "Hot fucking damn."

* * *

They showered after, separately, awkwardly.

Grant broke the silence. "Might be good if I knew your name." He smiled. "Now that I'm not calling you Sir and all."

Sir smiled. "Darien. Darien Rios. And you're Grant."

"Grant Grandmaison."

"Grandmaison." Darien wrinkled an eyebrow. "French, yeah?"

"French Canadian," Grant said. "Whole family."

Darien started to laugh. "That's kind of funny."

"What is?"

"Grandmaison, working at the big house." Darien grinned. "Do you hear that a lot? Inside?"

"Nah. Every now and then I'll get one or two who'll think of it, but most don't." Relatively few French speakers made it to Upstate. Thinking about work made his head hurt, just a little bit. He looked at his watch. "Shit, man. I'd better book for home, if I'm going to get any sleep before I have to go back there. Can you give me a lift to my truck?"

"You sober enough to drive?"

Grant grinned. "I think I sweated all the alcohol out of my system." He glanced toward the sweaty, rumpled wreck that was Darien's bed. "Or something."

Darien laughed. "Fair enough." He stood up. "I think it was more something than sweating, though, seeing as I did all the work."

"I'll make it up to you next time." The words were out before Grant thought about it. "That is," he said, stammering, "if you'd like to have a next time."

"I'm by the club pretty regular," Darien replied. "I'm sure I'll see you around."

Part Three

Most COs pride themselves on being observant. They have to have a good eye. Noticing details -- a suspicious bulge in a waistband, a new, shallow depression in a corner of the yard -- can be, and often is, the sole difference between life and death.

But even the most observant corrections officer doesn't come close to an inmate. Captive eyes don't miss a trick. With nothing but time on their hands, inmates watch everything, everywhere. They're looking, all the time, even when it seems like they're not paying the least bit of attention.

They keep an especial eye on the COs. Knowing where the guards are at any moment creates opportunities -- namely in those locations where the guards aren't, or can't get to, in a timely fashion.

They watch for more than mere presence. They've got an eye open for opportunity. Inmates are always watching, in the hopes of spotting a chance to get something, anything, over. A CO with things on his mind might not notice the contraband you're smuggling into your cell. A CO with a pounding headache and half-hung over makes attempting escape seem a little less impossible.

The relationship between captive and captor is, by its very nature, complex. Each party has competing goals, objectives that are diametrically opposed to the other. It's a constant source of tension. It makes the COs hyper aware of the inmates, and, much to Grant's chagrin, the inmates hyper aware of the COs.

* * *

"Grant, man, buddy!" Albert lived in the first cell on the tier, a six by nine room he called his corner office. He was blessed with a mouth four times larger than his brain, and knew far too well how to use it when he wanted to make some noise. "What the hell happened to you?"

Grant forced a smile. "What do you mean, what happened to me?" You never want to show weakness inside -- an injury is just opportunity unrealized to an inmate. He shrugged, feeling the square-edged kiss from Sir's belt twinging, sharp and bright on his stomach. "I'm fine."

Albert laughed. "You Po-Pos is all liars." He leaned up against the cell front, squeezing his face against the bars. His cheeks puffed against the metal, fleshy bulges that made Albert look happier than he really was. "Now don't be lying to me, Grant. Don't you disrespect me that way."

"No disrespect intended, Albert."

Albert pushed back from the bars, turning to walk to the back of the cell. His motions were stiff and awkward, a grotesque parody of how Grant was currently feeling. "You's walking like someone bust you upside the head, and you tell me nothing happened to you?"

Albert dropped his voice a full four notches, making it just as loud as a normal man shouting would be. "Who was it, Grant? If it was one of them NLR bastards, I'll have my boys take care of it for you."

The occupants of the next two cells were suddenly very intent upon Albert and Grant's conversation. Albert might have the mouth, but the Vagos shot caller who was his cell mate really had the power. Albert's words had changed the conversation from an everyday annoyance to something the inmates would want to know about.

Grant waved his hands. "Nothing like that. Easy there, Albert." He shook his head. "Woke up on the wrong side of the bed, that's all. No need to call out the troops."

"Right, Po-Po." Albert turned his back. "Might as well hit it, you gonna be like that."

The klaxon blare of the alarm cut further conversation off. Grant took off running down the tier, taking the stairs two at a time to descend to the common area. Three COs were already on top of Big Harry, one of the largest inmates to ever call this facility home.

Big was perhaps an understatement. Big Harry stood six foot four, in bare feet, and was pushing the scales at three-ninety-five last time medical had been able to persuade him to set foot on a scale.

"Come on, Harry," Captain Mitchell hit the floor at the same time I did, barking at Big Harry. "You don't want to go to the SHU. Settle down!"

Big Harry wasn't having it. "Motherfucking asshole took my blanket down!" He rolled on his stomach, sending two COs flying. One hit the wall hard, taking half a moment to catch his breath before jumping back into the fray.

The other crashed directly into Grant.

"Jesus, man!" Grant breathed. The CO outweighed him by a good hundred pounds, and Grant was not a small man.

"Sorry," the guy muttered, before launching himself back onto Big Harry. Grant was close behind him.

"Harry, we'll put the blanket back." A CO was shouting directly into the big man's ear. "But you've got to cut this shit out."

"Promise?" Big Harry was getting to all fours, carrying nearly a thousand pounds of CO along with him for the ride. "Do you promise?"

"We promise. God damn it, Harry! Lay down and cuff up!"

Harry dropped to his stomach, suddenly docile. "I get my blanket back?"

"Yeah."

Tree trunk arms folded, sliding under the assembled COs. "Cuff me up then." He turned his head to glare at the thin CO standing off to one side. "But if that motherfucker pulls my blanket out again, I'm gonna rip his head off and shit down his neck! Is that understood?"

"That's enough, Harry." Captain gave them the nod, and they got Big Harry to his feet. "Let's get you down to medical, make sure you didn't injure yourself with this little episode."

"Yeah," a voice beside Grant mumbled, after Big Harry'd been led through the Sally Doors. "Want to make sure precious doesn't have a boo-boo."

Grant looked over. It was the CO who'd crashed into him earlier, a guy named Mark something, just come to midnights a little over a week ago. "Ain't that the way it goes?" he asked, with a shrug. "Nine times out of ten."

"Not if I had anything to say about it, it wouldn't," Mark replied, gruffly. "But I don't."

Grant eyed him. There was a sharp edge to Mark's voice, something rank and bitter -- but the guy had just gotten knocked around pretty good. It happened. "Well, let's get the mother-loving report done, anyway, and get that out of the way."

"Yeah," said the thin CO who'd been standing nearby. "That'll be fun."

"What happened, anyway?" Grant asked. He knew Mark, but this guy, he couldn't place. "I'm Grant Grandmaison."

"Rusty Hayes," the thin man replied, extended a hand. He might have been thin, but he was strong as hell -- the pressure in the handshake was proof of that. "Just came over from Bare Hill."

"Mmm." Grant said. "Things are a little different here in Upstate. Our guys are," he continued, pausing for the right word, "twitchier."

"I see that," Rusty nodded, dipping his head for a moment. He had close-cropped sandy hair, tight against his scalp. "But it's looser here too, seems like."

"What do you mean?"

"He had that blanket stuffed up into the vent, blocking the air flow," Rusty said. "God knows what he had hiding in there. Could have been anything. But he's going to get the blanket back?"

Grant smiled. "Normally, no. But this is Big Harry you're talking about."

"And he's different why?" An eyebrow arched upward. "There's bigger guys down the street and they've still got to comply."

"Yeah, but they're not crazy in the head," Mark cut in. "Big Harry, he's fucked right up."

"That right?" Rusty was looking to Grant for the answers.

"In a way, yeah." Grant nodded. "The blanket's in the vent to keep the angels out," he explained. "Big Harry's haunted. He thinks the angels of his victims come back through the vent at night to, uh, violate him."

"Violate him?" Rusty laughed. "You're serious."

"I am." Grant had seen the big man down, more than a few times, screaming and crying and begging to be saved from his invisible assailants. "Puts him right over the edge, it does."

"Serves him right, you ask me. Man does what he done, he deserves a little torment." That was Mark, still edgy.

"That may be," Grant agreed. "But do you want to deal with this shit every night for the rest of his life?" He turned toward Rusty. "Big Harry isn't going anywhere, ever. He's got three lives, back to back. So he keeps the blanket. Sometimes you've got to have some kind of compassion, you know?"

"I guess," Rusty said.

"At least until they let us shoot all these bastards," Mark added.

* * *

An incident that can take five minutes out of the day can result in five hours of paperwork. Grant sighed and sat down with his stack of papers. At least he was getting off easy -- as a bit player in Big Harry's takedown, all he'd have to do was the basic stuff.

Rusty, on the other hand, would be documenting the incident for hours.

What a way to start a new assignment. Grant found himself watching the new guy out of the corner of his eye, and he liked what he saw. An easy-going attitude, a quick smile. None of the dark intensity he was usually attracted to -- nine times out of ten, Grant would seek out men with some Spanish in their veins. Men like Alejandro, he thought with a sigh, who would have nothing to do with him, or men like Darien, who'd not taken time out of the evening to discuss his heritage with him.

Rusty, however, looked like his name. Short sandy hair matched the spray of freckles on his neck. Pale skin, bright green eyes. Thin as a thought, but if he'd been pulled up to Upstate from Bare Hill, he had to be tough.

Tough was good.

Grant shook his head. There was a time and a place for everything, and work was definitely neither when it came to checking out men. Corrections wasn't exactly the most liberated field in the world, anyway. That's why Grant, although not exactly closeted, was extremely discreet about being gay.

Besides which, Rusty was probably straight anyway.

* * *

Four a.m. meant it was time to wake up the inmates who worked in the kitchen. Good guys, most of them. Working in the kitchen was a privilege, and those that managed to win a spot tried to hold on to it.

The six that lived in Grant's dorm never gave him any trouble. He could count on them being up and ready to go at first light, ID's ready and dressed for work.

But this morning, Russell didn't come out of his cell.

"Russell?" Grant called, shining his flashlight into the narrow, darkened space. He'd never had to call the older man twice before. "You all right, buddy?"

There was no response. Russell's cellie, Edgar, sat up, blinking into the light. "What the fuck, man?"

Russell was lying in his bed, eyes closed, not moving. Not even his chest.

"Oh, man," Grant groaned. He hit his radio, calling for help. Every instinct he had was telling him to go check the old man, but you never go into a cell alone. It makes you too vulnerable.

He heard the Sally Doors opening, control letting assistance into his dorm.

Edgar, by this time, had picked up on what was happening, and swung out of his bunk. "Russell! R-man!" He turned toward Grant, eyes wide. "He's dead, man! He's not breathing!"

"Come here and cuff up," Grant replied, "So we can get to him."

Edgar did, complying far faster than was his usual wont. "He didn't say he wasn't feeling bad or nothing."

The medic team was speeding up the stairs, there before Grant had Edgar all the way out of the way. The stretcher banged against the stair rails on the way up, sending steel-tinged echoes through the tier.

"Come on, guys," Mark waved his arms at the assembled kitchen crew, who were backed up against the wall. "Past time you all get you to work."

Nobody moved. They were all staring toward Russell's cell, watching the medical team push into the cell.

"I said get moving!" Mark barked.

They stood in place, although a few managed to tear their eyes away from the scene in front of them to glare at the CO.

"I know, guys," Grant said, stepping away from the cell door. "I'm worried too, but we need to let the docs do their thing. Nothing we can do here." He nodded to Jose, the senior inmate among the kitchen crew. "I'll make sure you know what happens."

Jose nodded. "Appreciate it, Grant." He gave the other four guys the nod. "Come on."

"Heartless motherfucker," one muttered, as they moved past Grant and Mark toward the door, but neither man said anything.

They weren't gone but a minute when one member of the med crew stepped out of the cell. "He's gone. Don't see anything out of the ordinary, but we'd better call up the camera crew before we move him."

Grant nodded. All inmate deaths had to be investigated, even if it was of natural causes. "I'll have control call down."

It was going to be a long, long day.

Part Four

It was damn near noon before Grant walked through the gates, dog-tired and sore as hell. Russell's thirty-to-life had ended earlier than anyone expected, an apparent heart attack having claimed the man in his sleep.

Grant had filled out yet another report, signed off on a mess of forms, and made sure word got to Jose about Russell's demise. Respect is a big thing in the institution -- if you gave your word to an inmate, you damn well need to follow through, or you risk losing that inmate's respect.

Sometimes that respect is all that stands between you and a sharpened piece of steel, ripped off the underside of a bunk. It's not much protection, but there's no sense throwing it away if you don't have to.

* * *

The sun was slanting directly through Grant's windshield, stabbing him in the eyes. Generally, he was through the gate and well on the way home before the sun started shining in earnest. Hell, for half the year, he was safely in bed before the sun even thought about rising and casting its wan winter light on the North Country.

No such luck today. Grant squinted, thinking for the millionth time that he should invest in a decent pair of sunglasses. The white line marking the side of Route 11 was barely visible in the light. Long as he kept his tires to that, he should be just fine.

That was the theory, anyway.

Grant had made it a little more than halfway -- he'd just cleared Mooers Forks, and had about ten miles, give or take, before he hit his driveway.

That's when the red lights came up in his rear view mirror, accompanied by an ear-splitting siren.

"Fuck me." Grant pulled over. "I don't need this."

The trooper pulled in behind him, lights flashing. Grant could see him pulling on his bullet proof vest before walking up to the driver's side window, obviously tense until he took in the blue shirt Grant was wearing.

"Hey, buddy." The trooper pulled his sunglasses off. "You're all over the road. What's going on?"

Grant sighed. "I'm sorry. Just pulled damn near a double, left my sunglasses in my locker, and I can't see for shit."

The trooper nodded. "How far you headed?"

"Champlain."

"You been drinking?"

Grant blinked. Right that moment, he was so tired and his head was pounding so loudly, he couldn't even remember what day it was. "Couple three days ago. Nothing today."

The trooper laughed. "Day hasn't even started yet."

"Nah, man, it's just about over." Grant shrugged. "If I can get myself home, that is."

"Go on." The sunglasses were back in place. "Dealing with them assholes in there, you deserve a break, way I figure." He turned toward the cruiser. "Just don't make me sorry I let you go."

"No sir," Grant said. "I won't."

* * *

He watched the trooper pull out, making a sweet little U-turn and speeding back toward Malone.

"Yup, them assholes." He pulled back onto Route 11 and headed for home.

On the way, Grant thought about Russell. Not a good man, really, when you consider what he'd done -- a man doesn't pull down 30 to life in a max for jaywalking -- but he'd never given Grant any trouble. Quiet, he liked to read. Every box he got from home was jam-packed with paperbacks: cowboy novels and mysteries.

Popcorn books, Russell had called them. Something to while away the hours. Filling time until the end.

A little bit of a tear surprised Grant, wetting the corner of his eye.

"What the fuck," he muttered. "Just a goddamned inmate."

An inmate that he'd seen five days a week for the past nine years, Grant reflected. Christ, he spent more time with some of his inmates than he'd ever spent with a lover.

"That is fucked up," he said, turning into his driveway. "I need to get my ass to bed."

* * *

He couldn't sleep. The bed was too wide, too empty, too goddamn sterile. Every time Grant rolled onto his back, he was instantly awake, his aching back reminding him of Sir's free hand with the belt.

Not Sir, Grant corrected himself. Darien.

The thought brought a smile to his face. That had been one intense session, a hook up the likes of which he'd never had before. You read about that kind of thing, sometimes, in the letter column of magazines, but Grant had never thought it was real.

And then it happened to him.

Grant curled on his side and smiled. Somehow, his hand found its way under the sheets. "You can call me Sir," he murmured, closing his eyes and thinking of Darien's dark eyes. The feel of the plug, the tight cuffs round his wrist, the sound of splintering footboards, there at the end.

It was good, it was intense, and it was suddenly interrupted by Rusty's image pushing its way into his consciousness. Thin little Rusty, pale as pale can be and naïve in the way only a new jack could be.

The way Rusty looked at him for authoritative answers when Mark was spouting off his philosophy.

Imagining Rusty saying "Yes, sir", the way he had to Darien.

"God," Grant groaned. The force of his orgasm surprised him, shooting out of him with an intensity he'd never expected.

The room was suddenly not so sterile, not so empty. On some small level, he'd recaptured the intensity of Darien's apartment.

In a way he'd never expected.

Covering his eyes with his free hand, Grant sighed. "I am so fucked up," he sighed. His head fell back on the pillow, the effort of holding it upright more than he could bear. "So goddamn fucked up it's not even funny."

It was the last thought to cross his mind for eight solid hours.

Part Five

"Another day, another dollar, eh?" Rusty slid into the chair next to Grant at the pre-shift briefing.

"Let's hope it's easier to earn today's dollar than yesterday's," Grant replied. It was kind of hard to look at the kid, especially after last night's dreams, but he had to keep it normal. "That was something."

"Is it always this…" Rusty asked, pausing to search for the right word. "Exciting up here?"

"Nah," Mark answered, taking the seat directly behind the pair. "It's not always this slow."

Captain walked in then, coming to the front of the room with a handful of papers and a bad day riding heavy on his shoulders.

"Evening, guys." He dropped the papers on the table. "It's been an interesting day here, and you know what that means."

"I take it interesting is bad," Rusty said, voice low.

"Usually," Grant answered.

"We've got Big Harry in Ad Seg, and he'll be there through Friday. Duwayne Hotchkins, 9-34760, has been moved over to that vacancy on your tier, Grant," Captain said, nodding in Grant's direction. "That relieves some of the overcrowding in B Dorm."

He sighed.

"For now, at least. Apparently, we're expecting seven new arrivals from downstate to be bussed in at first light. Not sure yet where we're supposed to put them, but we'll figure that out by the time they get here."

Captain kept talking, detailing the tale of two girlfriends who tried to smuggle some methamphetamine into the prison during visiting hours.

Grant didn't hear a word of it. His mind was otherwise occupied, inspired by the clean soapy smell of Rusty sitting next to him. What would that close-cropped hair feel like, if he could just reach out and touch it? What would the back of the thin man's neck taste like, if he could somehow steal a taste?

"And so that's how we'll handle that," the Captain concluded, his voice rising a fraction to indicate the briefing was at an end. "Any questions?"

Grant blinked, realizing he had missed something. He hoped, hoped against hope, that someone would ask a question, so he could piece together what had been announced.

Of course, no one did.

The prudent thing, the sensible thing, would be to raise his hand and ask what he'd missed. But that would make him look twelve kinds of stupid, so Grant stifled the impulse.

Instead, on the way out of the briefing room, he turned to Rusty.

"So, what I miss in there? I was, uh, a little distracted there at the end."

Rusty looked at him out of the corner of his eye, with the strangest little smile dancing at the corner of his mouth. "I noticed that."

Grant could feel the blush climbing up his neck, and willed it down. This was not the place to show his embarrassment.

"Um, yeah." He coughed. "So what did Cap say?"

"Nothing you got to worry about. They're moving six guys over to the common area, and using that space to bunk them up. Apparently the new guys are NLR, so they can't really go up on your tier, but they don't want to keep them all together, either."

Grant sighed. "You'd think they'd do this during daylight hours." Moving six inmates was not going to be fun, especially when they had to be woken up to make the move. "Nothing's ever easy, is it?"

"It might be," Rusty said, "If you're not too intent on making it difficult." He smiled, and stepped off to the second tier doors.

Grant wasn't sure what to make of that.

* * *

Course, the guys didn't give him much of a chance to think about it. Moving six inmates out of four cells in the middle of the night was guaranteed to cause upset, and it did. Grant was one tier up, and he could still hear every pissed off word coming from the cells below.

"Jesus Christ! You pigs couldn't do this earlier? I just fell asleep!"

"Just keep moving," Mark barked. A pair of guards were throwing all the inmate's possessions into clear trash bags, to be brought down to the common area. "Faster you get there, faster you can get back to bed."

"Fuck you!" The inmate turned around and knocked an elbow into the side of Mark's head. A long string of Spanish profanities followed. Mark went down, hard, and the inmate started kicking him in the side of the head, bare toes angled directly toward wide eyes.

"Get down! Down on the floor!" The guards rushed out of the cell to stop the incident, knocking the inmate off of Mark.

His cellie, who'd been cuffed up and was standing quietly against the wall, decided that this was an ideal time to take off running. He'd pushed past the conflict and was halfway down the stairs by the time the alarm went.

Rusty met him coming down.

"And where do you think you're going?"

The inmate wasn't about to stop for conversation. He tried running over Rusty, apparently thinking the wiry CO wouldn't pose a challenge.

He was wrong.

Rusty got hold of the guy's t-shirt and with strength unsuspected, pulled up. The inmate was already moving fast and off-balance -- Rusty's move sent them both off-balance and tumbling down the stairs.

Twisting like a cat, Rusty made sure that when they landed, he was on top.

"I asked you a question," he barked, planting a knee in the middle of the inmate's back. "Where do you think you're going?"

The inmate mumbled something.

"I believe you said, 'Nowhere, sir' because that's the answer, isn't it?" Another CO had arrived, and was snapping leg shackles onto the would-be escapee. "Nowhere."

The pair of them hauled the inmate to his feet, turning him to the wall. They'd almost made it when the inmate pivoted, quick as a cat, and sank his teeth into Rusty's neck.

He screamed. Blood was going everywhere. The inmate didn't let go, despite the other CO clubbing him upside the back of the head with a hardwood baton.

Guards were coming from everywhere, dozens of them, bearing down on the conflict as fast as they could. Inmates were screaming and shouting, encouraging the inmate and hollering so loud it nearly drowned out the alarm. Trash flew out of every cell, littering the floor and cascading toward the ground floor like so much perverse snow.

And then, a barked command, and a shot.

The inmate fell where he stood, taking a good chunk of Rusty's neck with him.

The dorm went silent.
You could have heard a pin drop.
Then Rusty fell over, flat on his face.

Part Six

The hospital wasn't allowing visitors. "Not yet," an implacable nurse told Grant, arms folded across her chest like so much riot gear. "Not until he's stabilized."

"And when will that be?" Grant asked.

She looked at him, sad. "I can't answer that question. All I can tell you is to try back in a while."

"Should I wait?"

"No," she said, turning away. "I wouldn't. He's not going anywhere, not for a while."

* * *

Grant went to the club.

"Am I still allowed in here?" he asked the bouncer. Goddamn, he was a big guy, towering over Grant. His shadow was large enough to provide shade for a picnic party on the beach.

"Depends." The bouncer smiled. "You gonna get all drunk and stupid and try to bust your knuckles on my abs?"

"Not today." Grant shook his head. "I promise."

"I'm gonna hold you to that."

"Actually, I'm sort of looking for Darien."

The bouncer gave him a blank look.

"The cab driver? Took me home the other day?"

"Oh," the bouncer said, face clearing. "You mean D?"

"Maybe."

The bouncer smiled. "It's his night off." He jerked his head toward the door. "You'll find him in there."

* * *

Darien was sitting at the bar, engrossed in conversation with the bartender and sucking down a beer.

"Is this a private party, or can anyone join?"

Darien raised an eyebrow and smiled. "This is a surprise." He nodded toward the stool. "Have a seat. I didn't think I'd see you twice in a week."

"Kind of a strange circumstance." Briefly, Grant detailed what had happened to Rusty. "They're not letting anyone in but family right now."

"COs are family." Darien's reply was sharp. "You'd think they would have picked up on that by now."

"Apparently they missed the memo." Grant shrugged. "Hopefully I can get in to see him sooner or later." He laid his money on the bar, telling the bartender, "Just a coke, please," when the man's bright eyes fell on him.

Bright green, the way Rusty's eyes were.

Shit.

"Let's hope so," Darien said, apparently following Grant's train of thought. His eyes flickered to the bar's surface for a moment, and then rose to meet Grant's. "Want to go somewhere, distract yourself from thinking about it for a minute or two?"

* * *

A narrow supply room afforded them a little privacy, enough space and silence for Darien to push Grant up against the wall and undo his belt.

"Hands over your head, big boy," he urged, pushing Grant's pants down over his hips. "Hold still and let me have you."

Darien fell to his knees, stopping only to let his hand run over the length of Grant's shaft. "Such a pretty cock. I was feeling bad that I didn't get a chance to do this earlier."

Then it was his mouth, hot and wet and demanding. Long, intricate twists of his tongue had Grant moaning aloud, one hand convulsively stuffed into his mouth to stifle the sound.

Darien's lips slid down to Grant's belly, planting the most intimate of kisses there. Then he drew his mouth back, teasing and taunting while pulling at the CO's balls, ever so gently.

"I can't," Grant whispered, "I can't hold back, Sir."

Darien sucked harder, pulling Grant's hips into his face. *Don't* was the clear, unspoken message.

Grant complied.

* * *

"You're amazing," Grant said.

"Not really. You just looked like you needed a distraction, from what -- from who -- you're thinking about."

"How did you know?" Grant asked. "What I needed?"

Darien smiled. "I've dated more than a few COs in my time. After a while, you pick up on what they need."

"Are you interested in dating another one?" Grant asked, hopeful.

Darien shook his head. "I'm not the dating kind."

Grant's shoulders slumped. "S'okay."

"Grant, listen." Darien's tone was sharp. "This is not about you. You're a fine looking man, hotter than hell. I'd be proud to have you as a boyfriend." He shrugged. "But I suck at fidelity. I suck at relationships. I suck at all the things that make couples work. It wouldn't take a month, and you'd never want to see me again."

"You don't know that."

"I do know that." Darien shook his head. "I've been me a long, long time."

"You're not willing to give me a chance?" Grant snapped. "Thanks a fucking lot."

"Grant, I don't want to lose you." Darien reached out and grabbed Grant by the shoulders. "If I date you, if we try to be a couple, I'm going to lose you. I'd rather be your friend -- your friend with benefits -- and have that with you than to have nothing at all."

Grant glared.

Darien dropped his hands.

"Well, think about it, anyway." He opened the store room door. "I know one thing for sure. The only one who can truly understand a CO, really get him, is another CO. You're never going to be happy with a civilian." The hallway light was bright enough to cast Darien into silhouette, obliterating his features. "Trust me. I know what I'm talking about."

Grant stood there, silent, until all he could see was Darien's back, going down the hallway. "You'd like to think so, anyway."

* * *

"Has there been any change?" Grant asked.

The nurse shook her head. "I can't really tell you anything. I'm sorry, I really am." Her eyes flickered down the hall, where two administrators stood talking. "He can't have visitors, yet."

"That's okay." Grant nodded. "I understand. Is it okay if I just sit myself over here and wait a bit?"

"Sure." The nurse's eyes drifted back down the hall. "If you want to hold on a while, I'll let you know when he's ready for company."

"Thanks," Grant replied. "I'd be appreciative."

An hour passed, and then two. Still Grant sat, watching and waiting, listening to the clock tick slowly. Minute after minute crept by, with no news.

And then, right about the time he was ready to head for home and crawl into bed, the nurse came over to him.

"If you want to go in and see him," she whispered. "I can give you ten minutes."

* * *

Rusty was bandaged up pretty heavily, thick cotton gauze coiled round his neck. An IV drip was going into one arm, and a whole jungle of wires was emerging on the other side, connecting him to a bank of monitors.

"Hey," Grant said. "How you feeling, man?"

"Been better." Rusty smiled. "Glad to see you, though." He lifted one hand. "Maybe I wasn't imagining things this morning."

"Nope." Grant swallowed. In for an inch, in for a mile. "I was the one imagining, and it looked pretty good." He took Rusty's hand. It felt natural. It felt damn good.

"You'll have to tell me about it," Rusty replied, "when I'm out of here." His eyes narrowed. "That might be a little bit, though, from what they tell me. Our buddy was Hep C positive."

"Fuck." Grant kept hold of Rusty's hand. "Nothing's ever easy, is it?"

"It might be," Rusty replied. "If you're not too intent on making it difficult."

Flesh and Blood by Tory Temple

The call came in right before his relief got there at eight in the morning, and Chance was glad for it. His crew was usually kept so busy answering medical calls and traffic accidents that fighting actual fire didn't happen often enough for his tastes, outside of the random house or car fire.

It was in a strip mall and it was big enough for five engine companies to respond. Chance's was the second on scene, and he felt the familiar rush of adrenaline as soon as they pulled up to the row of burning buildings. His crew leapt off the rig and turned to him immediately, waiting for direction, even though Chance knew that all of them were capable enough to figure out what to do on their own.

Still. Barking orders gave him a hard-on.

He took one look at the flames and tried to assess who was needed where. One of the chiefs from downtown was already shouting at two guys on the roof, so Chance sent Jim over to check if he needed to go up too, and Trey and Randy were working on the hose line.

The third engine pulled screaming into the parking lot, and Chance noted briefly that it was Engine Nineteen, Tucker's station. However, it was a C-shift day, which meant Tucker would be home, not at work. Chance regretted that he hadn't had a chance to call him to say he wouldn't be home any time soon, but Tucker would figure it out anyway. He'd probably call the station looking for him and Chance's relief would tell Tucker where he was. Chance was betting he'd be pissed off that he missed the opportunity to play in the flames.

He had no more time to think about it before one of the other captains yelled at him and pointed toward the ladder that was leaning against the side of the building. Chance nodded once, checked to see if his crew was following orders, and started scaling the ladder to the roof.

They battled flames for nine hours, stopping only briefly to gulp bottles of water or wolf down the sandwiches that magically appeared from some of the neighboring restaurants. Chance was drenched in sweat inside his turnouts before noon and wished desperately for a dry t-shirt, but there was no time to change before he found himself back on the roof, holding a hose line.

The only truly frightening part of the day occurred when the captain at Station Four got caught under one of the falling rafters inside a building. Chance hadn't been anywhere near the incident at the time; he'd been in the cab of his engine, on the radio with Station Two's engineer. There had been shouts and the sound of running feet and Chance looked up in time to see the captain being carried out and loaded into the back of a medic van.

The guy hadn't been brought to one of their local hospitals, but one that was farther away because of the reputation it had for its excellent burn unit, and all the men on scene had grown quiet when they'd found out. Being transported to a burn unit only meant one thing: pain. Chance had a sober moment when he realized not only was that captain's career in jeopardy, but his life was as well.

It was nearing six o'clock before one of the chiefs finally dismissed Chance's engine. Two other companies stayed to assess damage and cool hot spots, but Chance's crew climbed wearily onto their rig and rolled out. They discussed the fire on their short trip back to the station, and Chance complimented all of them on doing what they'd been trained to do.

C shift greeted them when they returned, grumbling about how they'd missed the call by only twenty minutes. Chance was just considering grabbing a fast shower before heading home to Tucker when Jim nudged him.

"Your boy's here."

His head whipped around, shower forgotten. It had been dark when they'd pulled in; he must have missed Tucker's truck in the lot. "Where?"

"Your office."

Chance headed down the hallway to the small office he shared with the other two captains, eager to see Tucker and tell him about their day. The adrenaline still flowed through him and he realized he was hard inside his shorts, same as he'd been when they'd arrived on scene that morning. Fire had that effect on him.

Tucker sat in Chance's chair behind the desk, his expression serious. He rose when Chance stopped in the doorway and came around the desk to stand in front of him, studying Chance's face. "You didn't call."

Chance raised a brow. "You think I had time to call?"

"You could've," Tucker insisted, a furrow appearing on his forehead. "You always got your cell. You coulda called when you stopped to eat."

Chance stared at him. This wasn't typical; Tucker knew better than anyone did what it was like when things were too busy to even take a piss, much less find time to call home. "Didn't C shift tell you where we were?"

Tucker studied his fingernails. "I called. They said -- they said a captain went down and they didn't know who. Called both hospitals and they wouldn't tell me."

Oh. Chance had nearly forgotten, the incident lost among his exhaustion and desire to get home. "It was Sheridan. Not me."

"Well, I didn't fuckin' know, now did I?"

Chance reached out a hand and curved it briefly around Tucker's jaw. "It wasn't me," he said again. "I wasn't even in the building."

Tucker leaned into the touch briefly before pulling away. "Yeah. I got that. M'outta here, I'll see you at home." He pushed past Chance and took off down the hall, heading toward the back door and the parking lot.

Chance followed him, all thoughts of a shower forgotten. "Hey," he said, once they'd reached the row of cars in the dark lot. Tucker ignored him and unlocked the door of his truck, so Chance tried again. "Tucker. Tuck. Stop a second." Chance reached for his arm before Tucker could climb behind the wheel. "I'm sorry you worried. But it was fucking crazy over there; I barely had time to eat or anything. Christ, you know how it is, right?"

Tucker looked up, eyes flashing in the darkness. "All I know is that I spent three fuckin' hellish hours sittin' in your office, waitin' to find out if you were hurt. Nobody would tell me *anything* at the goddamned hospitals 'cause I ain't your fuckin' flesh and blood. That's fucked up." He was breathing hard and still had one foot inside the cab of his truck, ready to bolt. "Don't nobody try to tell me we ain't fuckin' family just 'cause we ain't like the rest of middle fuckin' America."

Chance couldn't be mad at him. Tucker knew how it went during a fire, he'd been on plenty of them, but Chance was aware of what worry could do to common sense. It changed the whole perspective of things. It was obviously up to him to calm some fears; otherwise, Chance knew the rest of the night would be spent with someone on the couch and someone alone in bed.

"Tucker," he said, keeping his tone soft and tugging gently at Tucker's arm so he had to step out of the truck. "Listen. Let it go, all right? I'm good." He leaned in and nuzzled at the soft spot under Tucker's ear, darting his tongue out for a taste. Chance felt Tucker's breathing catch for a second before resuming at a calmer rate. "Are you going to take me home with you, or what?"

"Your car's here," Tucker said, closing his eyes when Chance continued to mouth the skin.

"So drop me off on your way to work tomorrow." He bit down lightly and was rewarded with a hand on his waistband, fingers curling underneath his shirt.

"Get in."

* * *

His erection had returned with a vengeance by the time they made it home, and once inside the foyer, Tucker kicked the door shut with his foot and put both hands on Chance's filthy t-shirt. "Bedroom," he demanded, pushing.

Chance spared a glance for the shower as Tucker propelled him into the bedroom. "I should clean up," he said doubtfully, but even he knew he didn't want to waste the time. Unless Tucker came with him, of course.

"No," Tucker said, crawling onto the bed and pulling Chance with him. "Later. 'Sides, you smell like fire."

Chance grinned and arched his neck when Tucker leaned down to suck a mark into the side of his throat. "I smell like sweat."

"That too. But mostly fire."

"Yeah? You like it?" His breath caught when Tucker's teeth worried at the mark he was making.

"Holy fuck, yes. And you do, too. Don't tell me you didn't get hard as soon as you smelled it this morning." Tucker left the spot on his neck and moved across to Chance's breastbone, dragging his tongue as he went and leaving cool trails that dried almost as soon as the air hit them.

"Maybe."

Tucker chuckled and paused in his licking to put his nose to Chance's skin, taking a deep breath. "No maybe about it. It's in your pores; I can smell it in your hair." He stopped and examined Chance's face. "And here." Tucker used a light finger to trace Chance's cheek and Chance remembered when he'd used his sooty glove to brush at the sweat of earlier. It had left a dark smudge of ash that he'd forgotten to wash off.

Tucker was studying him, his eyes dark with an emotion that wasn't often present, though Chance knew it was always there beneath the surface. It made Chance feel too exposed, too defenseless, too vulnerable under Tucker's hot gaze, and he reached up to pull Tucker back down for a kiss.

Tucker's hands were warm on his chest and Chance wanted to absorb him, wanted to take away the worry that still lingered in his touch and tell Tucker things were fine, but as usual, the words got stuck and he was afraid they wouldn't come out right anyway. It was a common occurrence, and Chance knew by this point that sometimes talking wasn't what was really needed.

So he did what he usually did when the words were too hard. He touched, instead. Chance used his fingers to still and soothe, he used his mouth to taste and warm cool skin, and Tucker responded to him with soft sounds and closed eyes.

They lay together for a long time, kissing and touching and not saying anything, until Tucker finally squirmed and slid down to rid them both of their shorts. Chance sat up to pull off his t-shirt and then there was a hard length pressing back up against him, Tucker rubbing into his hip and biting at Chance's shoulder.

One warm hand came down to palm his cock, and Chance gasped when Tucker's thumb brushed the head and gathered the moisture there. Tucker stroked him in a practiced fist until Chance was writhing on the sheets and making noises that would have embarrassed him if he weren't so needy. "Come on," he finally begged, so Tucker chuckled and reached up to the bedside drawer.

"I like it when you ask. Don't get to hear it that much."

The only answer he could formulate was "More," and then one slick finger was stretching him and pressing against the area that made things go hot and bright all at once. Another finger, and another flare that made him arch and reach for his cock, squeezing tightly just under the head in order not to come.

Tucker stopped what he was doing. "You okay?" he asked with a wicked grin, and laughed when Chance flipped him off. "Just checkin'."

Tucker kept it up until he had three fingers inside, and the burn was sweet enough to make Chance whimper and toss his head on the pillow, grabbing at Tucker's wrist and pushing his heels into the bed. "Better hurry," he warned, voice hoarse.

And then Tucker was up and over and pushing Chance's leg back and sliding in, using too much lube but it didn't matter because everything was tight and slippery and warm. Chance's cock jerked hard and he wasn't even touching it and Chance knew this wasn't going to be one of those times he congratulated himself on his stamina. He'd been too on edge all day to make it last now; the only thing he could hope for was that Tucker wasn't that far behind him.

Dark blue eyes had turned almost black, the pupils edging out any color left in the iris. Tucker kept one hand on Chance's knee and the other one came down to encircle his cock, pulling at Chance while he thrust slowly enough to drive both of them crazy. Tucker shifted and drove in hard, once, hitting the perfect spot and Chance bit back a curse.

The buildup was making him dizzy and it was a little scary how fast he'd gotten there, but then again, it was usually that way with Tucker. One more harsh thrust against his prostate at the same time Tucker pressed his thumb into the slit of Chance's cock, and his orgasm was jerked out of him suddenly. The pleasure almost hurt in its intensity and he could feel every muscle trembling when his back arched, his come landing on his stomach in hot splashes.

He was still shuddering with the aftershocks that wouldn't stop when Tucker came with a gasp and a hard thrust that drove Chance into the mattress. There were muttered curses as he froze, and Chance could feel the faint pulsing as Tucker spilled into him.

Chance was too limp to do anything but say "Oof," when Tucker toppled onto him, smooth and hot and slick against his chest. Chance brought up his arms to hold Tucker close and listened to their hearts beat opposite rhythms while they recovered. The faint scent of smoke still hung in the air, clinging to Chance's discarded clothes, and he breathed it in.

Eventually, Tucker lifted his head and slid to the side, propping his cheek on his hand and scrutinizing Chance.

He felt himself redden under Tucker's stare. "What?"

"I know you didn't have time to call," Tucker said, subdued. "I was bein' an ass."

"No," Chance shook his head. "You were worried. I would have been, too." It came with the job, although most of the time they tried not to think about it. They all knew that you couldn't let the worry consume you. It was no way to live your life.

"It's just 'cause I lo-- ... y'know." He shrugged one shoulder and looked down, playing with a loose thread on the bed covers.

"Yeah," Chance said, his voice low. "Me too."

* * *

The incident was forgotten within a couple of days, although Tucker was oddly quiet for a week or so. Chance watched him carefully when he thought Tucker wasn't looking, until Tucker finally rolled his eyes and pushed Chance into a wall.

"Stop doin' that."

"Doing what?" He tried not to blush.

"Lookin' at me all worried and stuff." Tucker leaned in and kissed him fast before moving away and picking up his gear bag to go to work. "I'm over it, we're all good. Okay?"

"Okay," Chance shrugged, embarrassed to be caught looking.

"Okay," Tucker said again, smiling a little, and left the house.

Chance went to the beach for the rest of the day, ignoring the pile of laundry that was mounded on top of the machine and the dishes that needed to be unloaded from the dishwasher. Household chores could wait; high surf couldn't.

Back home for a quiet night alone, and Chance considered calling Bonnie to see if she wanted to come over and watch movies on the couch. Then he remembered that it was her one-year anniversary with Matt, or something like that, so he abandoned that idea and settled for making himself a turkey sandwich with a Heineken for dinner.

He really didn't mind being alone, most nights. It was just the way things were, with Tucker and him on different shifts, and Chance didn't see the point in being upset over it. They each had long careers ahead of them in the fire service and there were going to be a lot of nights when the bed was empty. Better to know that and deal with it than pine over being alone for twenty-four hours at a time.

Chance settled on the couch with his beer and the remote, lifting a hand to stroke his cat's head when Smokey leaped up to sit next to him. "You and me, Smoke," he whispered, smiling a little when Smokey narrowed his eyes to slits and began to purr quietly.

The television ended up grabbing his attention with the end of a Padres baseball game, and Chance was halfway through his second beer when he heard a key in the front door. Taking his bare feet off the coffee table and sitting up, Chance was alarmed to see Tucker shove his way in the front door and drop his gear bag.

"Hey," Chance said, rising to his feet. "What's wrong? You okay?"

"No," Tucker snapped, brushing past Chance and heading straight for the kitchen.

Chance followed in time to see him root through the refrigerator for one of the Mexican beers he preferred, pop the cap off, and take a long pull. After three deep swallows, Tucker turned to him, fury still coming off him in waves. "Got sent home. *Goddammit*."

Chance leaned against the counter and studied him. It was times like this when he had to work hard not to let the superior rank of his job take over, and for the millionth time Chance thanked God that he didn't have to be Tucker's captain. "You got sent home. Are you sick?"

Tucker drained his beer and slammed the bottle down on the counter. "Do I look sick?"

"You look pissed."

"The man's a genius. No wonder they promoted you." The last was said with a caustic tone and arched brow, and then Tucker disappeared down the small hallway. Chance could hear the shower being turned on and sighed with distaste. Now came the difficult task of finding out what had happened without making it seem like Chance was lecturing.

He ventured into the bathroom and watched the steam start to rise over the top of the glass shower doors. Tucker dropped his clothes where he stood and stepped into the water, turning his face to the spray and then bracing both hands on the tile under the nozzle. Chance watched him bow his head and let the water run down over his hair and flow across muscular shoulders.

Tucker and water always made for an instant turn-on -- oh, who was he kidding, Tucker himself was the real turn-on -- and Chance had to remind himself that he needed to find out what had happened before there was any kind of sex. But damn, watching Tucker's skin grow sleek and wet under the water made Chance's cock stand up and take a lot of notice.

Eventually, Chance realized that Tucker hadn't changed position at all. He still stood with his head down and hands braced against the wall, letting the spray beat down on him. Chance watched him for another minute before stripping off his own t-shirt and shorts and getting into the shower behind him.

The water was scalding and Chance winced, trying to get used to the heat. Tucker's skin was already turning red and Chance wanted to reach over and nudge the tap a little lower, but Tucker didn't seem bothered by it so Chance left it alone. He settled for standing slightly off to the side and placed one hand at the small of Tucker's back. "You okay?" Chance said again, although the answer was very obviously 'no'.

Tucker shook his head once and reached around to take Chance's hand. He pulled it around his waist and tugged a little, urging Chance to step up and press himself against Tucker's slick skin. Once they were touching, Tucker eased Chance's hand lower, wrapping it around his erection and holding tightly.

Chance closed his eyes and leaned his forehead between Tucker's shoulder blades. All right, maybe sex would come first. His own dick seemed to appreciate that idea, anyway, considering how he was rubbing up against Tucker's ass without even realizing it. Chance tried an experimental stroke down Tucker's cock and got an appreciative groan in return, so Chance gave up pretending he didn't want to mess around and went with it.

He reached for the soap and, keeping one hand on Tucker's cock, used the other hand to lather up suds on Tucker's back. Chance watched the bubbles drip and slide down the tanned skin, stopping only for a moment at the curve between back and ass, then gaining more momentum and sliding over the firm cheeks. Chance kept a steady rhythm with his right hand, using the method he knew would bring Tucker close but not quite there, pausing every now and again to gather up the fluid beading at the tip.

When Tucker's small gasps could be heard above the noise of the water and he was pushing his ass back against Chance's cock, Chance let go only long enough to drop the soap and grab the lube they kept in the soap dish. Slicking up with a practiced hand, he traced a line down Tucker's crack until he reached his hole. Probing gently, Chance lubed him up well and grit his teeth against Tucker's needy whimpers.

"Cap," Tucker finally begged. "I don't want it slow or pretty. Please."

Chance withdrew his hand immediately and lined up. "You're not getting slow," he said, and shoved in hard.

Tucker's head went back and his fingers scrabbled for purchase on the wet tile. "Oh God, please," he repeated, water streaming down from his hair and over the back of his neck.

Chance leaned forward and caught the drops with his tongue, licking at Tucker's neck and using sharp teeth to bite at the tender skin. He pulled out nearly all the way before driving back in, angling his hips just right and feeling the head of his cock push up against Tucker's gland. "Please what?" he growled, his nails biting into Tucker's hips and leaving little crescent marks.

"Please fuck me," Tucker nearly sobbed, one hand going down to tug at his prick. "Don't make me ask again."

Chance nodded and pushed him flat against the tile, pinning him in place before starting to pound into him. Chance knew he was being rough and didn't care; it was what Tucker wanted and needed. Chance usually spent most of his life giving Tucker what he needed, anyway.

Faster, and then faster still, until the shower was filled with steam and the sound of their loving. Pants and gasps and cut-off groans mingled with the water, and Chance could feel the tightness just behind his balls. With effort, he detached a hand from Tucker's hip and brought it around to help Tucker stroke off. "Tuck," Chance ground out. "Right now. Gonna go."

Tucker bucked back against him and clamped down hard around Chance's cock, and then he was trembling in Chance's arms and coming over their fingers. Chance could feel the pulses deep in Tucker's ass and then he was coming as well, the orgasm drawn out of him and making him shudder and hold on to Tucker's wet skin as best he could.

They both tried to use the wall to keep them up, but eventually shaky muscles gave out and they sank down to the floor of the shower together. Tucker turned into him without a word and Chance held on tightly, gathering Tucker up as much as the small space allowed.

They sat under the shower spray for a long time, long enough to lose the hot water. When Tucker's skin turned cool and they both started to shiver, Chance got them both up off the floor and into warm towels. Tucker dried off without a word, though most of the previous anger he held seemed to have dissipated. Chance watched him out of the corner of his eye as they both dressed in clean clothes, and when Tucker sat down with a heavy sigh on the bed, Chance joined him there.

"Can you tell me?" Chance asked quietly, lifting a hand to brush Tucker's wet hair from his forehead.

Tucker eyed him. "You gonna give me a lecture?"

"No," Chance said.

"Really?"

"... maybe," Chance admitted, and Tucker snorted. "I'll try not to."

Tucker sighed in defeat. "You're gonna find out anyway," he muttered. "Got suspended for a shift."

Chance blinked. Shift suspension was uncommon; it usually only happened if the firefighter in question had done something fairly serious. "Okay," he said carefully, his mind already running through any one of a number of scenarios.

"So we go on this call for some guy who's dehydrated, right? He just started some fuckin' exercise program, and since he weighed almost three hundred pounds, looks like he needed it." Tucker shook his head. "We get to the house and the guy's wife says the doctor didn't tell him he needed to drink more water if he was gonna sweat so much."

Chance rolled his eyes. He had no doubt Tucker was telling the truth. Chance had been on his own share of medical calls that were caused by general ignorance or stupidity. "All right, so?"

"So Chris was off yesterday, and I had an overtime medic with me. Chuck Moore, you know him?"

Chance nodded. Chuck was a tall, African-American fireman that he'd worked with before. Good guy and a good medic. "Yeah. Chuck."

"Chuck kneels down next to him to start some saline in his IV. I'm standin' up, talkin' to Rich about whether or not we should just load him up and take the guy in, when the guy has a goddamn tirade about Chuck stickin' him with a needle. I think maybe he's got a needle phobia or whatever, but no."

Tucker stopped and Chance could see the anger start to creep back in. "And?" he prompted, now having no idea where this was going.

"And so the guy's a fuckin' bigot, Chance. Used the 'N' word and everything. He didn't want Chuck to touch him." Tucker shook his head and stared at the carpet in front of him. "Didn't even faze Chuck at all, but you know what I thought?"

Chance watched him. "Tell me," he said softly, knowing this was more than what it seemed like.

"I thought, 'if this asshole don't like black people, then he prolly don't like fags either'. And what would the fucker say if he knew that I sucked cock? Huh? Would he let *me* touch him? 'Cause he sure wasn't havin' none of Chuck, I'll tell you that. Set up a huge fuss until I finally just grabbed the saline from the box and stuck the asshole myself."

"Uh huh," Chance said, trying to follow him. "And then?"

"Wasn't saline," Tucker muttered. "Was morphine. I grabbed a thing of morphine by accident 'cause I was thinkin' about what this guy would do if he knew I took it up the ass."

Chance opened his mouth to say something and then snapped it shut, trying to process. Giving the wrong drug to a patient was a potentially fatal mistake. Not so in this case, fortunately, since the small vials of morphine that were kept in the drug boxes were only big enough to dull a patient's pain, not substantially reduce it. But it explained why Tucker had been sent home and was suspended for his next shift. "Christ, Tucker," Chance finally said.

"I know," Tucker responded, still staring at the floor. "I fucked up 'cause I wasn't payin' attention. I know. But Chance, Jesus! Just another goddamn example of someone who don't see people as... *people*! The fuck difference does it make if Chuck's got dark skin or Andy don't accept Christ as his savior or if I like to fuck guys? *The fuck difference does it make?*"

"It doesn't," Chance said, lifting a hand and running his knuckles down Tucker's cheek. "It doesn't make any difference. We know that, you and me. That's all that matters."

Tucker shook his head and rose to his feet. "No," he said sadly, "it ain't all that matters. I want it to be that way, but it just… ain't. I'm gonna find some food." He padded out the bedroom door in sock feet and Chance watched him go, heart aching.

* * *

Tucker's shift suspension came and went, and aside from knowing that Tucker had a written reprimand placed in his file, Chance didn't hear any more about it. Things were smooth for another month or so, with Tucker showing no more uncharacteristic behavior either at home or at work. Chance breathed a little easier.

Until, however, he got a call from Rich, Tucker's captain.

"Chance," Rich greeted him, his tone calm. "Can you meet us at the hospital?"

"Why?" Chance asked, sitting up and dropping the soft rag he'd been using to wax his surfboard.

"Bringing Tucker in for stitches. He's all right, just dropped a knife while he was cooking dinner. We're out of spare suture kits around here."

Chance closed his eyes, knowing how furious Tucker would be at having to go in. "You guys can't glue it?"

"Too wide. And the knife went right down the front of his shin; it's in a place that glue wouldn't hold. We're bringing him in now; can you make it?" Rich sounded resigned and Chance guessed Tucker had already started to fuss.

"Yeah, I'll be there. Is he pissed?" It was a stupid question to which Chance already knew the answer.

"Why the fuck do you think I called you?" Rich snorted, and hung up.

Chance grimaced and went to pull on a clean t-shirt.

The hospital was less than fifteen minutes away, and Chance pulled around to the emergency room, parking right behind Engine Nineteen and trusting that the firefighter's association sticker on the back of his car would excuse him from any tickets. He strode through the automatic doors and hoped there was a nurse on duty that would recognize him out of uniform.

He got lucky enough to run into Karen, an ER nurse that had been at the hospital longer than the twelve years Chance had been on with Oceanside Fire. "Hey," Chance greeted her, relieved to see her behind the counter.

She pointed through the double doors with a raised eyebrow. "Follow the noise," Karen said. "He's giving everyone who comes near him a hard time. Good thing he's cute."

Chance snorted and pushed his way inside. Cute, yes. Rational, not always.

He did as Karen had advised and followed the sound of Tucker's voice, audible above the controlled chaos of the emergency room. A quick scan of the place showed Tucker's crew lounging against the walls, trying to contain their amusement at Tucker's situation and make eyes at the nurses at the same time. Rich sprawled in the chair next to the bed where Tucker sat. Chance could see Tucker's shin still leaking slow drops of blood and could tell at once that Rich had been right; glue wouldn't have done the job.

Chance went to the other side of the bed and refrained from kissing Tucker's forehead, settling for resting a hand on his shoulder and squeezing. "Hurt?" he asked, trying to gauge how deep a cut it was.

"No," Tucker said sullenly. "And Rich didn't hafta call you. I woulda called and told you when we got back to the station."

"You're not going back," Rich said, and gave Chance a pained look. "You think you can work with your leg like that? Come on, McBride. You're not an idiot. You even bend down wrong to assess a patient and that thing's splitting wide open again."

Tucker muttered something under his breath that Chance assumed was probably uncharitable, but Rich just rolled his eyes and watched one of the young nurses bend over the towel cart.

When the on-call plastic surgeon finally arrived, Chance was unsurprised to see Tucker's crew wander into the room to watch. Most firemen had a fascination with things that the general public would find hard to stomach. "Cool," Trey said, watching as the doctor probed the edges of Tucker's wound.

"Fuck off," Tucker said, but they all crowded closer anyway. Chance stayed where he was, refusing to move.

When all sides of the bed had people leaning in to examine Tucker's leg, the plastic surgeon stood up abruptly. "Out," he barked. "Now. All of you."

"Thank God," Rich muttered, and rose from his chair. "Here, Chance. Sit."

"No," the surgeon said. "I said out."

"No," Chance echoed, and stayed where he was.

The surgeon narrowed his eyes. "Are you family?"

Tucker's crew averted their eyes and slunk out of the room, Rich leading the pack. Chance knew they were avoiding the entire issue of Tucker's sexuality, an issue that didn't often come up but was a touchy one when it did. Better to pretend they didn't hear anything.

"He's family," Tucker answered.

"Flesh and blood?" the surgeon pressed, eyeing Chance.

"What's the fuckin' difference?" Tucker shouted. "He's my partner!"

Chance sighed heavily. "Tuck. The privacy law. He has to follow it just like we do. You know he's only protecting himself."

Tucker furrowed his brow and stared at the crimson droplets of blood on the white sheet. "Fine. Wait out front."

Chance leaned in and kissed Tucker's temple, smoothing his hair back. "Right out front. Promise."

Tucker didn't answer and Chance waited until the surgeon looked up from where he was prepping his needle. "Yes?" the surgeon said, noticing Chance's stare.

"Fuck your privacy law," Chance snapped, and stalked out of the room.

He paced the small waiting room for twenty minutes before they wheeled Tucker out, a bandage taped snugly to his shin. "Can walk," he muttered to the nurse behind his chair, but she rolled her eyes and offered Chance a wink.

"You get a ride to the curb, my friend," she said to Tucker, and Chance hid a smile and followed her. She deposited Tucker there with a pat to his back as he rose from the chair. "You don't come back for medical again, hear?"

"Hear," Tucker said, without his usual wink or dimple, and Chance stayed close to his side as Tucker limped around the building to where his crew still lounged on the waiting engine. "Y'all can go," he grouched as soon as they saw him. "Still say you coulda glued it."

Rich grinned down at him from the captain's seat. "See you in ten to fourteen, McBride."

Chance grabbed Tucker's arm in time to prevent the rude gesture, and they both watched as the engine pulled out. "Are you hungry?" Chance asked him, pulling his keys from his pocket.

"No," Tucker said shortly. "Just get me home."

Being home did nothing to improve Tucker's mood. He moved as fast as his injured leg would allow and went straight to the bedroom, shucking his clothes and crawling beneath the covers.

"No food?" Chance asked again.

"No food."

"Beer?"

"No. Leave me the hell alone, Chance."

Chance heaved a sigh and steeled himself. "Tucker. Is it because you hurt yourself?" He knew it wasn't, but Chance still tried to see if he could head off the oncoming storm.

Tucker lifted his head from the pillow and stared at him for a moment before dropping his head back down and contemplating the ceiling. "You know it ain't."

Chance moved into the room and sat down with caution on the edge of the bed. "I know. But Jesus, Tucker, you know that privacy law as well as that surgeon did. You know he was covering his ass, that's all."

"That ain't all!" Tucker burst out, glaring at him. "How come you don't wanna see what's in front of your face, Chance? It's another goddamn example of how people don't wanna recognize what we got as real! As somethin' that's valid!"

Chance studied him for a long moment, taking in the snapping indigo eyes and the muscle jumping in Tucker's jaw. "Tucker," he said softly, "*we* know. It's real for you and me. Why isn't that enough?"

"Because it ain't. Because I'm sick of bein' treated like less than normal just 'cause I like dick. And mostly 'cause I ain't ashamed of what I got, and what I got is you." He sank down farther in bed and yanked the covers up to his chin, staring into the darkness of the bedroom.

Chance looked down at him. "Tuck," he murmured, reaching out to draw down the covers and reach for Tucker's hand. "Tucker."

Tucker turned and looked at him, the anger fading from his eyes and leaving only hurt and confusion behind. "Ain't ashamed of what I got," he whispered again.

"Me either," Chance smiled, and stripped his t-shirt off before climbing in next to Tucker. "Not ashamed."

Tucker turned and snuggled into him, burying his face in Chance's chest and snaking an arm over his waist. "Hey, Cap?"

"Yeah," Chance said into his hair, cock already responding from Tucker's nearness.

"Don't really wanna think about it."

Chance nodded and eased Tucker to his back, knowing what Tucker wanted and agreeing to the unspoken request. "Then don't." He slid down a little, mindful of the bandage on Tucker's leg, and kissed his way over Tucker's hip to the line of muscle leading to his groin. Tucker let out a soft sigh and Chance felt him relax a little bit, some of the tension seeping out.

Chance spent a long time pressing soft, open-mouthed kisses to the area around Tucker's dick, nuzzling and licking the skin but purposely ignoring the pretty cock that was hard and twitching in front of him. His own erection was making itself known as well, and that was a little harder to ignore.

He waited until Tucker was moving restlessly on the bed, fingers plucking at the sheet and stomach muscles bunched and tight. "Come on," Tucker finally groaned. "You ain't bein' nice. I'm injured."

"I'm nice," Chance laughed, and took Tucker all the way in without warning. He felt Tucker's cock hit the back of his throat and Chance swallowed, knowing exactly how Tucker would react.

He wasn't disappointed. Tucker arched off the bed with a strangled groan and two hands tangled in Chance's hair, all muscles clenching and straining. "Yes," Tucker murmured to the ceiling with his eyes closed. "God, yes."

Chance would have grinned but his mouth was busy, so he contented himself with humming a little and sucking hard. Down, down, as far down as he could go, and then back up to the head of Tucker's cock. Soft licks to gather up the sugary bitterness at the tip, one little pause to grip the base and press his tongue into the slit. Chance loved on him as best he knew how, trying to give Tucker something else to concentrate on other than his earlier round of emotion.

When Chance felt the fingers in his hair start to flex and grip, he knew Tucker was just about there. Chance held the base of his prick firmly in one hand, paused to lick a finger on his other hand, and drew a teasing line down Tucker's crack. When Chance heard Tucker take a quick breath, he lowered his head to swallow Tucker again and slid in a finger at the same time.

Tucker's reflex was to yank sharply on Chance's hair and then he was coming, spilling down Chance's throat in long, heavy pulses as he gasped and trembled. Chance caught it all and swallowed neatly, licking and sucking and drawing out anything Tucker had left. When he was sure Tucker was finished and lay panting beneath him, Chance kicked his shorts off and rose up to straddle Tucker's waist.

Tucker's hands came down to rest on Chance's thighs as he watched Chance begin to stroke himself. "Pretty," he whispered, his cheeks still flushed and eyes bright. "Here, baby." He brought a hand to rest on Chance's, helping Chance pull and tug at his cock until Chance felt the warning heaviness in his balls.

"Tucker," he ground out, and then pushed into their hands with a grunt and came over their joined fingers.

Tucker swiped one finger through the stickiness and held it up for Chance to see. As Chance tried to get his breath, he watched Tucker dart out his tongue to lick his finger, and Chance's spent cock gave a renewed twitch. Chance groaned and sprawled out on top of him. "I need ten minutes."

Tucker chuckled and wrapped strong arms around him. "I'll give you twenty. Thanks."

Chance lifted his head and looked at him. "This is what matters, Tucker," he said quietly. "This. I told you that before."

Tucker's arms tightened around him, but he didn't answer.

* * *

They went to Chance's mother's house for a weekend, an idea that in retrospect probably wasn't such a good one. But she'd asked, using the tone that always without fail hit Chance's guilt meter, and he'd mentioned it to Tucker.

"Your momma don't like me," he'd said with a raised brow.

"She doesn't like me either," Chance answered, falling into their usual routine. "She likes Casey."

"Your brother's an asshole."

"He's also not-- " Chance stopped himself from saying 'gay' and decided on something else. "He's also not a disappointment."

"Uh huh," Tucker said knowingly. "You're a real disappointment to her. Finished top of your class in school. Youngest captain in the department. Practically perfect in every way. No wonder she's disappointed." His tone suggested exactly what he thought of Chance's mother, and Chance couldn't blame him. His mom was… difficult.

"Look," Chance sighed, trying for patience. "She gave me the whole 'you didn't come for Thanksgiving or Christmas' speech, which means someone in her bridge club probably noticed I wasn't there. She wants us to come."

"Us?" Tucker took a swallow of his beer and eyed Chance over the rim of the bottle.

"I said I wasn't coming by myself. She said she figured that." There was no point in trying to lie and make Tucker think Chance's mother was thrilled with the prospect of her son's partner being there too. Tucker had met her enough to know otherwise.

"Sure, Cap," Tucker said with a smile Chance knew was meant to be sarcastic. "Let's go visit your momma."

At the time, Chance had been relieved to have Tucker capitulate so easily. It was just two days, after all. A six-hour drive that would get them there on Friday afternoon and then they could leave on Sunday morning. It wouldn't be bad.

Except now they were actually here, and Chance had been in a constant state of tension since their arrival. His mother had greeted him with a perfunctory kiss to the cheek and a nod to Tucker. Tucker had nodded back and grinned at her, but Chance's mother remained the only human being on earth who seemed immune to both Tucker's dark blue eyes or quick dimples.

Friday passed without incident, and Tucker had behaved himself and refrained from commenting on the fact that they were expected to sleep in separate rooms. It didn't stop Tucker, however, from winding up in Chance's bed at midnight with a twinkle in his eye and a firm hand on Chance's cock, and Chance had had to bite down hard on Tucker's shoulder to keep from crying out when Tucker made him come.

Saturday they were expected to attend lunch at the club, which Tucker again did without comment. Chance's mother introduced them to various women that Chance had silently dubbed the tennis crowd, each one looking exactly like the last. Brown, leathery skin and enormous diamond rings seemed to be the requisite. More than one of them gave Tucker a second look, Chance was amused to note, especially since his mother had introduced him only as "Chancellor's friend from California". Chance figured "the man he sleeps with" didn't have the same ring to it, and the neglected, rich housewives eyed up Tucker every chance they got.

Tucker remained on his best behavior for the rest of the day, which Chance realized later should have been a warning that trouble was brewing. Tucker rarely restrained himself in tense situations without having a rather impressive meltdown. The storm stayed out of sight until dinner, which they ate in his mother's formal dining room.

"Not for at least five more years, Mom," Chance explained for the millionth time.

"But Chancellor. You could *try.* There is no harm in taking the chiefs' interview now."

"Except for the fact that I don't want to." He forked up a bite of saffron rice and shrugged. "I've only been captain for two years. And I don't even know if I want to be a chief. Those poor bast--um, poor guys have a hell of a lot of paperwork." It wasn't really true; Chance knew he did want to be a battalion chief one day. Just not today.

"Plus, their hours suck," Tucker piped up.

Chance's mother turned her head to regard Tucker. "If Chancellor wants to get ahead, he'll be working long hours."

"He already does work long hours," Tucker replied, and Chance wondered if his mother picked up on the fact that Tucker was very subtly mimicking her accent. "He works a lot of goddamn overtime and brings home a crapload of paperwork. We're on different shifts; I barely see him as it is."

"I don't know why that matters," his mother said, lifting her wineglass to take a delicate sip. "The two of you aren't married."

Chance said "Mom," very sharply, at the exact same time that Tucker stood and pushed his chair back.

Tucker lifted up his t-shirt sleeve to reveal the Maltese Cross tattoo that he'd had since before Chance had known him. The small, scripted C in the middle of the fireman's helmet had been an addition to his ink almost a year and a half ago, and Chance had gotten an identical tattoo on his own bicep with the letter T in the middle. Rings and vows in front of a clergyman, no. But married? Definitely yes.

"That says different," Tucker snapped, pointing to his arm. "The fact that we live together says different. The nights either one of us is home by ourselves and lonely says different. Chance married me the day he put my name on his arm."

"That's your version of married," his mother said. "Who else recognizes it? Tell me that."

Tucker looked like he'd been punched. The only indication Chance had that he was still furious was the white-knuckled grip Tucker had on the edge of the table. "Mom, enough," Chance barked, standing up as well. "You either accept this or you don't. Enough of the pretending to be fine with it."

"I was never fine with it, Chancellor," his mother said calmly. "And I'm only speaking from the world's point of view. You're very lucky to live in such a tolerant place, because if you step outside your little bubble someday, you'll find that not everyone is as friendly to couples such as you and Tucker."

"Tolerant?" Tucker asked, sounding incredulous. "That's what you think?! That me and Chance live in a place that has tolerance for queers? Lemme tell you somethin'."

Chance didn't give him time to finish, knowing instinctively that Tucker had reached his breaking point and whatever came out of his mouth wasn't going to be remotely polite or restrained. He grabbed Tucker's arm and moved, hauling him from the room and out the front door.

The warm Arizona night engulfed them as Chance dragged Tucker to the porch. Tucker let himself be steered firmly until they reached the steps, at which point he yanked his arm out of Chance's grip and glared. "The fuck were you thinkin'?" he shouted, hands balling into fists. "What on God's earth made you think that both of us comin' out here would be okay? Christ, Chance! Stop lookin' for her fuckin' approval, 'cause she ain't never gonna give it to us!"

"I don't care about her approval!" he shouted back, knowing it was a lie and Tucker would know it too.

"You do," Tucker said, narrowing his eyes and moving closer. "'Course you care. Otherwise you wouldn't have brought me. You wanna see if one of these times she's gonna welcome me with open arms and embrace what we got. Well, I'll tell you what, Chancellor. She's just like the rest of the goddamned world, and she ain't wrong. She ain't wrong when she says no one else recognizes what we got as real."

Chance opened his mouth to say something and then realized he didn't have anything else to say. Tucker had his mind firmly made up, and Chance had to admit that recent circumstances hadn't done anything other than illustrate Tucker's point. "I'm sorry," he finally offered in a low voice, studying the porch floor. "You were right. I should have come by myself. I'm sorry, Tuck."

Tucker was nuzzling at him and wrapping arms around Chance's waist before Chance realized the man had even moved. "S'okay," he murmured, drawing Chance in close. "I shouldn'ta yelled. Sorry, baby. I know how your momma is."

Chance nodded and closed his eyes, burying his face in Tucker's neck and breathing in his familiar, loved scent. "Yeah. Okay."

They stood together for a while, long enough for Chance to worry that someone would come looking for them. He raised his head and looked around uncertainly. "So."

"So," Tucker said, catching Chance's gaze. "What the hell do we do now?"

"Now… we drink." The thought occurred to him out of the blue, and suddenly seemed like the most fantastic thing he could think of. Getting completely loaded sounded like a fuck of a great idea.

Tucker grinned at him and held his arm out with a flourish, so Chance took his hand and headed down the steps of his mother's porch. "Liquor store down the street," Chance said, and headed that way.

A round trip to the local liquor store found them back in front of Chance's mother's house, looking at it with distaste. "Not drinkin' here," Tucker said, holding his bottle of Jack Daniel's as if it were treasure.

"No," Chance agreed. "Not here. I know where."

The small park wasn't far, and it was thankfully deserted. Chance sat himself down on a swing and held out a hand for the bottle. Tucker handed it over without a word and took a seat on the adjacent swing, waiting for his turn.

The whiskey burned going down and warmed his belly instantly. Chance took another swig and passed the bottle back, watching as Tucker lifted it to his lips and took a healthy drink. Chance focused on Tucker's throat, watching it work as he swallowed. They spent a good ten minutes in silence, just passing the bottle back and forth until the liquor no longer burned like fire in Chance's throat, and things were going a little tilty at the edges.

When Tucker slid off his swing and sat in the sand beneath their feet, Chance blinked at him. "What're you doing?"

"Too much work to stay up on that swing. Come down here, baby. Come lie in the sand with me. It's like the beach." And he fell backwards with a thump, lying on his back and gazing up at the night sky.

It definitely wasn't like the beach, since Chance had been craving exactly that all weekend. It was rare for him to spend a day away from the water. There were two high tides a day and he took full advantage of both of them, except on workdays. Being landlocked in Arizona had set his teeth on edge.

Chance got off the swing and eased himself down in the sand next to Tucker. "This isn't like the beach," he grumbled, picking up a fistful of playground sand and letting it trickle out of his fingers.

"Sure it is," Tucker coaxed, slurring his words only a little. "Lie down and use some imagination." He sat up and pushed at Chance's shoulder until Chance sighed and lay back.

The spinning slowly came to a stop as Chance focused on the stars overhead. "I don't hear waves," he noted.

Tucker snorted and wiggled closer to him, taking his hand and entwining their fingers. "Yeah, you do," he said. "Just shh a minute. Hear it? Close your eyes and listen."

Chance closed his eyes and let himself float on the pleasant numbness of the Jack Daniel's. He was drunk, Tucker was drunk, and Chance figured they were both pretty glad to be that way. "I'm listening," he said. "No waves. My beach. I miss my beach," Chance mourned.

"Cap, jeeze," Tucker laughed. "You're one of those drunks who gets sad and cries. Snap out of it, pretend you hear the fuckin' surf, and then kiss me or somethin'."

"Okay," Chance agreed instantly. "Except I'll skip the listening to the beach part and just kiss you instead." He lifted the hand that Tucker was still holding and tugged, urging Tucker over to sprawl out on top of him.

"Hi," Tucker grinned, when he was covering Chance with most of his body. "Good job."

Chance smiled up at him and brought Tucker's head down to meet his mouth, nipping and licking at the corners and spreading his legs a little bit to fit Tucker more snugly in between. They were both hard already, of course, since it never took longer than half a minute of being near each other. Chance rolled his hips up a little and Tucker groaned.

"I ain't gonna fuck you right here in the sand. Sand burns."

Chance laughed. "But the being drunk and in public part doesn't bother you?"

Tucker looked confused. "No. Should it?"

Chance chuckled again and slid a hand down the back of Tucker's worn jeans, making a noise of pleasure when he discovered no other barriers between denim and skin. "Okay. No fucking in the sand. No fucking outside, actually." Visions of being arrested flickered through his fuzzy brain, of the night he and Tucker had spent in jail while in Kentucky. Once was enough, thanks.

Chance made a move to get up but Tucker pressed down with his body weight. "I said I wouldn't fuck you. That don't mean we ain't gonna have some fun out here. We deserve it."

It was either the alcohol or the hard cock pressing into his hip, but Chance was caught by the dark, flashing eyes and the soft curve of Tucker's mouth. Chance felt himself nod and shifted a little bit, one foot coming up to hook around Tucker's calf and pin him where he was. "Fun," he whispered back, thrusting upwards.

"There you go," Tucker murmured, bending his head to kiss Chance again.

Tucker tasted of whiskey and something sweeter, something that always reminded Chance of country and fresh air and fragrant meadow grass. Chance groaned and brought up both hands to tangle in Tucker's hair, holding his head in place as they kissed with clashing tongues and warm lips. "We're in the goddamn park," Chance tried one last time.

"Yup," was all Tucker said, grinding down on him and rubbing in all the right places. "You can tell Bonnie I made you come under the swings on the playground."

Chance half-laughed, half-moaned, and then gave up. It felt too good and Tucker knew how to do this to him, so there was no point now in trying to stop. Especially since Chance found himself digging his heels into the sand and gripping Tucker's ass with fingers that flexed and grabbed. "Tucker," he whispered, asking for more of something but not knowing exactly what that something was.

Tucker knew, however. Tucker always knew. He leaned in and licked at the sensitive spot under Chance's ear, then bit down on the tender skin with something that was bordering on pain. Chance sucked in a breath and arched his neck, feeling his balls throb and then pull up tight.

"Shit," Tucker muttered, and froze. Chance could feel the very faint pulsing between their layers of clothes and then Chance was coming too, one hand reaching down to grab a fistful of sand as he shuddered under Tucker's weight.

They lay panting together under the swings until Chance felt Tucker smile against his neck and kiss the spot he'd bitten. "See? Bein' drunk and rollin' around on the ground's got its merits."

Chance groaned. "Tell me that in the morning when we have to drive home. Six hours in the car will do wonders for my head."

Tucker chuckled and rolled off, shaking his head. "One of these days you're gonna learn to live in the now, baby. 'Stead of always thinkin' the worst about the future."

"Yeah," Chance said softly, getting to his feet. "So will you."

He got no response to that.

As he'd expected, Chance had a fierce hangover the next morning when he said goodbye to his mother. Tucker had gotten up -- after defiantly and drunkenly spending the night in Chance's bed, and fuck his mother -- and gone immediately out to Chance's truck to wait.

"Chancellor," his mother said as she sipped her morning coffee, "I think perhaps Tucker misunderstood our conversation last evening."

"No," Chance said, striving to keep his voice even. "He understood you perfectly. So did I."

She sighed and set her coffee cup down carefully on its matching fine china saucer. "It is not my intention to alienate you," she said.

Chance put both hands on the breakfast table and leaned forward. "If you alienate Tucker," he bit out, "you alienate me. When will you get it? We're a package deal from here on out. I am not Casey, Mom. I won't ever be rich. Or straight," he added as an afterthought.

She arched a sculpted brow. "I am aware you're not your brother."

"Yeah. You make that clear each time I see you. I love you, Mom, but I won't subject Tucker to this crap again. That means you don't get me, either." Chance pushed off from the table and stalked to the door, listening to the silence behind him.

He walked straight to his SUV and climbed into the passenger seat, leaning his head back against the headrest and closing his eyes. "Drive," he told Tucker.

They drove.

* * *

Another few weeks passed uneventfully, though by now Chance found himself always on edge, waiting. He watched Tucker as surreptitiously as he could, knowing Tucker's tendency for showing signs of stress in physical ways. Chance hoped that what he was watching for could be avoided.

Except Tucker came home from work one morning, white as a sheet, eyes standing out in stark relief against his pale face. "Bed," he managed to say as Chance rose from his chair at the kitchen table.

"What is it?" Chance asked, although he already knew. "Tuck. Tell me."

"Head," Tucker answered, clearly able to manage only one-word responses, and then disappeared down the short hallway to the bedroom.

Chance sighed and muttered "damn", under his breath before following Tucker. Chance had known as soon as he'd seen him. Tucker suffered from migraines, and although they didn't occur often, they were harsh and debilitating when they did hit. They were stress-related headaches, and nothing was more frustrating to Chance than Tucker's refusal to see the doctor for an upgraded prescription. "He wants me to *talk* to someone," Tucker would say with a disgusted tone, as if seeing a therapist was akin to being hanged. "I ain't gonna talk to no shrink about how to manage my stress. Got you for that, don't I?" Chance had finally let the subject drop when six months went by with no headache, but as he followed Tucker to the bedroom now, Chance realized he'd been waiting for Tucker to have one for days.

Tucker had managed to strip his shirt off and crawl beneath the covers, but the blinds remained open and the morning sunlight streamed through. Chance closed them quietly, immersing the room in semi-darkness, before sitting on the edge of the bed next to Tucker. "I'll get you ice," Chance whispered to him, stroking a hand down Tucker's bare back. "You want to try and take your meds?"

A barely-discernible nod came from under the covers, so Chance went and fetched a bag of ice wrapped in a towel, along with a bottle of water. He returned to the bedroom and urged Tucker to sit up and take his prescription medication, hoping it would stay down long enough to have some effect. "Gonna puke it up," Tucker muttered, taking it anyway.

"Probably," Chance agreed, reaching out and dragging the small wastebasket closer to the bed. "Call me when you do."

"You'll hear it," Tucker answered, lying back down and shoving his head under a pillow.

Chance rested the small, ice-filled towel on the back of Tucker's neck, using his other hand to squeeze at the tense muscles. There was nothing else he could do for Tucker, and Chance tried to shove down the helpless, frustrated feeling he always got when he was unable to offer any kind of comfort.

Ten minutes went by in near silence. The only sounds in the room were the small noises of discomfort Tucker made now and again and the sound of the slowly melting ice cubes. Chance hoped that Tucker had taken the meds in time for them to be effective, but he wasn't holding his breath. Not when Tucker was lying still as stone beneath Chance's hand, reluctant to make even the smallest of movements that would worsen his headache.

When the retching started, Chance took it in stride. He dutifully held the trash can for Tucker as he threw up his breakfast, wincing in sympathy as Tucker made a disgusted face and tried to spit the taste out of his mouth. Chance didn't worry the second time Tucker puked either, since it was pretty routine behavior with his headaches.

Chance felt his brow furrow, however, when Tucker threw up a third time and then a fourth. By the fifth time there was nothing left in the man's stomach, so all Chance could do was watch helplessly as Tucker dry-heaved over the trash can and then sank back down in bed, miserable.

"Tuck," Chance finally murmured, smoothing Tucker's sweat-damp hair from his forehead. "Do you want to go in?" Tucker would know Chance was referring to the emergency room for a shot of Oxycontin.

"No," Tucker said at once, with all the force he could muster. "M'fine. Lemme sleep and it's all good."

But the usual grogginess that signaled the conclusion of his headache didn't come, and when ninety minutes passed with no change in Tucker's condition, Chance didn't leave Tucker the choice. "We're going," Chance insisted, managing to drag Tucker to a sitting position. "You walk or I carry you."

"Christ, don't fuckin' carry me," Tucker muttered, getting to his feet and glancing around for his discarded shirt. "I seen the way you manhandle people outta burning buildings."

Chance ignored the insult and only found himself grateful that Tucker still had the wherewithal to crack jokes, humorless though they might be. "Let's go," Chance sighed, practically carrying him down the hall anyway. "Hospital."

Tucker didn't make a sound on the way to the emergency room except for a tiny whimper when Chance drove as slowly as he could over bumps in the road. When they pulled into the parking lot, Chance was afraid Tucker wouldn't be able to walk in under his own power and was wondering how mad he'd be if there was a stretcher brought out for him.

Apparently the thought had occurred to Tucker also, because he was able to force himself to his feet and stand fairly well on his own outside Chance's SUV until Chance could come around and help him in.

They were recognized by the ER receptionist at once, since Chance had purposely chosen to bring Tucker to the hospital their fire department delivered patients to. Chance was hoping for a quick in and an even quicker out, and prayed there were no medical emergencies that would bring in paramedics from the closest stations. The last thing Tucker needed was for guys he worked with to see him like this.

Chance wasn't any kind of religious guy, but he still sent up a quiet thank you when the girl behind the counter sent them back immediately and one of the nurses Chance knew bustled over.

"Poor chicken," she said, making a noise with her tongue when she saw Tucker's pale face and lack of ready grin. "Here you go, sweetheart. Down here." She swept aside a curtain and patted a bed for him, indicating Chance should take the chair next to it.

"Thank you, Sarah," Chance said to her, meaning it.

"You're welcome, honey," she said gently. "You don't look any better than he does."

She set off again and Chance blinked. He hadn't given any thought to how he himself felt, but now that she had mentioned it, Chance could feel the tension in his shoulders and the headache lying at the base of his skull. A massage would help, or probably a good blowjob. Unfortunately, the one person who could give Chance both of them was in much worse shape.

The doctor arrived within minutes, most likely prompted by Sarah, and Chance made a note to bring her flowers or cookies or whatever women liked. Bonnie liked those chocolate truffle things from the fancy store, so maybe Chance would stop in and get Sarah some. Anything to say thank you for how quickly Tucker was being seen today, because Chance well knew just how long this could have taken without her intervention.

The doctor prepped the needle of Oxycontin and looked over at Chance. "How many times has he had this?" the doctor asked.

"None," Tucker answered, and the doctor glanced down at him.

"This is an opiate," the doctor advised, needle poised just above Tucker's thigh.

"He knows," Chance said. It was the reason Tucker always resisted going to the ER for migraines. Too many shots of Oxy and his prescription medication would cease to work at all, not to mention the real danger of becoming addicted to the medication in the shot. Chance knew Tucker's head had to be close to exploding for him to have agreed to come in this time. "Give it to him," Chance prompted when the doctor hesitated.

The needle sank deeply into Tucker's thigh and Chance knew it had to hurt. The shot had to penetrate the muscle to work, but Tucker continued his uncharacteristic silence and didn't even flinch when the needle was withdrawn.

The doctor left them alone for a while with a curt nod and Chance sat watch. It wasn't long until Tucker was able to open his eyes and blink at the ceiling, and only a few minutes after that, he sat up carefully and looked around the busy emergency room.

"Wow," Tucker said, after letting out a long breath. "That one kinda sucked."

"You scared the shit out of me," Chance snapped, unaware of it until now. But it was true, he realized. He'd been terrified for Tucker, unable to stop his pain or even do anything to lessen it. And although Chance knew it hadn't been Tucker's fault, somehow Chance still held him responsible for not doing anything to manage his own stress.

"... m'sorry, baby," Tucker said, a wrinkle between his brows and look of sorrow on his face. "Didn't mean to scare you."

The guilt washed over Chance immediately and he shook his head. "No. I'm sorry. Not your fault. How's your head?"

"Better," Tucker said, the relief evident. "I might live."

"Lucky me," Chance said wryly, and was rewarded with a quick flash of dimple.

"Yeah, lucky you."

Their drive home was slower and less tense than on the way in. Tucker lounged in the passenger seat with his eyes closed, but his fingers tapped lightly on his jeans leg in time with the soft music on the radio. Chance was pleased to note the color creeping back into Tucker's cheeks.

"Want food?" Chance asked him, when they'd closed the front door behind them.

Tucker shook his head and looked slightly ill. "In a while. Maybe some of that soup that's still in the fridge from the other night."

Chance smiled at him. "Whatever you want."

"I want a shower." Tucker blinked and looked decidedly weary.

"Go," Chance nodded. "I'll heat up the soup and bring it to you in bed."

"You'd make a good cabana boy," Tucker grinned at him. "Put a towel on before you bring it to me." He turned and made his careful way down the hall before Chance could flip him off.

When the bathroom door closed behind Tucker, Chance leaned on the wall and scrubbed a hand over his face. He rolled his tight shoulders and was reminded again that he needed a good rubdown, especially since he could feel knots forming under his shoulder blades and along the line of his neck.

He looked toward the bathroom again, thoughtful. Maybe giving would be as good as getting. Chance pushed off the wall and went to the bedroom, pulling open the bottom drawer of his dresser and digging through the clothes. The small bottle of cinnamon massage oil was still there, a gift from Bonnie last Christmas. Chance had raised his eyebrow at her but she'd just shrugged and smiled sweetly at him. He'd put it in his drawer and nearly forgotten about it.

A quick trip to the kitchen and Chance warmed the bottle in the microwave, returning to the bedroom in time to see Tucker wander in, a towel wrapped low on his hips. "Might skip food," Tucker yawned. "Least 'til I sleep for a while." He yawned again, widely enough to make his eyes water.

Chance nodded and reached out for his hand. "Lie down," he urged, tugging Tucker to the bed. "Here, on your stomach."

Tucker eyed him but didn't argue, crawling onto the bed and stretching out with a sigh of relief. "Stay with me," he murmured.

"Right here," Chance answered, stripping off his t-shirt and then climbing on the bed in just the swim trunks he'd had on since returning from the beach that morning. He straddled Tucker's hips and reached for the small, warm bottle of oil.

Tucker raised his head and looked back over his shoulder. "What're you-- ohhhhhhh," he groaned, feeling Chance's oil-slicked palms on his back. "Yeah, that," Tucker mumbled, dropping his head back down to the pillow.

Chance grinned and spread his hands wide, digging in with his fingers and feeling Tucker's muscles relax instantly. The smell of cinnamon filled the room, spicy and sharp in Chance's nose. Damn, he should have dug the oil out long before this. Maybe Bonnie had known what she was doing.

Tucker lay perfectly still beneath Chance's weight, making tiny sounds of pleasure as Chance's hands worked to loosen some of the tension that lay in his neck and shoulders. Chance used his thumbs to press on the soft spot at the base of Tucker's skull before sweeping his hands down to Tucker's shoulders and kneading there.

Tucker yelped when Chance's fingers found a particularly tight spot on his left shoulder, but shook his head when Chance pulled his hand away. "No, keep goin'," he mumbled into his pillow. "Get it out."

So Chance did, working at the spot with oil and gentle fingers until he felt the knot finally give way. On impulse, Chance leaned forward and touched his lips to the place before sitting up again and moving on to the next spot of tension.

He slid down further and placed his hands on Tucker's lower back, pressing his thumbs into the muscle on either side of Tucker's spine and sliding his palms up and down along the ridges. Chance reached for more oil and took a moment to appreciate how Tucker's skin glistened with it, how it turned the flesh soft and pliable and warm. *Definitely* should have taken the oil out before now.

Chance hadn't realized he was hard until he sat up and moved forward. His cock brushed across Tucker's bare ass as he re-settled himself on Tucker's hips. He ignored his erection, telling himself this wasn't the right time. Not less than an hour after returning from the hospital, anyway. It was just that Tucker was lying naked underneath him, pliant and relaxed, and Chance's cock obviously didn't know the difference.

He continued to knead Tucker's back and upper arms, but stopped abruptly when he found himself rocking with purpose against Tucker's ass in an effort to get some friction on his dick. Chance swore under his breath and cursed his lack of control where Tucker was concerned.

Tucker looked over his shoulder again. "S'matter?" he slurred, obviously relaxed and near sleep.

Chance shook his head and blushed, glancing down at his crotch. "Sorry."

Tucker followed his gaze. "You're sorry? 'Bout that? Sheesh, baby." He coaxed Chance to rise to his knees and Tucker turned to his back, then tugged Chance back down on top of him. Chance felt Tucker's matching erection instantly. "Then am I s'posed to be sorry too?"

"You're always like that," Chance said, rolling his hips a little.

"So are you, Cap," Tucker laughed, his eyes soft. "Guess it works out."

"I guess it does," Chance admitted, leaning forward and cradling Tucker's head with his arms. "Feel okay?"

"Would feel better if you were in me," Tucker whispered, making Chance's breath catch.

He sat up only long enough to get rid of his trunks over the side of the bed, then returned to cover Tucker with his body and drop a gentle kiss on his forehead. "Okay," Chance agreed, as if he had any kind of choice in the matter. "But tell me if you start to hurt."

"Ain't gonna hurt," Tucker said, holding Chance's hips and thrusting up the littlest bit. "'Cept it ain't gonna last, either, unless you hurry up about it." He softened the admonishment with a smile, one that revealed only a hint of dimple but sparkled in his eyes.

Chance reached over for the small bottle of oil and studied the label. The *"and lubricant"* part caught his eye, right underneath the *"Cinnamon Massage Oil"* part, and he hoped they were right. If this stuff burned going in, it would really fuck up the moment.

A small puddle of it in his palm and then new, fresh spice was filling his nose and making a heady scent throughout the bedroom. Chance dropped a hand and coated himself with it, holding his breath and waiting for any kind of burn, but none came. The oil just warmed instantly on his skin and created a pleasant slickness that made Chance shudder.

He looked up to find Tucker watching him, his tongue sliding over his bottom lip and his eyes glowing. "Now me," Tucker murmured, drawing one leg up and bringing Chance's oiled fingers to his hole. "Please. Now me."

Chance nodded and swallowed hard, using his fingers to probe gently and slide inside Tucker with care. "Tell me if this stuff burns."

Tucker's eyes widened and he took a quick breath. "No. It don't burn, it--" he broke off and closed his eyes. "It's warm. It's all warm and-- oh, Jesus." His breathing came faster and shorter as Chance slid in another finger and prepped Tucker as best he could.

Tucker was restless and shifting on the bed when Chance finally withdrew his hand and leaned up and over. He guided himself to Tucker's entrance and waited until Tucker opened hazy eyes and looked at him. "Okay?" Chance asked, even though he knew it was always okay. More than okay.

Tucker nodded and reached for him, coaxing Chance forward even more and breaching Tucker just a little. Both of them gasped and then Chance was sinking in as far as he could, unable to wait or even pretend he had some semblance of control. Tucker was too warm and slick and tight for Chance to hold off, so he didn't.

He was able to take several long, smooth strokes before Tucker was twisting and whimpering in an effort to get Chance to hit his gland, so Chance changed his angle a bit and thrust in hard. Tucker's reaction was instantaneous. He cried out and arched his back, fingers digging into Chance's forearms. "More," he begged, and Chance couldn't deny him.

Chance dropped his head to the hollow between Tucker's neck and shoulder and braced himself, driving in deep. He felt the sweat bead on his forehead and was able to keep it together long enough to squeeze a hand between them, searching for Tucker's cock. Chance found Tucker hard as iron and leaking so much that Chance's fingers slid over him easily. He took Tucker in his palm and began to tug and rub in time with his own thrusts.

Tucker had gone silent, his eyes squeezed closed and teeth digging hard into his bottom lip. Chance could feel him reach and strain and tense every muscle, and Chance would have frozen that moment and stared at him forever if his own need wasn't so pressing. But his brain was screaming at him to just get off already, and Tucker picked that moment to clamp down hard around him. Chance figured he didn't really have much choice left.

Three more tight, short strokes and then both of them were gasping and clutching at each other with shaking fingers, leaving marks behind that would still be there in the morning. Chance knew both of them had intended it that way. Tucker clenched around Chance's cock and then there was a warm rush of fluid over Chance's hand and belly as Tucker came in long, soft pulses. It was enough to set Chance off and he heard himself groan Tucker's name, shuddering and jerking hard inside his body as Chance spilled into him.

Soft breathing was all Chance heard for a long time. He lay atop Tucker with his full weight, knowing Tucker would complain if Chance got too heavy. Tucker didn't say a word, so Chance pressed his face into Tucker's neck and let himself be lulled into a half-sleep, surrounded by the smell of cinnamon and sex and Tucker.

Chance moved only when he felt Tucker stir slightly. "Gotta change the sheets," Tucker mumbled, nuzzling up into Chance's hair. "And a shower might be good."

A shower would definitely be good, especially when Chance lifted his head and found himself half-covered in cinnamon massage oil and come. Not a great combination. He wondered if they should bother even washing the sheets or just toss them out with Thursday's trash.

They stumbled to the shower together, turning the water on hot and spending long minutes under the spray with soap and shampoo and gentle fingers. Tucker was mellow and relaxed, all signs of his migraine gone, and Chance was able to breathe easily for the first time that day.

Early evening found them on the couch under a blanket, a bag of chips between them and the remains of two Heinekens on the table. Tucker was a warm and sleepy weight next to his side, and Chance didn't want to move, ever.

"I wanna go somewhere," Tucker said, barely audible over the sound of the television.

Chance picked up the remote and muted the sound. "What?"

Tucker looked up at him, appearing much younger than his age. "I wanna go somewhere. You and me. Somewhere… somewhere where shit don't matter."

Chance knew what he meant. "Okay," he agreed. "I have a four day break from work that started today. Could go tomorrow and come back Saturday, if you want?"

Tucker nodded. "Got a shift tomorrow. Could call in sick, then I don't gotta work 'til Saturday either."

"Where are we going?" Chance had a moment of longing for somewhere tropical and warm, but it wasn't possible with only two and a half days.

Tucker was quiet for a moment, playing with his bottom lip while he thought. "Could go to Vegas," he said thoughtfully.

Chance considered that. They'd gone out to Las Vegas a couple of times together, but it had been at least a year since their last trip. Both of them liked the city, although Chance was usually worn down by the lights and cigarette smoke after a few days. It never seemed to bother Tucker, however, and Chance usually had to drag him home before Tucker gambled away their retirement.

"All right," Chance said, smiling down at him. "Vegas."

* * *

They left by eight the next morning, Chance reluctantly giving up his morning surfing when Tucker coaxed him into the shower at seven with promises -- and delivery -- of a blowjob. They packed quickly, throwing t-shirts, shorts, and jeans into duffel bags. Chance thought about the hotel's pool and hot tub and tossed in his swim trunks at the last minute, hoping for the opportunity to use them. Maybe while Tucker was gambling away their savings account.

It was a weekday morning, so the usual crowd that headed out to the river and desert on weekends wasn't present. The ride was easy and Tucker was agreeable enough to let Chance listen to whatever music he wanted, which was enough to put Chance in a good mood. They didn't stop for lunch and made excellent time, arriving in Vegas just before noon and opening their hotel room door by twenty minutes after twelve.

"Pool," Chance said, at the same time Tucker said, "Craps table." Chance sighed and held up his bathing suit. "I didn't get to surf this morning," he reminded Tucker. "At least let me check out the wave pool they've got here."

Tucker gave him a disgusted look. "You can do that at home."

Chance crossed the room and kissed him hard, holding Tucker's head in place with both hands and using a lot of tongue. By the time he pulled away, both of them had started to breathe a little bit harder. "Pool," Chance murmured, nuzzling at Tucker's nose. "Please. I'll take you out tonight."

Tucker smiled and nuzzled back. "Yeah, you will. After you feed me."

Two hours under the baking desert sun found both of them making good use of the hotel's lush tropical pool. Chance checked out the other swimming pool, the one the hotel made a huge deal about being the world's best wave pool, and pronounced it average before returning to the one where Tucker lounged in a chair under a palm tree. "Come on," he urged, and Tucker needed no further prompting to jump into the cool water with Chance in tow.

They swam and ducked under the waterfall and splashed and wrestled, Tucker using every opportunity to press up close to Chance and grope him under the water. Chance was hard and wanting by the time they finally climbed out of the water and reached for their towels. Chance quickly wrapped his towel around his hips, noting with embarrassment that it did nothing to hide his arousal.

Tucker just chuckled and wrapped up in his own towel, completely unashamed of his own erection. "It's Vegas," he shrugged, walking close enough to Chance so that their fingers brushed. "Who's gonna care?" He pushed the elevator button for their floor and grinned when the doors opened to reveal an empty car. "Wanna do it in here?" Tucker asked him with a sinful grin, pulling Chance to him and leaning against one wall.

Chance ground down on Tucker's hip, not able to help himself and feeling the dampness from their swimsuits and towels. "No," he said, kissing Tucker anyway and rubbing against his thigh.

"Feels like you do," Tucker murmured against Chance's mouth, holding Chance's hips and starting a lazy grind of his own.

"We're almost there," Chance muttered, somehow unable to tear himself away from Tucker's mouth and marveling that the elevator had made no other stops on the way up.

Tucker laughed as the doors opened on their hallway. "Got lucky on that one, Cap. Was about to jerk you off right there."

"Room," Chance said abruptly, seizing Tucker by the wrist and dragging him down the hall, belatedly regretting asking for a room that was far from the elevators.

Tucker dangled the key card from his fingers and Chance snatched it, jamming it in the lock and wrenching the door open. Before it had even closed all the way behind them, Chance had Tucker up against the wall and was biting down hard on the soft, slightly salty skin of his neck. "I hate it when you do that to me," he growled, flinging both of their towels aside.

"What's that?" Tucker asked, his head going back with a thump against the wall and his hands coming up once again to grip Chance's hips.

"Get me all hot in front of people," Chance answered, starting to pant and abandoning the idea of getting rid of their trunks. "Get me going in places where we can't do anything about it." He rolled his hips and was gratified when Tucker let out a low groan.

"Aw, baby, you just don't see it right," Tucker gasped, hooking one foot around Chance's calf. "It's foreplay. See how ready you are?"

He was ready, all right. Ready enough to-- Chance sucked in a sudden breath when his stomach clenched and his cock twitched, and then he was coming in an unexpected rush as he thrust up hard against Tucker's hip.

Tucker laughed softly at him before closing his eyes and snaking his hands down to hold Chance's ass firmly in place. "Stay there," he muttered, rubbing up hard.

Chance stayed, leaning heavily against Tucker since his legs were still shaky anyway. Chance bent his head and suckled hard at the bite mark he'd just made on Tucker's neck, tonguing the spot and tracing the very faint teeth marks. Tucker swallowed hard and then moaned low in his chest, and between them Chance could feel the faint pulsing of his orgasm.

They slid down to the floor in a tangle, chuckling and kissing and wet swimsuits sticking to hot skin. "Good start to vacation," Tucker grinned, and Chance had to agree.

Chance tried to get himself into the shower, he really did, but that meant they had to pass the bed to get to the bathroom. And suddenly the bed looked soft, so he sat down on it, and then Tucker was crawling up next to him and tugging Chance backwards to lay his head on the down pillows. "Nap," Tucker mumbled, stripping off his trunks and dropping them over the side.

Chance sighed and peeled off his own clammy suit, nestling in close to Tucker and closing his eyes. It was only two-thirty. Plenty of time.

Two-thirty turned into four-thirty and then five. The sun was low in the sky when Chance stirred. Tucker had grown cold, apparently, and was nestled beneath the covers, only his dark hair visible above the sheet. Chance slid over and wrapped around him from behind, burying his face in Tucker's neck and breathing him in. There was a very faint scent of chlorine from the pool still present, reminding Chance they were in need of showers before they ventured out for the night.

"Tuck," he whispered, bringing up a hand to push Tucker's hair back from his face. "We slept all afternoon. Wake up."

Tucker moved slightly, turning his face into Chance's hand and nuzzling there. "No one's awake during the day in Vegas," he mumbled. "They sleep so they can party at night."

Chance grinned and watched Tucker stick out his tongue to lick Chance's palm. "It's almost night. I need a shower, and then food so I can have the energy to keep up with you."

"Aw, you keep up good on your own," Tucker laughed, but he threw off the sheet and sat up. "Guess you could talk me into a shower," he said, glancing at Chance and using the power of his ridiculously long eyelashes. As if Chance needed convincing.

Chance rolled out of bed on his side and came around, tugging Tucker to his feet and pulling him toward the bathroom. "Shower," he said firmly. "Clean."

"You can do better at sweet talkin' than that," Tucker said wryly, but Chance just pushed him toward the large shower with frosted glass doors.

Half an hour and mutual handjobs later found both of them clean and relaxed. And hungry, judging by the growl Tucker's stomach made as they were leaving the room. "I want steak," he announced, punching the elevator button. "And not off a buffet, either. I want good steak."

Chance blinked, surprised but not argumentative in the least. Tucker's tastes were usually much less discerning than Chance's, despite the fact that Tucker was the best cook he knew. The lavish Vegas buffets were usually right up Tucker's alley, allowing him to eat as much as he wanted. The food itself was what Chance would categorize as good but not great, but Tucker never seemed to mind. The fact that he wanted to pass up a buffet in favor of a good steak in an actual restaurant was a pleasant change.

Tucker took his hand as they left their hotel through the front door. The temperature had dropped from the punishing heat of the day, but the air was still warm and balmy. Chance squeezed Tucker's fingers, relieved and happy to see him more carefree than Tucker had been for weeks. Chance had a moment of regret for not taking him here earlier. Clearly it was doing Tucker good.

Finding a cab was never a problem; the cabbies just lined up in front of every hotel and guests literally stepped out the door and into a cab. They found one easily and Chance gave the driver the name of one of the more pricey steakhouses in the area. Tucker raised an eyebrow at him but Chance just shrugged. "You'll win me back the cost of dinner, right?"

Tucker winked at him. "Sure, sweetheart. Either that, or I'll pay you back in trade."

The taxi pulled out onto the insanity of Las Vegas Boulevard and Tucker was distracted at once by the towering buildings and glittering brilliance of the city. Chance watched him lower his window and stick his head out, taking in the lights and noise as they drove, and Chance was reminded again of how the differences between himself and Tucker were actually what brought them together.

The ride to the restaurant was brief and there was a short wait for a table. They spent it at the bar, Chance with a beer and Tucker with a shot of whiskey, and once they were seated at their table Chance let himself enjoy the excellent cut of steak. Red meat once in a while wouldn't kill him.

Dinner was washed down with two more beers, and by the time they found themselves back on the street, Chance was feeling pleasantly mellow. He pulled Tucker into the back of another cab and looked at him expectantly. "Well? You want to go back and gamble for a while?" Chance didn't usually visit the craps tables, but he wasn't half-bad at cards and figured there'd be room at one of the poker tables.

"Later," Tucker said, and there was no missing the mischievous light in his eyes. "Wanna go somewhere else first."

"Where?" Chance asked, laughing. He knew where.

Tucker leaned forward and gave the club name to the driver, who merely nodded in a bored fashion and headed east.

Chance snorted and Tucker looked back at him with a wide grin. "You like the view there, too. Don't pretend it's all me."

"I know," Chance admitted. "But there are better places."

Tucker shrugged. "Maybe so. But this is one of the only places that'll give me liquor while I watch."

That point was inarguable, so Chance just leaned back with a shake of his head and a faint smile, and a renewed resolve never to let it get back to his chief that he was about to enjoy a night in a male strip bar.

The taxi pulled up to the innocuous front door of the club. The only thing to distinguish it from the other dark buildings surrounding it was a red velvet rope in front of the door. Tucker whipped out cash and paid the cover charge for both of them before seizing Chance's wrist and hauling him past the main downstairs stage and up a small set of stairs. Chance knew Tucker was headed for the smaller, more intimate stage that only held one dancer at a time instead of two or three.

It was a weeknight, so the club was definitely not at weekend peak. A few patrons were scattered throughout the stage area, but Tucker was able to find two chairs easily. He sprawled into one and signaled for a drink, pointing to the chair next to him. "Sit," he grinned.

Chance sat, amused. The view was always pretty, but somehow strip clubs weren't really what got him going. He would rather have the real thing under his hands; would rather have someone he could touch and kiss and lick. Still, watching Tucker was usually worth the couple of hours they spent there, so Chance settled back and signaled for his own drink.

The dancer currently on stage was young and lithe and almost done with his act, since the only thing he had left to do was remove his tear-away pants. Chance studied him and decided he'd been dressed as a construction worker. A yellow hard hat sat in the corner of the stage and a makeshift tool belt was draped over a table. Great, that meant it was theme night. Each guy would be dressed in a different outfit. Again, not really Chance's thing, but he eyed the oiled chest anyway. Skin was skin.

The next stripper was dressed as a sailor, and Tucker made an appreciative noise at the nice contrast between tanned, oiled skin and the white uniform. Chance had to admit the guy had nice hips, and laughed out loud when a dollar bill appeared in Tucker's hand.

The sailor finished, ending his song dressed only in a skimpy white thong with a red anchor directly over his cock. Tucker eyed his ass hungrily as the sailor left the stage. "He was nice," Tucker commented.

"He was tan," Chance agreed, knowing it was probably fake, either from a bottle or from a tanning bed.

Tucker looked up expectantly as the next dancer appeared, but he and Chance both groaned and rolled their eyes at the same time. The stripper was dressed as a firefighter, complete with yellow turnout pants, suspenders, helmet, and carrying rolled-up hose. Chance watched him dispassionately, already bored.

Tucker snorted his disgust and looked toward the bar for another drink. "That's the last fuckin' thing I need to see."

Chance nodded in agreement. It wasn't that the guy wasn't hot, because damn, he had a broad chest and thick arms. His eyes were blue, a piercing blue Chance could see even from a distance, and when the dancer turned around, his ass was small and tight. But still… God, dressed like a firefighter? Who got off on that shit? He slumped lower in his chair and waited for Tucker to get back with his beer.

Tucker appeared over his right shoulder and handed him a cold bottle, which Chance accepted gratefully. "This guy ain't done yet?" Tucker asked, dropping back down in his chair and taking a long drink of his own beer.

"Nearly," Chance answered, glancing up at the stage in time to see the dancer take off his suspenders and drop his pants.

"Think I'm 'bout done anyway," Tucker sighed. "Nobody impressed me."

Chance burst out laughing. It wasn't too hard to impress Tucker, not as long as you had a nice ass and firm package. "Aw," he grinned. "Just let me finish this bottle and then we'll go. I'll see if I can impress you."

Tucker twinkled at him. "I'm thinkin' yes," he said, and stood up from his seat just as the firefighter finished his set and another stripper strolled onto the stage.

Chance tipped his head back and drained his beer, leaving the bottle on the table next to him and rising to his feet. "Let's get out of here," he said, but got nothing in response. He looked over to see if maybe Tucker had already headed for the stairs, but Tucker was still standing there, staring transfixed at the stage.

"Wait," Tucker said, sinking back down and perching on the edge of his seat. "Not yet."

Chance blinked at him and then looked toward the stage. The next dancer had sauntered lazily to the middle of the floor and wasn't doing much except rocking his hips to the music that was just getting started. He was dressed in leather chaps, a vest, boots, and a hat that bore a startling resemblance to the Stetson that Tucker wore when he was on his farm in Kentucky.

"A cowboy?" Chance asked him, hearing the doubt in his own voice.

Tucker just made a shushing motion with his hand and sat back, his eyes wide and his mouth parted slightly, so Chance studied the man onstage. He was certainly good-looking, of that there was no question. But all the dancers here were good-looking, so it couldn't be just that. This one was tall and lean with corded muscle down his arms and over the flash of thigh Chance could see between the slits in the chaps. Dark hair and even darker eyes, with tiny laugh lines that appeared when the guy winked directly at Tucker before unbuckling his belt.

Tucker said something that sounded like "alksdjf" when the stripper undid his belt and dropped his chaps on the floor, revealing an American flag-striped G-string. Chance blinked again and looked at Tucker, who was gripping the arms of his chair and shifting around. He was sporting a hard-on that Chance could swear hadn't been there two minutes ago and was licking his lips as if he wanted to eat the guy for dinner.

Okay, then. Tucker was impressed. Chance waited until the dancer looked in his direction before tilting his head slightly toward Tucker and flashing some bills. The dancer nodded once, indicating that yes, he was available for private dances, before grinding his way toward the other side of the stage and the dollar bills that were being waved at him.

The song ended shortly after that and Chance was relieved, if only because Tucker had sunk down low in his seat and was absently rubbing himself over his jeans while he watched the stripper. Chance figured it wouldn't be too much longer before

Tucker started doing it more blatantly, which would definitely be illegal in the public areas of the club.

"Come on," Chance hissed, fastening his hand around Tucker's upper arm and yanking him out of his seat. Chance dragged him toward the bar and threw two twenties at the bartender. "That last guy," he said, jerking his head toward the stage.

The bartender took the cash and nodded. "On your right," he said, thumbing over his shoulder toward the small rooms behind the bar.

Tucker made another indecipherable sound and Chance couldn't help chuckling. It wasn't often the man was rendered speechless. Chance half-dragged, half-walked him toward the room that the bartender had indicated and pushed aside the heavy velvet curtain, letting it fall back into place behind them and essentially cutting them off from the rest of the club.

The room was small, but not too confining. It was big enough to hold a long couch that stretched from one wall to the other. The only other furniture in the room was a low table with a lamp. Chance pulled Tucker to the couch and sat, dragging Tucker down with him. "Keep your hands to yourself," he admonished. "I just paid forty bucks for this; don't get us kicked out before he's done."

Tucker nodded frantically. "Yeah. Okay. Don't touch. Okay."

Chance considered him. "On second thought, here." He lifted Tucker's closest hand and placed it on his own thigh. "Touch that."

The dancer chose that moment to lift the curtain and stroll through the doorway, an easy grin on his face and the cowboy hat in his hands. Tucker squeaked and the hand he had on Chance's thigh tightened. "Oh, shit," Tucker muttered under his breath, his eyes never straying from the stripper as the man crossed the floor to stand in front of him.

"He's the one?" the dancer asked Chance, laughing.

Chance snorted and eyed Tucker, hoping he would close his mouth before the drool ran out. "He's the one. I apologize in advance for any roaming hands."

The dancer leaned way over and flipped a switch on something under the couch, and a country song came piping through unseen speakers. The song was similar in beat to the one he'd danced to onstage, and Tucker's fingers tightened even more on Chance's thigh. Chance was betting there'd be bruises there come morning.

The stripper still held his hat in his hands as he started to move, muscles rippling in the dim light and smooth skin shimmering.

"Here you go," he winked, and leaned forward to place his black hat on Tucker's head. "You hang on to that for me." He punctuated the statement with a quick smile, flashing teeth that were blinding white, and drew closer to Tucker.

Chance glanced down and saw that Tucker had grown even harder in his jeans, if that was possible. It made his own cock twitch in response, or maybe that was the stripper. Chance examined him as he danced for Tucker. Damn. If nothing else, Tucker had good taste, because the dark eyes and pretty skin were enough on their own. Add in the quick grin and the tight muscle, and there was a deadly combination. Apparently, the whole cowboy thing had something to do with it as well.

Another ten minutes of the bump and grind had Tucker shifting around and gripping Chance's leg in an effort to keep some form of control. Chance was privately relieved when the dancer finished, if only because he had his doubts about Tucker's hold on his sanity.

"Half an hour," the dancer grinned at them both when he was finished. "Leave the towels in the bin." He indicated a wicker hamper near the door and walked toward the exit, stopping when he was halfway there and circling around to come back to them. "Forgot something," he smiled at Tucker, taking his hat from Tucker's head and placing it on his own. "Cowboy doesn't go anywhere without his hat." And then he turned to go, giving Tucker one more wink over his shoulder before disappearing out the door.

Chance braced himself just in time. Tucker launched himself at Chance, pushing him down onto the couch so they were lying across it. "Now," Tucker whispered urgently, "now, please, now now now." His hands fumbled at Chance's fly while he rubbed against Chance's hip, hard as rock in his jeans.

"Okay," Chance laughed, "hold on. Tuck, hold on a second." He managed to push Tucker back into a sitting position and then tossed a towel down on the floor between his feet. Unzipping his own fly, Chance knelt between Tucker's legs and went down on him in one smooth swallow.

"Oh God, yes," Tucker whispered, his head going back against the couch and his hands coming up to entwine his fingers in Chance's hair. He trembled with the effort of not thrusting, so Chance brought both hands up and slid them beneath Tucker's ass, encouraging him to move.

Once given the invitation, Tucker moved. His hands gripped Chance's head and his hips came off the couch in desperation, and

Chance could feel his own cock swell at the tiny whimpers Tucker probably didn't even know he was making. Chance took him in as far as he could, swallowing the drops of fluid Tucker was leaking and giving him long sweeps with his tongue.

Chance pulled off long enough to lick one finger, then lowered his head again to press his tongue against Tucker's slit before sliding that finger in. He heard the resulting gasp and felt the sharp tug in his hair and knew Tucker was nearly done. Chance turned his hand and pressed up with the finger that was inside, and then there was a sudden, warm rush in his mouth, and Chance could feel Tucker's heart beat with every pulse.

Chance swallowed as best he could and used soft, coaxing licks to draw it out for Tucker, cleaning him up as thoroughly as possible before rising up and straddling Tucker's thighs. Chance shoved his own jeans down as far as he needed to in order to get his cock out, and then he was holding himself in one hand and bracing the other on the back of the couch behind Tucker's head.

"On me," Tucker whispered, and Chance glanced up to see Tucker watching him, eyes bright and cheeks still pink from his climax. "On me, baby." Tucker tugged his t-shirt up by the hem, exposing his flat stomach. He dropped a hand over Chance's and helped him stroke, sweeping his thumb over the head of Chance's cock and pressing on the sensitive underside.

"Tucker," Chance moaned, visions flitting behind his eyes of Tucker writhing beneath him only moments before. "Tuck. Help." Chance was straining, he could feel himself reach for his orgasm and not quite get there.

"Show me," Tucker was murmuring in the low, soft voice he used when he wanted Chance to come for him. "Lemme see how pretty you are. Come on, you're right there, I can feel."

Chance bowed his head again and gripped the back of the couch until his knuckles turned white. One more tight stroke and then there it was: the white-hot, cramping flash of pleasure and the resulting full-body shudder. Chance kept his eyes open and watched his come fall on Tucker's belly in a perfect arc, leaving white streaks where it landed.

"There you go," Tucker grinned, when Chance lay panting against him. "We all need a little help sometimes. You okay?"

Chance nodded against his chest and felt the familiar heaviness in his limbs that signaled sleep coming on. They didn't have the luxury, however, of taking a power nap, so Chance reluctantly sat up and checked his watch. Eleven minutes to go before they'd be expected to vacate the room.

He stretched over as far as he could while Tucker held onto his hips and secured one of the towels that were kept discreetly under the furniture. Chance swiped at the mess on Tucker's stomach and managed to clean both of them up fairly well before rising shakily to his feet and zipping up. "Ready?" he asked, dropping the towel in the bin and holding out a hand.

Tucker crossed the room and took Chance's offered hand. "Ready. Thanks." He punctuated it with a kiss, squeezing Chance's fingers and nuzzling up behind his ear. "That guy was... wow."

Chance laughed as they left the room and made their way toward the stairs that would take them back out to the street. "He was wow, yeah. More wow than me?"

Tucker snorted and Chance could feel the blush creeping up his cheeks. It was an uncharacteristic remark, and Tucker knew it. "Cap," he laughed, "there ain't no one more wow than you. Swear."

Chance's cheeks grew even hotter and he regretted saying it. His self-confidence usually precluded such statements, but then again, he'd never seen Tucker react like that before. Chance made a mental note later to possibly use Tucker's memory of the stripper to his full advantage in the bedroom.

They took another cab back to the Strip and wandered among the crowds for a while before deciding to head downtown. The gambling was cheaper and Chance preferred the older casinos to the newer, flashier ones that primarily attracted families and the much younger crowd. Tucker didn't care where he spent his money, so they hailed yet another taxi and had the driver bring them to the older part of the city.

Three hours later found Chance with an extra ninety dollars in his pocket and Tucker close to two hundred in losses, so Chance let him finish his third drink and then dragged him bodily away from the dice table. "We have another day and night," Chance reminded him, laughing at the pout Tucker tried to use for leverage.

"But I ain't outta money!" Tucker protested, letting Chance steer him toward the door of the casino, despite his objections to leaving.

"That's a *good* thing, Tuck," Chance said with an eye roll. "Trust me."

They slept well into late morning the following day and had pretty much the same routine as the day before, minus watching men take off their clothes. Chance didn't know what would happen if he let Tucker within the vicinity of the dark-eyed cowboy again, but he wasn't willing to find out.

Their second night was spent necking in the Jacuzzi tub in their room. Chance didn't usually think of himself as one for bubble baths, but he did admit to Tucker there was something to be said for getting a hand job amidst mounds of strawberry-scented bubbles. The fruity scent lingered in the air for hours after their bath, and Chance fell asleep that night craving fresh strawberries.

Chance roused Tucker just after dawn the next day, put a Styrofoam cup of coffee in his hand and ignored his grumbling about the early hour, and had them both packed and in the car before eight a.m. "It's a four hour ride home," he informed Tucker as they pulled out onto the freeway. "I want to make it by noon, since I still have to wash clothes for work tomorrow."

"Since when does 'wash clothes' mean 'catch the three o'clock high tide'?" Tucker asked, leaning over to fiddle with the radio.

Chance glared at the road. Tucker just laughed.

It was a good sound.

* * *

The upbeat mood Tucker had found in Las Vegas stayed with both of them longer than Chance expected. Tucker was cheerful for long enough to make Chance almost forget the reason he'd taken him there in the first place.

Almost.

They both returned to work on their usual days. Chance had suggested neither of them pick up overtime shifts for a while in order to make the most out of the three nights a week they were able to spend together. Tucker had readily agreed, and Chance's life began to regain the steady, calm balance that he preferred.

On his fourth shift after returning from Vegas, Chance hopped down from the fire engine to the garage floor. His crew had been called by dispatch to a small house fire, but they were all disappointed to get there and only find remnants of smoke and a forgotten pot smoldering on the stove. The chagrined homeowner had apologized profusely, but it didn't stop Chance's crew from grumbling on the way back about the lack of actual fire.

Chance knew it was mostly their adrenaline that was making them edgy. It didn't happen that often, but getting geared up and ready to fight fire and then not being able to was disappointing and frustrating. The times it did happen often found firemen in the small yard of the station, shooting baskets and yelling at each other. Sometimes they'd use the station's workout room, too. Anything to burn off the displaced energy.

Chance wasn't immune to the pent-up adrenaline. He had caught himself drumming his fingers on his leg as they drove back to the station, and now he felt jittery and tense as he hung his gear back up in his locker. There were two guys already heading to the basketball court and he considered joining them before deciding to use the treadmill and weights in the workout room instead.

He'd only just sat down at one of the weight machines when a familiar dark head poked in the door. "Should take off your shirt," Tucker grinned at him. "You get a better workout that way."

"No, I don't," Chance laughed, pleased to see him. "Hey. When did you get here?"

"Before you guys got back," Tucker shrugged, strolling into the gym and letting the door close behind him. "Fire?"

"No," Chance groused, tilting his head up for Tucker's offered kiss. "A lot of smoke."

"Aw," Tucker teased, kissing him again. "Getcha all riled up for nothing?"

"Pretty much," he answered, liking the taste of Tucker's mouth against his own, but hyper-aware of the station full of firemen.

"Can fix that," Tucker whispered, tongue darting out to lick at a corner of Chance's mouth.

"Tuck," Chance warned, knowing that here wasn't the time or place but unable to stop one hand from creeping up to snag Tucker's t-shirt and drag him a little closer.

"Don't gimme the 'Tucker, not here' bullshit again," Tucker murmured against his mouth. "We've done it here before plenty. First time was right here in this room, as a matter of fact." Tucker straddled Chance's legs and sank down onto his lap, letting Chance feel the firm erection in his jeans. It matched Chance's own, making Chance groan softly when Tucker dragged his cock over the bulge in Chance's shorts. "Uh huh, see?" Tucker laughed, putting both hands over Chance's head and bracing them on the weight machine. "I'll make it fast."

If the way he was already clutching at Tucker and rocking his hips was any indication, Chance didn't think "fast" would be a problem. He threw a quick glance toward the door, at least relieved it was closed all the way before reaching up to yank Tucker's head down for a hard kiss. "Why do you do this to me?" Chance asked, using his other hand to settle Tucker more firmly on his lap.

"For fun," Tucker twinkled at him. "'Cause you don't get enough fun." He ground down hard and buried his face in Chance's neck, rubbing in just the right way.

"Tucker," Chance gasped, his eyes fluttering closed and both arms wrapping tight around Tucker's waist. His cock throbbed in his shorts and he shifted around on the uncomfortable seat of the machine, trying to get closer or tighter or more pressure or just something, *anything* to relieve the aching tension. "Tuck, please."

"Shh," Tucker whispered against his neck, never ceasing the slow, steady grind. "So tense all the time. Just relax and let it happen, baby doll. Feel it? Better hurry, there's a whole crew of guys out there."

Chance didn't know if it was the thought of being caught or the way Tucker was sliding just right against him, but suddenly his dick was twitching and his balls were lifting and then he was shaking against Tucker as he came in slow pulses.

"Like that," Tucker grinned, and Chance could feel Tucker's teeth on his skin. "Just… like… that." Tucker froze on the last word and held his breath, eyes squeezed shut and muscles trembling. He moaned, a low, satisfied sound, and Chance watched and thought him beautiful.

There was no time for afterglow, unfortunately. Chance had a moment of wishing they were on their couch or in bed or even the shower, anywhere that they could spend more than twenty seconds trying to still their heavy breathing.

Twenty seconds, however, proved to be too long. Before Tucker had even made an attempt to shift his weight and get off Chance's lap, the gym door opened and one of the firemen who worked on the second engine came in. Chance didn't know him well; he was an overtime guy from another station who'd kept to himself all day. His name was Adam and that was about the extent of the information he'd offered. Chance hadn't cared; the guy wasn't on his crew so Chance had no reason to bother with him.

Adam stopped and blinked at Tucker, who was still straddling Chance's lap. "Oh," he said slowly, eyes narrowing in on Chance. "Yeah, they said you two were…" He trailed off and waved a hand around.

"We were what?" Tucker asked easily, rising to his feet and turning to face Adam.

"Tuck," Chance said in a low tone, trying to head off the scene he could see unfolding.

"Screwing," Adam said, the disgust evident. "Fucking. Whatever. Good job, Shanahan," he said, nodding to Chance. "My wife and I aren't allowed to do at work whatever you just did with him," he continued, indicating Tucker. "You think the rules are different for you because you're quee--"

The last of his sentence was cut off by Tucker sending a hard right to Adam's cheek, knocking the man into the wall by the door. "Fuck you," Tucker spat, drawing back to hit him again.

"Tucker!" Chance shouted, leaping from where he sat to cross the room in two steps. He grabbed Tucker's arm a split second before he would have landed another punch.

Tucker wrenched away from him and turned to the door, pausing for only an instant to look back at both of them. Chance felt something inside him break at the pain-filled expression on Tucker's face. "It's never gonna change, Cap," Tucker said, his quiet tone filling Chance with more dread than if he'd been screaming. "We're never gonna get away from it."

And then he was gone, leaving Chance alone to deal with the mess.

* * *

Tucker wouldn't answer the phone later that night, although Chance didn't really expect him to. The house was quiet and empty when Chance got home from work the next morning, which was also sort of expected, although Chance had to tamp down the immediate sense of panic at finding the bed still made and Tucker's cell phone on his dresser.

Chance had spent most of the previous evening talking calmly to Adam and the captain of the other engine, explaining what had happened and leaving nothing out. By the time ten p.m. had rolled around, he'd managed to convince Adam not to press charges against Tucker for battery. There was still the matter of Tucker being written up -- again -- but that wouldn't result in any sort of legal mess.

"That guy's a dick," the other captain had whispered to Chance after Adam had gone to put some more ice on his swollen jaw. "No one at his own station likes him either."

Chance made a non-committal noise, knowing it didn't matter. The damage had already been done.

He paced between his living room and kitchen, wanting to go to the beach to surf but not daring to leave the house in case Tucker tried to reach him. Chance ignored the fact that Tucker didn't have his phone with him. People still used pay phones, didn't they?

The evening shadows were stretching long and spidery across the floor before Chance heard Tucker's key in the lock. Chance stayed where he was on the couch and waited.

Tucker came in, still wearing the same t-shirt and jeans as the previous day and looking suspiciously like he'd slept in his truck. He approached slowly and stood before Chance, his hands shoved deep in his pockets and his eyes uncertain. Chance's heart hurt to see the shadows under Tucker's eyes, the lines of strain around his mouth, but he said nothing.

"Am I in trouble?" Tucker asked, shoulders hunched.

"At work, yes. They'll probably call tonight or tomorrow."

"What about with you?"

Chance let out a deep breath very slowly and raised one arm. Tucker went immediately, curling into Chance's side and burrowing into his warmth. "Tucker," Chance said, and then stopped. There was nothing left to say that hadn't been said; nothing that would make Tucker think any differently than the way he'd been thinking for months. Chance was out of words, so he just sat and held Tucker close.

"I'm sorry," Tucker whispered after a long time, when the only light left in the room was the flickering of the television.

Chance just tightened the arm that was around him and said nothing.

A long time later, when Tucker had fallen into an exhausted sleep next to him, Chance carefully took off Tucker's tennis shoes and lifted the blanket from the back of the couch. He covered Tucker with it and turned the TV off before going to the kitchen and pulling out his small address book from a drawer. Despite the late hour, he made several phone calls, spending at least fifteen minutes on each one. Finally, satisfied with the results, Chance returned to the living room.

He knelt on the carpet and ran gentle fingers through Tucker's hair, brushing his silky bangs from his forehead. "Bedtime," Chance whispered. "Unless you want to stay on the couch."

Tucker stirred. "With you," he mumbled, scrubbing at his eyes with the heel of his hand.

"Okay. With me." Chance stood and held out a hand.

Tucker sat up and reached for it, heaving himself off of the couch and following Chance to bed. He dragged the blanket behind him and wrapped up in it when they reached the bedroom, waiting obediently until Chance had drawn down the sheet for him.

They undressed, leaving clothes in a pile on the floor, and climbed in. Tucker resumed his position under Chance's arm, curling in close and sighing heavily. "M'sorry," he said again, sounding defeated. "I fucked up, I know."

"You did," Chance answered, but not finding the energy or heart to go any further with the lecture. What else was there to say? Tucker already knew. He'd get an earful from his own captain when he returned to work, and Chance had learned too much over the past couple of years to try and lecture Tucker at home. It wouldn't do anything but draw a divisive line between them. "Just sleep," Chance sighed, drawing Tucker closer and pressing a kiss to his hair.

But neither of them did.

* * *

He sent Tucker out on a few random errands, pleading tiredness and showing Tucker the stack of paperwork he'd brought home to do.

Tucker sent him a suspicious look. "You never let me shop for food by myself. You always gotta boss me around and buy that fat-free shit."

Chance handed him a very specific grocery list. "Buy exactly what's on here and you'll be fine."

Tucker scrutinized the list. "I don't see ice cream."

"That's because it's not there. And you'd better go, the dry-cleaning place closes at five."

Tucker picked up a pen from the kitchen table and wrote something else on the piece of paper. He held it up long enough for Chance to see the words "ICE CREAM AND NOT THE LOW-FAT KIND" scrawled defiantly across the bottom before shoving the list in his back pocket. Tucker grabbed his keys from the counter and gave Chance one more distrustful look before leaving the house.

Immediately, Chance picked up the phone and made three separate calls. "He's out of the house," was the general message for each one, and then he hung up and went out to the back patio to turn on the grill.

By the time the recipients of his phone calls had arrived, the sun had begun to set and the smell of rich barbeque drifted throughout Chance's house. His four guests made themselves comfortable on his couch or in a kitchen chair, all of them with beer in hand.

Chance drank two himself while waiting for the familiar sound of the key in the lock. He told himself it wasn't because he was nervous, although of course he was. The idea had seemed like a good one when he'd thought of it, but now he was less than sure of Tucker's reaction.

He had just about convinced himself this was a terrible idea when he heard Tucker's truck in the driveway. Grabbing a third beer, Chance stationed himself in the living room and waited for the front door to open. It was only a minute longer before Tucker shouldered his way inside, loaded down with plastic grocery bags. "Hey Cap," he called, before looking up. "You're fuckin' crazy if you think I'm gonna buy that ground turkey crap instead of real…" Tucker trailed off when he spotted the group in the living room. "The hell?"

"Hi, sweetheart," Bonnie said, rising to greet him with a kiss to his cheek. "We just came over to say hi."

Tucker blinked at her. "Hey, Bon. Uh… all y'all?"

Matthew Perkins, Bonnie's boyfriend and Chance's old captain, got up from the couch and took the shopping bags from Tucker's hand. Matt handed him a beer instead and grinned. "Go sit down," he said, drawing an affectionate hand across Bonnie's back as he headed toward the kitchen.

Tucker looked at the beer in his hand and then at Chance before his eyes slid past to land on the third person on the couch. "Rich?"

Tucker's captain grinned at him and lifted his beer bottle in mock salute. "Hey, man. Thanks for letting me drink your beer."

Chance watched as Tucker blinked again, and then the fourth person Chance had called strolled into the room from the kitchen. "Pup," the man said easily, nodding in Tucker's direction.

"….. Coop?" Tucker asked, his eyes wide and disbelief evident in his voice. "Jesus Christ, tell me you didn't leave Ned and Johnny in charge of my goddamn farm."

"Our farm," the older man corrected, taking a long drink from his bottle. "And you think I'd run off to goddamned California if I thought those two couldn't handle it? It's three days, they won't run it into the ground."

Tucker stared at the man who'd been a hand on his father's tobacco farm since before Tucker was born, and who now owned half of it. "You said... you told me you ain't never got on a plane before."

"Nope," Coop shrugged, rubbing a hand over his grizzled chin and thinking about it. "Never did. Huh, guess now I could go visit my sister in Sedona. Flyin' ain't hard at all."

"Not when someone else pays," Chance reminded him with a grin.

Coop snorted and sat down on the couch next to Rich. "Told you when you called. I ain't never flown before, but I sure as hell know how much those tickets cost. Ain't no way I was gonna buy one two days 'fore you wanted me here."

Tucker turned back to Chance. "You called him," he said carefully, and Chance could tell he was trying to puzzle it all out.

"And me," Bonnie said with a bright smile. "And Matt and Rich." She took Tucker's beer bottle and opened it for him before handing it back. "Drink some of this, honey. Then Chance can tell you what's up."

"Yeah," Tucker said, raising the bottle to his lips but never taking his eyes from Chance's face. "I think he better."

Bonnie made a sound that sounded like "heh" before sitting back down next to Rich. Matt reappeared from the kitchen and came around the couch to stand behind Bonnie, hands resting on her shoulders, and when all five of them turned to look at Chance, he figured that was his cue.

He crossed the floor and took Tucker's hand, leading him to the empty chair next to the couch and encouraging him to sit. Tucker did, albeit suspiciously, darting glances toward the group on the couch. "Am I dyin'?" he asked, only sounding like he was sort of kidding.

Chance knelt down next to his chair and kept tight hold of his hand. "No. Tuck, I... I asked them to all come here for you."

"For me," Tucker repeated, watching Chance's face.

Chance nodded and plowed ahead, not knowing or caring anymore if this had been a good idea. "For you. I wanted -- *we* wanted -- to just show you once and for all that it doesn't fucking matter how the rest of the damn world sees us. What matters is you. What matters is me. What matters is what we make together. And the people in this room know it, so they're here to tell you that." Chance glanced up at his friends, the small group of people that he called family, and all of them nodded.

Chance gave Bonnie an imploring look, silently asking her to go first. She got up immediately from the couch and knelt down on the other side of Tucker's chair. "Hello, sweetheart," she smiled up at him, and Chance was grateful all over again for her friendship.

Tucker gave her a slight, uncertain grin, letting one dimple flash quickly and then disappear. "Hi, Bon. Cap pay you to come over?"

"No," she said seriously. "He doesn't have to. Tucker, I love you. I love you for what you've made Chance into. He laughs now. He manages to take a day for fun once in a while. He knows how to relax. All of those things were hard for him before you. I love how the two of you tease and argue and then kiss each other when you think I'm not looking. What you have with him is beautiful, Tuck. We all want you to know that."

Tucker was watching her as she spoke, his expression serious. "You came over to tell me that?"

Bonnie nodded and offered him a small smile. "I did, yup. And it goes for Matt too, since all he'd probably do is punch you in the arm or something."

Chance saw Tucker raise his eyes to where Matt still stood behind the couch. Matt nodded at him. "She's right, I'd probably just hit you." Tucker let a smile lift one corner of his mouth and Matt went on, "She's also right about the rest. I knew Chance before you did, and the things you've done for him have made him into the man I know now. Thank you."

Chance looked up at Matt, grateful and surprised by the warm words. He next turned his eyes to Rich, Tucker's captain at Station Nineteen. Rich cleared his throat and Tucker looked his way. "Oh boy," Tucker mumbled, a blush rising in his cheeks. "Couldn't wait for me to get back to work to yell at me, huh."

Rich chuckled and leaned forward to set his beer on the coffee table and clasp his hands in front of him. "McBride, you're a pain in my fucking ass. But you're one of the best firemen I know, and I've worked with a lot of damn firemen. That's all I give a shit about. I don't care who you live with, I don't care where you lay your head, and I sure as fuck don't care where you stick your dick. You're a good paramedic and you do your job, and to me, the one you come home to is as much your family as anyone." Rich nodded and sat back with a shrug. "That's all I've got."

The look on Tucker's face was indecipherable. Chance couldn't decide if Tucker was staring at Rich in amazement or disbelief or both, but when Coop cleared his throat and nervously scratched the back of his head, Tucker jerked his gaze that way immediately. "Guess that leaves me," Coop growled, not meeting anyone's eyes.

Chance tightened his grip on Tucker's hand. The decision to call the older man had not been an easy one. Although Tucker returned to Kentucky once or twice a year, Chance knew the trip was always difficult for him. There were demons there for Tucker, ones he had chosen to share with Chance and ones that he still kept secret. Chance never pushed him on the issue, but he always made sure to be home whenever Tucker returned from several days on his father's farm. Having Coop here was a very delicate boundary that Chance hoped he hadn't made a mistake in crossing.

Coop raised his head and stared directly at Tucker. "You look like your momma," he said. "She had them same dimples you got."

Tucker furrowed his brow and squeezed Chance's hand, waiting. "Yeah?" he asked.

"Yep," Coop said. "Pretty as anything, she was. Inside and out. Your daddy fell hard for her." He paused and rubbed the back of his neck, thinking, before looking back up at Tucker. "You don't got your momma and daddy no more, pup. That means you hold real damn tight to what you do got, and looks to me like what you got is sittin' here in this room. This is your family. *I'm* your family." Coop stopped again and nodded toward Chance. "That man became your flesh and blood the day you put that ink on your arm, Tucker. And your momma and daddy would say the same."

There was a long silence after Coop stopped speaking. Chance waited, holding Tucker's hand, until Tucker turned his head to look at Chance. "For me," he said softly. "You called 'em all here for me."

"Well… yeah," Chance answered, searching Tucker's face. "I did. Because you weren't listening to me. I thought maybe you'd listen to them."

Tucker looked back at the small group of people before turning to Chance again. "What… what do I say?"

"To me or to them?"

"To all of you."

Chance leaned in and spoke quietly. "To them, you say thank you. To me… you can say thank you later."

The corners of Tucker's eyes crinkled as a smile tugged at his mouth. "Later," he murmured, bringing up a hand and brushing his thumb over Chance's cheek. He rose from the chair and faced the people who had come for no other reason than to prove to Tucker who his family really was. "All y'all," Tucker started, and then seemed to come up short. "Y'all… might as well drink more of my beer." He finished with a shake of his head and a flush staining his cheeks, and Chance let out the breath he hadn't known he was holding.

It was near to midnight when Bonnie finally yawned and tugged on Matt's shirt. "Come on," she said, finding his keys on the kitchen table and jingling them. "Some of us have to work tomorrow."

"I'm not 'some of us'," Matt laughed, but he waved at Chance and stopped to clap Tucker on the back before letting Bonnie pull him out the door.

Rich followed suit, offering to drop Coop off at his hotel, and then all of them were gone and Chance looked at Tucker in the empty kitchen. "Well," Chance said, looking around at the empty bottles and remains of dinner.

"Well," Tucker said softly, getting up from a kitchen chair and crossing the floor. "You and me."

"You and me," Chance echoed, wrapping arms around Tucker's waist and pulling him in close.

Tucker nuzzled at him before bringing up his hands to play with the hem of Chance's t-shirt. "Thanks, Cap," he said, strangely subdued.

Chance reached out and lifted his chin. "When I said you could thank me later, I didn't mean like that." He kissed Tucker gently and was rewarded with a half smile.

"I know," Tucker said, meeting his gaze. His eyes were wide and dark, the indigo color blending into the black of his pupil. "But thank you anyhow."

"You're welcome."

Tucker leaned forward and kissed him, lips parted and soft. Chance moved his hands from Tucker's waist to slide up under the back of his t-shirt, pulling him even closer. "So," Tucker said against his mouth, "where do you wanna be thanked proper?"

Chance glanced around the kitchen. "Here's good," he smiled, already feeling his cock starting to firm up in his jeans.

"Here?" Tucker quirked a brow. "Ain't too romantic in here."

Chance pulled back and looked at him. "We've done it in here a hundred times."

"I know," Tucker grinned. "I don't really give a shit about romantic."

"Me either."

By way of answer, Tucker lifted Chance's t-shirt over his head, following suit with his own and then pressing sleek, silky skin up against him. Tucker leaned forward and dropped a kiss to the center of Chance's chest, darting out his tongue and licking there before fastening his lips to the spot and starting to suck.

Chance closed his eyes and let Tucker push him back against the counter, Tucker's mouth still sucking up a mark on his chest and his thigh sliding between Chance's own. Chance barely noticed when he started to rock against him, seeking friction and pressure. "Tuck," he whispered into the quiet kitchen, "please."

Tucker lifted his head and examined the red-purple stain over Chance's heart, tracing it with a finger. "That'll keep for a couple days," he said, seemingly satisfied. "You know, just so people know."

"So they know what?" Chance asked, shuddering just a little when Tucker leaned his entire weight against Chance and pressed him even more fully against the counter.

"Who you belong to," Tucker murmured before kissing him again, hard this time, his tongue shoving into Chance's mouth and his teeth biting into soft skin.

Chance moaned and held his head in place with one hand, kissing Tucker back and using his other hand to attempt to pop both buttons on their jeans. He was relieved when Tucker brushed Chance's hand out of the way and did it for him, yanking both pairs down and then they were kicking away denim and there was only heated skin.

They spent long minutes making out against the counter, hands roaming and touching and relearning, and Chance realized how easy it was to lose your way long before you ever knew you were lost. Tucker's fingers skimming his abdomen and his cock pressed heavy and hard into Chance's hip were recognizable landmarks, and he clung to them as he mapped out a path with his mouth from Tucker's ear to the soft spot under his jaw.

"Want," Chance whispered to him, shivering when he felt the pads of Tucker's fingers trace along his cock.

"Need," Tucker returned, bringing one of Chance's hands to feel his own hardness. "See? Need you."

"Need you," Chance repeated, realizing there was a difference. The want was always there, but the need was more crucial; it had become a part of both of them. "Tucker."

Tucker patted the kitchen counter, so Chance lifted himself and sat on the very edge, drawing up one leg and watching Tucker dig lube out of the drawer next to the sink. They'd decided years ago to keep lube in most rooms of the house and hadn't ever regretted the decision.

Especially not now, not when Tucker was slicking two fingers and circling Chance's hole as Chance's head fell back against the cabinets. Chance bit down hard on his lower lip and reached for Tucker's hand, silently encouraging him to go deeper. Tucker complied easily, probing and stroking from the inside, and Chance closed his eyes and traced Tucker's fingers in his ass. "More," he sighed, the word barely escaping, but then Tucker's hand was gone and there was a sense of loss Chance hadn't expected.

The emptiness was replaced soon enough by something more blunt and full, and Chance was relieved. He brought his leg up further onto the countertop and reached for Tucker, his hand sliding onto Tucker's hip and pulling him in. Tucker drew a breath that hitched in the middle, but then there was more lube and pressure and Tucker slid into Chance with one warm glide.

They stayed absolutely still for at least ten seconds, eyes locked on each other. Tucker's gaze was intent and serious and Chance looked right back, trying to communicate a million things to him without saying anything at all. They were silent and unmoving, Tucker's hand frozen on Chance's thigh and the other one over the mark he'd made on Chance's chest.

Chance thought maybe they could have stayed that way forever, the two of them bound together in a moment of understanding, but someone's muscles gave an involuntary quiver. He didn't know if it was him or Tucker, but suddenly it didn't matter because Tucker was moving and Chance was groaning and clenching tight around him.

"So pretty," Tucker was murmuring, and Chance pried open his eyes to see Tucker watching him as he moved. "You are so goddamned pretty."

There was no time for his blush to rise, however, because then Tucker had Chance's cock in a tight fist and was stroking him in perfect time with his own thrusts. "Yes, like that," Chance groaned, unable to do anything but strain and reach for what he needed.

"I know," Tucker answered, breathing faster and dropping his head down low. "Better hurry."

There was a moment of suspended clarity right then, a single instant when the bond between them became more than just "real". It was something Tucker needed, something both of them had always known but just misplaced for a while, and Chance felt it snap back into place in that tiny fragment of time. He would have liked to hold that moment for a while longer, to maybe examine it and see if he could find it again when he needed to, but Tucker chose that second to change the angle of his driving thrusts.

Chance cried out and began to tremble when he felt the head of Tucker's cock brush over his gland in unison with the strokes on Chance's shaft. Everything tightened at once and Chance felt the warning twinges begin. "With me," he gasped out, clenching around Tucker's cock as hard as he could. "God, please. With me."

Tucker slammed his free hand down on the counter and threw back his head. "Fuck!" was all he managed to get out before Chance felt him begin to pulse and shake. Tucker squeezed his hand hard around Chance's cock and then Chance was coming too, long arcs of fluid that splashed over Tucker's hand and onto his chest.

Chance's loose limbs and shaky muscles wouldn't let him stay on the counter, so Tucker eased out of him and did a half-hearted cleanup before helping Chance slide to the floor and curling around him. They lay kissing and nuzzling there together, and the floor was hard and Chance was sticky and he didn't care about any of that at all.

Eventually, Chance didn't know or care how much time later, they rose from the floor and rinsed off in the shower before crawling into bed and nestling close together. Tucker entwined his fingers with Chance's and raised their clasped hands to his mouth. "Thanks for the reminder," he murmured against Chance's knuckles.

Chance skimmed the back of his other hand against Tucker's cheek. "Family," he said softly. "Okay?"

Tucker nodded. "Family."

Trace Evidence by Alexa Snow

"I'll bet you five bucks it's a squirrel," Leo said under his breath.

Mitch stifled a laugh, and the end of his stick, which he'd been using to push dead leaves out of the way, broke off. "Damn it."

"There's some more over there." Leo gestured over his shoulder.

Sure enough, there was a small pile of branches at the base of a tree, some of them big enough for Mitch's purposes. "What I don't get," he said, going to retrieve one, "is why people can't just hang around. It's a waste of our time to spend a couple of hours out here."

"It's not going to take that long," Leo said. "At least she gave us a general idea of the area. If she hadn't done that much, we'd be searching the whole park."

Mitch sighed and selected a new stick, breaking some smaller branches off of it until it resembled a cartoon version of a broom. "True. And at least she didn't try to make an anonymous call. That's so annoying." 9-1-1 logged the phone numbers people called from, so there wasn't a way for people to make truly anonymous calls, although most of them didn't seem to realize that.

"Yeah, see? We got lucky." Leo grinned at him, working his way to the left where the ground dipped.

"'Lucky' would be having this kind of call come in on a day Joel and Bernie weren't both out sick, so they could deal with it like they're supposed to," Mitch griped.

"Drawback of working in a small town," Leo said. He stopped and frowned. "Huh. You smell that?"

Mitch moved over closer and sniffed cautiously. "I don't think so." He sniffed again. "I -- huh. Yeah, maybe." He scanned the area and caught sight of a slight rise near the base of a tree -- it could be nothing, tree roots making the ground buckle upward or whatever, not that he was any kind of an expert. But it could be something. "What about over there?"

"Could be."

They walked over slowly. It was strange, Mitch thought, wanting to get it over with and not wanting to find out at the same time. The smell got a little stronger as they got closer, which was definitely a sign that they were headed in the right direction. Unfortunately.

Once they were within a couple of feet of it, Mitch could hear the faint buzz of flies. "That's not a good sign," he said.

"Nope."

Mitch poked at the pile of damp leaves and buzzing insects with his stick, and some of the leaves slid off, revealing a layer of equally damp cardboard under the leaves.

And, peeking out from under the cardboard, the curve of three darkened fingertips.

"Christ," Mitch said.

The smell of rotten flesh wasn't too bad, not yet, but that was probably because he hadn't lifted the cardboard up. Steeling himself, he reached out with his stick again and did just that; the stench rose thick and sweet, gagging him, and he could see a young girl's face, eyes open and staring, the skin around her lips swollen and beginning to crack.

Leo made a choked sound and staggered back a few feet. "Fuck," he said. "Jesus."

"Yeah." Mitch let the cardboard settle back down, covering up the body. For a few seconds, the urge to cover the cardboard back up with leaves and pretend he hadn't seen it was strong, but it passed. He glanced at Leo, who looked distinctly green. "You want to call it in?" That'd give Leo the chance to walk away, at least.

"Sure." Leo cleared his throat and turned away, unclipping his radio from his belt.

Mitch stayed where he was, letting the reassuring sound of Leo's muttered voice soothe him as he looked out across the park. It was still early -- not much past seven thirty -- but there were people in the park. Joggers, people riding their bikes on the bike path. Women wearing business suits and high heels walking their little designer dogs. All of them going about their days, totally unaware that anything was wrong, that the dead body of a young girl lay less than a quarter of a mile away.

"They're sending a team," Leo said, coming closer. "We just need to hang tight until they get here."

"We'll have to talk to the woman who called it in," Mitch said.

"Yeah." Leo glanced at the base of the tree. "How old do you think she is?" He cleared his throat again. "Was."

Mitch shook his head, then shrugged. "Fifteen? Seventeen?

There's gotta be a missing persons out on her."

"Yeah. Hopefully it won't take long to identify her." Leo clipped his radio back onto his belt and glanced at the damp cardboard again, then took out his wallet and opened it up. "I owe you five bucks," he said, taking out a bill and offering it to Mitch.

"Keep it," Mitch said. The thought of winning a bet because of a dead girl turned his stomach.

"No, come on, take it." Leo grimaced and pushed the money into Mitch's hand. "You can buy me lunch."

"If we have our appetites back by then." Mitch seriously doubted it at that moment, but he'd been on the force long enough -- and Leo's partner long enough -- to know that chances were good they'd have recovered by noon.

Leo was digging around in his pocket again. "Want a mint?" he asked.

"Not if it's been in your pocket," Mitch said. "I'd take a mint, but I don't want one that's covered with lint."

"Longfellow," Leo quipped. "Here -- it's wrapped."

"Okay." Mitch took it and unwrapped it, putting it into his mouth. The minty fumes helped cover the sickly-sweet odor. "Thanks."

"No problem."

Shoulder to shoulder, they stood and waited for the team from forensics to show up.

* * *

The woman who'd put the call in to the station was named Anna Gerow. They didn't have a work number for her, and it was almost the end of the work day when Mitch and Leo had enough time to talk to her anyway, so they turned up outside her house around five-thirty and waited in the squad car. She lived less than a quarter of a mile from the edge of the park.

Anna turned out to be one of those business suit women: pretty in a natural sort of way, with her hair gleaming and her skirt a little wrinkled, presumably because she'd been sitting on it most of the day. She was unlocking her front door when Leo and Mitch walked up to the house, and she turned, looking worried, then relieved, then worried again as she realized who they were.

"Oh," Anna said, turning the door handle but not pushing the door open. Mitch could hear a dog whining and scratching on the other side. "You're from the police, aren't you? Did... did you find something?"

"Yes ma'am," Leo said. "Are you Anna Gerow?" They always had to ask, even when the answer was really obvious.

"Yes," she said.

"I'm Detective Banks." Leo gestured at Mitch. "This is Detective Anderson. Could we talk with you?"

Nodding, Anna said, "Of course. Come in. Unless you need me to go somewhere with you?"

Mitch shook his head. "That won't be necessary. We just needed to ask you a few questions about this morning."

"Okay." Anna bit her lip, which smeared her lipstick. Imperfect, Mitch instinctively liked her a little more. "Just... don't let the dog out." She slipped inside, managing to grab the dog's collar on the way in, and backed up to leave room for Mitch and Leo to enter. Once the door was shut, she let go, and the dog, which couldn't have weighed more than fifteen pounds, scrabbled its way over and started jumping up on Mitch, who was closer. "Sally! No! Down!"

"It's okay," Mitch said, crouching to pet the dog. It licked at his palms eagerly, ears down, tail wagging furiously. Its fur was soft and brown. "I like dogs."

"I'm sorry," Anna said anyway. "She gets lonely during the day. I try to come back at lunchtime when I can, but this morning my schedule got thrown out of whack and I didn't... well. Anyway. Would you like some coffee?"

"That'd be nice," Leo said. They knew that it helped to give people something to do in situations like this -- it'd calm her down a little if she was nervous. A distraction.

In the kitchen, Anna said, "Please, sit down." Sally, who'd followed them eagerly, immediately sat, and Mitch laughed as he and Leo pulled out chairs.

"There, see?" he said. "She's a good dog. She follows orders."

"That's the first time in months," Anna said, smiling. "I took her to a couple of obedience classes, but it didn't work out. She was a bad influence on the other dogs."

"I've been thinking about getting a dog," Mitch said. Of course, Clay wasn't crazy about the idea, which was why it hadn't gone further than the 'thinking about it' stage.

"Sally came from the animal shelter," Anna said. "There are so many dogs that get euthanized every day because people are only interested in purebreds. I went in one day just to look, but... you know how that goes. She started wagging her tail as soon as she saw me, and that was that. Love at first sight." She finished setting up the coffee maker and came over to sit down at the table with them. "You must have found something," she said seriously. "Was it a person?"

Leo nodded. "It'll be on the news tonight," he said, then glanced at the clock on the wall. Mitch took out the little notebook he used during questioning. "About now, actually. The body hasn't been identified. We were hoping you could tell us everything you remember about this morning."

"I don't see how it will help," Anna said. "I never actually saw anything. I just knew something was wrong by the way Sally was acting." The dog stood up on its hind feet, front paws resting on Anna's thigh, and she patted it absently. "We were walking -- we do it every morning, same time, same place -- and all of a sudden she started whining and pulling on the leash. She wanted to go off the path into the woods, but I know she's supposed to stay leashed, and she doesn't always come when I call if she's excited..."

"What time was this?" Mitch asked.

"We leave the house at six fifteen," Anna said. "So it might have been six thirty? And I called as soon as I got back."

Mitch checked his notes. "You called it in at six forty-two," he said.

"And were you the ones who... found the body?" Anna asked.

"Yeah," Leo said. "Less than an hour after you called."

"Do you know what happened? I mean, was it an accident?" Anna sounded hopeful, as if she didn't expect the answer to be yes.

"It's hard to say for sure," Mitch said. "Did you see anyone else when you were walking Sally?"

"Not near where she got all worked up," Anna said. "I mean, I passed a few people, but that's all."

"And did any of them seem out of place to you?"

"You mean, were they acting suspicious? No. They were all either running or walking dogs, like me."

They knew that the body hadn't been there long -- less than a day, the medical examiner had said. But it never paid to cut corners, which was something Leo and Mitch both understood. Their agreement on that issue was one of the reasons they worked so well together.

Leo leaned back in his chair. "And when Sally started acting strangely, was there anyone nearby?"

Anna frowned, apparently trying to remember. "No, I don't think so. That path is sort of the back way into the park -- most people go in on the other side. Sometimes Sally and I are the only ones in that part of the park, especially in the mornings."

The coffee maker spat and hissed, and Anna got up to pour the coffee into three mugs that looked like they'd seen better days.

"Cream or sugar?" she asked.

"We both take it black," Leo said. He'd always taken it black; Mitch had started to for convenience's sake, then gotten used to it. She brought the mugs over to the table and sat back down.

"Should I be worried?" Anna asked. "Do you think I should start walking Sally somewhere else?"

"I don't think you need to worry." Mitch thought about it, then decided it was worth the small risk to tell her a little bit of the truth. "We don't think... whatever happened, happened at the park."

She blinked and sipped at her coffee. "That means someone moved it," she said. "The body, I mean."

"Yes," Leo said. He gave Mitch a look, but it was hard to figure out what it meant. "That's really all we can say at this time. If you want more information after the body has been identified, give us a call and we'll tell you what we can."

"Was it... was it a man or a woman?" Anna asked.

That much would be on the news. "A woman," Mitch said. "She was young."

"Oh." Sally jumped suddenly up into Anna's lap, and she patted the dog without seeming to pay any attention to her. "I worry, sometimes," she said. "Living alone. My mother says if I had to have a dog I should have gotten something bigger. Something that could protect me."

"This is a really safe neighborhood," Leo said. "And the crime rate in Franklin's pretty low compared to other parts of the state. I really wouldn't worry."

"Easy for you to say," Anna said, eyeing him. Leo had wide shoulders and a solid build, and he worked out six or seven days a week. Even people who didn't know he was a cop wouldn't consider messing with him.

"Here," Leo said, eyeing her back. He drank down his coffee in a few long swallows -- Mitch still didn't understand how he could drink it like that -- and took his wallet out of his back pocket. "Take my card, okay? If you ever hear anything suspicious and you want someone to check it out, give me a call."

Anna grinned; it was definitely a grin and not a smile. "Detective Banks," she said playfully, taking the card. "Are you flirting with me?"

"No ma'am," Leo said. "And to prove it, Detective Anderson here will give you his card, too."

"Ah. Because you always tell people they should call you whenever they're nervous?" Anna took Mitch's card when he offered it and set it on the table beside Leo's.

"Absolutely. It's part of the job."

Mitch drank some more of his coffee and put the cup down. "Speaking of the job," he said, "we should get going."

"Well, thank you," Anna said. She started to stand and Sally jumped down onto the floor. "If there's anything else I can do -- not that I think there is -- let me know."

"We really appreciate your cooperation," Mitch said.

"Sally. Sally, come here." Anna crouched down in the front hallway to restrain the dog. "Okay. Have a good night."

"You, too," Leo said. "Don't forget to call if you need anything."

"I won't forget," Anna said, and Mitch shut the door behind them as they stepped out onto the porch.

"You're unbelievable," he told Leo.

"What?" Leo said, feigning innocence. "I'm just doing my job." He whistled as they walked to the car.

* * *

"I'm home," Mitch called, tossing his keys onto the table and shrugging out of his jacket.

"Oh, good, it's you," Clay called back, probably from the kitchen. "I thought you were a stranger breaking in to ravage me."

Mitch toed off his shoes and went into the kitchen, which was warm and smelled good. "You shouldn't joke around about stuff like that," he said.

Turning his head to look at Mitch, Clay rolled his eyes. "If you can't joke around about stuff like that, it'll make you crazy. Bad day?"

"Yeah," Mitch said, then reconsidered. "No. Bad morning. We found the body of a teenaged girl in Meeker Park."

"Oh, no." Clay sounded genuinely dismayed, and stopped stirring whatever was on the stovetop long enough to hug Mitch. "That sucks."

"Yeah, it really does." Mitch sighed and pulled away. "Do I have time to grab a shower before dinner?"

"Sure. The risotto's got another ten minutes." Clay hesitated, then said, "Mitch? Are we okay?"

"What?" God, some careful analysis of their *relationship* was the last thing Mitch needed right then. "Yeah, of course we are. Why wouldn't we be?"

"I don't know," Clay said. "Never mind. Go take your shower."

Under the hot water, Mitch leaned his forehead against the tile wall and let his shoulders slowly slump down into their lowest position. Tonight wasn't the first time Clay had asked if everything was okay, and the truth of it was, the answer was no. Everything wasn't okay. But damned if Mitch could figure out what was wrong, and until he did there didn't seem to be much point in freaking Clay out. He'd want to know how to fix it.

Mitch was starting to wonder if there was anything to fix.

It wasn't that he didn't love Clay -- he did. But they'd been together for five years now. Fuck, maybe he was just getting the Seven Year Itch a couple of years early? Lately it just seemed like everything Clay said or did annoyed the crap out of Mitch, which he was starting to realize was no way to live. It wasn't like Clay had changed; the stuff that annoyed Mitch now was the same kind of stuff Clay had always said and done. But suddenly things that had once been cute... well, they didn't seem so cute anymore.

Maybe Mitch was just getting old. Considering he was only thirty-eight, that thought was depressing enough that he didn't manage to drag himself out of the shower until the water went cold. He toweled dry, pulled on some sweatpants and a t-shirt, and went to the dining room, where Clay was pouring wine into two glasses.

"Is this okay?" Clay asked. "I know we don't usually have wine, but I needed some for the risotto, and then I thought--"

"Yeah, it's fine," Mitch said, cutting off the explanation because he really didn't care.

"I'll go get the salad," Clay said.

They ate salad without much more than small talk, but the wine went to Mitch's head enough that by the time Clay served the risotto and accompanying whole-grain bread -- Clay was always finding some new hobby, and the current one was gourmet cooking -- he was feeling a lot more relaxed and less irritated.

"So then," Clay said, "they called up and said the arrangements were too cheerful! Can you believe that? After three consultations about how they wanted every color of the rainbow? I guess they only wanted somber shades or something."

"They should have gone to a place that specializes in funerals," Mitch said.

"Well, it's not like we don't do our fair share of those," Clay said. "It just doesn't make any sense. I don't understand why people can't just be clear about what they want. Is it that difficult to be direct? Especially when you're paying for it."

He got up to pour more wine, still talking, and there was just something about how he looked in that moment -- blond hair tousled, the familiar shape of his chin. Mitch couldn't resist; he had to reach out and touch him.

"Well, hello." Clay raised an eyebrow at him, glancing at Mitch's hand on his hip.

"Hi," Mitch said. Fuck it. He slid his chair back and grabbed Clay's wrist, then tugged at him until Clay collapsed into his lap with a yelp.

"Mitch," Clay said softly, melting against him with such appreciation that Mitch felt guilty for having been so distant lately. They kissed.

"This is a really great dinner," Mitch said.

Clay's blue eyes were happy. "It is?"

"Yeah," Mitch said. "And you're a really great boyfriend." Who cared if it was the wine talking -- he was horny and he wanted to get laid.

He was also, he knew dimly, an asshole, but right then he didn't want to think about that.

"Screw the food," Clay said. "Let's go to bed."

Mitch had Clay's shirt off before they'd even reached the bedroom, licking at his little nipples just to hear him gasp. Clay's hand was inside Mitch's sweatpants, rubbing his cock and playing with his balls. It had been a while, Mitch realized, though he couldn't have said for sure how long. Too long, apparently, if the temptation to just spin Clay around and fuck him against the wall meant anything.

"Here, sit," Mitch said impatiently. He unbuttoned Clay's slacks and shoved them down, then pushed Clay onto the bed and knelt between his thighs, sucking on his dick in short, quick pulls until Clay was crying out and coming in his mouth, shaking and clutching at Mitch's shoulders.

"Oh, God, fuck me," Clay said, still coming, still trembling.

"Mitchell, please."

No arguments there -- Mitch struggled out of his own pants and grabbed the lube. He slicked himself up as quickly as possible and climbed on top of Clay, kissing him as he worked his way inside that tight, perfect ass. Clay arched underneath him, gasping open-mouthed and loudly as he tried to relax. It was an incredibly tight fit just like always; Clay never seemed to loosen up all that much. "Yeah," Mitch gasped. "Fuck, yeah. Love fucking you."

Clay moaned and lifted his head for another kiss. "I love you," he said. "Love... oh, Mitch."

"Good," Mitch agreed. He pushed in a little deeper, everything hot and slippery and Clay *moving* under him, hips rocking, taking it like he loved it, which had been one of the things that had made Mitch want him -- not for sex, not *just* for sex, but for himself. To have, to keep. And now...

Now it was all so fucked up, and he didn't even know why.

He forced his attention back to Clay's body, and to what it did to his when he was thrusting inside it. Clay's hands grabbed onto his ass and that, along with the slow burn of the wine in his gut, was all it took -- Mitchell came, eyes closed, lowering his weight down onto Clay. Clay murmured soft words in his ear, stroked his hair tenderly.

Mitch kept his eyes closed even when he pulled out and lay down next to Clay, and when Clay said his name a little while later, he pretended to be asleep.

* * *

In the morning, Mitch got up early and crept out of the house while Clay was still sleeping. It wasn't hard to do, since he'd actually fallen asleep before going back to finish dinner, and not only was he well-rested, but his stomach was growling. He called Leo from the driveway to see if he wanted to meet at the gym.

"'Lo?" Leo mumbled sleepily.

"Shit," Mitch said. "Did I wake you up?"

"No," Leo said, yawning. "The phone did."

"Very funny. Sorry. I was going to ask if you wanted to meet at the gym."

"Meet *you* at the gym?" Leo asked. "*You*?" It was clear from his tone of voice how astonishing a concept this was.

"Fuck you," Mitch said, and hung up on him. The phone rang

before he'd even gotten behind the wheel of his car, and he answered it. "What?"

"Man, what crawled up your ass and died?" Leo said. "Yes, fine, let's meet at the gym. Just stop swearing at me."

"You just said ass," Mitch pointed out, grinning despite himself.

"I was referring to a part of your anatomy," Leo said. "I wasn't *calling* you an ass." Mitch could hear running water. "Anyway, I can say it nicer if it means you won't hang up on me. What's wrong?"

Mitch sighed. It would have been easy to come up with some excuse -- that he hadn't slept well, that he was still stressed about yesterday -- but he didn't want to lie, not to Leo. "Can we talk about it later?"

"Sure. I'll meet you at the gym in twenty, okay?"

"Okay. Thanks, Leo."

"No problem, man."

Mitch grabbed an orange juice and a muffin at the nearest coffee place, avoiding the actual coffee because if he had caffeine before he worked out it gave him heartburn. He'd only been on the treadmill for five minutes when Leo came in. Leo was wearing a worn t-shirt and sweatpants so thin they were practically see-through, and Mitch couldn't help but wonder what kind of looks Leo would get wearing something like that in public. Interested ones, probably.

"Hey," Leo said. "You didn't have coffee, did you?"

Mitch grinned. "No. All other evidence aside, I don't actually *want* to be miserable."

Leo got onto the treadmill next to Mitch's and started it up. "Are you?" he asked after a minute. "Miserable?"

That took a little thinking about. "I don't know," Mitch said. "Maybe sometimes."

"That sucks," Leo said, glancing at him. "You should fix that."

"I would," Mitch said. "If I could figure out what was wrong."

They ran in companionable silence for a minute before Leo suggested, "You could talk to someone."

"I'm talking to you," Mitch said.

Leo frowned at him. "Which is fine," he said. "But I'm not a professional."

"Sure you are," Mitch said.

"I'm not a professional *therapist*," Leo clarified.

"Look," Mitch said. He'd been running long enough that keeping his sentences short was now necessary instead of just fun. "I don't want to talk to anyone. I'm no good at that. Talking to you... that's the best I can do."

"Okay, fine," Leo said. "Talk to me. Just don't get mad if it doesn't end up being all that helpful."

"I don't talk to you because I think... you're going to do a good job analyzing me," Mitch said, panting for air now. "In fact... I might talk to you... because you don't."

"Stop talking and run," Leo said severely, so Mitch, glad for the order even though he had five months longer on the force than Leo, did.

* * *

Just before noon, the body that Mitch and Leo had found in Meeker Park was identified as that of sixteen-year-old Paige Sadler, who'd been reported missing two days before. That was the good news; good only, of course, because it meant that her family wouldn't have to wait years wondering if she were alive or dead.

The other good news was that Mitch and Leo didn't have to go tell her family -- it was something Mitch hated doing, and for the most part he managed to pass the job off onto someone else. Witnessing that kind of shock and grief definitely wasn't why he'd become a cop.

The bad news -- and there was always bad news in their line of work, of one type or another -- was that they had no leads on who might have dumped the body in the park. None at all. They knew it was murder; the cause of death had been a blow to the head, but there was also evidence of severe bruising around the throat, and the girl had been sexually violated both vaginally and anally. But there wasn't anything to go on. There were no fingerprints of any kind nearby, what with none of the surfaces lending themselves toward holding them. The rapist and murderer had worn a condom, and there was nothing but soil and bits of leaf under the dead girl's nails. The only hairs they'd found on her and in the area had been identified as her own. They had nothing. No semen, no blood, no skin, no hair.

According to Paige's family, she'd been a loner. No real friends, no boyfriend. At a loss for better people to question, Mitch and Leo went to Paige's high school to talk to some of her teachers and classmates.

The principal at Paige's school hadn't known her personally other than to see her in the hallways; he pulled her file and the three of them looked over it together.

"She didn't get in much trouble," Mitch said. It was an understatement; her record was completely clean, her grades unremarkable.

"If she had, I'd have known her," Principal Weinburg said wryly. He was a small man with thinning hair and a friendly, warm manner. "The problem kids are the ones I see the most."

"I think we'd like to speak to a couple of her teachers in private," Leo said. "And then maybe we could go into one of her classrooms and ask a few questions? We won't be formally questioning anyone, obviously -- we're just hoping we might get pointed in the right direction."

Principal Weinburg nodded and checked his watch. "Mr. Clark has a free period now; he teaches Junior English. I'll send him in."

When Mr. Clark appeared, he looked appropriately somber, but quickly admitted that he'd barely known Paige despite the fact that the school year was nearly over. "She didn't really participate in class."

"Was she failing?" Mitch asked, even though he'd seen her grades.

"No, not at all. She seemed bright enough -- not one of the best students, and I don't think I remember her ever raising her hand or joining in a discussion, but she did the work."

Leo scribbled something down on his pad. "Did she get along with the other students?"

"I wouldn't know," Mr. Clark said. "I never saw her talking with anyone." He hesitated, then added, "She seemed... sad. Lonely."

"Yeah," Leo said. "It sounds like she was. Look, thanks very much for your time, and if you think of anything else, please call." He handed the man one of his cards.

"It was no problem." Mr. Clark hesitated in the doorway. "I hope you find whoever did this."

"We will," Mitch promised, although he was beginning to have serious doubts.

Paige's chemistry teacher didn't have anything more helpful to say, unfortunately, and when Mitch went in to talk to Paige's US History class, the kids seemed either bored or a little too interested.

"Did some sex freak get her?" a boy asked.

"We're not releasing information about the cause of death at this time," Mitch said.

"That means yes," the boy said, glancing around. Two of the other boys nearby grinned at him. "That's crazy, man."

"Why do you say that?" Mitch was aware that some of the girls were uncomfortable with the topic, which didn't surprise him; he wasn't all that comfortable with it himself.

"Because no one normal would have wanted to have sex with *that*. She was ug-ly."

The history teacher gave the kid a warning look. "Eric."

"I'm just sayin'." Eric slouched down in his seat and stopped talking.

"What kinds of words would you use to describe Paige?" Mitch asked.

The kids looked around at each other, and then one girl, a blonde in a bright red shirt, offered, "Shy?"

Mitch nodded, hoping to encourage more. "You mean she didn't talk to any of you?"

"Not really." The blonde flipped her hair back.

"What other words?" Mitch asked, but the kids just shrugged and looked down at their desks. "Okay, who were her friends?"

"I don't think she had any," a short boy with glasses said.

"How about a boyfriend?"

"Her?" Eric snorted.

Not wanting to get into another discussion like before, Mitch decided it was time to call it quits. "All right. Thank you for your help. If anyone thinks of anything later that might be important, you can leave me a message here." He stepped over to the blackboard and wrote his cell number, then nodded at the teacher and left.

Leo was waiting outside in the hall. "Anything?"

"No. Apparently she was ugly and had no friends." Mitch rolled his eyes at the ceiling and was temporarily distracted by the sight of a pencil sticking out of one of the panels.

"I didn't even get that much," Leo said. They started walking down the hallway. "The consensus seems to be that she was quiet and no one really paid all that much attention to her."

"Poor kid," Mitch said. Clay's earlier years had been like that, he knew, and he felt a sudden surge of confusing feelings -- sympathy, guilt, frustration.

Most of the rest of the afternoon was taken up by a couple of routine calls and some paperwork. Mitch made sure to check in with the medical examiner, who didn't have anything new to report even after having run some more tests "just in case". He was just leaving the building when his cell phone rang.

"Hello?" he said.

A slightly familiar woman's voice said, "Detective Anderson? This is Anna Gerow. I reported the suspicious smell in the park yesterday morning?"

"Right," Mitch said, waving to Leo as his car pulled out of the parking lot. "What can I do for you?"

"Well, this isn't a business call," Anna said.

Almost automatically, without realizing how rude it might sound, Mitch said, "I'm not available for anything but business calls."

Anna laughed; she had a nice laugh. "No, no, not like that. I've been volunteering at the animal shelter where I got Sally and remembered you'd mentioned something about wanting to get a dog. We just seized eighteen from a backyard breeding set up in Fairview and I was thinking maybe you might like to adopt one?"

"Huh," Mitch said, heading for his car. "Look, I hate to say no, but this really isn't a good time. For a dog, I mean -- the phone call's fine."

"You'd know better than I would," Anna said. She sounded disappointed, though. "There's nothing I could do to convince you? We could meet for coffee and talk about what kinds of things you're looking for in a dog... see if any of the ones we have might be a good fit?"

"I'm actually just on my way home." Mitch unlocked his car and got in, then shut the door. "My partner's waiting for me."

"And I take it you're not referring to Detective Banks."

"No," Mitch said. There was just something about Anna that was disarming, that made him willing to open up. "But he'd want you to call him Leo. And I'm Mitch."

"Well, Mitch, I was sort of thinking we could help each other out, here." Anna said. "I find you a nice dog, you save one from being euthanized. Everybody wins."

"Okay." Suddenly, Mitch wanted nothing more than to meet her for coffee, not to mention put off going home, even if it *was* atypical to socialize with someone who was involved with an active investigation. "If you really want to talk about the dog thing, I can be at The Hatch in ten minutes."

* * *

Mitch ended up talking to Anna for more than two hours, conveniently forgetting to call home to let Clay know he'd be late. The phone rang in the middle of their third cup of coffee -- Mitch picked it up, glanced at it, saw his home number, and switched it off.

"Work?" Anna asked.

He shook his head.

"Your mother?"

Again, Mitch shook his head.

"Who is it you're trying to avoid?"

Saying it out loud made him sound like a jerk, but he did it anyway. "My boyfriend."

"He'll be worried," Anna said, frowning. "You have a dangerous job. Here, give me the phone and I'll call him."

Mitch stared at her. She sure was a lot more than met the eye. "No?" he tried.

Anna crossed her arms over her chest and looked at him sternly. "You have two choices," she said. "Give me the phone and I'll call him, or go home."

The thought of Anna talking to Clay was more than he could handle; Mitch went home.

Before he'd shut off the car in the driveway, Clay was standing on the front porch. "Are you okay?" he asked, and his tone of voice made it clear how worried he'd been.

"Yeah," Mitch said. "Fine."

"I tried calling, but I couldn't get through. I left you like a dozen messages. Where *were* you?" Clay was practically wringing his hands.

"Nowhere," Mitch said, but he knew immediately that wasn't going to fly. "I met someone for coffee, okay? I wouldn't have if I'd realized you'd freak out about it."

"I wouldn't have freaked out if you'd *called me*." Clay followed him into the house and stood in the entryway as Mitch took off his shoes. "I thought you'd been *hurt* or something."

"If I were hurt, someone would call you," Mitch said. "Leo, for example."

"What if he was hurt, too?"

"Then someone else would call you. You're on all my contact lists at work, you know that. Why do you have to be such a drama queen?" He said it more viciously than he'd ever spoken to Clay before.

Clay looked so shocked that under other circumstances it would have been funny. As it was, it made Mitch's stomach twist and ache.

"Why do you have to be such an asshole?" Clay asked, and flounced off the bedroom, slamming the door loudly.

"Fuck this," Mitch said, and shoved his feet back into his shoes. "I'm going out!" he shouted through the house. "I'm leaving my phone off, so don't try to call!"

He took a bitter, cruel pleasure in kicking the door shut on his way out.

* * *

Mitch grabbed a salad at a drive-through, ate it in his car, and went back to the gym. It was pretty much unheard of for him to hit the gym twice in one day, but he didn't know what else to do with himself and it'd kill an hour and a half at least. There was no way he was going home any time soon, that was for sure.

He did turn his cell phone on, but that was just because he'd hate to miss a call from work. Obviously.

After forty minutes on the treadmill and half an hour on the Nautilus machines, Mitch -- grateful that he carried more than one change of clothes in the trunk of his car -- took a quick shower and drove to the grocery store, where he got a pre-made sandwich from the deli, a bag of potato chips and a bottle of water. He ate sitting outside at one of the two metal table-and-chairs that he was pretty sure were supposed to be for customers but which apparently only got used by employees on their cigarette breaks, judging by the overflowing ashtrays.

He didn't check his messages until he'd finished eating, and doing so only made him feel worse. What had started out as fairly cheerful messages from Clay quickly turned worried and then almost frantic as Mitch worked his way through them.

As he was sitting there, he caught sight of two men who'd just gotten out of a car in the parking lot. The driver had come around to the passenger side and was talking to the other man, who was leaning against the car like he needed its support. The driver was a couple of inches taller than the passenger and had at least thirty pounds on him, but the way he put an arm around the smaller man and started to guide him toward the store made him seem gentle.

"We've got to do something," Mitch heard the smaller man say as they got closer.

"We will. But not tonight. You haven't slept for two days, Nick. We're going to get some pills or something, find a hotel room and put you to bed." The bigger guy steadied the other one -- Nick -- as he swayed, then they continued on.

As they were passing Mitch, Nick looked up and into his eyes, and Mitch revised his previous assumption that the man was drunk or high. Probably not, he thought. Sick, maybe, but not drunk. Not with sharp green eyes like that, eyes that saw right into Mitch like they knew him.

The two men went inside, and Mitch sighed, got up, and went home.

* * *

The bedroom door was opened just a crack, the room itself dark when Mitch slipped inside. They had blackout curtains on the windows because there were times he worked nights and the only way he could sleep was if he could block out the sunshine, so he was an expert at navigating the space even when it was pitch black.

"Go away," Clay said, and Mitch's heart skipped a beat.

"Look, I'm sorry," Mitch said. He wasn't sure that he actually was, but it was the right thing to say, and he was tired. He wanted to go to sleep.

There was a click as Clay turned on the light. Mitch blinked. Clay was sitting up against the headboard, the blankets pooled around his waist and his eyes red-rimmed. "Let's not do this."

"What, go to bed?" Mitch asked, still standing where he was.

"All of it. Talk, fight. Just go sleep on the couch. We can figure everything else out tomorrow." Clay was wearing Mitch's old, worn T-shirt, the one he wore when he was upset or had a cold. The one he called his comfort shirt.

Mitch wasn't sure he wanted to think about what it meant that Clay was wearing it. "Figure what out?"

"What we're going to do," Clay said. "How we're going to split stuff up, I guess."

"Split stuff up?" Mitch was confused.

"I'll need a little time to figure out where to go," Clay said, and somehow Mitch got it, was across the room and on the bed, trying to pull a resisting Clay into his arms. "Don't, okay?" Clay sounded heartbroken. He pushed Mitch away and got out of bed. "Fine; you sleep here, I'll sleep on the couch."

"Clay..." But he was already gone.

* * *

They did try to talk in the morning, but it was awkward and uncomfortable, and after ten minutes of it Clay said, "I don't think I'm ready to do this." For a moment, Mitch hoped he meant splitting up, but then Clay added, "Tomorrow night, okay? We could probably both use a little time to think."

Mitch went to work -- he was still buckling on his holster when Sean MacPherson, who worked the desk during first watch, came in. "You're on the Sadler case, right?" he said.

"Yeah," Mitch said, just as Leo came in the other door. "Cutting it close."

"I know. I hit the snooze button three times," Leo said. "Hey, Sean."

"Hey, Leo. I was just telling Mitch that there's a couple of guys out front saying they might have some info on the Sadler case."

"Might?" Mitch said.

Sean shrugged. "They're not really all that forthcoming. You want to talk to them?"

"Sure. Put 'em in room three," Leo said.

Mitch waited for Leo to get himself together, then they went to room three, which only held a couple of tables and some chairs.

And the two guys Mitch had seen the night before outside the grocery store. They were both standing.

"Hi," he said, once he'd recovered from his surprise. The smaller man, Nick, obviously recognized him, too. "I'm Detective Anderson -- this is Detective Banks."

"Do they partner you up in alphabetical order?" the bigger guy asked. He had curly brown hair, kind of tousled and long, like it'd been a while since he had a haircut. "I'm Matthew Cole. This is Nick Kelley." He gestured at Nick.

"I saw you," Nick said. "Last night."

"Yeah," Mitch said, remembering what he'd overheard. "I saw you, too. Do you want to sit down?"

They did, and so did Mitch, although Leo remained standing.

"You're from out of town?" Mitch asked, and Leo gave him a

funny look. "Like he said, we sort of bumped into each other last night."

"We're from out of town everywhere we go," Nick said ruefully.

Mitch frowned. "And you think you have some information that would help us?"

"Nick has... some pretty unique abilities," Matthew said, not really answering the question. Nick kept glancing at Matthew like he wanted reassurance, and Matthew reached out and patted Nick's hand where it rested on the table. "We travel all around the country. We've worked with a couple of police departments before."

"What are you, some kind of forensics expert or something?" Leo asked.

Nick shook his head. "No. But I know what happened to that girl," Nick said. He leaned forward, looking at Mitch intently. "The one you found in the park. I saw her."

"You saw the report on the news, you mean," Leo said bluntly, and then, when Mitch looked at him, he said, "Oh, come on, Mitch. You can see where this is headed. He wants us to believe he's some kind of psychic or something."

"Of course we saw the report on the news," Matthew said. "But not until after Nick knew what had happened. I have some names and phone numbers here--" He took out his wallet and started looking in it. "If you don't think we're telling the truth -- and believe me, I know how it sounds -- call them. They'll tell you we're for real."

"What do you want, to be paid?" Leo was frustrated now; he was never the most patient of guys, and this was just the kind of thing that ruffled his feathers.

"It *is* our job," Matthew pointed out, but Nick was shaking his head.

"I just want to help," Nick said. He licked his lips and frowned, lifting his chin, and sat back in his chair. His eyes went a little unfocused and he inhaled sharply. "She's here."

"Oh, for God's sake." Leo stormed the few steps to the door and opened it. "Thanks very much for coming, but we won't be needing your 'help'."

Matthew was leaning over and whispering something to Nick, who was clutching at Matthew's hand and trembling visibly. If it was an act, Mitch had to admit it was a good one. "I can't," Nick said. "No, I'm not -- I know. I want to, but it's--"

"Easy," Matthew said. He glanced at Mitch and then Leo. "He

can help you."

"No!" Nick's voice rose suddenly; he jumped to his feet, the force of his movement causing the light wooden chair to skitter backwards across the floor, then tip over with a clatter. Mitch was standing, too, watching Nick warily.

Leo, on the other hand, had had enough. "Out," he said. It was clear he was talking to Matthew more than Nick. "Get him out of here now."

"You're making a mistake," Matthew said, but he must have been able to tell how serious Leo was, because he was already herding Nick toward the door. Nick was fighting him, muttering something at Mitch, but it was impossible to tell what he was saying, and even when Mitch did catch a few words in a row, they didn't make any sense.

"Make sure they leave!" Leo called to Sean. He looked at Mitch and shook his head. "Why do we always get the crazy ones?"

"I think they must be drawn to you," Mitch said, but he was more shaken by what had just happened than he was letting on.

"Seriously. People watch a couple of those stupid shows on Court TV and think all they have to do is fake a couple of 'visions' to get rich and famous." Leo was disgusted. Mitch could hear Nick shouting something; it went muffled suddenly when the front doors closed. "Good riddance."

They went out on a couple of calls -- routine stuff, nothing all that interesting if you didn't get excited over a minor a case of shoplifting at a small local jewelry store. The teenaged boy had grabbed a handful of bracelets off the shelf and bolted out the door only to trip over the curb and sprain his ankle. He'd been caught less than two blocks from the store, hobbling along with the jewelry still clutched in his grip. The store owner had decided not to press charges, but one of the patrol officers thought it might help to scare the crap out of the kid, and Leo had a reputation for being the guy to do the scaring. By the time Leo finished with him, the kid was sobbing and apologizing. He left for the emergency room with his enraged mother, who promised he wouldn't get into any more trouble in the future.

Toward the end of their shift, Mitch sat down at one of the office computers to do some research. They still hadn't been able to get any leads on the Sadler case, to the point where Mitch was idly wondering if they should have spent a little more time talking to Nick Kelley. Anything would have been better than nothing, right?

An hour searching the database for similar and unsolved murders in the general area didn't turn up much. There'd been a case where a young woman had disappeared the year before; she was still missing, but the boyfriend was a suspect. There were two cases of young men being killed, their bodies found some weeks later, in towns on either side of Franklin, but the database didn't have much more information than that. Taking note of the detectives' names, Mitch slept the computer and turned in his chair to discover that Leo was standing behind him.

"Jesus!" Mitch said, startled. "Warn a guy when you come in, okay?"

"Sorry," Leo said. "You turn up anything?"

"I don't know." Mitch rubbed his forehead and sighed.

"You look like hell," Leo said. "What's going on?"

He'd been trying to hide it all day, but Mitch should have known that Leo would be suspicious no matter how good a job he did. "Clay and I might have broken up last night."

"What?" Leo stared at him. "And what do you mean 'might have'?"

"I mean I don't exactly know."

"You had a fight?" Leo asked.

"Yeah. There was door slamming. And shouting." Mitch was starting to feel like he needed either a cup of coffee or a drink. "I don't know."

"You said that already." The look Leo gave him was a concerned one, and Mitch wasn't sure he liked that too much. "You want to grab some dinner or something?"

Mitch shook his head. "Nah. I'd be shitty company. And I'm not hungry. I guess I'm going to go home and talk to Clay."

"Yeah, you're sounding really hyped up about that idea." But Leo patted him on the shoulder. "Okay. See you the day after tomorrow?" They had the next day off -- normally Mitch would be looking forward to the chance to sleep in and spend some time at home, but right now it didn't sound all that good.

"Yeah," he said.

He sat there for a while -- the next shift had already come on duty half an hour before, and the building was pretty quiet at that point -- then went out the back since that was closest to where he'd left his car. He'd just reached the driver's side when a hand on his arm startled him; he swung around, one fist curled automatically, to find Nick Kelley's wide eyes staring back him.

Good reflexes meant being able a pull a punch as well as throw one. Mitch lowered his arm slowly while his heart beat a too-quick pattern in his chest. "Don't do that," he said.

"I'm sorry," Nick said. He glanced around. "And about this afternoon; I'm sorry about that, too. But I was hoping I could talk to you. Please."

"Where's your guardian?" Mitch asked, and Nick's lips curved into the first smile he'd seen on the man.

"That's a little more true than you know. He's back at the hotel -- it's a couple of blocks that way." Nick gestured toward the west. "We've been pretty busy lately. He was tired."

Mitch looked at Nick, took in the dark hair, the finely carved nose, the sharp green eyes. Something about the man brought out his protective side -- the same way Clay had brought it out in him when they'd first met. "Should you be out on your own?" he asked. It was kind of blunt, sure, but the answer might be important.

"Maybe not," Nick said. "Matthew keeps a pretty close eye on me for good reason." He shivered, although it wasn't that cold.

"Get in," Mitch said, pointing to the passenger side of the car.

"Thanks."

In the car, Nick didn't seem to know what to say.

"Are you hungry?" Mitch asked.

Nick shook his head. "I just needed... I wanted you to know that it's true. What I can do. I know you don't have any leads on who killed her -- Paige -- but I do. I know things."

"Why should I believe you know things because you say you can talk to ghosts?" Mitch asked. "For all I know, you and Matthew killed her."

Earnestly, Nick said, "We were miles away from here when she was killed. We didn't get into town until last night, and she's been dead for a couple of days -- she's pretty clear on that."

That sounded convincing, but on the other hand, it wouldn't have been hard to look up the details of when Paige's body had been found. "You're going to need to do better than that," Mitch said.

"Paige knows who killed her," Nick said. His eyes did that funny, unfocused thing again, and his voice got distant. "He followed her home from school for days. She was just starting to get worried about it when he talked to her for the first time. He said she was beautiful -- she knew she wasn't, but she still liked to hear it."

"What was his name?" Mitch said, caught up in the possibility despite himself.

"She didn't know. He said she could call him Joe, but she knew that wasn't his real name by the way he said it. He wasn't anything special to look at. Not too tall, not too short. Not too fat, not too thin. But he was nice to her." Nick sounded like he was repeating something he'd been taught, but when he met Mitch's gaze he looked sharp again. "Until he killed her."

"None of that's enough to even give us a place to start, let alone identify him," Mitch pointed out.

"There's more. There's a lot more." Nick shivered and turned toward Mitch, reaching for his hand. He looked like someone who'd been at the end of his rope way too long. His fingers were cold in Mitch's.

Mitch didn't flinch away despite the intensity of the moment. He was powerfully drawn to this man. "Tell me."

"I want to," Nick whimpered and trembled and there was nothing for it; Mitch hugged him, not caring about the awkward position or the fact that anyone could walk by and see them, and after a few seconds Nick shuddered and relaxed. "She's gone again." He sounded relieved and disappointed.

"They do that a lot?" Mitch asked.

"What, come and go?" Nick pulled away, pressing his fingers to his temples. "Sometimes. It depends on how strong they are."

Mitch was fascinated despite himself; he was starting to believe. "And what does that depend on? How old they are? Were. How long it's been since they died?"

"Lots of things." Nick rubbed his mouth. "She's not the only person he's killed."

"Shit," Mitch said. If this hadn't been a one-time thing, that meant the killer could -- and probably would -- strike again. "Can we ask her more questions? Find out more?"

"If I can. If she comes back."

"Is there a chance she won't?"

Nick sighed. "There's always a chance. But she probably will. They usually seem to stick around until whatever it is that's keeping them here gets taken care of."

"And that's where you come in." Mitch thought for a minute. "Is there some way we can get her to come back sooner? What about one of those, you know, Ouija boards?"

Leaning back in the seat, Nick shook his head. "I've never tried.

Do you have one?"

"Well, no."

Nick gave him a long, appraising look.

"What?" Mitch said.

"What about the place where her body was found?" Nick said. "I know it's not where she died" -- and that was information that hadn't been released in the news, information it would have been damned hard for Nick and Matthew to come across -- "but it's probably the next best place if we want to talk to her."

"Okay," Mitch said. Going into something like this without backup went against his training, but then again training had never covered what to do with someone who was claiming to be a psychic. And he knew what Leo's reaction would be if he called him. So instead he started up the car and put it into reverse. "Let's go."

* * *

The park was only a couple of minutes away, but Mitch's phone rang before they got there. He flipped it open, saw that it was Clay calling, then sighed and answered it anyway. "Hi."

"It's me," Clay said.

"I know," Mitch said.

"I was thinking about going out for a while after work," Clay said. "But if you were going to come home... back. To the house? And you wanted to talk--"

Mitch interrupted him. "I can't. I'm working."

"Your shift ended half an hour ago," Clay pointed out.

"I know, it's just... something came up. I'm going to be tied up for another hour or two." Mitch glanced at Nick for confirmation of the time frame they were looking at, and Nick nodded.

"Probably not more than that," Nick said quietly.

Not quietly enough -- Clay overheard. "Are you *seeing* someone?" he asked, his voice rising into a near-shriek.

"No!" Mitch said. "Not like that."

"You're so full of shit, Mitchell Anderson," Clay snapped, and hung up.

"I really, really am," Mitch said, shutting the phone and dropping it down into the cup holder.

"God, I'm sorry." Nick leaned forward and put his face in his hands.

Mitch reached over and rested his hand on Nick's shoulder. "It's not your fault. Things have been screwed up for a while. Now we're just... I don't know, trying to figure out how to untangle our lives so we can go on alone."

Nick looked at him. "It doesn't sound like that's what you want," he said.

"I don't know what I want," Mitch said honestly. "I guess I want every little thing he does not to get under my skin. Things that used to be cute--" He winced at the word choice, but went on, "Now they just annoy me." He slowed down as the neared the public parking lot that was adjacent to the park. "Here we are."

"Okay." Nick took a steadying breath. "Are we close to where her body was found?"

"Not really. It's on the other side, over there." Mitch pointed. "Don't worry, I have a flashlight and stuff. It'll be fine."

Nick smiled grimly. "Oh, don't worry, Detective Anderson. I stopped being afraid of the dark a long, long time ago."

Made sense. "Well, good. And it's Mitch."

They walked across the park through the twilight -- it was strangely quiet, when this time of day should have been one of the most crowded. Mitch supposed it was because of the news reports; things like that spooked people, and probably with good reason. The fact that they didn't know Paige hadn't been killed in the park didn't help. Despite his claims that he wasn't afraid of the dark, Nick stuck close, to the point where his arm bumped Mitch's a couple of times.

"You okay?" Mitch asked the third time it happened.

"A little nervous," Nick admitted. "I don't usually do this without Matthew."

"We don't have to," Mitch said. "We can go back and get him, if you'd--"

"No," Nick said. "As long as I can trust you. I can, can't I?" He looked at Mitch, expression serious.

"Yeah, you can. I'll make sure nothing happens."

Nick made a little dismissive sound. "You can't do that. Just don't leave me here. If I start to freak out, try not to let me hurt myself, and if I stop talking, wait it out. I'll be back sooner or later."

It was all starting to seem more complicated than Mitch had been counting on. "What do you mean, hurt yourself?"

"If I get... lost enough, I could walk myself into a tree," Nick said. He glanced around. "Oncoming traffic's less likely to be a threat here."

"I think I can stop you from doing that much." Mitch slowed down as they neared the wooded area where he and Leo had found Paige's body. "It was over here."

"Paige?" Nick said, like he wasn't talking to Mitch, and Mitch froze.

"Is she here?" It felt natural to ask, but as soon as he had, he was glad they were alone, because from a practical standpoint it made him sound kind of crazy.

"No. I don't know." Nick tilted his head to the side, listening. "I know she wants to tell me. She wants us to catch this guy. She's confused, scared. He... he took her to his apartment. It's close by. Small. The walls are off-white, and the paint is scuffed in some places." He took a few uncertain steps in the direction of the tree where Paige's body had been hidden, and Mitch reached out and took hold of his elbow. Right away, Nick turned toward him. "Help me," Nick whispered, and Mitch wasn't sure if he was talking to him or to Paige.

"I will," he said anyway. "I'm right here. Whatever you need."

Nick's head tilted down, his forehead coming to rest on Mitch's chest, and Mitch's hand went up automatically to the back of Nick's neck.

"It's okay. Nick? Tell me what to do."

"Don't let me," Nick said, but left the thought unfinished. "I need to get closer."

Mitch walked with him until they were only a couple of feet from the tree. The police tape was gone, but if you knew what to look for you could see where the leaves and ground had been disturbed. The last rays of sunshine were fading away, Mitch's eyes adjusting to the darkness. He looked around, but they were still alone.

As far as he could tell, anyway.

Nick pulled away from Mitch and went right to the tree, laying his palm against it. "I know," he said. "He took her to his apartment. It wasn't the first time. They... they had sex. That wasn't the first time, either."

"Did she consent to it?" Mitch asked.

"Yes," Nick said. "She didn't like it, though. It hurt. But he said nice things to her. He was nice to her, at first. He said she could make him happy. She wanted to." He was leaning against the tree now, and Mitch went closer in case he needed more support than that.

"What did he look like?"

"I told you. Not tall, not short. Average weight. Brown hair. Brown eyes." It could have been a description of half the men in town.

"Okay," Mitch said. "Was there anything special about him? The way he looked, I mean. Tattoos, scars, piercings?"

After fifteen seconds or so, Nick answered. "There's a tattoo on his wrist -- like a cross, but with a circle. A Celtic cross."

"What about the apartment? Where does he live?"

Nick -- or maybe Paige -- seemed to have stopped listening. "She used to leave her bedroom window unlocked for him. He'd sneak in while she was at school and leave things under her pillow. Little presents."

"And then he killed her," Mitch said, hoping to get things back on track, partially because the last thing he wanted was to hear about how this killer had been such a *nice guy*.

"She didn't--" Nick twitched and cried out, stumbling away from the tree and wrapping an arm around his head as best he could. "Don't -- don't touch me. I just need -- I have to know. Please. Please. I can't help if I don't..."

Mitch knew he should have asked more questions before they got so deep into this. This was too fucked up, and he had no idea how to deal with it. "Nick. *Nick*."

"They had sex," Nick said, no inflection in his voice. "He wanted to do it again and she said no. He -- he--" He broke, collapsing to the ground like his feet had been cut out from under him; Mitch lunged for him but was too late. He knelt beside Nick instead, afraid to touch him, afraid not to. "It wasn't the first time, and he's going to do it again."

"Who else has he done this to? Do you know? Does she?" Mitch settled for being as close as possible but kept his hands to himself.

Nick's head shook back and forth slowly, weaving. It was darker than it had been, and Mitch couldn't tell if his eyes had that glassy, unfocused look he remembered from before. "She knows, now, that she wasn't the first. I don't know how -- it's not like they can read minds, they can't, they don't know what he -- oh *shit*, oh Christ, no, no, *no*--"

He sounded so desperate that Mitch couldn't stop himself from reaching for him, one hand curling around Nick's upper arm. "Easy," he said helplessly. "It's okay. Just... breathe, or something.

It's not real."

"Not real?" Nick laughed, high and hysterical. "God, do you have any idea how much I wish it *wasn't*? It is, whether you believe it or not. I can *hear* them, and I'm *not* crazy. Don't leave me."

"I won't," Mitch promised. "I'm not. I'm right here. What does she know?"

"He told her. After she was dead. About the others, and how he did the same to them..." Nick raised his face to Mitch's. "There were three of them," he said. "And two of them were men."

"They... *what*?" Mitch was shocked.

"They were all different," Nick said. He pressed the heels of his hands against his eyes and rocked forward and back a little, and he sure as hell looked -- and sounded -- crazy. "But he must have seen the same things in them, the same... whatever it was that made him want them. He wanted them, and he takes what he wants. He--" Nick jerked away from Mitch suddenly, falling onto his back and arching like he wasn't getting any air, hands scrabbling furiously at the ground for purchase. The choked wail he made was enough to make Mitch's skin prickle.

He moved, getting an arm around Nick and pulling him half into his lap. "Nick," he said urgently as the other man whimpered and struggled, then abruptly quieted, curling up with his head pressed to Mitch's thigh. More uncertain now, Mitch repeated Nick's name.

"Sorry," Nick muttered. He gave a whole-body shiver. "Mitch?"

"Yeah," Mitch said. "I'm here. Are... are you okay?"

Nick swallowed but didn't otherwise move. "Not really. Give me a minute."

"Okay." Hesitantly, he stroked Nick's hair, and Nick gave a little sigh that sounded appreciative. "There's no rush. Take all the time you need."

"S'cold." It was more an observation than a complaint, but Mitch slid his hand down and rubbed Nick's arm instead, trying to warm him up. "Thanks for staying."

"I told you I would," Mitch said. "Anyway, who the hell would just leave you in the middle of something like that?"

"You'd be surprised," Nick said wryly. He sighed again and struggled to sit up, bracing a hand on the ground next to Mitch's leg.

Mitch helped him; he didn't realize until Nick was sitting up straight that the other man was still practically in his lap. He could feel Nick's other hand resting on his hip.

"You sure you're okay?" Mitch asked.

"Better than I was." Nick was close enough that Mitch could feel breath across his skin. "Sometimes it takes a lot out of me, but I'm used to it."

Considering how it had looked from his side of it, Mitch didn't see how it was the kind of thing anyone could get used to. He even believed, at that point, that everything Nick had told him was true. The way Nick had cried out, the almost-seizure he'd had, not to mention the way he was still shaking and clinging to Mitch... no one was that good an actor. "Have you ever gone to a hospital?"

"Once. I passed out and Matthew couldn't wake me up -- I think he panicked. I woke up in the emergency room. I was fine, though." Nick leaned in closer, seeking either warmth or just contact, and Mitch didn't complain. They sat there quietly, listening to the sounds of cars in the distance, with Nick's hand at the waistband of Mitch's slacks moving every once in a while, the subtle unconscious caress and the smell of Nick's hair, unfamiliar hotel shampoo, making Mitch slowly, painfully hard.

He wanted Nick. He didn't exactly understand why, but it was there, and it wasn't just physical. It was that need to protect Nick, to take care of him, to make everything better. Nick's partner Matthew couldn't even be bothered to show up tonight, or Nick had snuck out without him (and there had to be a reason for that). Mitch was the one who was here.

Mitch slid a hand up Nick's arm and over his shoulder to the back of his neck. His fingertips brushed into Nick's hair at the nape; Nick lifted his face, and Mitch kissed him.

Nick's lips and nose were cold, but his mouth parted willingly against Mitch's, his hand tightening at Mitch's waist. Mitch wrapped his other arm around him and pulled him closer, delving his tongue into Nick's mouth for a first taste of the warmth there; Nick made a small, eager sound and grabbed hold of the front of Mitch's shirt.

"Jesus, you feel good," Mitch muttered.

Nick turned to face him, legs straddling Mitch's lap. Both his hands came up to Mitch's face as the two of them found a better angle. "Mitch... we can't do this," Nick said.

"Sure we can," Mitch disagreed, although they sure as hell couldn't -- shouldn't -- do it here.

"No, we can't." Nick kissed him again, though. It made it hard to take him seriously.

Mitch decided that the best way to keep Nick from continuing to say they couldn't do something that they obviously *were* doing was to kiss him, so he focused on doing that. Nick felt fantastic, solid but not heavy, and he clung to Mitch like he *needed* him, which just turned Mitch on that much more.

"No," Nick said against Mitch's lips, and then again with more emphasis. "No."

Disappointed, Mitch let go of Nick's arms and leaned back. "Okay," he said. "Whatever you want."

Nick got up and backed away. "Can we go?"

They walked back to the car without saying anything. Mitch unlocked the passenger side door for Nick and waited for him to get in, then shut the door; he didn't realize until he'd walked around to the other side how weird all of this was, and then he had to pause for a second and take a deep breath.

"I'm sorry," he said, after he'd started driving back toward Nick's hotel. "I didn't -- I don't do stuff like that."

"It's not that I didn't like it," Nick said. "But Matthew wouldn't. And I'm pretty sure your boyfriend wouldn't be too crazy about it, either."

"We broke up," Mitch said. "I think. Which would make him not my boyfriend."

"You don't know what's going on," Nick said. "You need to talk to him and work things out before you start messing around with other people."

Mitch tried to let that sink in. "I know," he said finally. "You're right. I've never -- I never cheated on Clay. *Never*. God." It made his throat hurt to think about it.

"Hey." Nick patted Mitch's arm. "Don't freak out. Just take a couple of deep breaths and figure out what you want to do. If it's over, you can move on knowing you did what you could. If there's still something there that can be fixed, you can work on it. Together."

When they arrived at the hotel, it was nicer than Mitch remembered, even though it had been a couple of years since the last time he'd been there. He shook his head at the desk clerk when they went by -- she must have recognized him, because she looked first alarmed, then relieved. It was a reaction Mitch was pretty familiar with. He walked Nick up to his room.

"I have a key somewhere," Nick said, fumbling in his pockets. He got the key card out, but it slipped from his hands and fell to the floor.

"I've got it," Mitch said. Bending down, he picked up the card. When he straightened back up again, he glanced at Nick, who looked so exhausted and miserable that Mitch did a double take. "Hey," he said gently, and hugged him. It was an impulse, a need to provide comfort. He inhaled and exhaled a couple of times, imprinting the scent of Nick's hair in his memory, then pressed an awkward kiss to Nick's temple before pulling away. "Here."

Nick took the key and smiled. "Thank you."

Shaking his head, Mitch said, "No -- thank you. For everything."

"I just wish I could have done more," Nick said, and before Mitch could reply, the door opened.

"Where the hell have you been?" Matthew asked. He was wearing sweatpants and a t-shirt that were rumpled from sleep, his curly hair mussed up.

"I left you a note," Nick said.

"Yeah, I know," Matthew said. "But you didn't say where you were going or how long you'd be gone. Is he under arrest?" This question was obviously aimed at Mitch.

"No." Mitch wasn't sure what was going on between Nick and Matthew, so he thought it was best to say as little as possible.

"Good." Matthew relaxed and stepped back. "Come on in."

Mitch followed Nick into the room, which had the standard two double beds but also a small sitting area with a sofa and chair. "This is nice."

"We gave up on cheap places years ago," Matthew said. "Not that we couldn't be doing better." He sounded a little bit annoyed, Mitch thought, and Nick's shoulders slumped.

"Seems like you're doing pretty good to me." Mitch wasn't just saying it.

"Yeah, well." Matthew shrugged and rubbed the back of his neck like he was trying to get a crick out. "Excuse me a minute." He went into the bathroom and shut the door.

"Sorry," Nick said quietly, once they heard the water running. "He's not really a morning person."

"It's dinnertime," Mitch said.

Nick grimaced. "You know what I mean. It takes him a while to wake up."

"What was all that about, anyway?" Mitch asked, keeping his voice low.

"Oh... he wishes I'd agree to doing stuff that'd make us more money. You know, interviews on TV, maybe one of those shows where the psychic does readings for members of the audience... that kind of thing."

"You don't want to?" Even as he said it, Mitch realized what a stupid question it was. "No, obviously not. So not all the ones on TV are fakes?"

"I don't know," Nick said. "Probably some of them are. But there are ones like me, except some of them have a lot better control over their abilities than I do." He sat on the bed Matthew had been sleeping in, the one with the covers down and rumpled.

"You're helping people, though," Mitch argued. "And you're trying. That's what matters."

"Even if it didn't," Nick said, "it's the best I can do." He sounded lost.

Matthew came back out of the bathroom, looking a little less sleepy. "So, what happened?" he asked.

"I thought if I could talk to him alone, maybe things would be different," Nick said.

"Were they?" Matthew sat next to Nick and put a hand on the back of his neck, cradling the base of his skull the same way Mitch had been not long before. The look he gave Mitch was calculated, making sure that Mitch knew who Nick belonged to.

"We went to the park," Nick said.

"The one where they found the body?" Matthew asked, frowning. "That was a shitty idea. You know what could have happened?"

"Mitch was there," Nick protested. "It was fine. He kept an eye on me."

"Right, because he's got a lot of experience taking care of you," Matthew said. He glanced at Mitch. "No offense."

"It's okay," Mitch said. "But he's right -- it turned out okay. Here we are." In his world, that was one of the things that mattered most -- the final outcome.

"And did you get anything out of it?" Matthew asked.

Mitch nodded. "It was a little confusing, but yeah." He looked at Nick. "Would it be okay if I called you? If I had more questions? I don't know how long you're going to be in town..."

"We stay until he's ready to move on," Matthew said.

"I don't know," Nick said. "If... I think she's gone, but that doesn't mean she is. And it doesn't mean the others aren't still around. Wherever they died."

"Oh, great, a serial killer?" Matthew sounded fed up; it made Mitch want to hit him, because none of this was Nick's fault.

It also made him feel guilty, because he recognized Matthew's tone as the same one he'd been using more and more often with Clay, and he'd been both oblivious to it and blind to how it must have been making Clay feel. "We don't know that for sure," Mitch said.

"Yes, we do." Nick was firm. "Well, I don't know exactly what makes someone a serial killer, but this guy's killed four people, and he's going to do it again." His voice was shaky, and Matthew put an arm around him like it was a reflex.

"He's not," Mitch said. "I won't let him. It stops here, okay? I promise you that."

The look Nick gave him was grateful and trusting. "Okay," he said. He swallowed and licked his lips, then got up and moved to the bedside table. Opening the drawer, he took out a piece of paper and a pen, then leaned over the table to scribble something down. "Here." He stepped closer and gave Mitch the paper. "Call whenever you need to."

"And you call me," Mitch said. "If you think of anything else. Like where this guy lives?"

Nick shook his head. "She didn't know how to tell me. It's an apartment building; that's all I know."

"Okay." Mitch nodded at Matthew. "Thanks for all your help. Have a good night."

"We will," Matthew said.

As soon as Mitch got into his car, he called Leo, who for some reason wasn't answering his phone. "Come on," Mitch said, listening to it ring, but it went to voice mail. "Leo, it's me. I've got a lead on the Sadler case and I need to talk to you." He exhaled. "Call me when you get this."

He sat in the parking lot for a few minutes, trying to decide what to do next. Part of him was tired enough to want to call it a day, but the thought of his inaction resulting in another death had him calling work instead. He got the Sadler' address and drove over there; Mrs. Sadler was in the middle of cooking dinner when he knocked on the door. She wiped her hands on her apron absently, like she didn't know she was doing it. The stains on it, a variety of organic shades, made Mitch wonder if she'd been cooking since her daughter had disappeared.

"Hello," she said, offering her hand.

"Hello, ma'am. I'm Detective Mitch Anderson." He held up his badge so she could see it.

"Oh." Her first name was Ellen, Mitch knew. "You're one of the men who found Paige."

"Yes, ma'am, and I'm very sorry for your loss. I was hoping you could spare a few minutes to answer a couple of quick questions?"

"Sure. Come in -- I was just cooking..." Mrs. Sadler looked slowly toward the kitchen -- just then, the sound of a smoke detector going off pierced the air. "Oh, no."

"It's okay," Mitch reassured her. "I'll get it." He quickly found the smoke detector, took it down, and silenced it, then moved to turn on the fan over the stovetop. Mrs. Sadler opened a window.

"I probably shouldn't be cooking," she admitted, sinking down into a chair. "I can't seem to concentrate on anything."

"I'm sure that's understandable," Mitch said. "Is there anything I can do to help?"

Mrs. Sadler turned her gaze on him, her expression going from kind of befuddled to much sharper. "You can find the monster that killed my little girl," she said.

"I will," Mitch promised. "Did Paige mention anything unusual in the couple of weeks before she disappeared? Anything at all? About any new friends she might have made...?"

"Do you think someone at her school did this?" Mrs. Sadler asked, a hand going to her throat in horror.

"No, no," Mitch said. "We've talked to some of her teachers and classmates, and we don't have any reason to think it had anything to do with school. But maybe... did she have any after-school activities? Music lessons, sports, anything like that?"

Mrs. Sadler shook her head slowly. Her brown hair, which had more than a few gray streaks in it, was pulled back from her face, making her look tired. Or maybe she just *was* tired. "She didn't seem interested in any of those things. She was a good girl. She never got into any trouble, she got good grades... who would do something like this?"

"I don't know, but I'm going to find out," Mitch said grimly. "I know this is a difficult time--"

"Her funeral is tomorrow," Mrs. Sadler said. "That's why I'm doing all this cooking. People will come back here afterwards, and I have to have something to feed them..." She started to cry softly, making no effort to hide the fact, the tears running down her face unchecked. "My husband went to buy a suit. His old one didn't fit anymore, and he couldn't go to our baby's funeral without a new suit..."

"I'm so sorry," Mitch said again. This was one of his least favorite things, dealing with people who were grieving, and the thought struck him suddenly that it was probably because it reminded him of when his parents had died.

He'd been sixteen, just old enough to have control of his emotions, and he hadn't cried. Everyone around him had -- his aunt and uncle were the worst. They'd handled everything from the funerals to the estate, opened their home to Mitch, but they'd cried through every step of the process, and somehow Mitch had never been able to forgive them for it. They should have been there for him, and he'd thought that should include keeping it together instead of falling apart and forcing him to be the strong one.

Mrs. Sadler was brushing away her tears now; Mitch handed her the box of tissues that was on the table, and she took it gratefully. "Thank you," she said. "You're so nice. I'm sorry -- what was it you were asking?"

Relieved that she had rallied, Mitch said, "If you could remember anything unusual, anything at all. Even something that didn't seem important might help."

She looked out the window over the sink at the darkened sky, then got up and went over to the windowsill. She picked something up and offered it to Mitch; it turned out to be a keychain with a nondescript key on it -- the keychain looked like stainless steel, rectangularly shaped with a darker carbon fiber insert in the center. Mitch reached into his pocket for a glove before he took it from her. "I just found it yesterday when I was straightening up her room," Mrs. Sadler said.

"This was Paige's?" Mitch asked.

"The keychain was. I don't know where the key came from. It doesn't look like one of ours." Mrs. Sadler sat down again. "About... maybe three or four weeks ago, she came out of her room after school with a little wrapped package in her hand. She said she'd found it on her pillow. When she opened it, the keychain was inside. I thought..." She looked down, maybe ashamed. "I thought she'd put it there herself. She didn't really have any friends, and I think she was lonely, sometimes... I thought maybe she was trying to pretend she had a secret admirer. It didn't seem like the kind of thing she'd pick out."

Mitch remembered what Nick had said about Paige leaving her window open, her lover coming in and leaving her presents -- had this been the first gift? Had the guy been stalking her for a while before he'd finally approached her? "What happened after that?"

"She didn't mention it again until the day before she... she disappeared. She was upset because she couldn't find it. She asked me if I'd seen it." Mrs. Sadler got up and took the cover off a large pot, then stirred the contents. "She turned the house upside down looking for it." She sighed. "I found it in a pile of clean clothes she'd never gotten around to folding."

"Do you mind if I check and make sure the key doesn't fit any of your locks?" Mitch asked.

She shook her head. "No, of course not. Whatever will help."

He went outside and, still wearing the glove, tried the key in each of the exterior locks including the padlock on the shed in the back yard; it didn't fit. He knocked on the door again, and after a minute Mrs. Sadler came and opened it. "Would it be okay if I kept this for a while?" Mitch asked, holding up the key.

"Yes. There's nothing else you need?" She seemed weary and emotionally distant now.

Mitch went over everything in his head. "No. Would you like me to put the smoke detector back?"

Mrs. Sadler smiled wanly. "My husband just called; he'll be home in a few minutes. He can do it."

"Okay." Mitch nodded. "I'll be going, then. We'll be in touch."

In his car, Mitch phoned the precinct in Greenville and asked to speak to the detective in charge of one of the unsolved murders he'd found on the computer earlier. He got lucky -- the guy was actually on duty and not far from where Mitch was at the Sadlers', and agreed to meet Mitch in the parking lot of a convenience store nearby.

"Jim Harper," he said, offering his hand as Mitch shut his car door.

"Mitch Anderson. Thanks for meeting me." They shook hands.

"No problem." Jim leaned against his squad car and crossed his arms over his chest. "I heard about the girl being killed. It didn't occur to me to connect the two cases."

"I don't know for sure that they *are* connected," Mitch said. "It just seemed worth it to dig a little deeper and find out."

"Teenaged girls being murdered -- that's pretty much as bad as it gets," Jim said. It was the kind of thing cops said to each other, knowing that it wasn't anywhere near as bad as it got.

"Yeah. So, what can you tell me? You know how that database is, three quarters of the entries are bare bones."

Jim nodded. "In this case, there isn't that much to tell. We couldn't come up with any evidence. I figured it was one of those cases that would never be closed."

"What about the basics -- how did he die?"

"Coroner said it was strangulation. There was a lot of bruising around the throat. Nothing else -- unless you count the fact that he was probably raped. Coroner thought that might have happened after he was already dead, though." Jim smirked in a way Mitch didn't like.

"The girl was, too," Mitch said. That was enough of a similarity to warrant further investigation, at least. "No evidence? Blood, hair, semen?"

"Nothing," Jim said. "If there had been, we'd have followed up."

"What about where the guy was found?"

"That was in the report," Jim pointed out. "Somebody's back yard, pretty much. Big property with a lot of trees, they didn't go out there very often but some neighboring kids were messing around and found the body under some rotting cardboard." There was that smirk again. "He was rotting pretty good by then, too."

Mitch didn't like to think about it. "Same with the girl."

"Really? Huh. Sounds like maybe we're looking for the same perpetrator."

"Sounds like," Mitch agreed. "Was there anyone you talked to, anyone who knew the victim? Friends, family?"

"No one," Jim said. "He lived over in those apartment buildings on the east side -- what the hell are they called... Maple Crossing?"

"Maple Gardens," Mitch corrected him. It was where Clay had lived when they'd met; the apartments were small but well maintained and the guy who ran the place was gay, so members of the GBLT community tended to gravitate there. "You remember what number?"

"Nah. Didn't matter all that much." Jim glanced at his watch and frowned. "Shit, I've got to go." He reached out and clapped Mitch on the shoulder in a way that was a little too familiar. "Keep in touch, okay? Let me know if you find anything."

"I will," Mitch said, thinking there wasn't much chance he'd ever talk to this guy voluntarily again.

At that point, he wanted little more than to go home, but he was already halfway to Maple Gardens, and it was hard to just drop things when every place he went seemed to take him a step closer toward being able to solve this case. He drove over and found the apartment manager's office, which was closed for the evening. There was a number to call listed on the door, though, so Mitch dialed it and waited.

"Hello?" a man answered after the third ring.

"Hello, sir. My name is Mitch Anderson; I'm a detective with the Franklin police department. Is this Derek Roach?"

The man sighed. "Yes. Please tell me apartment twelve isn't playing that stupid Evanescence album at top volume again."

"They're not," Mitch assured him. "I'm investigating the death of Lawrence Driscoll. I know it's been a while, but I was hoping I could ask you a few questions?"

"Sure. Shoot." There was a brief pause, then Derek said, "Probably not the best word to use with a cop, right? Sorry."

"It's okay." Mitch grinned. "I'm standing outside your office now. Do you want to come down and meet me, or...?"

"You're right underneath me," Derek said. "Which I swear I didn't mean in a suggestive way. I'm upstairs, apartment three -- do you think you could come up? The thing is, I'm in the middle of microwaving a frozen dinner and if I don't eat it while it's still hot, it'll metamorphose from food into some sort of plastic."

"I'll come up," Mitch said, already starting up the stairs. "Be right there." He hung up, remembering those frozen meals from when he'd been a bachelor and knowing Derek wasn't really exaggerating how bad they could be. At the top of the staircase, he turned right and found #3, then knocked on the door.

Derek opened it and eyed him appreciatively for a second or two before stepping back. "Come on in." The microwave beeped and Derek headed for the kitchen to retrieve his food as Mitch shut the door. "I'd offer to make you one of these, but I don't think you'd really want one."

"Probably not," Mitch said. "I'm spoiled -- my partner's into gourmet cooking right now. It's all braised this and truffled that."

Holding the plastic tray of steaming food with a brightly colored oven mitt, Derek gave him a look that was understanding now. "And you don't mean your cop partner," he said.

"No, I don't."

Derek relaxed, letting out an audible, relieved sigh. "Well, thank goodness. It's always good to know where a person stands." He set down his food and pulled his hand slowly from the oven mitt, which clashed with his shiny purple shirt. "And from where I'm standing, I'm hoping your partner knows how lucky he is."

"He used to live here," Mitch said, not wanting to get into it. "Clay Walker?"

"Oh, yeah, I do remember him." Derek took a fork from a drawer and waved it in Mitch's direction. "Lucky, lucky boy. Too bad he met you before I did."

It was flattering, Mitch told himself. "So, about Lawrence Driscoll..."

"Right, right." Derek stirred his food, which looked like a combination of pasta and vegetables. "He lived alone, he was a nice guy. Never any trouble. He was shy, I think. His family didn't want anything to do with him -- they wouldn't even come pick up his things after he died, just told me to throw them away. Not that I did, of course. I kept a few things myself, but most of it went straight to Goodwill."

"Did he ever have people over? Dates?"

Derek ate a bite of pasta, then licked his lips thoughtfully. "Not that I ever saw. But a few weeks before he went missing, he stopped coming home after work some nights. I wouldn't have noticed except his parking space is next to mine and I, for one, have a *very* busy social life."

"I'm sure you do." Mitch shifted his weight. "Is that all you can tell me? What about when you cleaned his place out -- was there anything unusual in there?"

"Honey, have you *seen* gay boys' apartments?" Derek raised an eyebrow and perched himself on a stool. "His was positively boring. Clothes, CDs, furniture, sure. But no fun sex stuff at all." He pouted.

"Okay, well. Thanks." Mitch handed Derek one of his cards; Derek's fingers lingered a little too long on his. "If you think of anything else, call me."

"Oh, believe me, I will." Derek put the card down next to a bowl on the countertop between them, and a glint of silver caught Mitch's eye.

"What's this?" he asked, recognizing it as a keychain that matched the one Mrs. Sadler had given him.

Derek shrugged. "I found it in his apartment when I was cleaning it out. I kept meaning to take the key off and use it myself, once I figured out it wasn't a spare to his place, but I never got around to it. I kind of forgot it was there."

Mitch pulled a glove and evidence bag from his pocket, slipped the glove on, and reached for the keychain. After so much time had passed, chances were good there weren't any useful fingerprints or anything on it, but it didn't hurt to be careful, and now that it seemed likely both key chains had come from the same place... There was a key on this one that looked like it matched the one on Paige's keychain, too. "Do you mind if I take it?"

"Why? Do you think it might be to a safe-deposit box full of money?" Derek smiled and waved it away. "No, no, of course, take it." He gave Mitch a hopeful look. "You know where to find me, so don't be a stranger."

On the drive home, all Mitch could think about was what might have happened if he and Clay hadn't met. They'd both been lonely as hell when they had, but that wasn't what he was focused on. What if Clay had still been living in that place when the killer was scoping out his next victim? What if Clay had been the one murdered and raped and left to rot under some fucking cardboard in some rich person's yard? The thought made Mitch feel sick; by the time he pulled into the driveway, his hands were shaking, and he was so damned grateful to see Clay's car there that it was like inhaling smelling salts, sharp and head-clearing.

He knew what he had to do.

The front door was unlocked. Mitch pushed it open. "Clay?"

"I'm here," Clay said, and Mitch followed his voice back to the bedroom, where a suitcase was open, half-packed, on the bed.

"Can we talk?" Mitch asked.

"I don't know." Clay sighed. He was holding a pair of dress slacks in his hands, still on their hanger. "Who were you with when I called before?"

"This guy named Nick Kelley," Mitch answered immediately. "It was a work thing. He's some kind of psychic, and we had no leads on this case with the girl. He was trying to help. That's all."

Clay looked doubtful. "He's not some boy on the side? You aren't sleeping with him?"

"No," Mitch said. "He's just in town temporarily, and he has someone. I'm not sleeping with him. I haven't slept with him, I swear. Can we go into the other room and talk?"

Clay sighed again, looking at the slacks he was holding. "Okay, what the hell. There's no way to pack these without getting them all wrinkled, anyway." He hooked the hanger onto the closet handle and followed Mitch out into the living room.

Mitch gestured at the couch, and Clay sat down.

Slowly, Mitch knelt on the floor in front of Clay and reached for his hand. Looking confused, Clay said, "What--"

"Let me," Mitch said, but he was ready to shut up if that was what Clay wanted. Clay didn't say anything, just looked at him wide-eyed and a little bit worried. "I know I've fucked things up, and I'm sorry. I've been stupid and stubborn. All I want now is the chance to make it up to you. Whatever you want me to do, I'll do it. I love you, and I don't -- I don't want you to leave. Please." His throat and chest felt tight. "I don't want to lose you."

He knew the look on Clay's face; it was the one that meant he was wavering, reconsidering. "Are you sure?" Clay said finally.

"Yes," Mitch said. "More sure than I've ever been about anything. Please, Clay. Things will be different, I promise."

"If they aren't, I'm going to take your gun and shoot you with it," Clay said, looking serious.

"Is that a yes?" Mitch asked hopefully.

"Oh, I suppose so," Clay said. "Since you seem to want it so much." His eyes were shining, and he was smiling and putting his arms around Mitch's neck, letting himself be pulled down onto the floor. "I never could resist a handsome man..."

"You'd better," Mitch said, kissing him. "Resist all of them but me."

"I don't want anyone but you," Clay said. "I never have."

"I know." Mitch should have appreciated that more; it meant a lot, knowing that he could trust Clay, and he *did* know that, absolutely. He kissed Clay's ear and Clay gave an appreciative shiver.

"I've even been rebuffing the advances of this guy who keeps flirting with me at work," Clay said, tilting his head to expose his neck.

Mitch nipped at the tender skin and grumbled, "Good. You want me to tell him to back off?"

"No," Clay said. "He's a good customer, he's just a flirt. Oh, do that again." Mitch did, and moved his hand down to cup Clay's dick through his jeans at the same time. "Ohhh. Are you going to fuck me, Mitchell?"

"Not here." Mitch threaded his fingers into Clay's soft hair and kissed him wetly and thoroughly.

"Why *not* here?" Clay begged. His lips were swollen and dark pink, and his pale blond stubble was scraping the hell out of Mitch's face, but Mitch didn't give care.

He pulled back, holding Clay's face -- Clay's beloved, incredible face -- between his hands. "Because you deserve better," he said, "than being fucked on the floor. You deserve silk sheets--"

"We don't have silk sheets," Clay interrupted.

"Would you shut up? I'm trying to be romantic here." Mitch smiled. "I want to take you to bed. Can I do that?"

Clay looked on the verge of tears, and his voice shook when he said, "Yes. *Yes*."

Mitch led Clay to the bedroom, where he kissed him again and again, unbuttoning his shirt -- he couldn't help but note that Clay's shirt, while stylish, wasn't flashy the way Derek's had been -- and peeling it off slowly. He kissed Clay's shoulder, reminding himself with lips and tongue how perfect Clay's skin was. "Jesus, I've missed this."

"Me, too." Clay clung to him. "God, Mitchell, I love you so much."

"I love you," Mitch told him. He undid the front of Clay's jeans and pushed them down, rubbing Clay's erection through his thin cotton boxer briefs. "Clay. My Clay."

"I am yours," Clay agreed. "Forever."

"Forever," Mitch said. "Tell me what you want."

"Just you." Clay's hands were fumbling at Mitch's clothes. "Naked, and on top of me. Please."

It didn't take long; their clothes tangled on the floor as Mitch shoved the suitcase out of the way and pressed Clay down onto the bed.

"What about the sheets?" Clay asked, gasping with laughter. "We're still on the comforter."

"Next time," Mitch growled. He closed his mouth closed over Clay's dick and sucked at it, a slow up and down as Clay's hips moved restlessly. He loved the sounds Clay made when he did this -- high pitched and anxious.

"Mitch. Mitchell." Clay's hand rubbed Mitch's shoulder. "Need you."

"You've got me," Mitch said reassuringly. "I'm right here."

"I meant *in* me," Clay said. "Now."

Mitch tried to remember where the lube was; he moved up, covering Clay with his body and kissing him. Clay's mouth opened, letting his tongue in. "Do you have any idea where the lube is?"

Mitch asked.

Clay pulled away. "Uh-oh."

"Uh-oh?"

"I kind of, sort of, might have thrown it out," Clay said.

"Are you serious?"

"No, I'm lying -- I thought it would make the night a little more fun," Clay said. "Yes, I threw it out. I thought..." He looked uncertain, suddenly, hurt, and it killed Mitch that he'd been the one to do that to him.

"I know," he said. He brushed Clay's hair back and kissed the corner of his mouth softly. "I know. It's okay. We'll make do. Stay here -- I'll be right back."

Mitch made a quick trip to the bathroom, where he found the bottle of unscented lotion he used when his hands got dry. By the time he got back, Clay had moved the suitcase to the floor, pulled down the covers, and was lying on his side, one hand slowly jacking his dick.

"Miss me?" Mitch asked.

"More than you know," Clay said. "Come here."

In a flash, Mitch was curled up behind him. He squeezed a little bit of lotion onto his fingers and tangled them with Clay's, slicking Clay's dick, playing with it and his balls until Clay was panting and shivering.

"Mitch, please," he begged. "God, I... I want you so much. Please."

"Oh, no," Mitch said, even though he was dying for it. "I'm not done with you yet."

He rolled Clay onto his back and knelt between his thighs, one hand on Clay's dick. Slowly, he rubbed some lotion back behind Clay's balls, teasing at his opening, then he slipped a finger inside and found Clay's prostate, pressing on it and stroking his dick. "Fuck," Clay said, eyes closed. "Fuck, Mitchell."

"That's it," Mitch said encouragingly. "Come on."

"Oh, God." Clay clenched around him, his dick twitching in Mitch's hand. "I don't... want to come 'til you're inside me."

When Mitch entered him, it was slow and hot and devastating, with Clay's legs up over his shoulders and their eyes locked. "Love you," Mitch told him, watching how Clay's eyes went glassy and unfocused with pleasure.

Clay gasped as Mitch went deeper; there was a fine sheen of sweat on his skin and his lips looked so kissable that Mitch had to lean in and brush his mouth over Clay's. "Mitch. God." He made a sound of protest as Mitch pulled out, then groaned when Mitch slipped in again. The lotion wasn't as slick as lube, but it felt just as good. Softer and warmer, somehow.

"Love seeing you like this," he said. "You're so hot when you're all turned on."

"You turn me on," Clay gasped. "Mitch... Mitch, I'm going to--"

"Yeah. Come on." Mitch wrapped his hand around Clay's dick and squeezed, working the tip, and Clay came, fluid shooting out over Mitch's fingers and onto Clay's chest and his ass pulsing around Mitch's cock. It felt fantastic -- so good that Mitch had to tighten his jaw not to come, too.

The last jolt of orgasm wrenched a soft cry from Clay, who went limp under Mitch and whispered, "Give it to me. Fuck me, Mitchell. You know how much I love--"

That was all it took -- Mitch thrust in a few more times, then threw his head back and froze as it ripped through him, hot and almost painful. He shuddered and moaned, his hips still until the end, when they jerked forward one more time.

If he hadn't had Clay's legs up over his shoulders, he would have just collapsed. As it was, he had to stay upright long enough to ease himself out of Clay and over to one side before letting himself fall down onto the mattress, face planted in a pillow.

He felt Clay's hand on his shoulder and somehow found the strength to turn his head. "You," he mumbled, "are amazing."

Clay smiled brilliantly. "I am?"

"Yes," Mitch said. He rolled onto his side and pulled Clay close. "And I obviously don't tell you that enough if you have to ask."

"I wouldn't mind hearing it more often," Clay admitted, starting to snuggle in, then reaching for some tissues and cleaning his chest off. "I guess we haven't been talking -- really talking, I mean -- enough lately."

"No, we haven't. But things are going to be different now." Mitch kissed Clay's hair and thought about it; it wasn't the kind of thing he could just say. He had to follow through. "I promise."

"I know," Clay said. "I believe you."

"I don't know why," Mitch said. He traced Clay's cheekbone with his fingertips. "I don't deserve you."

"You used to say that a lot," Clay said, frowning. "I think maybe you said it so many times you started believing it, but it's *not true*. You deserve to have someone, and to be happy. You can't just...

start pulling away because you're afraid things aren't going to work out. Because then they *won't*."

Mitch stared at him in awe. "How the hell did you get so smart?"

"I read more than one book a year," Clay said flippantly. He hitched himself up onto one elbow and ran his fingers along Mitch's chest. "What was it, do you think? That started things going wrong?"

It was a fair question, so Mitch thought seriously about the answer. "I don't know. I wish I did."

"If we don't know, how do we stop it from happening again?"

"Sheer stubbornness?" Mitch suggested, and Clay grinned.

"You're good at that." Clay lay back down, cushioning his head on Mitch's shoulder. "What about... what do you wish were different?"

"Nothing!" Mitch said. "I like things the way they are. When we're okay."

"But there must be things you want," Clay said. "Oh! I know."

"You do?"

"This woman called, before. Anna? She said you want to get a dog."

Mitch frowned. "Yeah, but you don't like dogs."

"No, I don't *know* anything about dogs," Clay corrected him. "I've never had one. Sure, some of the bigger ones make me kind of nervous. And I don't really like the little designer ones, either. They're too Paris Hilton."

"Only if you intend to start carrying one around in a purse," Mitch said.

"Anyway, stupid," Clay said, smacking him with the flat of his hand. "What I'm trying to say is, if you really want a dog, let's get a dog."

"Are you sure?"

"Yes, I'm sure. As long as I get a say in which dog to get," Clay said. "And you have to get me a book, like, 'Dogs for Dummies', or something."

"I haven't had a dog since I was a kid," Mitch said. "I'm going to need a book just as much as you."

"Anna gave me her number. She said, if we were splitting up, I should think about getting a dog of my own."

"Yeah, well, I'm glad you're not going to have to." Mitch shut his eyes and hugged Clay as tightly as he could in the position they were in.

Clay sighed and relaxed against him. "Me, too."

* * *

The next day, which happened to be Mitch's day off, they met Anna in the parking lot outside the animal shelter where she volunteered.

"You must be Clay!" Anna said as soon as she saw them. She hugged him, and, Clay being Clay, he hugged her back even though it was the first time they'd met. "I'm so glad to see you. Mitch!" She hugged Mitch, too, and he let her. "Good for you for working things out," she whispered. Then, in a regular voice, "Come on, let's go inside so you can meet the dogs."

Inside, there was an entryway and a desk, then doors that led to rooms that housed different types of animals. Mitch and Clay followed Anna into the dog room, which was instantly deafening. "Oh my God, it's like a nightmare," Clay said, covering his ears.

"Even people who have dogs can find this part kind of overwhelming," Anna said. "I can get you ear plugs if you want?"

"No, I think I'll live," Clay said. "Will they do this the whole time?"

"They'll calm down in a few minutes," Anna reassured him.

The nearest dog was watching them with hopeful eyes, tail wagging furiously. It was some kind of shepherd mix, Mitch thought. He went over and crouched down. "Hey, girl," he said, and her pink tongue came out and licked at the chain-link fencing between them.

"He's too big," Clay said from beside him.

"It's a girl," Mitch said.

"Okay, *she's* too big. She must weigh a hundred pounds."

"Only sixty," Anna said. "She is big, though, and she has some behavioral issues."

"What does that mean?" Clay asked. "Does she rip people's faces off? Or shit all over the house?"

Anna laughed. "No, but she hates other dogs. She needs a more experienced owner."

"Which would not be us," Clay said. "Okay, what do you recommend?"

"Well, I had a couple of thoughts for you guys," Anna said, leading them around to the left and stopping in front of a cage holding what looked like a black lab. "This is Prue -- she's three, so still young enough to make a good transition to a new home, and she's a sweetie. The biggest behavioral issue you'd have with her is she might lick you to death."

"I don't like licky dogs," Clay said. "Besides, I can't have a dog named after one of the Charmed Ones in my house. It's too creepy."

Mitch gave him a fond look. "What is it with you and that show?"

"Other than the fact that its extended run is proof that television executives are actually controlled by the devil?" Clay countered.

"You could change her name," Anna said. "People do that all the time."

"And then wonder why the dogs have behavioral issues," Clay said. He was getting way more into this than Mitch would have anticipated.

"Women do it all the time," Mitch said, and Clay looked at him funny. "Change their names? When they get married."

"Oh." Clay waved his hand. "That's voluntary. It's totally different. Next?" He looked at Anna hopefully.

Anna led them past two more dogs to another cage with a solid-looking dog that was clearly some kind of bull terrier. It had the square jaw, short fur, and brindled look Mitch was familiar with. "This is Butch."

"He certainly is," Clay said admiringly.

"He's five and was living in a house with two other dogs, three cats, and six kids."

"Now *that* sounds like chaos," Mitch said.

"It must have been. The guy lost his job and they got evicted. One of the other dogs went to live with a friend and the other is staying with the wife's brother -- they're hoping to get him back. Butch was the newest addition to the family, so he and the cats ended up here. He's a nice dog; friendly, lots of energy, well-trained." Anna stuck a hand into the cage and Butch sniffed at her hand politely, wagging his tail with what Mitch would have sworn was a grin on his face.

"Isn't that a pit bull?" Clay asked.

"We don't have a pedigree on him, but probably. He definitely seems to be some kind of terrier mix. But he's a really nice dog."

"I don't like pit bulls," Clay said, shaking his head. It was said in the tone of voice Mitch knew meant there was no arguing with him.

"Okay," Anna said. "The next one I thought might be good for you guys is over here." They'd moved from big cage territory into an area with cages that were more medium sized, just like the dog in question, who was white with a soft, crinkly coat, black ears and little black spots all over. Its tail had long, feathery fur. "This is Freckles. She was a stray, so we don't know anything about her background. But she's healthy, she's had all her shots, and she's been spayed. She's a little shy, but I think she'd come around pretty quickly once she had some stability."

Clay was already kneeling in front of the cage talking to the dog softly. "Good girl. Good dog." He turned his head and looked at Anna. "Can we take her out?"

Mitch and Anna exchanged a glance. "Sure," Anna said. "Let me go get a leash and we can take her for a walk."

The dog's ears perked up at the word "walk". "She's smart," Clay said. "She knows what we're saying."

"That might be taking it a little far," Mitch said. "She's pretty, though." Not really what he'd been picturing in terms of a dog, but if Clay liked her, that was good enough for him.

Freckles had crept forward slowly and was crouching on the floor near Clay, looking at him with her huge brown eyes. "It's okay," Clay said. "You're a good girl. Do you want to go for a walk?" Again, the dog's ears twitched upward. "See! She knows."

Coming back with leash in hand, Anna unlatched the cage and went in, fastening the clip to the red collar Freckles was wearing. The dog stayed crouched low to the floor, slinking more than walking, as they walked over to an outside door that led to the grassy yard behind the building, but as soon as she smelled the fresh air, she walked more normally.

"I was starting to wonder if there was something wrong with her legs," Mitch said.

"Dogs are smarter than you think," Anna said, handing the leash to Clay. "Their senses of smell are so much better than ours -- if we think a room full of dogs smells funky, imagine what it must smell like to them. They can read our body language, little movements we aren't even aware we're making... they know who to trust."

Now that they were outside, Freckles was looking around with interest, occasionally glancing up at Clay for reassurance. "Good dog," Clay told her, and she wagged her tail tentatively.

The dog stopped to sniff something, and Mitch went a little closer and crouched down. "Hey, Freckles," he said, and she watched him warily for a few seconds before taking a few steps and touching her nose to his hand. She let him pet her; it was clear she enjoyed the attention even though she was still a little nervous.

"She doesn't have any diseases or anything?" Clay asked.

"Clean bill of health," Anna said. "And she seems to get along with other dogs -- she's obviously not an alpha dog, but there's nothing wrong with that, and it means you won't have any trouble with her if you ever decide to get another dog."

"We haven't even gotten a first dog yet," Mitch protested, but he could tell by the look on Clay's face that the decision had already been made.

* * *

The first three hours with Freckles were a whirlwind of shopping, which Mitch was pretty sure made Clay like getting a dog all the more. They went to two super pet stores, where they bought two new collars (Clay couldn't decide which one he liked better) and two leashes (one regular leash and one of the retractable ones).

"What's wrong with this leash?" Mitch had asked, holding the one that had come from the shelter. Freckles was sitting on the floor next to him, and even she was starting to look bored.

"It's a *charity* leash," Clay said.

Mitch gave him a look. "We paid almost $200 to adopt the dog," he said. "Besides, how else were we supposed to get her to the car?"

"She needs a much nicer one," Clay said, hands on his hips as he checked out the selection. "What do you think of pink?"

"She's a dog, not a baby," Mitch said. "And we're not going to get any of those stupid ear bows."

"God, no," Clay said. "But what do you think about toenail polish?" He looked sideways at Mitch. "I'm kidding."

"Good." Freckles whined and Mitch bent to pat her; her tail waved back and forth against the floor. "Please tell me we're not going to be here all day."

"Definitely not. I don't like any of these -- we'll have to go to the other place across town."

It took two trips for Mitch to bring everything from the car to the house. Food and water bowls, a cushioned bed, a huge bag of kibble, some towels "just for Freckles" because Clay didn't want to let her use any of the house towels -- "They're new!" -- and at least a dozen dog toys. Clay stayed with Freckles, who didn't seem inclined to explore; she stuck close to Clay, not going more than a couple of steps from him.

They had the nicest day Mitch could remember in a long time -- an hour and a half in the yard tossing a ball back and forth demonstrated that Freckles was happy to chase the ball but had absolutely no idea what to do with it after that. At one point Mitch threw the ball and accidentally hit her with it; she just shook her head, looking puzzled, and Clay laughed so hard he fell down onto the grass.

"You'll get grass stains on your pants," Mitch told him, grinning.

"So?" Clay laughed some more, then reached a hand up to Mitch and yanked him down on the ground, too. "Hey there, good-looking."

"Hi," Mitch said. He kissed Clay slowly, then yelped when something cold and wet pressed against his wrist. Startled, Freckles leapt back, then, tail wagging, returned and licked Clay's cheek.

"Gah! Dog kisses!" Clay shrieked. He rolled away, covering his face. "Get her away!"

Mitch would have figured Freckles would be freaked out by Clay's over the top reaction, but the dog was wriggling around Clay excitedly and trying to lick him more. Clay shrieked and rolled around, one arm wrapped around his head and the other trying to fend off the dog while Mitch watched with amusement.

"Help me!" Clay said.

"You love it," Mitch told him, and Clay didn't deny it.

They took a long walk, and by the time they got back Freckles was exhausted. She collapsed on her new bed and was snoring within minutes. Mitch and Clay started dinner -- it had been a while since they'd cooked together, and Mitch had forgotten how fun it could be. Of course, they ended up getting distracted in the middle and having incredibly hot sex right there against the kitchen counter. By the time they got back to the food, the chicken was a little more done than it should have been, but Mitch was so relaxed and happy that he couldn't have cared less.

"Can you move the dog bed in there?" Clay called from the bathroom, where he was brushing his teeth.

Mitch, in the bedroom drying his hair with one of the non-dog towels, said, "Um... no?"

"Oh, come on." Clay appeared in the doorway still holding his toothbrush and wearing only his bathrobe. "She'll be lonely."

"And we'll be up half the night listening to her whine," Mitch said firmly. "No. It's better for her to get used to the way it's going to be, and she's *not* sleeping with us." Besides, he'd already gone through his nightly routine of making sure the house was locked up tight, and the dog had been sleeping heavily in her bed. Hopefully she'd be fine until morning.

"Okay, okay," Clay said. "You're the big dog expert." He left and came back a minute later, taking off his bathrobe and hanging it up. Mitch slipped behind him and slid an arm around his waist, kissing the back of his neck. "Mm."

"You're not too sore?" Mitch whispered, dragging his lower lip along Clay's ear. They'd really gone at it earlier; he'd gotten kind of carried away.

Clay murmured appreciatively and pushed his ass back against Mitch's hardening erection. "No. Oh, that's nice." Mitch was teasing at his nipples with both hands, pulling them into tight little points and enjoying Clay's breathy gasps. "Oh. Let's go to bed."

"Yeah," Mitch said.

Stepping back, Mitch smiled as Clay turned around. He loved looking at Clay when he was naked -- and so did his dick. Clay was already hard, too, and he gave Mitch a long kiss before sinking down to his knees.

"Jesus, Clay," Mitch breathed, threading his fingers into Clay's hair.

Clay sucked at his balls first, getting them wet, his mouth hot and perfect. Mitch groaned when Clay moved on to his cock, sliding his lips down over the head and along his shaft. Clay knew exactly how to suck him, alternating between gentle teasing and more forceful until Mitch's toes were curling and his hands were clenched into fists. As much as he loved fucking Clay's mouth, he wanted more.

"Come here," he said, pulling Clay to his feet and over to the bed.

"How do you want me?" Clay asked.

Mitch kissed his neck and shoulder, then turned him around so he was facing the wall, curling Clay's hands over the headboard. "How about like this?"

"Mm. This is good," Clay said. "We still forgot to buy lube."

They'd used olive oil in the kitchen earlier -- Mitch eased a finger inside Clay and found him slick and ready despite their shower. "I think we'll be okay," he murmured, rubbing deeper until

Clay whimpered. "What do you think?"

Clay's back curved down into a beautiful arch. "Yes," he gasped. "Yes, please, God."

Kneeling between Clay's thighs, Mitch lined up his cock and pushed inside him, shuddering at the clench of tight heat. "Fuck." He held onto Clay's hips and found a slow rhythm, being careful not to be too rough. It was incredible, watching his cock sliding in and out of Clay's ass, hearing the soft little moans that Clay made.

"*God*, Mitchell." Clay was trembling. "God, fuck me."

Mitch jerked his hips forward and Clay gasped. "Like that?"

"Yes. Like that. More." Mitch could see Clay's hands tighten on the headboard; he slid his own hand around and found Clay's dick, working it with every thrust.

"Jesus, you feel so good," he muttered, moving faster -- he couldn't help it.

Clay was moving with him now, his dick hard as rock in Mitch's grip. "So do you. Mitch..."

"Oh God, I'm gonna come--" It shocked Mitch with its suddenness; before, he'd held off for a long time, keeping himself away from the edge by concentrating his attention on leaving a series of love-bites on Clay's neck, but now it slammed into him, his entire body lighting up with it. It was all he could do not to scream as he shot deep into Clay in fierce pulses.

He was shaking when it was over, one hand on the mattress to help keep him upright and the other still holding Clay's dick loosely. His fingers were damp where they touched the head of Clay's erection. Somehow, Mitch managed to go back to thrusting, and he tightened his grip and brought Clay off in about six strokes, groaning against Clay's spine when Clay came.

"I think I'm gonna fall down," Clay gasped, and Mitch pulled out and helped him lie down instead, both of them breathing pretty heavily for the first few minutes until they recovered.

"Should have waited to take a shower," Mitch said.

"You can grab a quick one in the morning before your shift," Clay murmured. "I wish you had two days off in a row."

"I have some vacation days to take." Mitch yawned and kissed the end of Clay's nose. "Maybe we can go away for a weekend or something."

"That'd be nice."

There was a scratch on the other side of the door, and the sound of the dog whining. "Go lie down," Mitch said sternly.

"I told you she'd be lonely," Clay said. "Couldn't we let her in? If she slept on the floor?"

"Fine," Mitch sighed and got up to open the door. "But when she stops listening to everything we say, it'll be your fault."

"I thought you said she didn't understand what we say," Clay said, and Freckles ran into the room and onto the bed.

"Oh, no," Mitch said. He went back to the bed and pointed at the floor. "Down. *Down*." Sulkily, the dog jumped down and curled herself into a ball. "Good girl."

Shutting off the light, Mitch slid between the sheets and got comfortable.

"'Night, Mitchell," Clay whispered. "I love you."

"Love you, too," Mitch said, and was instantly asleep.

* * *

"I really, *really* have to go," Clay said against Mitch's lips.

"I know," Mitch said, kissing him again. They were standing in the driveway next to Mitch's car -- it was already an unusually warm day despite the early hour, the sun shining brightly -- and somehow they couldn't seem to tear themselves away from each other. "Me, too."

Clay sucked on Mitch's lower lip. "I don't want to be late."

"Me, either." Mitch leaned on his car and slid his hands from Clay's back down to his ass, kneading at it. "Here. I'm going." They kissed again, more deeply, and Mitch wished they had another ten minutes. Five, even.

"You can't leave until you let go of me," Clay said. He pressed forward, showing Mitch that they were equally turned on.

"But I don't want to let go of you," Mitch said. "I want to stay here."

"We can't." Firmly, Clay pulled away, reaching out to touch Mitch's lip with his thumb. "You look like you've been making out."

"So?" Mitch said. He grinned and forced himself to pick up his keys, which he'd set down on the roof of the car. "Okay, okay. I'm going."

"Good." Clay backed up toward his own car. "I'm going to come home on my lunch hour and check on Freckles. I don't know how long she can hold it."

"Okay. Wait." Mitch jogged four steps to Clay and kissed him one more time. "Let's go out for dinner. Somewhere nice."

The look Clay gave him as he drove away was starry-eyed -- Mitch had forgotten how much he liked that look. He thought about it on the way to work, pleasantly distracted, and didn't remember Paige Sadler until he pulled into the parking lot. A heavy weight settled over him and he had to force his mind back on track.

He actually wasn't late, and spent ten minutes writing up the information he'd managed to collect into a brief report for the case file and for Leo, listing the sources without specifying which details had come from where. He knew Leo wasn't going to like hearing that he'd talked to Nick, but with Mrs. Sadler, that other cop Harper and Derek the apartment manager on the list he figured there was at least a slight chance he'd be able to gloss over the Nick thing.

"You talked to *who*?" Leo said.

A very slight chance, apparently.

"Look, it's not like I sought him out," Mitch said. "He showed up and asked if he could talk to me. What was I supposed to do, arrest him?"

"No -- you're supposed to have enough sense to refuse to listen to anything he has to say," Leo told him. "He's a fake, Mitch. A fraud. He's just hoping something he says turns out to be a lucky guess and someone -- maybe us, maybe Paige Sadler's family -- will be grateful, and gullible, enough to offer him something for it."

Mitch shook his head. "I don't think so. Anyway, plenty of these leads didn't even come from him. Here, look at the key chains." He pulled the evidence bags out of his pocket -- he'd put Paige's in an evidence bag too at that point --and handed them to Leo.

Turning them over in his hands, Leo frowned. "These came from two different places?"

"Yeah," Mitch said. "One from the Sadler house, one from Derek Roach, who found it in Driscoll's apartment."

Leo held the bags up, comparing the keys. "Huh. They look the same."

"That's what I'm telling you -- we're looking for the same killer." Mitch took the evidence bags back. "I've gotta see if they can lift any useful prints off them, but I'll admit I'm not all that hopeful."

"You never know," Leo said. "Hey, I heard Anna sold you and Clay on one of those mutts of hers. I'm glad you and Clay worked things out."

Mitch blinked. "Thanks. Um. Where did you hear that?"

"From Anna," Leo said slowly, like that was the only way Mitch was going to understand what he was saying. "We went out last night. Just for drinks, but it was cool. I like her."

"You do."

"Yeah. Don't you?"

"Oh, no. I mean, yes. I like her fine." Mitch wondered how the conversation had gotten away from him. "Look, I'm going to see if I can get in touch with the detective who dealt with the Harris case, see if I can come up with anything else that will help."

Leo shrugged and nodded. "Okay. Hey, Al's out and Mike's looking for someone to go check out that breaking and entering thing that happened at the mall last night. You mind if I go?"

"Nah -- this could take me a while." Mitch was already sitting back down at the desk, intent on getting to work.

A call to the detective on the Harris case didn't turn up anything but some numbers -- the body had been found on January 3rd and the medical examiner had said the man had probably died approximately forty-eight to seventy-two hours before, which meant some time around New Year's Eve. It was a similar M.O., although in this case the cause of death had actually been strangulation, and the man had been raped after he'd been killed.

Mitch logged into the database and looked up the girl who'd gone missing the year before, the one whose body had never been found. Her boyfriend had called the police and filed a missing person's report in mid March, saying he hadn't seen her for two days after a few weeks of relationship trouble. If Nick was right, she might have been a victim of the same perpetrator, but there sure wasn't any way to prove it.

Sitting back in his chair, Mitch searched the database some more, looking for missing persons cases that had never been solved or anything else that might seem familiar, but didn't have any luck. He was considering calling Nick's number, just to see if there was anything at all Nick could tell him that might help, when Leo came in.

"Jeez, are you still here?" Leo said. "I figured you'd have moved on to something else by now."

"I guess I'm ready to," Mitch said, getting up and stretching. "I'm not getting anywhere here."

Leo clapped him on the shoulder. "There's a report of a bunch of cars being broken into in the Bookshed parking lot. Let's go see what's what -- you can get some fresh air."

"Okay," Mitch agreed.

Taking reports from the people who'd discovered their cars broken into took a hell of a lot longer than it should have, and was a hell of a lot more boring. Mitch stood patiently as a young woman with a long multi-colored scarf and a baby on her hip tried to list the CDs that had been stolen from her car. "Um... Sarah McLachlan," she said. "Sinead Lohan -- I got that one in England."

The car looked like anyone could have taken anything out of it at any time; one of the doors was tied on with rope. "You're sure it was locked?" Mitch asked her.

"Oh, absolutely. I'm really just glad no one stole the car seat." The young woman smiled and joggled the baby, who broke into a wide, toothless grin. "I know it doesn't look like much, but it's all we have."

Feeling a rush of affection for the girl, Mitch nodded. "Okay. Hopefully we'll catch whoever did this and we'll be able to return your property to you..."

"But you can't make any promises. I know." The girl reached for the back door of the car and Mitch jumped to open it for her. "Thanks."

Mitch's phone rang. He glanced at Leo, who was taking someone else's statement, and at the other people who were waiting to give theirs, then decided he could spare a minute or two.

He flipped the phone open. "Mitch Anderson."

"Hello, lover," Clay said.

"Clay," Mitch said, smiling. "What's up?"

"I just wanted to let you know that our dog is evil," Clay said. "She ate my slippers. I thought that was, like, a cartoon dog thing."

Mitch laughed. "You weren't kidding when you said you didn't know anything about dogs."

"What, that's seriously normal?" Clay sounded horrified. "Dogs are bad, Mitchell. Really, really bad. Why did I agree to this?"

"I'll buy you some new slippers," Mitch said.

"Good. I want ones with fur linings. Although I won't be needing them tonight. What's with this weather? It's too early for it to be this warm."

"It's nice," Mitch said. "You shouldn't complain."

"I'm not complaining," Clay said. "I opened the windows before to let the fresh air in."

"And when you say 'before' you mean just now, right?" Mitch said, knowing Clay meant before they'd both left for work.

"Not exactly," Clay admitted.

Mitch sighed. "You promised you weren't going to do that anymore."

"I meant to shut them," Clay said. "I'm going to shut them right now." Mitch could hear the muffled sound of footsteps on the hardwood in the hallway. "Okay, shutting the windows. And I--" Clay stopped, and Mitch waited.

And waited.

"Clay?" Mitch said.

"Oh, Mitchell, what did you do?" Clay said.

"What are you talking about?"

"What is it? It's not a car, is it? No, because then there'd be a key." Clay sounded excited, almost breathless.

"Clay. I don't know what you're talking about," Mitch said again.

"The box, stupid. Don't pretend you don't know."

Mitch was staring down at the clipboard he was holding, the one with the report the young woman with the baby had been making. "What box?"

"The one on my pillow," Clay said, exasperated now. "The one with the stainless steel keychain in it."

In his pocket, Mitch could feel the press of the key chains and keys against his thigh.

"Clay," he said. "Listen to me," and something in his tone must have gotten through because Clay stopped whatever it was he'd been babbling and listened. "Get out of the house, right now. Get in your car and lock the doors and drive over to the station *now*."

"Mitchell?" Clay said uncertainly. "What are you--?" There was a crash. In the background, Freckles started to bark. It was the first time Mitch had heard her bark, and it didn't sound like a happy, playful bark; it was snarling, vicious.

Mitch shouted Clay's name once, then ran for the squad car, the clipboard he'd been holding clattering onto the pavement behind him.

He was behind the wheel and had the car in gear by the time Leo ran over. "What the hell is going on?" Leo asked, jumping into the passenger seat, but Mitch was too frantic to pause long enough to say more than, "Clay," as he pressed the gas pedal to the floor. He pulled away, tires burning on the pavement.

"Clay? Clay, you answer me right this fucking minute!" Mitch said tersely into the phone, but the other end of the line had gone dead. He was five miles from the house.

Too far.

"Give it to me," Leo said, and took the phone when Mitch shoved it at him. "Clay? Clay, are you there?" He shook his head when Mitch glanced at him. "Nothing. What's going on?"

"He found one of these key chains in our *house*," Mitch said. "In our fucking *bed*. And then I heard -- there was a crash, and the dog started barking..."

"Just concentrate on driving," Leo told him, and picked up the radio to let the station know what they were doing and where to send back-up.

Mitch could barely pay attention to what Leo was saying. He was gripping the wheel so hard that his hands hurt, and his heart was with Clay, his brain playing over and over again the last words Clay had spoken, that scared, tentative lift in his voice, the sound of the dog snarling as vicious as any Mitch had heard before.

He took a corner so sharply that the driver's side tires left the pavement for a second or two; the car fishtailed when it came back down, but he regained control. His heart was beating too fast -- and it didn't usually do that even when something work-related sent a spike of adrenaline through him, because he'd been doing this long enough that it was old hat. Only this *wasn't* old hat, because it was Clay.

His fucking stupid brain couldn't stop reminding him of all the details of this case: the victims being struck on the head, strangled, being *raped*, and if whoever this fucking asshole was did so much as leave a *bruise* on Clay, Mitch was going to kill him. He took another corner, again too fast, and Leo grabbed onto the dashboard and didn't say anything. Usually the only thought Mitch spared other cars on the road when he was in pursuit or a hurry was gratitude that they were slowing down and getting out of his way, but right then he wanted to smash through them on purpose just to feel the satisfying crunch of metal on metal.

It had been a long time since Mitch had realized -- if he ever had, really -- how fragile life was. That was fucked up, because he'd seen Paige Sadler's body less than a week before. It should have sunk in. He should have known. Instead, he'd just continued on, not thinking about it, pretending he was somehow protected because he was a cop.

Mitch turned down their street with the sound of the siren echoing in his head, screeched to a stop in front of the house instead of wasting time slowing down to pull into the driveway, and flung open the car door. He ran full-out, not paying any attention to Leo behind him, took the front steps in two bounds, and tried the door -- unlocked, of course, and if Clay was okay he wouldn't be for long because Mitch was going to fucking *kill* him.

Shouldering the door open, Mitch shouted, "Clay!" There was no answer, but a moment later he heard the click of the dog's nails on the floor; he drew his gun, the solid weight of it giving him some small measure of comfort as Leo came up behind him, quiet.

"Clay? Answer me!"

Nothing. Freckles came around the corner through the kitchen, limping a little bit, and whined at them. It took a second or two for Mitch's eyes to translate what he was seeing -- the dog's muzzle and front bright and tacky with blood.

"Fuck. Clay!" Mitch moved past the dog and down the hallway toward the living room with Leo shadowing him. He glanced automatically toward the back door -- it was open, broken glass scattered across the floor.

"Clay!" Mitch shouted it again, not expecting an answer this time, and rounded the corner to see the bloodied body of a man he didn't know -- *brown hair, brown eyes, average height, average weight* -- lying on the floor, and Clay beyond him, face-down, crumpled, still.

Leaving the perpetrator for Leo to deal with, Mitch went immediately over to Clay and knelt down on the floor, hand shaking as he touched him. "Clay?"

Clay made a little sound like a protest; he was warm, his pulse regular, but Mitch was afraid he might be hurt in ways that weren't obvious.

"Stay still," Mitch said, not sure if Clay could hear him. He glanced over at Leo, who was standing over the guy with his gun drawn, nudging him with his foot. There was no response, even though the guy's eyes were open and staring at the ceiling and he seemed to be breathing. He was bleeding from his inner thigh, a puddle of red across the floor, and he was wearing gloves that didn't quite cover the tattoo on his wrist.

Leo nudged the guy again. The man groaned and Leo told him, "Don't move."

Mitch quickly set his gun on the floor within easy reach and unclipped his radio from his belt, then requested an ambulance. Through the open front door, he heard the distant sound of sirens --

back-up on the way.

Freckles came over and sniffed at Clay, her gory muzzle almost enough to turn Mitch's stomach. The perp twitched and the dog growled; her lips lifted, showing her teeth, and Clay made another soft murmur and rolled over.

It was too late to keep him still, but Mitch lay a hand on his shoulder anyway. "Easy, baby. I'm right here."

"Mitchell?" God, it was the sweetest thing Mitch had ever heard, Clay's voice, even sounding the way it did. Fuck, there was bruising all around his throat and his lips had a faint bluish tinge. Mitch realized that the roughness in Clay's voice went with the red marks around his throat. The bastard had had his hands around Clay's neck.

"Everything's okay," Mitch told him. "There's an ambulance on the way." He could actually hear sirens in the distance.

"It was that guy. The one that's been flirting with me at work." Clay's eyes opened. "The dog bit him. She protected me."

"I know." Freckles, standing beside them, wagged her tail like nothing was wrong. Shifting over a little, Mitch leaned in to meet Clay's gaze and hopefully hold it. "Just look at me, okay?"

"Okay," Clay said hoarsely. "Why? What's--" He turned his head and saw the guy bleeding all over their floor, Leo standing there. "Oh my God."

"No, no, look at me." Mitch got down lower and Clay looked at him again. There were tears in his eyes. "It's okay."

"Is he dead?" Clay asked.

Mitch shook his head. "No. Did he hurt you?"

Clay's hand went up to his throat and he swallowed painfully. "I think... I think I hit my head. And he was choking me. Then the dog bit him, and--" He shut his eyes, trembling. "I pushed him. He fell."

"Shh," Mitch said. "It's okay, baby. We can talk about it later."

The sirens outside were loud now, and Mitch heard the squeal of tires and then a couple of the guys from the station calling for him and Leo..

"Back here!" Leo called, and a few seconds later Bernie and Joel appeared, weapons drawn. Mitch could see them sizing up the situation in about two seconds.

"The ambulance was right behind us," Joel said. He holstered his gun and came into the living room, then knelt beside the perp. "Jesus." The guy's eyes were shut now, but Mitch could still see the shallow lift and fall of his chest.

"Yeah," Mitch said.

"Good dog," Joel said, either in general or to Mitch.

The ambulance arrived -- two of the paramedics immediately started to take care of the perp, bandaging up his leg and then bundling him onto a stretcher. "How's he?" one of them -- Mitch was pretty sure his name was Danny -- asked, nodding at Clay.

"I'm okay," Clay said. He was sitting up now, leaning against Mitch. "I don't want to go to the hospital."

"We need to get you checked out," Mitch said.

"I'm *fine*." Clay was still hoarse, but his color was better. "There's nothing they can do."

"You're going if I have to put you into the ambulance myself," Mitch said, then lowered his voice. "Please, baby. For me? You could have a concussion."

Clay nodded and pressed closer to Mitch, resting his forehead on Mitch's shoulder. "Okay, I'll go. But not in the ambulance."

"Not in the ambulance," Mitch agreed.

Danny came over and checked Clay's vitals, then asked him a few questions. Finally, he said, "Throat's pretty swollen, but he's getting enough air, and his eyes look okay. I'll catch up with you later on, see how you're doing."

"Thanks," Clay said.

The paramedics loaded their patient into the ambulance and left.

"There's blood on the couch," Clay said, frowning.

"There's blood everywhere," Mitch told him. "Don't worry about it. As long as it's not yours, I don't give a shit."

Clay looked upset. "But the couch is new."

"Baby," Mitch said, cradling Clay's chin in one hand and lifting it a little. "Stop worrying about the fucking couch. We'll get a new one, okay?"

"I like this one." Clay said. His eyes met Mitch's; they were a little glassy.

Mitch nodded. "I know you do. Come on; let's get you up off the floor."

Clay was shaky on his feet, and he clung to Mitch, hanging on like letting go wasn't an option. "He came into our house," Clay whispered. "I was just -- he broke the glass in the door, and he--" Leo came back into the room and he stopped.

"Sorry," Leo said. "Why don't you guys go on; we can get a report from Clay later. I'll call Anna to come over and take care of the dog."

"Thanks," Mitch said, and led Clay toward the front door.

The ER was busy, and even though police tended to get preferential treatment -- even if they weren't the ones who were hurt -- they ended up waiting a long time. Mitch sat with Clay, holding his hand, until the doctor came into the exam room and checked him over. "You're going to have a rainbow of bruises," the doctor said.

"I like rainbows," Clay said with a wan smile.

"Good." The doctor pressed his fingertips lightly against Clay's throat. "Does that hurt?"

"Mm. A little." It made Mitch want to kill the guy.

The doctor rolled his chair back and stood up. "Everything looks good otherwise; there are no signs of concussion, and at this point you're not likely to keep swelling. Take it easy for a day or two -- nothing strenuous -- and if you have any problems, which I don't think you will, call your regular doctor or come back here."

Leo was waiting for them out in the hallway. "Don't worry," he said immediately, holding up a hand. "I left Bernie at your place until the door's fixed."

"What about the guy?" Clay asked, leaning against Mitch's side.

"They had to give him a couple dozen stitches," Leo said. "And he's got a hell of a concussion, but that comes in handy because he's already confessed to way more than he should without a lawyer present, if you know what I mean." Mitch did. "He'll be here overnight at least. Under guard, of course. Once the doctors say he can be released, he'll be officially taken into police custody."

"Good," Clay said. "What about Freckles?"

"Anna came over to your place and got her cleaned up."

"No, I mean... is she going to get in trouble?" Clay sounded anxious.

Leo shook his head. "Nah. The guy broke into your house and attacked you -- she was defending her territory and you. Worst case scenario, she'll have to be under a sort of house arrest for a while. As long as she doesn't show further signs of aggression, things'll be fine." He looked at Mitch instead of Clay. "We need to go down to the station."

"Yeah, I know," Mitch said.

"It's okay," Clay said, subdued. "I know we have to. There are probably, like, a dozen forms and things to fill out, right?"

"Not that many," Leo said. "But it's important to do it as soon as possible. While everything's still fresh in your mind."

Clay nodded. "Okay. So let's do it."

They used the same room they had with Nick and Matthew, but this time the vibe was totally different. Instead of being distant and professional, Leo was solicitous, getting Clay a cup of coffee and asking more than once if there was anything he needed. Mitch let Leo take over, and sat with Clay instead of on the other side of the table. He knew he wasn't going to like anything he heard.

"Okay, Clay," Leo said. "You know we caught the guy, so this is really just a formality. We're not in a hurry; take all the time you need." He picked up his pen. "Can you tell me what happened?"

Clay's hands were on the table, his fingers laced together. "I was on the phone with Mitch," he said. "The windows were open -- it was such a nice day and I wanted to let some fresh air in. But I needed to go back to work -- oh God, I never called!" He turned anguished eyes to Mitch. "Daphne's going to be so pissed off."

"Not when she finds out what happened," Mitch reassured him. "I'll call her later, okay? Don't worry about it."

"Easy for you to say," Clay said. "You don't have to work with her." But he made an obvious effort to focus on what they were doing. "So Mitch told me to shut the windows. I did, and then I saw the box on my pillow. I thought Mitch left it."

"Did you open the box?" Leo asked.

"Yes. There was a keychain inside." Clay frowned. "I don't know where it went."

"We found it at the scene," Leo said. "It's been taken into evidence." That was right, Mitch thought -- Leo would have recognized that the keychain matched the other two.

"Okay. Anyway, I think I asked Mitch what it was. At first I thought it was some kind of surprise -- like, he was going to give me a key to something new to go on it. But Mitch freaked out and started telling me to go, to drive to the station, and then..." Clay's hands tightened and he swallowed, remembering. "I heard a crash, and the dog started barking, and I turned around and someone -- that guy, he grabbed me." He had tears in his eyes, but seemed determined not to let them fall.

"His name is David Knowles," Leo said, nodding. "Did you know him?" It was a typical and effective method of diffusing the emotional upset of recounting something traumatic; go off on a tangent.

Clay shook his head. "Not really. Not -- I didn't know his name. But I'd seen him before. A bunch of times."

"Near your house?" Leo asked.

Another head-shake. "No, at work. He'd come in for a while, pretty regularly, to buy flowers. He always paid in cash, and he always took them with him when he went -- that's why I never knew his name. He'd be in often for a month or so, then there'd be no sign of him for a few months, and then he'd start coming back again." Leo made a note. "Then, the past couple of days, he... he started talking to me. Asking me personal questions, stuff like that."

Leo was calm and patient. "What kinds of questions?"

"If I lived nearby," Clay said.

"And did you tell him where you lived?" Leo asked.

Clay looked scandalized. "Of course not." He swallowed. "Well. I gave him a general idea. But I didn't tell him what street or anything."

"It's okay," Mitch said, resting his hand on Clay's thigh.

"I'm not that stupid," Clay said.

"No one thinks you're stupid," Leo said firmly. "What other kinds of questions did he ask?"

"Um..." Clay tried to think. "What I liked. He said... he said I looked sad. Like I needed a friend. I... I think I told him my boyfriend and I were having problems."

Leo leaned forward a little bit. "What did he do when you said that?"

Clay flushed, remembering. "Started flirting with me."

"Did you encourage it?" Leo looked apologetic for having to ask, but if he didn't, someone else would later.

"No," Clay said. "I tried to discourage it, but without being rude."

"And when was the last time you saw him before today?"

Clay's shoulders were slumping; he was starting to look tired. "I think yesterday. At work. He asked me out. I said no. He kind of smiled, and he said he'd change my mind."

Leo nodded as he took some more notes. "And today, after he grabbed you, what did he do?"

"He said... he said it was my turn," Clay said. "He pushed me up against the wall. I hit my head. And then... I think he was choking me. Freckles jumped on him and bit him, on the leg, and he kicked her. She slid across the floor and crashed into the table. He was bleeding, kind of a lot, and I turned to grab the dolphin statue off the coffee table -- I remember thinking you'd be glad if I broke it on his head," he said to Mitch with a little grin. "But he grabbed me again, and his hands were really strong. I couldn't breathe. I was trying to do something, I don't know, hit him, knee him in the balls..."

Hitching his chair closer, Mitch pushed Clay's coffee cup against his hand. Clay picked it up and sipped the coffee.

"And then," Clay said. "I think he tripped over the dog or something, because he fell and hit his head. And then I think maybe I fainted. I sort of remember hitting the floor. I know Freckles was growling... I don't know. And then Mitch was there." He turned adoring eyes toward Mitch, who put an arm around Clay's shoulders.

"Good," Leo said approvingly. "You're doing great, Clay. Now, when you say you'd seen him before at work, about how many times do you think he came into the shop?"

* * *

There was still a squad car in front of the house when they got back -- Leo insisted on following them home, and Mitch hadn't argued when it'd been clear that Clay found the idea comforting -- as well as a blue van with a local company's logo on it. Anna's car was across the street, and when she heard them coming up the steps she appeared in the entryway with Freckles.

"Is she okay?" Clay asked.

"She's fine. I had one of the shelter vets come over and look at her just in case -- he said she's a little banged up, but nothing's broken. He even helped me give her a bath." It wasn't until Anna mentioned that part that Mitch realized the blood that had been all over Freckles' fur was gone. "She's a good girl." Freckles wagged her plume of a tail and looked up at Anna.

Clay bent to pat her. "Leo said she won't get in trouble."

"I talked to the shelter's legal consultant," Anna said. "We can prove that she's up to date on her shots. It'd be a good idea not to take her out of the yard for a couple of days, probably, until we can make sure everything's taken care of. But she's not in trouble."

"Good," Clay said.

"Hey, Mitch," Bernie said, joining them. "Everything's all set -- we got all the photos and prints we need, and we had to take a couple of things into evidence, including one of your sofa cushions. Jameson had one of the cleaning crews come in; they just left. Figured the last thing you'd need would be to come back to a big mess of bl... uh. A big mess."

Mitch smiled tightly. "Thanks, Bern."

"And the glass lady's just finishing up; once she is I'll clear out of here. Unless you need anything?" Bernie seemed eager to help -- Mitch appreciated it.

"I think we're okay," he said. He glanced at Clay, who nodded.

"Kind of tired," Clay said, then, to Mitch, "We can postpone that dinner out, can't we?"

"Sure."

"Cool. I think I'm gonna go grab a quick shower."

Mitch didn't realize until everyone else had gone that Clay had been in the bathroom a long time. He locked the front door -- glancing out into the driveway and catching Anna and Leo standing close together, Anna's face tilted up toward Leo's, which made him smile -- and double-checked the back one before knocking on the bathroom door. "Clay?"

"You can come in," Clay called. "Is everyone gone?"

"No, I thought we could maybe put on a show," Mitch said, going in. The air was thick with steam. "Yeah. It's just us."

The water shut off, the handle squeaking a little bit as Clay turned it, and Mitch grabbed a towel and offered it to Clay as he slid the shower curtain aside.

"Shit," Mitch said, startled again by the sight of the reddened skin around Clay's throat.

"Does it look awful?" Clay asked. He brought a hand up and touched the skin lightly.

"No, not awful," Mitch reassured him. But as soon as Clay stepped out of the tub, he couldn't stop himself from pulling him into an embrace.

Clay patted Mitch's back awkwardly. "It's okay. I'm fine."

"You have no clue how scared I was," Mitch said. Clay smelled like shampoo and soap, and he was warm and pliant from the shower; it was Mitch's heart that was beating too fast.

"Probably not as scared as me," Clay said.

"The thought of that bastard putting his hands on you..." Mitch felt Clay shiver and cursed himself for reminding him. "He's never going to touch you again, I swear."

"I know." But Clay was shaking now -- a delayed reaction Mitch should have expected after how well he'd held it together throughout the afternoon. "I think I need to sit down."

"Let's get you to bed," Mitch said.

He lay down with Clay and held him, running fingers through Clay's short hair as it dried. After a while, Freckles jumped up on the bed and lay near the foot of it, worried dark eyes watching them, and neither of them shooed her away. A couple of times Mitch suggested that he go make some dinner, but Clay insisted that he wasn't hungry. "Stay with me until I fall asleep."

It didn't take all that long -- Clay relaxed into a heavy sleep, and after half an hour or so Mitch slipped out of bed and went to the kitchen. Freckles followed him. He put food in her bowl and watched her as she ate it. Each time Mitch moved, the dog looked up at him, and finally he couldn't wait anymore.

"Come on, girl," he said, and went into the living room with her at his heels. "Sit," Mitch told her, and she did, watching him expectantly. "Good girl. Lie down."

Freckles lay down, ears pricked at attention.

"Fuck me," Mitch breathed. The dog's head tilted to one side; she looked confused. "That wasn't an order," he said, smiling. "Stay."

Leaving her there, he went to the closet near the front door and took out an umbrella he'd had so long he didn't remember where he'd gotten it. He went back to the living room holding it like walking stick, watching Freckles' reaction. She hadn't moved from where he'd left her, and she blinked at him patiently, apparently waiting for further instruction.

"Good dog." Mitch raised the umbrella, pointing the end of it at her. She didn't seem nervous. He raised it higher, over his head, standing over the dog menacingly. Freckles just blinked up at him. Mitch made a threatening sound and swung the umbrella downward toward her like he was going to hit her. Her ears went back, but her eyes were wide and worried and the tip of her tail was wagging; she showed no signs of aggression whatsoever. It was like she'd lived with Mitch all her life and trusted him implicitly.

Mitch dropped the umbrella down onto the floor and knelt, taking Freckle's head in his hands. "Good girl. Good dog." He patted her until she was panting and grinning, trying to lick his face. Then he got up and went back to the bedroom, where Clay was still sleeping peacefully.

Reassured in more ways than one, Mitch called for a pizza from Clay's favorite place, a grilled chicken and mushroom, and then looked in his wallet until he found the folded piece of paper Nick had given him and phoned the number scribbled on it. It only rang twice before Nick answered it.

"Hello?" His voice was like a rush of warmth -- hearing it made Mitch feel good.

"Hi, Nick. It's Mitch."

"Mitch. Hi," Nick said. "I haven't heard from her again. Paige, I mean."

"Oh," Mitch said, sitting down on the half of the couch that still had a cushion. "Okay. Maybe you won't." He sounded a little bit smug, and Nick must have picked up on that.

"You caught him?"

"In a matter of speaking," Mitch said. "Yeah, he's in custody. He broke into my house and attacked Clay."

"God. Is he okay?" Nick sounded shocked.

Mitch looked toward the bedroom, listening, but it was quiet. "He's okay. A little bruised, but when I think how things could have turned out..." His voice broke, just a little bit.

"You were lucky," Nick said softly. "You *are* lucky. You know that."

And, because there was nothing else to do but agree, Mitch said, "Yes. Very lucky."

"Then I don't have to tell you not to mess with that," Nick said. "Are you staying together?"

"Yes. I was lucky there, too." More than he deserved. He knew that.

"Did you tell him?" Nick asked. "About what happened with you and me?"

Mitch cleared his throat and glanced up to see Clay standing there in the doorway, eyes dark and worried. "No," he said faintly. "Not yet."

"But you will?" Nick pressed.

Mitch nodded, still looking at Clay. "I will. What about you?"

He could practically hear Nick's indecision, but after a few seconds, Nick said, "It won't matter. It won't change anything. What Matthew and I have... it's not like that. But yes, okay? I'll tell him." He sighed. "Listen, Mitch... take care of yourself, okay? And him."

Getting up, Mitch walked over to where Clay was leaning against the door frame. "Yeah. You don't have to worry about that." Carefully, he said, "I love him."

"I know you do," Nick said.

"Thanks, Nick. For all your help, and for... for everything."

"You're welcome," Nick said, and then, "Goodbye, Mitch." It was harder to hear than Mitch would have thought, but somehow he managed to say goodbye, too, and hung up the phone.

Clay was watching him. "Who was that?"

"Nick," Mitch said. "The guy from work. The psychic." He hesitated, trying to decide if this was the wrong time to tell Clay more or if it was just that he was afraid to, but Clay beat him to it.

"Something happened," he said. "Between the two of you."

Mitch nodded. "I kissed him."

Instead of freaking out or pulling away -- both of which he would have been entitled to do -- Clay said, "Tell me why."

"Sit down first," Mitch said, tugging at Clay's hand gently, because Clay was trembling in a way he was pretty sure had nothing to do with emotion.

Clay made a face. "Not on the couch," he said.

"The cushion's gone anyway," Mitch said. "Kitchen?"

They went into the kitchen and sat, Mitch sliding his chair close to Clay's so that their knees were touching. Clay looked at him expectantly.

"He was... the whole psychic thing was intense," Mitch said, trying to put it into words. "It was like it hurt him. I think it *did* hurt him. He collapsed onto the ground -- it was at the park, where we found the girl's body -- and I was holding him, trying to, I don't know, comfort him."

"Of course you were," Clay said gently, and Mitch looked at him. Of all the reactions he'd been expecting, this wasn't one of them. "What, did you think I was going to freak out?"

"Um..." Mitch didn't know how to respond to that. "Yeah. Kind of."

Clay held his gaze. "You just kissed him? I mean, nothing else?"

"Nothing else," Mitch said. "I swear."

"Okay." Clay reached out and took Mitch's face in his hands. "I love that you want to comfort people. I've always loved that about you. It'd be pretty hypocritical of me to be mad at you about it now." Something flashed behind his eyes. "But it never goes any further than that. Ever. Do I make myself clear?"

Mitch leaned in and kissed him quickly. "Yes. Totally clear. It's never going to happen again. I promise."

The doorbell rang and Clay flinched.

"It's just the pizza guy," Mitch reassured him, patting his knee. "I got your favorite."

"Chicken and mushroom from Emilio's?" Clay asked.

"Of course. I'll go get it." The dog followed Mitch to the door -- she hadn't even barked when the bell rang, Mitch realized -- and stood beside him while he paid, not seeming even slightly bothered by the presence of the delivery guy. By the time Mitch went back to the kitchen, Clay had put out two plates and a handful of napkins.

Clay looked at the pizza doubtfully when Mitch opened the box. "I don't know if I can eat."

"Sure you can," Mitch said, leaning over to put a slice of pizza onto Clay's plate. "You need to. You've got to keep up your strength."

"I'll have to go to court, won't I?" Clay said.

Mitch nodded as Clay plucked a slice of mushroom off his slice of pizza and ate it. "Maybe. It depends. But probably not any time soon. These things can take a long time."

"I know. Do you think he'll get life? I mean, he'll at least go to prison for a long time, right? There's no way he'll get off?" Clay sounded worried but kept his gaze unwaveringly on his food.

They'd already talked about this. "Clay. Sweetheart." Mitch waited until Clay looked up at him. "He killed three people, maybe four. He attacked you. And you heard what Leo said about him confessing to some of it already. Besides, we have a witness -- you. He's not going to get away with this. You don't have to worry about it."

Clay made a little face. "But stuff happens sometimes, right? Cases fall through. Don't they?"

"There's no reason to think that'll happen here," Mitch told him. "Whatever judge ends up hearing this one's going to take it very, very seriously. Trust me."

"I do," Clay said. He sighed. "I don't want to eat right now. Could we just go to bed?"

This probably wasn't the time to argue with him, so Mitch led Clay back to the bedroom. Freckles followed them and lay down next to the bed as they got in, silent but watchful.

"Just hold me?" Clay asked.

Mitch did, wrapping Clay in a fierce embrace and kissing his temple. "It's gonna be okay, baby. I promise."

"I know. I love you."

"I love you, too," Mitch said into Clay's hair, knowing it more certainly than he'd ever known anything in his life.

Nothing else was as important, and he was going to do whatever it took to hold onto this -- onto Clay -- for as long as he could.

Contributors

Chris Owen:

Chris Owen lives and writes in eastern Canada, where the winds blow cool and calm on the good days, wicked and fast on the bad. There's rain and sun, and in the winter there's snow... a lot of snow. A nice fire to keep warm, a nice pen with good flow, and a decent notebook are all that Chris really requires. Which is not to say that the PowerBook isn't the best thing ever. Chris went to a bunch of schools, learned a lot of things, and now makes stuff up because not to do so is unthinkable.

CB Potts:

CB Potts is a bad woman. She makes her editors crazy, her readers cry, and small furry animals shrivel into small balls of despair. Despite this, she does have some redeeming qualities, including her award winning recipe for Random Male Flambee and an unerring ability to be one number off on the lotto. Rumor has it she has quite a sense of humor, but as of this writing, we've seen no evidence of it.

Should you be interested in this madness, and quite frankly, we don't know why you would be, but to each their own, and far be it from us to judge how you want to waste your time, you can discover more at http://cbpotts.livejournal.com

Tory Temple:

Tory Temple lives and works in southern California. She spends much of her time either at the beach or hanging around fire stations, both places rife with ideas for books. She loves peanut butter cookies, jeans that fit right, and various shades of pink. Tory's website, Stems and Petals, can be found at http://ragingpixie.bitchenvy.com/stems

Alexa Snow:

Alexa Snow is an emotional person who appreciates practicality in others. She's prone to crying at inconvenient times, drinking too much coffee, and staying up too late playing with words (either reading or writing.) A background of schooling she wasn't all that interested in resulted in a Bachelor's degree in Sociology and a vague sense of wasted time; she is grateful that writing gives her a deep sense of satisfaction. Alexa lives in a tiny old house in New England with her husband, young son, and a small collection of pets that includes an asthmatic cat. Other titles published by Torquere Press include "Clear Cut" and "Sleeping Stone."

Printed in the United States
146068LV00005B/64/A

9 781603 701655